Dear Reader:

The novels you've enjoyed over the past years by such authors as Kathleen Woodiwiss, Johanna Lindsey, Laurie McBain, and Shirlee Busbee are accountable to one thing above all others: Avon has never asked its writers to fit any particular mold. Rather, Avon is a publisher that encourages individual talent and is always looking for writers who are writing books they *want* to write.

In 1982, we started a program to help readers pick out authors of exceptional promise. Called "The Avon Romance," the books were distinguished by a ribbon motif in the upper left-hand corner of the cover. Although most titles were by new authors, they were quickly discovered and became known as "the ribbon books."

Now "The Avon Romance" is a monthly feature on the Avon list. We offer you historical novels with many different settings, each one by an author who is special. You will not find predictable characters, predictable plots, or predictable endings. The only predictable thing about "The Avon Romance" will be the superior quality that Avon has always delivered in the field of romance!

Sincerely,

Page Cuddy

PAGE CUDDY
Editorial Director

RENÉ J. GARROD

THE WILD ROSE

AVON
PUBLISHERS OF BARD, CAMELOT, DISCUS AND FLARE BOOKS

THE WILD ROSE is an original publication of Avon Books. This work has never before appeared in book form. This work is a novel. Any similarity to actual persons or events is purely coincidental.

AVON BOOKS
A division of
The Hearst Corporation
1790 Broadway
New York, New York 10019

Copyright © 1985 by René J. Garrod
Published by arrangement with the author
Library of Congress Catalog Card Number: 85-90679
ISBN: 0-380-89784-9

First Avon Printing, November 1985

AVON TRADEMARK REG. U. S. PAT. OFF. AND IN OTHER COUNTRIES, MARCA REGISTRADA, HECHO EN U. S. A.

Printed in the U. S. A.

WFH 10 9 8 7 6 5 4 3 2 1

For Delmar,
my husband and inspiration

Chapter 1

The last wisps of morning fog clung tenaciously to the rooftops of buildings of clapboard, canvas, and adobe huddled on the hillsides. The sun had already melted away most of the thick white blanket that had cloaked the city at dawn. Floating in the green-gray waters of the bay, ships from a dozen nations creaked against the pilings of the wharfs lining Montgomery Street, while the gentle breeze that rocked their hulls blew the pungent taste of sea and salt to the lips of the slender, dark-haired young woman who stood momentarily stranded in the middle of one mud-mired street.

"The streets of California are paved with gold," her father had told her. She wrinkled her nose, her gray eyes darkening a shade as she pulled one dainty, boot-clad foot from the thick brown liquid earth that encased it. Paved with gold, indeed. Unless gold had suddenly changed its color and texture, someone had pulled off the biggest hoax in history.

Miranda Austen had long since grown used to her father's exaggerations, though she vowed this one about California topped them all. Streets of gold, nuggets the size of a man's fist . . . she had sat unbelieving through countless tales of men made rich overnight. Despite her calm reasoning, her father had remained convinced that California was the pot of gold at the end of the rainbow.

Though Miranda loved her father, she was not blind to his faults. Until her mother's death four years ago, her only memories of him consisted of his sporadic visits to their country home. Her father had found life in the country much too dull, while her mother's fragile health did not allow them to join him at their London house. Since her mother's death she had lived in London, keeping house for her father and gently trying to dissuade him from some of his more outrageous schemes. One year he had invested heavily in an untried racehorse. The next, an ill-fated shipping line caught his fancy. Once he even had been enticed to join a venture to import young cacao trees and grow them in a giant orangery. He had had such high hopes of cornering England's chocolate market. Miranda smiled ruefully. It was only providence and a respected family name that had kept them out of debtor's prison on several occasions.

She had learned to accept the ups and downs of their fortunes philosophically and had taught herself to stretch whatever household money her father allowed her to meet their needs. Often times were lean, but she had always managed to keep food on the table. Clothing purchased during good times was often altered to fit the styles at some later, less prosperous, date.

They had been enjoying a period of relative prosperity when her father had burst in one evening, waving a well-worn newspaper clipping of a *London*

Times editorial, his pale blue eyes gleaming with excitement. "Mandy, my dear, you are going to be a rich woman, richer than the queen herself!" He paused to catch his breath, unmindful of the several strands of graying hair falling across his brow. His cheeks were flushed, and sometime during the course of his journey home, his portly figure had escaped the stricture of the last two buttons of his vest.

Smiling at his boyish enthusiasm, she asked, "What have you come upon this time, Papa?" Despite her father's impetuousness, Miranda did not attempt to curb his excitement.

"Gold! They've discovered gold in California. It's so thick, they are scooping it up by the shovelful. Miles and miles of the stuff just free for the taking."

Glancing up from the shirt she was mending, Miranda asked, "And just where is this California?" The even level of her voice was in vivid contrast to her father's exuberant tone.

"On the west coast of the North American continent. It's a real paradise by all accounts, and I'm going to take you there. It will give you a chance to see a bit of the world. I'll strike it rich, then we'll come home, and I'll build us a house so big, it will take two days to walk from one end to the other."

At this point Miranda began to lose her indulgent smile. "Papa, you can't be serious. We can't chase halfway around the world on the word of some demented journalist. For once, please be sensible."

"I know you have reason to doubt me, but I've checked this one out thoroughly. The club is alive with the news. Tomorrow some of the members are getting together to view a nugget on display at the

Bank of England. Why, they say it's so pure, it makes a man weep just to look at it.'' Edward Austen pulled out his handkerchief and dabbed at his glistening eyes in a mock display of emotion.

"Let's just think about it for a while, Papa.'' Miranda laid her sewing aside, her dismay growing as she realized that her father was seriously considering taking her to this California.

"Don't worry, Mandy. I'll take my time," her father assured her. "I'm a man of business." He brought his index finger to his temple. "And men of business are always careful to investigate the details." He tucked a bottle of port under his arm before leaving the room, giving her little confidence that he would use even a moderate amount of prudence.

Two weeks later they were steaming down the Thames toward the gold fields of California, her worst fears realized.

Miranda returned her full attention to the placement of her feet as she continued across the boggy thoroughfare to the other side of the street. She stepped up onto the makeshift sidewalk, which was constructed of boxes, crates, rolls of sheet lead, and anything else that happened to be on hand. It was a relief to be on solid ground again. She smiled politely as two men tipped their hats in greeting. She was quickly becoming accustomed to the informal friendliness practiced in this country.

Upon reaching her destination, she lifted the flap of the tent and stepped inside. The room was crowded with tables and chairs. Toward the back, a large black cookstove heated the ingredients of the midday meal. Miranda chose a table near the stove, then, after giving her order, sat back to observe the other patrons. They were all men.

Miranda wondered if she would ever get used to living almost exclusively in the company of men. Though she was treated with singular politeness, she couldn't even walk down the street without drawing attention. It had been the same since leaving London.

She had been dismayed when she'd discovered she was the only woman passenger aboard the *Royal Mail* steamship sailing from London to Chagres, Panama. It had done little to improve her already jaundiced view of the trip. Not until six weeks later, after she had survived over a week in the steaming, bug-infested Panamanian jungle and emerged on the Pacific coast, did she finally meet a fellow female traveler.

Miranda smiled as she thought of her friend Lizzy Decker. They were worlds apart, both in background and temperament, but had become instant friends the moment they had laid eyes on each other. She sipped her soup as she recalled their first meeting.

She and her father had arrived on mule earlier in the day at the camp surrounding Panama City. She had been returning to the encampment after a much-needed bath in the blue waters of the Pacific, when she heard, mingled among the clatter of provisions and the low drone of male voices, the distinct sound of a feminine voice singing a lively tune. Straining her ears to locate the source, Miranda's excitement grew as she recognized the words as English. Without further delay she ran toward the voice, hoping it wasn't some cruel trick of her imagination.

Lizzy looked up from her labors, halting her song in mid-note. The two stood silently staring at each other, afraid to trust the evidence of their own eyes. The woman Miranda viewed was taller than average and of stocky build. Her mousy brown hair was pulled away from her face into an untidy bun at the nape of her neck. She possessed a plain face of unmemorable features, but as it broke into a smile, Miranda thought it was the most beautiful sight she had ever seen.

The two threw themselves into each other's arms in an embrace so warm, any onlooker would have sworn he was witnessing the reunion of long-separated sisters. Their words tumbled over each other as their questions poured out, then, laughing, they both stepped back to catch their breath.

"My name's Elizabeth Decker, though I've been called Lizzy for as long as I can remember." Lizzy spoke with a distinct American accent as she held out her work-worn hand.

"I'm Miranda Austen," Miranda returned, clasping the offered hand. "How ever did you get here?"

"I imagine the same way you did. The mosquitoes flew me over." Lizzy giggled gaily at her own joke.

"They are dreadful, aren't they?" Miranda raised her eyes heavenward as she absently rubbed one bite-riddled arm.

"Hey, you're not supposed to scratch those things. It makes them fester," Lizzy cautioned.

"I know that's true, but I just can't seem to help myself. I'd go mad if I couldn't relieve this itching once in a while."

"You're right. I'm full of good advice, but when no one is looking, I scratch for all I'm worth," Lizzy admitted. "Though don't you go lettin' my husband know."

"Then you accompanied your husband?"

"Yes, ol' Ed was bit by the gold bug like half the other men in the States. He was determined to go, though we'd been married less than six months. Well, I'm no fool. He may have been feelin' the chains of matrimony bitin' into his freedom. I don't have your pretty looks to hold a man to me. Now I said to myself, 'If I let this man go, he may just never come back,' so I made him bring me along."

"Surely he wouldn't have left you." Miranda could not understand how she could calmly discuss her husband's possible disloyalty.

"You've a lot to learn about men if you believe that." Lizzy smiled at her naïveté. "I have no doubt 'fore long he'd find himself another pair of soft arms to comfort him. After that he'd probably forget he even had a wife back home."

The voice of the proprietor broke into Miranda's musings. She smiled at him apologetically as she assured him she did not require any further service and immediately pulled her cloak around her shoulders and left the café.

Retracing her steps, Miranda crossed the street without mishap and, a few minutes later, was safely inside the room she and her father shared above a mercantile store. She removed her cloak and exchanged her boots for slippers, taking the time to wipe the boots free of mud before placing them near the door. She resigned herself to another boring afternoon.

Her father rarely spent any part of his day with her, and though in London it would have been unheard of for a young woman to walk the streets alone, she had quickly learned that unless she was willing to forego her midday meal, she would have to brave the streets alone. So far she had not ventured farther than the eating-house where she and her father habitually shared their morning and evening meals, but in face of her father's negligence and her own growing boredom, the thought of a stroll around town was becoming increasingly inviting.

Miranda pulled a chair over to the window and sat down. Keeping her face a discreet distance from the pane, she observed the inhabitants of the city bustling to and fro.

She wished her father were more like other fathers. She could not imagine one of her friends' fathers suggesting, let alone bringing, his daughter to such a place.

It was bad enough that it had not even occurred to her father how unsuitable it was to have her accompany him; but now that they had arrived in California, he left her on her own day after day while he frequented saloons and gaming hells, trying to gather information about the gold fields. Her situation was very distressing, particularly since she was fast approaching her nineteenth birthday, and most girls of her age were securely married. Her father seemed oblivious of his duty to help her find a suitable mate, and it was becoming very easy to envision herself as an antiquated virgin.

Several hours later the squeaking of the door hinge brought Miranda's attention back to the room. Her father stepped in, his cheeks flushed and his thick, gray hair wind-tossed.

"Hello, Papa," Miranda said, greeting her father as she helped him shrug out of his coat, and noting with dismay that he had lost another button. "Did you find out anything?"

"We're in luck. I found just the man I was looking for; name's Lucas Adams. He has been here since autumn and is very knowledgeable. We're to meet him tonight for dinner."

"Has he agreed to take us to a suitable place to find gold?"

"Everything is settled on that score." Edward Austen's pale eyes shimmered with excitement as he envisioned himself surrounded by mountains of glittering gold. A chill ran down his spine. "The man drives a hard bargain, but I believe him to be honest."

Her father absently stroked his clean-shaven chin. "Wear something pretty tonight. I want you to make a good impression." He glanced around the room as Miranda scraped his mud-caked boots. Its only furnishings were a cot, a small dressing table, and two well-worn chairs.

"I'm sure glad I brought you along, Mandy," he commented. "If it hadn't been for you, I'd be staying in one of those wretched tents. There will be time enough for that."

Miranda did not doubt the truth of his statement.

They had searched the town over for decent lodgings, finding even the most undesirable boarding-houses filled to overflowing. They were beginning to despair of finding a place at all when they had stopped in a store to ask advice. The storekeeper was a weathered man in his mid-forties, and though he was sympathetic, he could offer them little advice. They were about to leave when he made his offer.

"I can't bear to turn the young lady away. She's too pretty to be wandering around without a roof over her head. If you like, I'll rent you my son's room for twenty-five dollars a week. He caught the fever and left for the gold fields last week."

They quickly agreed to this arrangement, having discovered earlier that the price of lodgings was outrageously high. As her father counted out the necessary payment in advance, Miranda had silently prayed their money would hold out until they found some gold.

They were to meet Lucas Adams at a café on Portsmouth Square. Miranda dressed with special care in a layered gray-blue silk that complimented the color of her eyes. It possessed a high, black lace neckline, with a bodice that molded to her petite figure, then flared at the waist into a full skirt. The same lace fringed the edges of long, wide sleeves that were gathered snugly around her wrists. Having no mirror, she simply tied her waist-length hair with a black silk ribbon and let it cascade in soft natural curls over one shoulder. Nodding his approval, her father helped her don her light wool cloak, then they set off to brave the muddy streets.

Miranda held her dress high as she stepped carefully on some boards recently placed in the street to aid traffic. The mercantile store was just off the square, so they had little distance to travel. Miranda dropped her hemline as they stepped into the prearranged meeting place, briefly surveying her skirt to be sure she had protected it from the mud.

Her father guided them to a small table to one side of the room. It was set with a patternless white china and devoid of table linen. The walls of the establishment were painted but bare. Window coverings had yet to be hung. It was obvious the proprietor had seen only to the essentials before opening for business.

The eating-house was fairly empty. As they sat waiting for their dinner companion her father sipped a small whiskey, and Miranda sat quietly observing the steady stream of miners who entered. Almost to a man, their dress was identical. Each wore a red flannel shirt, corduroy trousers stuffed into high-topped boots, and a broad-brimmed hat. Many carried guns strapped to their waists, occasionally accompanied by a large, rather evil-looking knife.

As Miranda's gaze shifted around the room, her attention was caught by a young woman entering from the back of the café. Her buxom figure strained against the fabric of her robelike gown. She had a friendly smile for each of the men but deftly avoided their eager hands as she made her way to a raised wooden platform in the middle of the room. Climbing the few steps to the top of the platform, she curtsied in each direction. The boisterous conversations ceased in anticipation. With a single fluid motion the woman dropped her garment to her feet. While the men roared their appreciation Miranda choked on her own breath, turning fiery red as the totally naked young woman took up a suggestive pose. Throwing her father a murderous look, she rose from the table to run blindly toward the door and headlong into the chest of a miner as he was entering the eating establishment.

"Get out of my way, you clumsy oaf!" She practically spat the words at the unfortunate fellow. "Why don't you watch where you are going instead of ogling that doxy?" Miranda pushed the man aside, then hurried down the street. This time her father had gone too far. He had no right to subject her to this kind of embarrassment. Why couldn't he at least show a little fatherly concern? She was tired of being subjected to his irresponsible nature, and when he returned to their room, if he dared, she would tell him so in no uncertain terms.

"Good evening, Mr. Adams. Have a seat." Edward Austen rose in greeting as a tall, bearded, suntanned man approached his table. "I'm sorry for that little display."

"Do you know the little whirlwind who attacked me at the door?" Lucas Adams raised one eyebrow as he chuckled in amusement. Whoever the girl was, he thought, she was a fiery little beauty.

"I'm afraid you just had the pleasure of meeting my daughter, Miranda. She's usually not so hot-tempered, but I'm afraid the entertainment unnerved her a bit," Edward Austen explained as he appreciatively eyed the young woman on the stand.

"That explains why she practically bit my head

off. Why didn't you mention you were bringing your daughter? I would never have suggested this place."

"I suppose it slipped my mind. Besides, I never dreamed this city offered such . . . sophisticated entertainment." Edward Austen's eyes never left the redheaded beauty.

"Don't you think you'd better go after her to make sure she's all right? She won't swoon in the streets or anything, will she?" Lucas asked. Refined young women had an annoying habit of becoming vaporish if they felt their sensibilities had been injured, and Edward Austen's daughter definitely looked refined.

"Miranda has never swooned in her life. She's not delicate-natured like her mother. No, I think it's best we enjoy our meal. It will give her time to cool off a bit. We can take her something to eat when we finish. Let's order now, and you can let me know what I need to purchase before we set out for the gold fields." Edward Austen dismissed his daughter from his mind.

They discussed the necessary provisions as they supped on salmon, baked beans, fried biscuits, and coffee. Freshly baked pie was included with the meal. Though they were charged the outrageous sum of a dollar and a half per meal, the men did not complain. The food was good and the proprietor allowed them to take an additional plate to Miranda after Lucas promised to bring the dish back later that evening.

"I imagine Miranda will have simmered down by now. I've never known her to stay angry for long," Edward Austen commented. He led the way up the stairs to their room, pausing at the door to knock lightly before entering.

Miranda jumped from the edge of the bed, prepared to launch into the tirade she had been mentally rehearsing for the last hour. The door swung open, and in walked her father, closely followed by the same miner she had bumped into earlier that evening. She felt herself go crimson as she recognized his rugged face.

"Miranda, this is Lucas Adams. Lucas, this is my daughter, Miranda," her father introduced them, keeping his eyes carefully averted from hers.

"Pleased to meet you." Lucas bowed slightly over her extended hand. "Though I believe I have had the pleasure already," he added with a grin.

"It's possible," Miranda replied, unwilling to be outdone by his cool manner. How dare he taunt her? Her hands clenched into fists. What pleasure it would give her to knock that maddening grin off his face!

The tension in the room was palpable as Miranda and Lucas stood assessing each other like two pugilists before a fight. After quickly running her eyes up and down his frame, she began a more studied inspection of his face. Laugh lines crinkled the corners of his smoky blue eyes. His straight nose was neither broad nor narrow. A full auburn beard concealed most of his remaining facial features. Lowering her eyes, she noted his broad shoulders and surmised he was no stranger to physical labor. A broad chest tapered to a trim waist and hips supported by lean, muscular legs. He looked as if he could easily ward off any dangers they might encounter.

Her gaze returned to his face, to find him regarding her with open amusement. Refusing to be the first to break eye contact, she stared at him in open challenge, her heart racing, trying not to show she had been favorably impressed.

"Here, Mandy, we've brought you some dinner," her father broke in as he began to feel uncomfortable about the way the two boldly stared at each other. "Lucas promised to have the plate back tonight, so eat up."

Miranda bit back a sharp retort as she took the plate. There would be plenty of time to confront her father after their guest had left. To air their family differences before this man would only invite his mockery.

Pulling a chair over to the dressing table, her father continued, "Sit over here. Lucas and I can fill you in on our plans while you eat."

Miranda set her plate on the table and slipped into the offered chair, though she kept a wary eye on their guest. The man's stare was much too bold to her way of thinking. She might have been as naked as the young woman in the café, considering the gleam in his eyes. It took every ounce of her self-control to appear calm. She sat picking at her food, barely tasting the few bites that reached her mouth.

Lucas gave her a brief summary of the current status of the known gold fields, along with his recommendation that they try the streams above Hangtown.

"Hangtown, what a pleasant name for a town," she commented dryly, giving up any pretense of eating.

"That's only a nickname it picked up after some miners there hung some miscreants at Elstner's Hay

Yard. Its original name was Old Dry Diggings. It is
the site of one of the biggest gold finds, though the
rumor is that it is beginning to play out,'' Lucas explained.

"If it is played out"—Miranda repeated the unfamiliar term—"why are you suggesting it as the best
site?"

"The gold is washed out of the mountains by rain,
then funneled into the streams. My guess is, the further upstream you go, the thicker the gold should be.
But, as I say, it's just a guess. I've been here for
months, and though I've done well, it's been because of hard work and not a lucky strike. If you
really want my advice, you should talk your father
into opening up a supply store. With prices what they
are, that's where the real money is—"

"Now don't you put any ideas in her head," Edward Austen quickly interrupted. "I didn't come
halfway around the world to open up some store."

"Suit yourself, but have you bothered to wonder
how your daughter will fare while you're out in the
gold fields? San Francisco isn't exactly London, you
know." Lucas thought it odd that he should have to
remind the man of his parental duties. Edward Austen seemed to have a habit of forgetting he had a
daughter.

"I'll know exactly how she is faring because she'll
be right with me. What kind of father do you take me
for? I'd never consider leaving her behind. Why, the
very thought is ridiculous." Edward Austen's cheeks
flushed slightly. "Miranda is a good daughter. She'll
be a great help."

"Believe me, she'll be better off in San Francisco. The gold fields are no place for a woman."

"Mr. Adams." Miranda interrupted their argument. "I have every intention of accompanying my father. I am perfectly able to take care of myself." If the gold fields were as unpleasant as this man said, her father would need her. He had survived the deprivations of their travels with much less fortitude than she. His previous ventures had been conducted from the comfort of an overstuffed chair set within the safe confines of his private study. Without her guiding hand there was no telling what kind of trouble he might get himself into.

"Since you have never been to the gold fields, you haven't the slightest idea what you're talking about. I'm convinced your father is a fool. Are you determined to persuade me it is a family trait?"

"Now look here, Lucas, I'll have none of your insults," her father chimed in, his face puffed red with indignation. "You agreed to act as our guide and adviser, but I will thank you not to tell me how to care for my own daughter."

"I agreed to act as *your* guide. You mentioned nothing about bringing along a daughter. As you well know, I didn't even know you had a daughter until this evening," Lucas calmly returned.

"Mr. Adams, are the mining camps any worse than the Panamanian jungle?" Miranda questioned, struggling to keep her voice equally calm. She did not appreciate his patronizing attitude. Mr. Adams had no right to pass judgment on her capabilities without a shred of evidence to support his view. If he sought to test her competence, she was more than willing to meet the challenge.

"I don't know. I came down from Oregon," was the honest reply.

"I managed to survive the jungle quite nicely." Miranda smiled triumphantly up at Lucas's face, ignoring the fact that she had been miserable the entire time they were crossing the isthmus. "I sincerely doubt California can offer me much worse."

"It's your decision." Lucas shrugged indifferently. "But if you hold me up or cause any kind of trouble, I'll leave both you and your father without a backward glance."

"Agreed."

Edward Austen breathed a sigh of relief. He needed Lucas Adams despite his outspokenness. Though he would never admit it to Miranda, he knew he had gotten himself into something he could not handle alone. He needed an experienced man along to insure his success. For some reason Lucas Adams rubbed his daughter the wrong way, but once they got to know each other, he felt sure they would get along.

After checking over the list he had given her father and adding a few items to accommodate a third person in their party, Lucas turned to Miranda. "I trust you will see to any items necessary to take care of your feminine needs?"

Miranda's cheeks burned as she nodded affirmatively. She detested his impertinence. What right did he have to ask such a personal question? Someone definitely needed to teach him some manners.

"When are we to leave, Papa?" Miranda asked, pointedly ignoring Lucas Adams.

"Lucas, what do you say?" Her father redirected the question.

"I would like to get started the middle of next week if you can be ready by then. I still have some business to take care of in town, but it should be completed by then." As he started for the door he added, "I'll check back every day or so to see how you're coming along with the supplies. Buy everything you can here. The prices are even higher along the way. If Miss Austen is finished with the plate, I'll be going now."

Miranda handed him her still full plate.

"Good evening, Miss Austen, Mr. Austen."

Miranda sank back into the chair as the door closed. "Wherever did you manage to find such a rude man? If that's what the gold fields do to one's manners, I think we had better start wearing guns, too, though in his case, I doubt if he had many manners to start with."

"Now, Mandy, you weren't exactly polite yourself. What's wrong with you tonight?" Edward Austen regretted the question the instant it slipped from his lips.

"What's wrong with me!" Miranda's gray eyes flashed indignantly as she bore down on him. "First you take me to dinner at some bawdy café, then you bring that arrogant man to our room so he can insult me further. Isn't it enough that you've brought me to this godforsaken land without subjecting me to the company of prostitutes and cads?"

"Calm down, Mandy. I had no idea that young woman was going to take off her clothes. Surely you believe I have more sense than to knowingly take my own daughter to such a place. Why, it cuts your poor old father's heart to the quick to have you even think such a thing." He avoided her eyes by gazing out the window.

"I'm sorry, Papa." Miranda relented. "I should have known you didn't do it on purpose. It was probably that callous Mr. Adams who chose the place."

"Well . . . yes, it was, but he would never have chosen it if he had known I was bringing you along. He told me so himself." Edward Austen could not fathom why his usually congenial daughter had taken such an instant dislike to their guide. The man might be a bit outspoken, but he was going to take them to riches beyond their wildest dreams.

"That he would patronize such a place at all says a lot about his character," Miranda returned. She was not about to forgive Lucas Adams's behavior so easily.

Chapter 2

The next day greeted them with the usual fog, but by midmorning a bright sun had burned off the mist. It promised to be a beautiful day. Miranda spent the morning mending some of her undergarments, but by noon she could resist the sun's beckoning rays no longer. Putting her sewing aside, she placed a small amount of coins in her reticule, then went downstairs.

Mr. Clark, the storekeeper, was busy with a customer, so she waited patiently, browsing through the stacks of goods until the man paid for his purchases and left the store, his arms heavily burdened.

"Mr. Clark, I am going to wander around a bit and enjoy some of this sunshine for an hour or two. If my father comes back before I return, will you tell him where I have gone?"

"Be glad to, Miss Austen. You have yourself a nice afternoon." Mr. Clark gave her a fatherly smile before turning to greet another customer who had just entered the store.

Miranda waved a farewell as she stepped out the door. She picked her way gingerly across the street. Her immediate destination was the small tent-café where she and her father took their meals. It was clean and respectable, which put it a cut above the majority of eating establishments in San Francisco.

The proprietor, a pleasant-looking man in his mid-thirties, served her a steaming bowl of oxtail soup as they exchanged pleasantries. Miranda had learned earlier that Hiram Jackson had come to California to try the gold fields but, after a few luckless weeks, had decided he preferred a less strenuous method of making an income. He had returned to San Francisco to open this café and was very pleased with the income his establishment generated.

Hiram lingered at Miranda's table, engaging her in conversation until he no longer dared ignore his other customers. Staring wistfully at Miranda, he sighed, then returned to his labors. Miranda smiled at his obviously smitten gaze. It was flattering to be the object of so many longing looks. The shortage of women in California guaranteed even the most homely girl the pleasure of instant popularity. While Miranda knew she was by no means homely, she did not attribute the wealth of male admiration she had received since arriving here to any great attraction on her part. She did not possess the fair hair and china-doll complexion that had marked her mother as a beauty. While her skin was fashionably pale, she felt her face a trifle too thin to be considered truly handsome. Large eyes and a slightly turned-up nose lent her an elfin quality. Miranda pressed her naturally rose-colored lips together thoughtfully. Her own contrasting features were pleasant enough, though hardly above average.

Her meal finished, Miranda stepped back into the

sunshine and began striding purposefully toward the edge of town. She had not seen Lizzy since they had left the ship nearly a week ago, and she was determined to discover how her friend was faring. She sorely missed Lizzy and felt in need of some of her sensible advice. Lizzy had a knack for making the best of a bad situation.

Lizzy had made the weeks waiting for the promised steamer in Panama City bearable. She had even maneuvered her husband into giving Miranda his place in their stateroom when the *Argonaut* finally did arrive.

There had been more passengers than berths on the ship. The captain had reluctantly agreed to take on extra passengers if they were willing to sleep on deck. Lots were drawn, and Miranda's and her father's lot had fallen to the deck. The voyage was expected to take from fifty to sixty days. Miranda could not imagine how she would be able to take care of her private needs in such public circumstances.

Then Lizzy had come to the rescue, a reluctant Ed in tow. After his wife leveled him with her second meaningful stare, he offered his berth to Miranda. She had made a brief protest, but Lizzy would hear nothing of it. Though Lizzy could claim only twenty-five years to Miranda's eighteen, she had begun to mother her from the moment they met.

It seemed likely that the Deckers had been forced to pitch a tent on the edge of town, considering the lack of available lodgings, so this was where Miranda began her search. She occasionally stopped a passerby to ask if he knew the whereabouts of the Decker couple but with no luck. All her inquiries earned her were a wealth of appreciative smiles, and several times she found it difficult to prevent some homesick miner from staying to converse with her the entire afternoon. Though the men here were overly friendly, with the exception of Lucas Adams, she had found them to be polite and courteous.

Miranda was about to give up her search when she noticed the unmistakable figure of Lucas Adams strolling casually toward her, attired in the standard red flannel shirt, trousers, and boots.

"Good afternoon, Miss Austen. What brings you out here?"

"I'm looking for a friend of mine," Miranda replied, noting how the sun caught the deep red undertones of his dark brown hair and beard. She wondered absently what he would look like without the beard.

"Maybe I can help. What's her name?" he offered.

"Lizzy Decker. She is here with her husband, Ed," Miranda informed him. In the light of day Mr. Adams's vigorous build was even more impressive. She mentally scolded herself for taking an interest in the man's physical attributes.

"Is she a rather large woman who likes to boss her husband around?" Lucas asked.

Miranda giggled at his accurate description of her friend. "Yes, that sounds just like her."

"Then I'm afraid you're too late. They took a wagon out of here yesterday morning. I believe they were headed south."

"Oh." Miranda turned slightly to hide her disappointment. "I guess she's all right then."

"She was managing just fine. She certainly keeps a tight rein on her husband, though, like she's afraid if she turns her back, some other woman will snatch him up. Considering the man's looks, I can't believe that's possible. He is definitely the least appealing human being I have ever laid eyes on."

"In Lizzy's case I've concluded that love truly is blind." Miranda's smile lit up her entire face. "I guess if she's gone, I might as well go back."

"If you'll allow me, I'll escort you to your room." Lucas offered her his arm.

"Thank you." Miranda placed her hand on the offered arm, eyeing him curiously as she tried to reconcile today's polite manner with the bold rudeness of the night before. She had to admit that she did attack him before they were even introduced. Maybe the incident put him out of sorts, though she wouldn't have guessed him to be the sensitive type. Well, it was best to enjoy his good humor of the moment in case he should suddenly turn surly again. Since her father had committed them to travel with this man, it would make things easier if they could deal civilly with each other.

The top of Miranda's head barely reached Lucas's shoulder as they strolled side by side, Lucas drawing the envious stares of many a man. He simply smiled, then patted her hand solicitously, obviously enjoying their envy. His manner was much too possessive, and it was beginning to annoy Miranda. After all, they were virtual strangers. There was something about Lucas Adams that kept her off-balance.

"You mentioned you came from Oregon?" Miranda ventured in an effort to begin a conversation.

"Yes, my brother and I live up there. We farm and have some lumbering concerns."

"Did your brother stay in Oregon, or is he here in California too?"

"He stayed home to tend matters there. It would have been impractical for us both to come. Since he has a wife and children to look after, I was the logical choice. Whatever I make down here we split fifty-fifty."

"I take it you're not married then," Miranda stated.

"No, I almost made that mistake once, but since then I've managed to avoid the marriage trap," Lucas replied, his thoughts momentarily drifting to Mary Blake. At the tender age of nineteen he had courted her with the devotion of a puppy. She had teased and tempted him, professing undying love, never letting him touch her. Then, one afternoon in a cool glade, she had reluctantly surrendered to the desire he felt would tear him asunder if he did not find relief. At least, at the time he had thought it was surrender. Now he realized she had deliberately seduced him. When she had come to him two weeks later to tell him she was with child, he had readily agreed to marry her. He smiled, thinking of how naive he had been. Even if he had fathered a child, no woman could possibly have known so early. Luckily he had learned the truth in time. The besotted father was unwilling to let another man claim his child. The man did not have the position and wealth of Lucas's family. It had been a blow to Lucas's ego to learn that was what Mary truly desired of him. Despite her tears of protest, he had immediately called off the engagement. The bitterness had eased, but still, in the eleven years since, he had had no desire to marry, finding the freedom of the single life much to his liking.

"You sound as if protecting your bachelorhood has been a constant trial for you," Miranda said, interrupting his thoughts. "Perhaps you have some hidden quality of which I have yet to be made aware. It must be difficult to be so in demand."

"Yes, it does try one's patience at times." Lucas grinned. "But I don't want you to get the wrong impression. I do enjoy women. I just enjoy my freedom too much to get tied down to one permanently."

"How fortunate for womankind," Miranda returned, smiling sweetly. "No one of us will have to put up with you for a lifetime."

"*Touché,* madam, but you will notice we have arrived at your destination." He came to a stop in front of Clark's Supply Store. "I would love to spend the afternoon bantering with you, but as I have an appointment, I must forego the pleasure. Good afternoon." Tipping his hat in a farewell gesture, he continued down the street.

Miranda stood for a moment, admiring his purposeful stride, before she caught herself and hurriedly entered the store. Though she had enjoyed their verbal sparring, it wouldn't do for her to become too friendly with Mr. Adams. His manners were too unpredictable.

"Is that gentleman an admirer of yours, Miss Austen?" Mr. Clark asked as she entered.

"No." Miranda felt her cheeks grow warm.

"He's a friend of my father's. I ran into him, and he offered to walk me back."

"Sorry I made the mistake," Clark apologized, a knowing twinkle in his eye. "I imagine with just a pinch of encouragement you could have him courtin' at your door."

"Thank you for your confidence, Mr. Clark, but I'm really not interested in him in that way," Miranda replied. Quickly changing the subject, she asked, "Has my father returned yet?"

"No, miss, but I expect he will be along shortly." Mr. Clark turned back to the task of restocking his shelves.

It was nearly dark by the time Miranda's father returned. She was just about to light a lamp when she heard the door squeak open.

"I can't believe the prices they are asking in this country." Her father plopped into a chair, shaking his head in disgust. "I imagine I'll just get Clark to provision us. His prices aren't any worse than the rest."

"Are we running short of funds, Papa?" Miranda questioned, her voice heavy with concern.

"Now don't start worrying. We've plenty of capital. It's just that with these prices I feel like I'm being robbed every time I walk into a store."

Miranda breathed a sigh of relief. At least money was one thing she needn't worry about.

"Papa, I'm hungry. Can we go to dinner now?"

"Sure, darling, but you'd better get your cloak. That infernal wind has kicked up again," he advised.

The next morning Miranda's father awoke with a cold. He went downstairs to discuss provisions with

Mr. Clark but returned shortly, groaning as he ascended the stairs. He immediately lay down on the cot and pulled one of the blankets over his shoulders.

"I'm afraid this damp weather has given me a doozy of a cold. I think I'll stay in today and try to sleep it off. Be an angel, will you, darling, and run down to the café? See if you can buy me a bowl of broth." He sniffed loudly.

"Of course, Papa," Miranda replied as she bent to help her father remove his boots, then tucked him snugly in bed. "I'll be just a few minutes."

"You're a good girl, Mandy. Give me a day or two and I'll be back to my old self. I'm too eager to get to the gold fields to lie around in a sickbed for long."

Miranda hastened to their usual café. The soup for the noonday meal was already simmering in a large cast iron pot, but it was too early for it to be ready to serve. The tent was empty except for Hiram Jackson, who stood leaning over the pot as he added a variety of root vegetables to the simmering broth. His eyes lit up as Miranda entered.

"Good morning, Miss Austen. Are you coming for a late breakfast or an early lunch?" His handsome face glowed as he smiled a greeting.

"Neither. I'm afraid my father isn't feeling well. He sent me to fetch him some broth. May I take a small pot back to our room? I promise to bring it back as soon as he is through."

"Of course you can. A man would have to have a heart of stone to refuse any request made by such a beautiful lady." Hiram's color heightened as he spoke, and he turned toward the kettle to hide his discomfort before adding, "I'm afraid the soup is not quite ready, but I'd be honored to keep you company if you'd care to wait.''

Miranda was about to explain that she would return later, but the eager look on Hiram's face stopped her. She was sure her father could manage alone for a short time. "Thank you, Mr. Jackson," she replied, seating herself in a chair near the stove.

Hiram wiped his hands on his apron, then sat in the chair opposite her. "When does your father plan to leave for the gold fields?" he asked, genuinely interested in anything that concerned her.

"The middle of next week. We are buying our provisions from Mr. Clark, but he still needs to purchase a couple of horses and a pack mule.''

"Will you be staying above Clark's store until he returns?'' Hiram ventured, hoping he could continue to look forward to her daily visits to his café. Already a plan was forming in the back of his mind; however, he sensed it would take time to win this lady's approval.

"I'm going with my father to the diggings," Miranda replied, hoping this admission would not evoke the same type of response it had from Lucas Adams.

"Oh, Miss Austen, you can't do that," Hiram cried, clearly dismayed. "If your father is concerned about your safety here, I'll be glad to keep an eye on you for him.'' Hiram remembered all too well the deprivations of life in the mining camps.

"Thank you for your concern, but you needn't worry about me. I'm going along to take care of my father more than anything. He's not used to rough living, and I doubt if he could manage without me.''

"You're a brave daughter to sacrifice so much for

your father," Hiram commented, his opinion of her rising to new heights.

"Oh, not so noble as you think," Miranda confessed. "I did everything in my power to keep him from coming to California in the first place. But since we are here, I may as well see it through to the end."

"M-miss Austen." Hiram was made bold by the knowledge that he had little time to execute his plan. "Would you allow me to call on you?"

Miranda, taken back by the suddenness of his question, wondered briefly if he had already spoken to her father, then rejected the idea. His question had been asked on impulse. The idea was not repugnant to her, though it seemed rather foolish, since she would be leaving in a week's time. Hiram Jackson's looks were above average. Though his face was boyish, he exuded a strong air of masculinity. He was clean-shaven except for a thin mustache that was a shade darker than his wavy strawberry-blond hair. Looking up into his deep blue eyes, Miranda could see all his hopes reflected in them. She could think of no way to deny him without hurting his feelings.

"I suppose you may come calling, though you will have to ask my father first," she answered, keeping her smile carefully devoid of emotion. She could see no harm in enjoying Hiram's company for a week; however, she had no intention of leading him to believe the relationship could become more permanent, if that were his intention. "If the soup is ready, I really should be getting back to my father. He will be wondering what is taking me so long."

As she rose, Hiram jumped up to assist her from her chair. Scooping a generous portion of the soup into a small iron pot, he covered the contents with a lid, then handed her the vessel along with the necessary eating utensils.

"How much do I owe you?" Miranda questioned as she began counting out some coins.

"Nothing." Hiram smiled broadly. "This meal is on me."

"Thank you, Mr. Jackson." Miranda smiled, feeling a bit guilty. She hoped she had not already given him too much encouragement.

"I'd be mighty pleased if you would call me Hiram," he encouraged.

"Thank you, Hiram," Miranda amended. "Now I really must be going." She walked quickly back to their room.

"I'm sorry, Papa, but I had to wait for the soup," Miranda explained as she set the steaming pot on the table. "I hope you aren't too annoyed."

"I suppose it couldn't be helped. How much did this pot of food set us back?" he questioned as Miranda handed him a bowl of the inviting broth.

"Nothing," Miranda replied. "He wouldn't let me pay for it."

Her father eyed her curiously.

"Papa, Hiram wants to call on me."

"Hiram, is it? What luck! That could cut down on our expenses considerably. You be sure to be especially nice to that young man," her father advised.

"Papa, you don't expect me to lead him on, do you? I can't believe you would ask such a thing. It would be cruel." Miranda was greatly offended by her father's suggestion.

"I'll tell you what is cruel: the prices they charge

around here. He won't be going to the poorhouse by feeding us. It seems to me a painless way to save a few coins. You don't find him repulsive, do you?''

''Of course not. He is a very pleasant man. I just don't want to deceive him.'' Though Miranda was thrifty by nature and necessity, she did not consider deception an acceptable way to cut costs.

''Then marry him if he asks you,'' her father retorted, irritated by her impractical attitude. ''That should soothe your conscience.''

Miranda bit back any further comments. She had no intention of leading Hiram Jackson on, no matter what her father said. Dishing herself a bowl of soup, she ate her meal in silence.

She spent the next two days nursing her father. He indeed had nothing but a simple cold, but he seemed to enjoy the luxury of lying in bed all day while his daughter saw to his needs. The first two days were an endless procession of requests for hot tea, back rubs, and glasses of whiskey, ostensibly to clear his stuffy head. She read to him, sang to him, and listened indulgently while he filled her ears with tales of men made rich in a day. By the third day he began to be bored by his idleness and decided to rise from his sickbed.

Miranda was greatly relieved. She knew he was exaggerating his complaints. During his illness Miranda had insisted he use the cot while she made her bed on the floor. She was looking forward to returning to the soft cot. In a few days' time a bed would be a luxury of the past.

The one good thing about her father's self-imposed confinement was that it gave her an excuse to avoid spending time with Hiram. Already she regretted agreeing to let him call. He made no attempt to conceal his adoring looks whenever she entered the café. Miranda knew, despite her good intentions, that he was going to be disappointed when she left. It would have been better to turn him away from the start, as she had no intention of staying in California any longer than necessary. Besides, she was not in the market for an American husband, no matter how adoring.

She had enough problems caring for her father. When she did marry, it would be to some stable English gentleman who could provide her with the security she longed for, not a man who would desert his home to follow some golden dream. That was exactly the type of man she wished to avoid. Hiram Jackson had guaranteed his failure to win her heart by the very fact that he had come to California. That fact did not keep her from liking him; it only prevented her from considering a serious attachment.

She began going to the café during peak hours to avoid any involved conversations with Hiram. She was quite sure he intended to ask for her hand. If possible, she would never give him the opportunity. Though her insistence that she pay for any food he provided them seemed to upset him, Miranda refused to take advantage of his affections in any way. She knew her father was not pleased with her decision, but when the need arose, the daughter could be as stubborn as the father.

Chapter 3

Lucas Adams had not contacted them since the day he had walked Miranda home. Though he had said he would check back every day or so, they hadn't seen a trace of him in three days. Miranda was beginning to wonder if he had changed his mind about guiding them to the gold fields. It would be just like the man to leave without a word, she thought as she rubbed the ache in the small of her back. Her father had not seen fit to vacate the cot, and another night spent on the hard wood floor had done little for her disposition. She awoke feeling stiff and out of sorts with the world in general.

Dressing quietly, she threw an exasperated glance at the peacefully sleeping form on the cot, then she hurried down the stairs. As she turned to catch a remark made by Mr. Clark, her attention was momentarily diverted from the doorway. To her chagrin she walked headlong into the flannel-clad chest of a miner. Even before she looked up into the grinning face, she knew to whom the broad chest belonged.

"You do have a penchant for running into me, don't you, Miss Austen." Lucas looked down at her distressed face, then added under his breath, "Are you trying to tell me something?'' He laughed as the color rose in her cheeks.

"No." Miranda struggled to regain her composure. "But it appears to me *you* have a penchant for blocking doorways."

"I didn't come here to argue. Have you eaten yet?" He deftly changed the subject.

"No, I was just going to get something."

"Good, we can get something together, then I have someplace I want to take you."

"Where is that?" She was not at all pleased that he had not asked if she was willing to accompany him.

"Why don't I leave that for a surprise? It will give you something to think about while we eat." Lucas counted on her curiosity to prevent her from refusing him.

"Can I trust you to be more discreet in your choice of breakfast establishments, or should I prepare myself to witness another lewd display?" Miranda asked rather acidly.

"Rest assured, I will be most gentlemanly in my selection. Now, if you will stop chattering long enough to take my arm, we will be on our way."

"Mr. Clark, tell Mr. Austen his daughter is with Lucas Adams should he become concerned with her whereabouts."

"Glad to, Mr. Adams. Now you two have fun," Mr. Clark admonished, throwing Miranda a conspiratorial wink.

"What was that all about?" Lucas questioned as they started down the street.

"He thinks I should encourage your affections."

He arched an eyebrow as Miranda gazed up into his eyes, her expression unreadable.

"And do you?"

"Hardly. You're not exactly the kind of man I'd want clamoring at my doorstep. I require my callers to be gentlemen." For once Miranda felt as if she had the upper hand in their conversation.

"Good. I have no intention of being saddled with some lovesick female," Lucas informed her. "Your father doesn't have enough money to pay me to put up with that."

Not sure she hadn't again been bested, Miranda let the conversation end on that comment.

"Here is a suitable place," Lucas informed her as he started to lift the flap of Hiram Jackson's tent café. Seeing Miranda's hesitation, he let the flap fall back in place. "Really, you are tiresome. This place is perfectly respectable."

"It's not that." Miranda bit her bottom lip, not knowing how to explain her reluctance. "I'd just rather go someplace else."

Lucas stood studying her face a few moments, then, as understanding dawned, he commented, "I see, you're afraid one of your beaus will be upset if he sees you with me."

"Hiram is not one of my beaus," Miranda blurted out before thinking. "But, you're right, I'd rather he didn't see me with you. Can we go somewhere else?" Lucas Adams exhibited a possessive attitude when she was in his presence. She felt quite sure he did it to annoy her, and it seemed foolish to subject Hiram to such a display. It could only bruise his feelings.

"Whatever you wish." Lucas did not press her further. "That place across the street will suit equally as well."

Lucas ate a hearty breakfast while Miranda nibbled on jam-covered biscuits. Before running into Lucas, she had been quite famished, but she found his presence had an adverse effect on her appetite. They ate in silence, Lucas being occupied with his meal and Miranda with her thoughts. She could not understand why Lucas made her feel so edgy. He was certainly coarse, but that did not explain why her stomach tied in knots whenever he was near. She had met coarse men before and had dismissed them easily from her mind. Why did thoughts of Lucas constantly plague her? It made no sense to feel such strong emotions toward a virtual stranger.

"If you're finished, we might as well be on our way." Lucas rose to assist her from her chair. "Do you always eat so little?" he asked, more with concern than sarcasm.

"I'm just not feeling very hungry this morning." Miranda shrugged off the question.

Lucas presented his arm, then guided her out into the street. The fog had already lifted, and it promised to be a beautiful day. Fortunately it had not rained in almost a full week, making the streets much easier to traverse. Guiding her to the front of an unobtrusive supply store, Lucas bade her wait outside. A few minutes later he returned with a paper-wrapped bundle, then wordlessly steered her toward the other side of the square.

As they walked along they passed a kaleidoscope of miners from a variety of countries, garbed identically, their origins easily distinguishable by the difference in their languages. A Chinese immigrant scurried by, his tiny, shuffling steps causing his long black pigtail to bob rhythmically on his back. It was still too early in the day for the prostitutes to begin plying their wares, but Miranda knew that by noon, every corner would hold a covey of those disreputable ladies. To her there was nowhere else on earth with such a diverse population. In a way it was exciting to be part of such an unusual blend.

"Ah, here is our destination." Lucas stopped before a low, unpainted clapboard building. Above the door hung a brightly painted sign announcing: COUTURE. Opening the door, he ushered her inside.

"Good morning, sir, ma'am, I'll be with you in just a moment." The proprietress turned her attention back to the customer she was serving. Miranda's eyes lit briefly on the customer. The liberal use of face paint and the cut of her gown made her profession all too obvious. Miranda looked up at Lucas in disgust.

Before she could open her mouth, Lucas leaned down to whisper in her ear. "Now behave yourself. I need the services of a seamstress. If the woman refused to sew for prostitutes, she could never stay in business. Prudish ways don't survive long around here."

Miranda could not argue with the truth of his statement. She could count on one hand the number of decent women she had seen since arriving in San Francisco. If women were rare in this country, women with any moral fiber were virtually nonexistent.

"Now, may I help you?" The proprietress, a thin woman in her mid-thirties, hurried over to them. Though her dull brown hair was beginning to gray, her skin still held the glow of youth.

"Do you know the type of dress the sunbonnets wear?" Lucas asked.

"Yes, sir." The woman wrinkled her nose.

Miranda was busy perusing the variety of silks and other fine fabrics lining the walls of the shop. It amazed her that such a rustic town could boast a shop with such a fine array of fabrics. However, Lucas's next statement brought her full attention back to him.

"I would like you to make these into two such dresses. The muslin is for aprons." Lucas handed the woman his package.

"Ah, you wish your wife to have more practical clothing as well." The proprietress noted the cut of Miranda's dark blue gown with a professional eye. The dress was beautiful but hardly suitable for any but the most refined of tasks.

"I'm not his wife!" Miranda spun around, immediately regretting she hadn't let the misconception stand as a knowing look entered the seamstress's eyes.

Misreading Miranda's stricken look, the woman quickly explained, "I do not let such things bother me. If I did, I would have been forced to close this shop long ago. Now, if you will step into the back, I will take the necessary measurements." She lifted the curtain that hung across the doorway at the back of the shop. Miranda followed, debating whether or not to try to explain that there was no relationship between Lucas and herself, then decided to keep silent.

If she had done that in the first place, she could have avoided embarrassment.

The seamstress was quick and efficient in taking the measurements, clucking her tongue in appreciation as she wrote the figures on a slip of paper. "It is a pity to hide your pretty figure in such a dress. Your clothes should all be well fitted to show off your daintiness," the woman complained.

Miranda shrugged her shoulders. She had no idea what type of dress Lucas was ordering, but it didn't sound the least bit flattering. She thoughtfully fingered the sturdy calico fabric as the proprietress refastened her gown. Each was patterned in a cheerful floral design, the dominant color of each piece being blue and green respectively. She could find no fault with the material but could not fathom why Lucas had bought it for her.

"Can the dresses be finished by Monday?" Lucas asked as they reentered the front of the shop.

"If it is necessary," the seamstress assured him.

"Good, then I will be back Monday to pick them up and to settle the bill. Good day." Lucas tipped his hat as he ushered Miranda from the shop.

"Why did you do that?" Miranda questioned as soon as they were outside.

"Do what?"

"Order those dresses. Surely you could see what the woman thought of me."

"She thought you were my wife until you burst in to inform her differently." The corners of his lips turned up in amusement. "You caused your own embarrassment. I was willing to overlook her mistake."

Miranda was irritated that what he said was true. She chose to ignore his remark. "You still haven't answered my question."

"The gowns you have are impractical for where we are going. As I have yet to see you clothe yourself in anything remotely suitable, I took it upon myself to remedy the situation."

"How gallant, but ladies of virtue do not accept gifts of clothing from strange men."

"*Ladies*"—he emphasized the word—"are better mannered than you are. It is impolite to reject a gift given in good faith."

"I just don't understand why you did it," Miranda tried to explain. He was confusing her again, and she didn't like it.

"Maybe I'm trying to bribe you," Lucas offered, a challenging glint in his eye.

Miranda blushed at the innuendo. "I can't be bought," she stated, her chin held high in the air.

"Any woman can be bought," Lucas countered, an edge of mockery in his tone. "The prostitutes sell themselves for gold, the ladies for social position. Perhaps no one has discovered your price as yet."

Miranda winced as he caught her wrist, her palm just inches from his sardonic face.

"Remember little girl, I'm a lot bigger than you," he warned her. "If you ever do succeed in slapping me, the repercussions will not be pleasant, I promise you. Now, compose yourself, and I'll take you back to your father."

Miranda pondered his warning in silence as she allowed herself to be guided down the street. She had never considered that Lucas might use the strength she had admired against her. The thought frightened her. Perhaps it would be wiser to find someone else to serve as their guide. It did not seem prudent to put herself at the mercy of a man with such a distorted view of women.

Of one thing she was certain. As soon as they reached the room she would have her father reimburse him for the cost of the material. She could pay the dressmaker herself when she went to pick up the finished garments. She would accept nothing from this man walking so confidently beside her.

When they had reached the front of Clark's store, Lucas, watching her through half-veiled eyes, commented, "I knew you could behave yourself if you really tried. Thank you for the pleasantly silent stroll." A smile tugged at the corners of his mouth as she struggled to retain her composure. It was delightful how easily his teasing angered her.

"Yes, the lack of conversation was pleasantly refreshing. We must do it again sometime," Miranda returned when she was sure her voice would not betray her agitation. To anyone out of hearing distance the exchange appeared quite friendly.

"I have a few things to discuss with your father. If you'll lead the way, I'll be right behind you." A firm hand on the small of her back nudged her gently into the store.

After ascending the stairs in silence Miranda entered the room, Lucas close behind her. It was immediately apparent her father was not in.

"I'll stop by later today." Lucas turned to leave.

"No. Wait just a minute." Miranda stopped him, bestowing her most enticing smile upon him as he turned back toward the room. Satisfied he would wait, she knelt before her father's trunk, laying aside his clothing until she found the small black box she was seeking. After removing what she considered a sufficient amount of coins, she carefully returned the box to its hiding place, then replaced the clothing before lowering the lid.

"This should adequately cover the cost of the material." Miranda looked triumphantly into Lucas's eyes as she folded his lean, brown fingers around the coins.

Lucas stood perfectly still. He slowly uncurled his fingers and stared at the coins. "It's too much."

Miranda missed the deadly tone in his voice. "Consider it an advance on the salary my father promised you."

Lucas closed the distance between them in one stride. Enveloping Miranda in his powerful arms, he crushed her tender lips with his. Though she did not respond, he found his first, brief taste of her sweetness much to his liking. Just as abruptly he released her, but not before he had deftly slipped the coins down the front of her bodice.

"You consider them advance payment." He grinned. "And get someone to teach you how to kiss." His voice was seductively soft, serving to make the sound of the door slamming that much louder.

Convinced he would not return, Miranda turned to the task of fishing the coins from her bodice. She muttered several unladylike oaths as one slipped out of reach. Pulling at her clothing, she did a little shimmy step until the cold coin slid down, clanking on the floor. She returned the coins to their box and went to lean against the windowsill, staring morosely out at the city. Her hand caressed the tender spot on her cheek where Lucas's beard had scratched her soft skin.

"Have someone teach me to kiss indeed," she complained to the world in general. "That wasn't a kiss, it was an assault." Why let his comment bother her? she chided herself. If she had her way, she would never set eyes on the man again.

She spent the remainder of the day in the room, waiting for her father's return. Once she stepped downstairs to question Mr. Clark, but her father had neglected to tell him when he expected to be back. Trudging up the stairs, she continued her wait with only her disturbing thoughts as companions.

It was imperative that she convince her father to hire a different guide. She held no illusions that Lucas felt anything for her. She felt sure he would continue to use his unwanted advances as a means to punish her if her actions should displease him. It would be impossible to tolerate such a man on a day-to-day basis.

The dinner hour was fast approaching when Edward Austen returned. Miranda immediately noticed his jovial mood. "What has you feeling so cheerful tonight, Papa?"

"I managed to pick up a couple of horses and a mule at a reasonable price. They belonged to two brothers who have had enough of this gold country. Those men were so homesick for their wives, I had no trouble at all dickering them down. Then I ran into Lucas Adams and spent a perfectly enjoyable afternoon gambling with the man. What a fellow! I don't think I've ever met a man I liked more."

Miranda's face fell. "Papa, I need to talk to you."

"Why so glum? You don't want to spoil a perfectly fine day, do you?" Edward Austen drew his brows together.

"Well, no. But, Papa, I want you to find another guide."

"Why ever for?" her father asked, thoroughly confused by her request. "I couldn't find a better man than Lucas Adams."

"But, Papa, he's mean and callous and seems to delight in insulting me," Miranda protested.

"He told me how you got your feathers ruffled about the dresses. He was just trying to be helpful, girl. Why are you refusing his generosity when you're always minding me to be careful of our finances?"

"Papa, you know it's not right for him to buy me clothing."

"This isn't England, Mandy. Things are different here. If the man wants to buy you clothes, that's his business. Now, I don't want to hear another word about it." Her father dismissed her argument.

"But, Papa, he kissed me." Miranda had not wanted to tell him, but she was getting desperate.

"So that's what's really bothering you." Edward Austen chuckled as he paused to rub his chin. "Listen, Mandy, you're a pretty girl, and women are scarce here. Why, I'd probably have done the same thing had the opportunity been presented to me. If it will make you happy, I'll tell Lucas you have an aversion to kissing. I'm sure he'll respect your wishes.''

Miranda's shoulders sagged in defeat. There was no way she was going to convince her father to change guides. Instead of being outraged at the liberties Lucas had taken, he was making excuses for the man. He would be no help at all in protecting her from Lucas's base nature. Well, she thought, sighing philosophically, she would have to provide her own protection.

''Grab your wrap, Mandy. I'll take you to get something to eat,'' her father directed. Miranda obeyed, following her father sullenly down the stairs.

For the next few days Miranda was able to avoid all but minimal contact with Lucas Adams. If he came to see her father, she would excuse herself and leave the room. The night her father invited him to join them for dinner, she politely declined to make it a threesome. Her father remained oblivious to her conspicuous absences. In all, she thought her efforts quite successful.

She had begun to spend most of her days sitting in Hiram Jackson's café. It was pleasant to be treated with politeness and respect by someone, and the visits helped her to avoid spending time in their room where she was more likely to have to tolerate Lucas's presence. As the time for their departure grew near he was spending more and more time with her father.

Hiram was overjoyed to have all this attention. Though Miranda was careful to do nothing to encourage an attachment, it was obvious his feelings for her were more than that of a friend. She felt sorry she would have to disappoint him but felt more competent to handle this relationship than the one with Lucas. Whenever she sensed Hiram was becoming too serious-minded, she would quickly change the subject or find some urgent reason to depart the café. If her luck held, she could still avoid the issue of marriage altogether.

On Sunday Miranda joined a handful of worshipers at a small Protestant church. Though the building was little more than a shack, it had been whitewashed both inside and out, and someone had erected a crude, makeshift steeple on the roof. The sermon was uplifting, though overly long, but in all, Miranda found the meeting enjoyable.

Monday afternoon she stopped by the dressmaker's to see if her dresses were finished. Lucas had not yet been by, and as she paid the woman for her work, she felt as if she had won at least a small victory. The dresses, fashioned identically, were nothing more than a long length of fabric gathered, then sewn to a high-necked, rounded yoke. Long sleeves were also gathered, then attached to thin, buttoned cuffs, while more buttons fastened together the sides of the yoke that parted in front to allow for ease in dressing. The style was similar to several nightdresses Miranda owned. The dressmaker had sewn a thin fabric belt to be tied around the waist, but otherwise the dresses had no fashionable touches.

"They do look practical," Miranda commented as she held up the blue calico.

"I sewed an extra ruffle on the aprons so you won't feel quite so drab." The seamstress patted her hand in understanding.

No wonder Lucas had thought her protests so ridiculous, Miranda mused as she carried her package
back to their room. No man in his right mind would
buy such a garment for his mistress. Was his desire
to see her properly attired for their journey really Lucas Adams's only motivation for purchasing the
clothing? Why had he taunted her? She didn't understand the conventions of a society that seemed devoid of rules. She was still deep in thought when she
entered the room to find Lucas and her father conversing earnestly over a map. They both looked up
as she entered the room.

"I see you've been shopping." Her father noted
the package in her arms.

"Yes." Not feeling up to a confrontation with Lucas at the moment, she did not comment further.

"We're mapping out our trail, so be a good girl
and let us work awhile longer," Edward Austen re-
quested before turning his attention back to the map.
Miranda walked quietly to her trunk. After unwrap-
ping the dresses she laid them neatly on top of her
other clothing. Glancing up, she could see Lucas
watching her out of the corner of one eye. She knew
by his uplifted brow that he had recognized the fabric
of the dresses. Ignoring him, she removed a needle
and thread from her sewing pouch, then gently closed
the lid of her trunk. When she looked up again, Lucas's full attention had returned to the map.

Miranda sat on the edge of the cot and began
mending a torn sleeve on one of her father's shirts.
She felt exhausted. She was tired of avoiding Lucas,
tired of sidestepping Hiram's attentions, and, most
of all, tired of California. She suddenly realized she

was very homesick. She longed for polite conversations in tidy parlors, afternoons of tea and scones, and for leisurely strolls through the park. These pleasures were all so distant, they seemed almost unreal. She brushed furtively at a stray tear. Afraid she was going to make a fool of herself, she lay the sewing aside, excused herself, and hurried from the room. There had to be someplace in San Francisco where she could find enough privacy to have a good cry.

Wiping away an occasional tear as it trickled down her cheek, Miranda walked briskly toward the wooded hills on the edge of town. She had to pass endless rows of tents before she was finally clear of the town. She walked until she was satisfied she would not be disturbed, then she sat down on a moss-covered rock and buried her head in her arms, gently sobbing out her misery. It was a blessed relief to let down her guard and allow herself the luxury of feeling thoroughly sorry for herself.

When her tears were spent, she stayed in the peaceful solitude of the forest glen until she noticed the sun was low in the sky. Reluctantly she rose, slowly retracing her steps. A small stream crossed her path. Kneeling, she splashed the cool water on her face and eyes to remove any evidence of her tears. She used the hem of her petticoat to dry her face and continued on her way.

It was fully dark by the time she reached the doorway of their room. She was grateful to arrive at this small haven, as the night life of the city had already begun in earnest.

"Where have you been?" her father demanded. He had become genuinely concerned about her.

"I'm sorry to have worried you, Papa. I went for a walk and lost track of the time," Miranda said, apologizing.

"Well, I suppose there is no real harm done. Lucas is out looking for you, but I imagine he'll have the sense to check back here before too long to see if you've returned on your own."

This news was thoroughly disheartening. Lucas was bound to be annoyed with her when he returned, and she just didn't feel up to one of his caustic tongue-lashings tonight.

"Why don't I go get us something to eat," her father offered. Miranda was seldom melancholy, and her mood concerned him. "You stay here in case Lucas returns while I'm out."

He returned in a few minutes bearing a pot filled with a thick chicken-and-vegetable stew and a small sack of warm biscuits. Miranda helped her father serve the meal and began eating with surprising gusto, the long walk having given her an appetite. They had almost completed their meal when, after knocking lightly to announce his arrival, Lucas entered the room.

"I'm sorry, I've looked—" he broke off in midsentence when he saw Miranda sitting at the table. "Where have you been?"

"I went for a walk. I'm sorry I troubled you," she replied, her eyes lowered to her hands in her lap.

"That must have been some walk. Next time let someone know where you're headed. It's not wise for a woman to walk alone after dark. After some men get a few glasses of whiskey under their belts, they become a mite headstrong,'' he advised, not unkindly. ''Since everything is all right here, I'll be on my way.'' He turned and strode out the door. Miranda sighed in relief, grateful that Lucas had let her off so lightly.

The next day was filled with last-minute preparations for their departure. On Lucas's advice, Miranda had persuaded Mr. Clark, for a small fee, of course, to store her trunk for her until they returned. She was relieved they were finally beginning their journey. The sooner her father was able to try his luck in the gold fields, the sooner they could return home.

She had decided to leave all but one wine-colored gown behind. Though the dress was far from practical, she could not bear to be without at least one fashionable gown. She folded it carefully and placed it in the leather pack her father had provided for her the day before. Chemises, drawers, petticoats, and nightdresses followed. When she came to her corset, she held the article up in indecision. Her waist was naturally slim. Even in her most close-fitting gown the garment was hardly necessary. Her eyes drifted to the two calico dresses. In such loose-fitting clothing no one could possibly know what her figure looked like, let alone whether or not she wore a corset. It seemed rather foolish to wear the constricting garment. Feeling just a little decadent, Miranda packed the corset into the trunk. She placed the blue calico in the pack, reserving the green for tomorrow's journey. Both muslin aprons followed, then a small cloth bag containing her grooming articles. A few more personal items went into the pack until her trunk held nothing but an assortment of gowns, her corset, and several of her more delicate petticoats. Satisfied she was as ready as she ever would be, she decided to go to lunch.

It was earlier than she thought when she entered the café. Except for two miners sitting at a corner table, the place was empty. Both men tipped their hats when she entered, but after giving her an appreciative grin, they returned to their conversation. Hiram came in from the back of the tent, carrying a large bag of potatoes. His eyes lit up when he saw Miranda sitting at one of the tables.

"Good morning, Miss Austen. May I get you something to eat?" He set down his burden, wiping his hands on his short apron as he approached her.

"Yes, a bowl of soup would be fine."

"If I'm not being too bold, may I join you? I could use a bite to eat myself before things get busy around here."

"Of course you may. I would enjoy the company," Miranda replied truthfully. Except when their conversations took a serious turn, she enjoyed Hiram's company immensely. He was polite, charming, and full of humorous tales he had picked up from his patrons.

Hiram excused himself and returned bearing two steaming bowls of vegetable soup and a plate of biscuits. "A man came in here looking for you last night," Hiram commented as he slid into the seat opposite her. "He said you were lost and he was helping your father look for you. I'm glad you made it home safely."

"I wasn't really lost. I just took a walk and lost

track of the time. It's apparent my thoughtlessness caused undue concern.''

"I admit I was a bit worried until your father came in and told me you were back," Hiram confessed.

"I'm sorry I worried you," Miranda apologized.

They continued their conversation as they ate the filling soup. Miranda laughed gaily as Hiram related a particularly amusing story he had overheard the night before. By the time they had finished eating, a few more men had wandered in for their midday meal. Hiram excused himself, served the men, then returned to her table.

"I had better let you get back to work." Miranda rose as another man entered the tent. She smiled at the one friend she had found since arriving in San Francisco. "I really am going to miss you."

"When are you leaving?"

"Tomorrow morning."

Hiram looked stricken. "Don't leave, Miranda," he pleaded, for the first time using her Christian name. "Stay and marry me. I promise I'll take good care of you."

Miranda hesitated a long moment before replying. It was a very tempting offer, but she had to refuse. "I'm very fond of you, Hiram, but I can't marry you." Miranda held up her hand to silence his protest. "You deserve a better wife than I could be for you. I don't belong here."

"But, Miranda . . ." He paused as she firmly shook her head.

"I hope we can always be friends," she said simply, placing a gentle kiss on his cheek before hurrying out the door. She wished she could have said yes to Hiram. Perhaps, if she had loved him, she could have gotten used to life in California, but she didn't. Without mutual love a marriage between them was sure to be disastrous. In time Hiram would forget the hurt and understand that she had given the only answer possible.

Miranda wandered idly about the town for most of the afternoon. When she returned to the room, her father had not yet arrived, so she determined to go look for him. She found him seated at a table in a nearby gaming saloon. In the opposite chair sat a thimblerigger, his hands deftly manipulating the three shells on the table while her father concentrated on the movements of his hands. The pile of English coins at the man's elbow left Miranda in no doubt of his skill. She groaned in frustration.

"Mandy, what are you doing here?" Her father looked up in surprise. "Damn. Now I've lost track of the pea. Here, have a seat." He motioned to the chair beside him, turning to concentrate on the three shells placed in a row before him.

"Why not let the little lady choose for you?" his nemesis suggested, raking his eyes appreciatively over Miranda.

"My father was just leaving," Miranda coldly informed him as she urged her father from his seat. She had to shout to be heard above the din.

"But, Mandy, I may be able to recoup my losses," Edward Austen protested as his daughter continued to nudge him toward the door.

"But we're already late for our appointment," Miranda prodded. "You can come back tomorrow.'' Edward Austen shook his head in confusion, but he followed Miranda without protest. When they reached the street, he turned to his daughter.

"Who is it we are supposed to meet? I can't seem to remember making an appointment with anyone.'' He ran his fingers through his hair.

"You didn't. I just needed an excuse to get you away from that dreadful man,'' Miranda admitted. "It really is getting late, Papa, and we are leaving in the morning.''

Edward Austen snorted in reply, but beyond his expression of displeasure, he did not censure his daughter for her actions.

As they approached Hiram Jackson's café Lucas Adams rounded the corner. Miranda's heart skipped a beat in response to his ever-present grin. Her father immediately asked him to join them for supper.

Miranda considered skipping the meal altogether but decided she was being cowardly. If she expected Hiram to remain her friend, she would have to face him again sometime. The café was almost full when they entered, but they were able to find a vacant table near the back of the tent.

It was some time before Hiram noticed them. As he approached their table he looked hopefully at Miranda, but as he neared, he could see in her eyes that he had not a glimmer of hope. His gaze switched to Lucas, and after openly appraising the man, he turned to Miranda, his pain clearly evident.

"Why didn't you tell me about him?'' he asked quietly. "It was cruel of you to lead me on.''

"But, Hiram—''

"If you are ready, I will take your order now,''

Hiram interrupted, squaring his shoulders as a businesslike mask stole over his face. "As you can see, I am very busy tonight."

Miranda gave her order, though she did not feel the least bit hungry. It had been a mistake to come back so soon. It was obvious by the way Hiram had looked at Lucas that he had jumped to the wrong conclusion. Hadn't she told him her father had hired Lucas Adams as a guide? She longed to call him back to explain, but a crowded café was hardly the place to iron out such a misunderstanding.

She tried to catch his eye as he placed a plate of aromatic stew before her, but he turned away.

"Well, Mandy, I suppose you set the man back on his heels and none too gently, it would appear," her father commented idly.

Miranda raised her eyes wearily to her father. She keenly felt the loss of her friend and was in no mood to explain to anyone, least of all her father. As her gaze shifted to Lucas she was startled by the contemptuous set of his lips.

"I merely refused to marry him," she defended, suddenly more interested in rearranging the contents of her plate than explaining the situation to either man. Obviously Lucas had concluded she was a merciless flirt. Though his unfair assessment upset her, she did not feel he deserved an explanation.

"You would have been wise to accept his offer," Lucas advised her coldly. "It would have saved you untold hardships."

"I don't love him," Miranda replied quietly, spearing a chunk of carrot but making no attempt to raise it to her lips. She wished he would drop the subject.

"Then you shouldn't have played your little game with him. He is a good man . . . but obviously not up to your little tricks," Lucas further observed.

"If I want your advice on how to run my life, I'll ask for it. Hiram is none of your business." Miranda stabbed viciously at a piece of beef and thrust the morsel into her mouth.

"Now, you two," Edward Austen broke in. "No need to get so miffed over a small flirtation. Let's just eat our dinner and retire. We have an early start in the morning."

The meal continued in silence. Miranda had to exert every ounce of her self-control to keep from flinging the contents of her plate into Lucas's face as he continued to stare down his nose at her. How dare he assume the worst when he knew nothing about the situation? She had not encouraged Hiram's affections. Though she might have acted foolishly in continuing to come here after she had realized his intentions, she had not wanted to hurt him. How had she managed to make such a muddle of things? All she had wanted was a friend.

When she had eaten all that was possible in her uncomfortable state of mind, Miranda rose and left, not bothering to excuse herself, going directly to their room. A short time later her father returned. After a minimum of conversation they both retired.

Chapter 4

The sun shone weakly through the thick blanket of fog that encased the city. Even at this early hour the streets were full of merchants preparing for a new day and bleary-eyed men staggering home after an evening of drink and games, or perhaps a night of pleasure in the arms of one of the city's less reputable ladies.

Miranda held her mount as Lucas secured a pack to the back of her saddle, pulling her cloak tightly around her slim shoulders in an effort to keep out the cool, damp air. The horse her father had chosen for her was a lively, but well-mannered, chestnut mare. In England Miranda had had some opportunities to go riding, and though her limited experience did not qualify her as an expert, she was a competent horsewoman.

"If you're ready, we should get started." Lucas directed the statement to her father as he tested the strength of the knot he had just tied. "We'll have to get there early if we expect to find spaces on the ferry."

Leading their animals through the streets, they

headed toward the docks. When they arrived, a group of miners had already gathered before the ferry, eager to be off. Some had horses or mules, but many were on foot.

Presently the captain came out of his cabin to briefly survey the group and signal his men to allow the boarding to begin. This procedure was conducted in an orderly fashion, though an occasional mule balked at the idea of leaving firm ground. In no time the ferry was filled to capacity, and they were on their way across the bay, disembarking a short time later at Benicia, ready to begin the overland journey to the gold fields.

"Come here and I'll give you a leg up," Lucas directed Miranda when they had led their animals clear of the loading area. Miranda complied, settling herself comfortably in her saddle. She started to thank Lucas, but he had already turned to walk toward his horse. Swinging himself effortlessly up onto his saddle, he gave a low whistle, and they started down the road. Lucas was in the lead, followed by his heavily laden mule. Miranda fell in behind him, with her father and the second mule completing their small caravan.

As they started up the river Miranda was filled with a mixture of excitement and dread. This was why they had traveled so far, and it was a relief to finally begin searching for the promised gold. In a few weeks' time her father would either realize his dream or admit defeat. She could not imagine him staying in this wilderness long if his fortune was not easily found. He was not accustomed to rough living and even less accustomed to hard work. Miranda had little doubt that within two months' time, rich or not, they would be on their way back to England. With this comforting thought she fortified herself for the hardships to come.

They rode in silence over rolling hills forested with huge oaks and towering pines. New leaves unfurled to clothe a variety of shrubs and bushes in their spring finery. The spicy-sweet scent of deer brush and pine mingled to perfume the air. As they passed, disturbing the serenity of the forest, squirrels scrambled up trees or into hidden burrows. The sun climbed higher, warming the air and dissipating the last wisps of fog.

The trio traveled at a leisurely pace, and as the trail was not treacherous and her horse surefooted, Miranda could focus most of her attention on the passing countryside. She had to admit that this was a beautiful land. Its wild, untamed quality served to enhance its beauty in Miranda's eyes. As they moved farther away from the mud and decadence of San Francisco, her soul began to fill with hope and a sense of peace she had never felt before. She was engrossed in her thoughts and the landscape until Lucas's voice, signaling the animals to a halt, brought her attention back to her horse. She gently reined in her mount, then waited for further instructions.

"This looks like a good stopping place to stretch and grab a bite to eat," Lucas stated as he dismounted. Miranda followed his lead, sliding unassisted from her horse's back. She rubbed the mare's nose affectionately before looping the reins over the branch of a tree.

"Are you getting tired?"

"No, not at all. Everything is so beautiful, I was hardly aware time was passing," Miranda replied truthfully. "I'm so glad I didn't stay in San Francisco."

"We've only been out a few hours, and this trail is an easy one. I'll be interested to see if your opinion remains unchanged after we have been out a week or two." Lucas was surprised by her answer. Most people viewed the ruggedness of the land as something to be conquered, failing to notice its majestic beauty.

"Damn wild country, this." Miranda's father joined them after securing his mount. "How long did you say it would take us to reach civilization again?"

"The better part of a week, though I don't know how civilized you'll find Sacramento City. Already tired? I can take you back to the ferry if you wish." Lucas doubted Edward Austen would ever travel beyond Sacramento City. The man was a dreamer, and most likely a week or two of the hard realities of trail life would convince him he'd be better off returning to San Francisco.

"I intend no such thing," Edward Austen replied, a bit put out by Lucas's condescending attitude. "I was merely making polite conversation."

"It appears your daughter appreciates the open spaces more than you do."

"I told you Miranda would be no trouble. She's an adaptable girl," Mr. Austen stated, glad for a chance to point out the wisdom of his decision to bring his daughter along. "She'll be a big help when it comes to cooking and such. It will give us that much more time to scoop up the gold."

"I've told you, you don't scoop up gold. It is hard, backbreaking work, even if you do find a rich claim," Lucas reminded him, annoyed at the man's continued naïveté. If he hadn't been offering such a generous salary, he would never have agreed to take Edward Austen on. But Lucas was too much of a businessman to turn down such a deal. At a salary of five dollars a day, he stood to make a goodly sum whether they found gold or not. If they did strike it rich, so much the better. He had only had to alter his plans slightly to accommodate the Englishman; he was a simple man motivated by a simple greed. Lucas doubted if he would be much of a problem.

His daughter Miranda was a different matter. Though she seemed sincere in her praise of the countryside, it went against his instincts to expose any woman to unnecessary hardships. Miranda's slight frame and fragile looks gave him little confidence in her ability to stand up to the deprivations of a miner's life for long. He had to admit she had spirit, but he had seen much sturdier women broken by the hardships of the Oregon Trail. In a way it made him sad to think of Miranda crushed by the rigors of rustic life. But it wasn't his problem. He mentally scolded himself for his sentimentality. If Miranda was cursed with a fool for a father, there was nothing he could do to change that. She would have to manage the best she could.

They sat in the shade of a large white oak to eat a meal of cheese and oven-baked bread. It was funny how such a simple thing as a loaf of bread, hitherto taken for granted, could become a delight when one knew one would soon be forced to do without it, Miranda mused as she enjoyed the midday repast. In the future they would have to be contented with fried biscuits.

Lucas seemed unusually quiet, but then, there really was little to say. She wondered if he was thinking about the incident in the café as he sat quietly studying her. Her eyes momentarily flashed with angry fires as she remembered how he had immediately assumed her guilty of Hiram's accusation. She looked up to find him still watching her, an amused expression on his face.

"What were you thinking of that made you so angry?" Lucas asked. It startled Miranda that he had accurately read such a fleeting expression. Her eyes met his, and she stared into their smoky depths, searching for some measure of the man. Her heart began to beat more rapidly, and she averted her gaze.

"It was nothing," she lied, hoping he would be polite enough not to pursue the matter further. Her strange physical reaction to him frightened and confused her.

"If thinking of nothing angers you so easily, I'll have to be careful not to do something to really get you riled."

"A wise decision, Mr. Adams," Miranda agreed, knowing full well that it didn't bother him in the least to anger her. He had already proven that on numerous occasions.

"I hope you two don't plan on continuing these verbal jousts the entire trip. It really does get tiresome," Miranda's father complained. "If you'll excuse me, I believe I'll relieve myself of your company . . . and a full bladder." He rose and headed off to the privacy of a nearby clump of bushes.

"Does your horse suit you?" Lucas turned the conversation to a safer topic.

"Yes, she really is perfect. I think we'll get along well with each other." Certainly they should be able to discuss a topic as neutral as horses.

"I'm glad. Having a stubborn horse can be a real problem out here. The trail won't be bad until after we leave Sacramento City, but we'll be traveling through some pretty steep canyons before we reach our destination. Assuming your father lasts that long."

"Is all of California so sparsely populated?" Miranda ignored his last remark.

"For the most part. We'll pass a few *ranchos* and some smaller mining towns; otherwise, there is nothing but temporary mining camps lining the streams and rivers. Men pitch their tents and pan until the color begins to run low or they hear of a richer strike, then they move on."

"It must be lonely for the men who didn't bring their families." Miranda recalled the way many of the men in San Francisco had looked at her. When they smiled, they were not seeing her but a representation of a loved one left behind.

"Most men had the decency to leave their wives and children safely at home." Lucas looked meaningfully in the direction her father had taken. "California is a wilderness. It is hard enough for a man to survive, let alone a woman. If the trip here doesn't kill them, a few months in the mining camps usually will. I wouldn't feel too sorry for the men, though.

There are women who are usually more than willing to share their more desirable charms . . . for a price, of course.''

"Have you always been so crude?" Miranda asked in irritation. It seemed impossible to carry on a civilized conversation with the man.

"Sorry, ma'am," Lucas tipped his hat in a mock show of gallantry. "This is a crude land. If you wanted polite conversation, you should have stayed at home, safe in your little English parlor."

"Do you think I want to be here sitting in the dust with some boorish oaf?" Miranda grabbed a handful of earth. Opening her palm, she let the dirt sift through her fingers and onto the toe of Lucas's boot. "Had the choice been mine, we would never have left England. But since we are here and my father has committed us to travel with you, I would greatly appreciate it if you'd keep your lewd comments to yourself. You have been contracted to guide us, not educate me on the prurient side of life. I'm sure you are most knowledgeable in the various aspects of such a life, but you will kindly spare me your expertise.'' Feeling her companion properly chastised, Miranda rose, brushing the crumbs from her skirt. She had left Lucas Adams no quarter to doubt her opinion of him or this venture. Her head held high, she walked with regal dignity toward her mount.

They traveled until sundown before stopping to make camp. Both Lucas and her father were well pleased with the distance they had journeyed that day. Miranda paused periodically to rub her tired backside as she began unloading some pots and pans from one of the mules. It was obvious her father planned to have her do the cooking, and she deemed it wise to begin that chore immediately. Since her experience in cooking over an open fire was limited to their journey across the Isthmus of Panama, she felt far from competent in her assigned task. If Lucas made one snide remark about her cooking abilities, she vowed she would pour his dinner on his head. Smothering a giggle, she pictured some previously unknown culinary concoction dripping down his face and beard.

"I'm glad you find your aches and pains so amusing."

Miranda jumped at the closeness of Lucas's voice. "I wish you wouldn't sneak up on me." She felt a guilty blush spread across her cheeks. Lucas reached around her to remove a pack containing a variety of food items.

"I'll get a fire started. I don't think your father is going to be much help with dinner."

Miranda surveyed the weary figure slumped against a tree and nodded in agreement. Gathering the pans in her arms, she followed Lucas.

Lucas laid the pack in the center of the clearing, then went off to gather dry twigs for kindling. In a few minutes he had a small blaze started, and after directing Miranda to keep feeding the fire from the pile of brush he had brought, he went off with an ax to gather more substantial fuel. Miranda rummaged through the contents of the pack, trying to decide what she should fix for their dinner. The beans would provide a filling meal, but they would take too long to cook. Without fresh meat she was at a loss as to how to fix a stew. She was greatly relieved when Lucas returned and, after adding a small armload of wood to the fire, began cutting chunks off a slab of bacon, apparently having already made his choice for their dinner.

"Do you know how to make skillet biscuits?" he asked as he set the bacon aside and began to whittle the ends of three long green branches to a sharp point.

"Yes." Miranda silently thanked Lizzy for teaching her this skill.

"If you'll make us some, they go well with roasted bacon. Tomorrow we'll stop earlier and I'll hunt some fresh meat."

Miranda turned quickly to her task, being careful not to spill any of the precious flour. After she discovered the price charged for such a basic commodity, the saying "Waste not, want not" had taken on new import. In a few minutes she had the dough prepared and formed into biscuits. Rubbing a large iron skillet with a little of the bacon fat, she balanced it on three rocks over the fire, then filled the heated pan with her small breads. Lucas sat on his haunches, roasting the bacon on the prepared sticks. The fat spewed and sputtered as it dripped into the fire, filling the air with a mouth-watering aroma. After Miranda had placed a pot of water over the fire to boil for coffee, Lucas handed her one of the sticks.

"Do you think your father plans to chew and swallow his own dinner, or does he expect us to do that for him too?" Lucas questioned, his voice thick with sarcasm. He had not expected Edward Austen to be an ideal traveling companion, but he had thought the man would make at least some effort to pull his own weight. Instead he let his daughter wait on him as if he were the only one who had spent the day in the saddle. Lucas could barely resist the urge to boot the man in the backside.

Miranda shrugged her shoulders. She was equally irritated at her father. They were all tired, and there was no reason he should be exempt from the duties of camp. It embarrassed her that her father did not seem to care how his selfish behavior appeared to others.

When the meal was cooked, her father roused himself and came to join them at the camp fire. "Damn hard day." He reached for the tin plate Miranda offered him, settling down on a log to enjoy his meal. As no one responded to his comment, he focused his entire attention on his food.

After dinner Miranda rinsed and wiped out the coffeepot and skillet before returning them to the pack. Lucas finished unpacking their animals, stringing the packs containing their food supply on a rope between two trees. In answer to Miranda's unspoken question, he explained that it would help to protect their supplies from bears. Miranda sincerely hoped none would be bold enough to raid their camp.

Until they reached a more permanent location they would sleep out in the open, weather permitting. She took the blankets Lucas handed her and unrolled her bedding near the fire. She was bone-weary and more than ready for a good night's sleep. Satisfied that her bed was as comfortable as possible, she started for the edge of camp.

"Don't go far, and if you hear the bushes rustle, run like crazy back to camp," Lucas called over his shoulder. "When I have time, I'll teach you to use a gun."

When she returned, she noted that Lucas had made his bed directly next to hers. He was watching her, clearly anticipating her disapproval. But she said nothing. In her father's presence she felt safe from any untoward advances, and the security of a skilled woodsman close at hand meant more to her than propriety. Snuggling down under her covers fully clothed, she settled in for the night, secure in the fact that Lucas could protect her from any unseen dangers of the forest.

"Now look here, Lucas. Do you think it's necessary to sleep so near my daughter?" Miranda's father complained when he noticed the proximity of the two bedrolls.

"Your daughter seems to have no complaints, and unless she does, I have no intention of moving." Confident that Lucas would handle her father, Miranda allowed herself a tired smile before drifting off to sleep.

They were up at dawn. The air was cool, but as they moved along the trail, it quickly warmed to a comfortable temperature. Miranda felt refreshed, and though her bottom was a trifle tender from yesterday's long ride, it did not cause her too much discomfort. The day passed uneventfully, and they made camp by the edge of the river by midafternoon. Lucas left Miranda and her father to set up camp while he went to hunt some meat for their dinner.

"Mandy, I'm not as young as I used to be." Her father rubbed at an aching muscle. "Just let me rest my bones for a few minutes, then I'll get up and help you."

Miranda sighed in exasperation. "Go ahead, Papa. I can manage."

It soon became apparent that the entire chore of readying the camp would fall on Miranda's shoulders. After unloading the lighter packs from the animals and gathering enough firewood to see them through the night, Miranda decided to take advantage of the privacy and stripped down to her chemise and drawers to sponge off at the river. Her father had long since fallen asleep against a tall pine.

The water was cold and caused her skin to prickle with goose bumps, but it effectively washed away the day's grime. "I wonder how long it will be before I enjoy the luxury of a hot bath again?" she wondered out loud.

"Quite some time, I imagine." Miranda whirled around at the sound of the familiar voice, coming face-to-face with an appreciative grin. "I rather like you dressed this way." Lucas took a step forward, making no effort to hide his obvious desire.

"If you lay a hand on me, I'll scream," Miranda warned.

"What good would that do you? If your father did bother to rouse himself, I could easily overpower him."

"You wouldn't—" Miranda's voice broke off as she became truly alarmed. After all, he had taken liberties before. What was there to prevent him from doing so now?

"No, I wouldn't." Lucas ceased his teasing when he realized she was taking him seriously. The silly chit was really frightened. "You better get dressed before I prove myself a liar. You make a very fetching sight, and I'm not a saint." He handed her her clothing and turned his back. Miranda quickly pulled her dress over her head, silently vowing to be more cautious of her surroundings in the future.

"I bagged a couple of partridges." Lucas offered her his arm. "You did a nice job setting up camp."

Miranda eyed him suspiciously. He was being entirely too complimentary.

"Don't worry, I'm not going to ravage you. Maybe steal a kiss or two, but I'll wait until you're willing for the other."

Her pulse quickened. "I wouldn't hold my breath." She sailed past him, tying her belt securely around her waist. His hearty laughter followed her as she stomped toward camp.

Her father was still sleeping soundly, and she resisted an urge to pour a pot of cold river water over his peaceful form. "Where are you when I need you?" she scolded. "I've finished the work. The least you could do is protect me from that man's advances." Edward Austen slept on, blissfully unaware of his daughter's frustration.

"I told you there would be no help from that quarter." Lucas reentered the small circle of their camp, throwing a disgusted look in her father's direction. Then, changing the subject, he continued, "There is time for your first shooting lesson today if you like. These forests are thick with bears and wolves. I don't like you wandering around without some way to protect yourself when I'm not near."

Miranda's eyes lit up at this prospect. She hated

being totally dependent on Lucas for protection. If she could become skilled with a gun, it would give her some measure of independence. "Thank you, I would like to learn." She made no attempt to conceal her enthusiasm.

"Good girl. Get your father's rifle and we'll go practice in that clearing."

Miranda was surprised to find the rifle so heavy. Following Lucas into a small meadow, she patiently awaited his instructions.

"The first rule you must learn is to never point a gun at a man unless you plan to shoot him. More people are killed by accident than design, just because there are a lot of careless fools in this world."

Miranda nodded in understanding.

"Out here it's best to keep your gun loaded at all times. In a pinch you probably won't have time to load it." Miranda listened intently as he showed her how to load the rifle, a task she found relatively straightforward. At last, after a few demonstrations, he determined that she was ready for a few practice shots.

"We'll use that stump over there for a target."

Miranda raised her gun to her shoulder as he had shown her, bringing the sights in line with the stump.

"Whenever you're ready."

Miranda nodded, closed one eye, rechecked her aim, and slowly squeezed on the trigger with her forefinger. The butt of the rifle slammed against her shoulder as the shot roared out. She was thrown off-balance and couldn't see if she had hit her target; she surmised by Lucas's healthy laugh that she had come nowhere near it.

"You may not have enough weight to handle that gun." Lucas continued to chuckle. "Try planting your feet farther apart, and remember to rest the butt of the gun against your shoulder. It will lessen the kick."

Miranda did as she was instructed, taking aim again. This time she retained her balance, but the butt of the rifle still banged mercilessly against her already bruised shoulder. The bullet fell short of its target, but at least it hit in the general area.

"Better." Lucas nodded his approval. They continued with their lesson, and as the hour wore on, Miranda started hitting consistently close to her target. The pain in her shoulder had become almost unbearable, and she squeezed back tears every time the wooden butt assaulted her anew. But she was determined to keep at her lesson as long as Lucas was willing. At last he called a halt to the day's instruction, and she gratefully set the rifle down.

"I'm afraid I'm not very good," she commented as she gingerly massaged her throbbing shoulder.

"You did fine for your first try. I don't imagine marksmanship is one of the skills deemed necessary for young English ladies. Does your shoulder hurt?"

"Just a little. It will be fine by morning." Noticing the sun's position in the sky, she added, "I expect I had better start plucking those birds you shot if we plan to eat tonight."

"I think we'll let your father do the cooking tonight," Lucas stated dryly. "A little work won't hurt him."

"Unless you're not feeling hungry, you'd better let me do it. I would hate to see what would remain of the birds by the time my father got through with them," Miranda suggested. Feeling she should try to defend her father, she added, "He really doesn't mean to be remiss, it's just his nature."

"His nature is going to have to change awfully fast if he plans to be a miner, but I'll bow to your superior wisdom as far as dinner is concerned. I'm in the mood for a tasty meal."

"Thank you for the lesson," Miranda called over her shoulder as she started toward the river to fill a large pot with water. She soon had the water boiling briskly, and after dipping the birds in the boiling liquid, she began pulling off the feathers, humming as she worked. Lucas set about unloading the heavier packs and securing them for the night.

Miranda was quite pleased with the meal she set before the men a short while later. She received compliments all around and would have thoroughly enjoyed the evening if she could have ignored the pain in her shoulder. Lucas noticed the way she favored her right arm and rummaged through his personal belongings for a bottle of liniment.

"Have your father rub this into your shoulder. It will help a little." He handed her the bottle, then turned his back toward her. Miranda pulled down the shoulder of her dress to permit her father to minister to her. She was not surprised to see the ugly blue-black swelling that marred her shoulder. Her father gently rubbed in the soothing ointment, and though he was inclined to comment, her beseeching looks kept him silent.

The next morning Miranda was dismayed to discover her shoulder had stiffened during the night, and she could not move her arm. She tried to accomplish her morning chores, but it soon became apparent that this was impossible. Lucas exasperatedly came to her aid as she tried to roll her bedding.

"Let me see your shoulder," he demanded. His tone did not allow for disobedience. Miranda slipped down the shoulders of her dress and chemise, careful not to expose herself more than was necessary. Lucas swore under his breath as he examined the bruise and pulled her garments back in place. Without further comment he rolled her bedding. When the animals were packed and they were ready to begin the day's journey, he motioned her toward his horse.

"You'll ride with me today," Lucas ordered. His hands encircled her waist, and he lifted her effortlessly onto his saddle. Miranda started to protest, but noting the angry glint in his eye, she snapped her mouth shut. He was already thoroughly irritated with her foolishness.

Swinging himself up on the saddle behind her, Lucas pulled her onto his lap as he grasped the reins. Miranda tensed at such intimate contact, but as Lucas seemed barely cognizant of her existence, she soon began to relax. She wondered briefly that her father voiced no protest, then, remembering his attitude when she had told him of Lucas's kiss, she realized she should expect none. Since leaving San Francisco, her father seemed perfectly content to leave all responsibility for her care to Lucas.

The steady motion of the horse and the warming sun soon lulled Miranda into a state of drowsiness. She sighed in contentment, only vaguely aware of the strong arms and pleasantly masculine scent that surrounded her; she felt strangely protected. She shivered slightly as she felt a gentle nibbling at the nape of her neck. She snuggled closer to make that vulnerable spot more accessible. Coarse hairs tickled her sensitive skin.

"I'm almost glad for your foolishness," Lucas whispered in her ear, pulling softly at her round, pink earlobe with his teeth. His words broke into Miranda's trancelike state, and she straightened in confusion.

"What are you doing?" She shook her head to clear her thoughts.

"I'm treating myself to a taste of your delectable neck," Lucas murmured softly. "Go back to sleep. I was enjoying myself."

"You!" Miranda blushed with the knowledge that she had welcomed the feel of his lips against her neck. Lucas laughed at her discomfort.

"Who are you more upset with, yourself for liking it or me for tempting you? Underneath your prim and proper exterior I think there lurks a woman who is not proper at all," Lucas teased.

"How dare you say such a thing!"

"Keep your voice down or your father will overhear you. Remember, he doesn't like us to argue." Lucas grinned. "Besides, I didn't mean to be insulting. I just sense an underlying wildness in you. It would be interesting to get to know that aspect of your character."

"I'm sorry, you're mistaken. I'm as proper as they come," Miranda asserted, not at all convinced of the truth of her words. After all, what was she doing riding contentedly in the arms of a man she had not even known a few weeks ago?

"Believe whatever you like." Lucas dismissed her protest and turned his full attention back to the trail.

Miranda tried to keep herself erect but soon found herself relaxing against Lucas's arms again. She forced herself to concentrate on the passing countryside in an effort to keep her mind from wandering in a more dangerous direction. She was only moderately successful.

They made camp early, Lucas insisting Miranda do no work the remainder of the day. She awoke the next morning feeling considerably better. Though her shoulder was still tender to the touch, she was able to move her arm without too much discomfort. They again departed early. Miranda was relieved that today she was able to ride her own horse.

One day began to blend into another, and five days after leaving Benicia, they boarded a ferry to cross the Sacramento River to enter Sacramento City. Edward Austen's eyes brightened at the sight of the town. Miranda knew the rustic life did not agree with him, and Lucas's constant chiding of his less-than-industrious nature had further dampened his spirits. Her father was not used to having his failings so bluntly brought to his attention. Miranda hoped a day or two spent in Sacramento would revive his usual optimistic spirit.

After crossing the quarter-mile-wide Sacramento River on the ferry, they led their horses through the center of town. The homes and businesses of Sacramento were built between trees and bushes, giving the town a grovelike appearance. As in San Francisco, most of the structures were merely poles driven into the ground with walls and roofs of sturdy muslin. The streets ran at right angles, and every corner was piled high with provisions. Miranda noted that here, too, there was a disproportionately high number of saloons for the size of the population.

The new arrivals led their mounts to the edge of town where Lucas began to unload the horses and mules. Miranda organized their camp while Lucas built her a lean-to. With so few women in their midst, the men could easily take care of all their needs in the open, but Miranda was glad to have a private place to dress and sleep. The shelter was no more than a piece of muslin secured over a framework of branches, but it was adequate for her needs.

"I'm going into town for a while. I should be back in time for dinner, but if I'm not, don't wait for me," Lucas told her, after finishing his tasks.

Miranda finished arranging the last few items in their camp after he left, and then she stood up, stretching her arms above her head.

"If you like, we can see the town together," her father offered.

"Yes, I'd like that." Miranda tried to brush the dust from her skirt before placing her hand on her father's arm and allowing him to lead her back toward the town.

Here, as in San Francisco, the population was of diverse origins: American, Spanish, Swiss, Russian, Chinese, Australian. The promise of gold had lured men from every corner of the globe. They stopped at a supply store and found that Lucas had been correct in advising them to buy what they could in San Francisco. Prices in Sacramento were considerably higher. Miranda was grateful that, other than replenishing their food supply, they would not have to purchase any provisions here.

They had passed the fifth saloon when Miranda's father could resist temptation no longer. "Mandy, I'm going to step in here for a moment for a little libation. I'm sure you'll be all right on your own."

"Go ahead and enjoy yourself. I'll be fine." Miranda waved her father away, feeling he needed a little recreation, and continued down the street. She found a crude bench under a large oak and sat down to watch the town's population pass by while she waited for her father.

A group of miners stopped to make her acquaintance and exchange pleasantries. She politely asked each about his luck in the gold fields and was pleasantly surprised to find their accounts most optimistic. Miranda was enjoyably engaged in conversation when she recognized the unmistakable figure of Lucas Adams coming out of a saloon with a pretty young blonde, whose profession was obvious, on his arm. Schooling her expression, she calmly continued her conversation as she covertly watched the couple stroll toward the rear of the saloon. So, he couldn't wait to relieve his needs with some woman. *Well, better her than me*, Miranda thought caustically. Her stomach was tied in a knot, and she felt a sudden need to be alone. After a few minutes she made some inadequate excuse, then rose, hurrying down the street and leaving her confused companions wondering what they had said to offend her.

She almost ran through the town in an effort to reach the haven of their camp. She hurt all over but could not adequately explain to herself why seeing Lucas with that woman had so upset her. She knew that men did such things. Why should it bother her that Lucas was like any other man? She had absolutely no right to censure his activities. But, despite all her logic, she remained thoroughly depressed the rest of the day.

Her father returned within the hour, but as he could not fathom his daughter's changeable moods, he soon gave up any attempt at conversation. Lucas did not return for dinner, a fact that only increased Miranda's sour disposition. As his companionship was clearly unwanted and he was feeling a bit under the weather, her father retired early, leaving her alone with her thoughts. She sat staring morosely into the fire, only half listening to the strains of lively music drifting from neighboring camps.

It was thus that Lucas found her when he returned to camp. She reminded him of a sad child as she sat on the ground, her arms wrapped around her knees. Her bottom lip protruded, forming a slight pout while her dark-lashed eyes held a faraway look. In truth, she was little more than a child, and Lucas felt a twinge of guilt for the way he had been treating her. Despite the fact that she had unwillingly been thrown into a totally foreign way of life, she did not whine or complain. And if the first leg of their journey was any indication, she would prove a more worthy traveling companion than her father. Seeking to comfort her, Lucas reached down to stroke one soft cheek.

"Don't you touch me!" Miranda whirled to her feet, standing to face him, her hands on her hips.

"What's wrong with you?" Her sudden venom startled him.

"Nothing. I just don't appreciate being pawed."

"If you consider a touch on the cheek being pawed, you've got a lot to learn about life." Lucas was irritated beyond reason. Miranda's reaction to his offer of comfort effectively squelched all protective feelings. "This is being pawed." He grabbed her with one arm and began stroking her bodice with the other.

"What's the matter? Didn't your little doxy satisfy you?" Miranda spat the words in his face.

"So that's what's got you so fired up." Lucas laughed, abruptly releasing her. "I've insulted your prudish sensibilities again."

"I am not a prude." Her body trembled in frustration. "If you want to spend your days like a rutting boar, it is no concern of mine."

"That's right, it isn't, so stop meddling in my affairs!"

"Meddle?" Miranda's eyes widened with incredulity. "I was sitting here minding my own business until you assaulted me!"

"You were spying on me earlier today," Lucas returned confidently.

"I did no such thing! I just happened to be on the streets when you, with your usual discretion, were parading that whore for all to see. I'm sure half the state knows you bedded the woman."

"Then what's the problem, woman?" Lucas ran his fingers through his hair. "If you don't care, why bite my head off?"

"Please, just leave me alone." Miranda's voice was barely above a whisper. She didn't know why she was reacting this way. There was no logical reason why seeing Lucas with another woman should make her so miserable. Not waiting for Lucas to reply, she ducked into the lean-to.

Lucas added another log to the fire and prepared his bed. Miranda was the most exasperating woman he had ever known. When she wanted to be, she could be an amiable companion, but her quicksilver moods made her impossible to fathom. One minute she was smiling sweetly, the next she might be trying to scratch your eyes out. Besides, hadn't painful experience taught him not to be taken in by an innocent face? Miranda had led that man on in San Francisco. Like any woman, she was prepared to use a pretty face to get what she wanted. Still, she was a fetching sight. He would have to be careful not to be taken in by her soulful looks, but that didn't mean he couldn't enjoy some of her charms. Satisfied with the direction of his thoughts, Lucas pulled his blankets over his shoulders and was soon sleeping peacefully.

Miranda was not so fortunate. She tossed and turned all night, unable to get comfortable. Her thoughts ran around in familiar circles, and by the time she finally fell asleep, she was no closer to understanding herself than when she had retired.

The next day she busied herself with washing and mending some of their clothes. In the afternoon she took a few coins from her father and started off for the city's center. She planned to buy some ribbons for her hair. She took her time choosing, finally deciding on a pair of blue-and-green ribbons to match her two dresses. She undid the neat bun at the nape of her neck and parted her hair down the middle. Deftly forming two thick braids, she tied one over each ear with a ribbon to form a loop. Feeling considerably more feminine, she left the store. Pausing outside, she scanned up and down the street until she realized she was looking for Lucas. She stamped her foot in frustration. *I don't even like the man,* she reminded herself. *He is an uncultured rustic with a decided lack of manners.* Almost immediately she acknowledged the falseness of this statement. While Lucas might be well skilled in the rustic life, his language and mannerisms gave evidence that he had a better than average education. She wondered about his parents and from what kind of home he had come. She was still thinking about him when she reached the camp. "Get out of my mind, Lucas Adams," she ground out between clenched teeth. "I don't want to think about you."

The next morning they were back on the trail. Early in the day they passed a *rancho,* its pastures filled with large, long-horned Spanish cattle. The fields were thick with wild, green grasses and colorful wild flowers. Deep orange poppies waved lazily in the morning breeze, growing so densely in places, they carpeted the hillsides with gold. As they traveled farther upriver they occasionally passed a small band of miners, knee-deep in the river's cold spring waters, concentrating on the contents of their large shallow pans as they swirled saucer after saucer of river sand. Their tired eyes would light up at the sight of Miranda. Without exception they would stop at each of these camps for a few minutes, to exchange news before moving on. Friendliness was the rule rather than the exception.

Their party settled into an uneasy truce. Miranda and Lucas were friendly, though there was an underlying wariness on Miranda's part. While Lucas's insouciant pursuit of her made her uncomfortable, her own growing attraction to him bothered her even more. Edward Austen was becoming adjusted to life on the trail, and he had reluctantly started to do his share of the work, which eased tensions between the two men. Miranda had persuaded Lucas to continue her rifle lessons after promising to let him know immediately if her shoulder was bothering her. She could now occasionally hit her target and had learned to brace the gun to minimize the jolting effect. It was a pleasant enough time, and Miranda was in no hurry to reach Hangtown. She couldn't imagine a place with such a name being anything but dreadful.

When they reached a fork in the river, they continued their journey along the southern branch. Lucas informed them that they were now following Weber Creek, named after its discoverer, Captain Charles Weber. They passed a string of small mining camps, always stopping to share news from downriver. The farther upstream they traveled, the more eagerly their party was received.

One morning when the weather was pleasantly warm and Miranda was paying more attention to the rugged terrain than the trail, Lucas suddenly reined his mount to an abrupt halt. The other members of the party followed suit.

"Poor devil." Lucas moved his horse in front of Miranda's but only partially succeeded in blocking her view of the decaying skeletal remains of what once must have been a hopeful miner. The corpse lay sprawled on the sand near a shallow, open grave. Though the skeleton was complete, several bones had been disconnected from the main body and were lying several yards away.

"What happened to him?" Miranda asked in a hushed tone as she turned her head away from the grisly scene.

"Probably wolves unearthed his grave. His friends didn't take the time to bury him deep enough. Lead your horse back a few yards, then wait until I call you," Lucas instructed as he dismounted. "The man deserves a proper grave."

Miranda did as she was told, feeling strangely weak; the sight of the carelessly dug grave brought home the reality of the harshness of the land for the first time. She sat in the shade of a tall pine, surveying her surroundings with new eyes. Presently she heard Lucas calling her, but before returning, she picked a small bouquet of lupine. She found Lucas and her father leaning on their shovels near a fresh mound of earth.

"He'll rest easy now." Edward Austen wiped the sweat from his brow with his handkerchief. "We buried him good and deep."

Miranda laid her small offering atop the grave, knowing by day's end that it would be wilted beyond recognition. "It seems so sad leaving him out here all alone. I wonder who he was."

"That's something we will never know. Let's just hope whoever buried him the first time had the decency to write his family," Lucas commented. "There is nothing more we can do here. Let's try to get a few more miles in before sundown."

They turned their attention back to the trail, all three sobered by the reminder of their own mortality.

Chapter 5

It was noon when they entered Hangtown. As they rode through the streets Lucas pointed out the tall oak growing in the center of town that had played such an important role in the event that had given the town its unpleasant name. Though there were still many of the familiar canvas structures, a good portion of the town's buildings were built of clapboard, the most prominent being the Eldorado Hotel. A surprising number of women were on the streets, leading Miranda to wonder why this seemingly uninviting town had attracted a higher percentage of the available female population.

They set up their camp on the edge of town. The procedure had by now become routine and took little time. Lucas and her father went into town to pick up the latest news and enjoy a drink or two while Miranda stayed behind to do some much-needed laundry. There had been no opportunity to do more than rinse out a few underthings since they had left Sacramento City. The chore took the better part of an hour, and Miranda's hands were thoroughly chilled by the time her task was completed. She carried the bundle back to camp and hung the items over low-lying branches to dry in the warm afternoon sun.

Before going into town, she changed from her now-damp green calico into her wine-colored gown. It felt good to be wearing a stylish dress again, no matter how impractical. The color was striking with her dark hair and brought out the natural rose color in her cheeks. She gave her hair a thorough brushing before tying it over one shoulder with a matching ribbon. Satisfied with her appearance, she started for town.

She had not gone far when she saw Lucas standing under a tree conversing with a small group of miners. Upon seeing her he waved her toward them, running his eyes appreciatively over her figure. Wary of his open admiration, she hesitated a moment before joining the group.

"This is Miranda Austen," he introduced her when she reached them. "Miranda, this is Joseph Bristow, William Caudill, and Benjamin Smith. They're all Missourians."

"Pleased to meet you, ma'am." Each man tipped his hat as he was introduced.

"Do you have claims near here?" Miranda asked politely. She had discovered that the two questions one always asked upon making a new acquaintance in this country were: "Where is your claim?" and "How rich is it?"

"We're up on the south fork of the American River. Just came down to replenish our supplies and enjoy a little civilization for a day or two," William offered.

"I hope you're doing well." Miranda's interest was clearly pleasing to the men.

"Well enough, I s'pose," William continued. "Though there're days I wonder if it's all worth it."

"Ben tells me they are holding a barn dance here tonight," Lucas informed Miranda. "It should be a lot of fun, and I'm sure they can always use an extra skirt."

"I'm afraid I have never been taught the barn dance, but I would love to come and watch."

The men greeted Miranda's statement with a round of laughter. "Beggin' your pardon, ma'am, but a barn dance isn't a kind of dance, it's a dance held in a barn." Ben Smith's explanation caused Miranda to join in their good-natured laughter.

"I'm afraid Miranda is very English," Lucas explained. "I guess it's up to us to Americanize her." The men readily agreed to take on what they considered would be a very pleasant task. After conversing a while longer Lucas excused Miranda and himself, suggesting it was time they find her father and see about dinner.

"I feel like splurging tonight," Lucas said as he guided her down the street. "I think I'll dine at the Eldorado. Would you care to join me, madam?" He stopped in the middle of the street to bow low over her hand.

"I would be delighted, sir," Miranda replied, catching his festive mood, thinking that sometimes he could be a charming companion.

It took little time to locate Miranda's father. While not drunk, his jovial mood was well aided by a generous amount of alcohol. A dinner out suited his

mood, and a few moments later the three stepped into
the Eldorado Hotel. The interior was lit with kero-
sene lamps, and the place was alive with the sounds
of laughter and clinking glasses as patrons engaged
in a variety of games of chance.

The ground floor was divided into two sections.
The large saloon and gambling hall dominated the
area. A thick haze of cigar smoke hung above
wooden tables set up to entice the miners to engage
in games of monte, dice, and roulette. To the left of
the bar a piano player filled the air with tinny music.
The smaller portion of the room was devoted to dinner guests. Its small, round tables were covered with
white linen and set with china and silver.

Lucas guided Miranda to a table in a relatively
quiet corner while Edward Austen followed a bit unsteadily behind. Miranda was not bothered by her
father's slightly inebriated state. Through the years
she had seen him in various stages of intoxication,
and while he might become a bit boisterous, he was
never crude or obnoxious.

They ordered a complete dinner and enjoyed a delicious meal. Miranda was thoroughly delighted to
be eating at a real table again. She and Lucas good-
naturedly teased her father, informing him of the upcoming dance; the prospect of a festive evening increased his good humor.

They were lingering over the last of their pudding
when a miner stuck his head in the door and shouted,
"Dance hall's ready." Immediately there was a wild
scramble for the door, accompanied by a chorus of
hoots and hollers.

"Shall we join them?" Lucas rose and offered

Miranda his arm. She allowed herself to be assisted from her chair, perfectly content to let Lucas play the gallant escort.

"I imagine he can find his own way." Lucas cocked his head toward Miranda's father, who sat grinning into his cup of coffee.

"I'm sure he'll manage." Miranda smiled tolerantly as they followed the crowd out into the street.

The dance hall was indeed a barn with the majority of its contents removed. At one end three musicians stood on a raised platform supported by bales of hay. Two sported fiddles, the third a banjo. Additional bales of hay set around the edges of the room served as seats for weary dancers. A bowl of punch was provided on a table in one corner while stronger refreshments flowed freely from private sources. Though the men far outnumbered the women, it appeared that every female in the area had been invited. The more reputable ladies of the town seemed willing to view the many prostitutes with a tolerant eye, and there was even a handful of children present. For tonight, everyone was willing to meet on equal ground.

"Form your sets," a large, red-bearded man yelled as he jumped onto the musicians' platform. Miranda found herself being dragged to the center of the room along with every other available woman as the dancers began forming squares of four couples each.

"Lucas, I don't know how to do this kind of dancing," Miranda pleaded in his ear.

"Don't worry. Just do what the caller says, and I'll pull you in the right direction." Miranda had no further chance to protest. As the musicians struck up a lively tune, she found herself immediately in Lucas's arms being swung in a small, tight circle.

"Swing your partners, now your corners all; promenade your own sweet darlin' round the hall," the strong voice of the caller sang out over the heads of the dancers. Miranda was whirled from one pair of strong arms to another while the onlookers kept time to the jaunty beat with their feet. Lucas laughed heartily at her bewildered look when, at one point in the dance, she found herself standing in the middle of the square without a partner. Her arm was hastily grabbed by a work-worn hand, and she was again twirling around the hard-packed dirt floor. By the end of the first dance she felt breathless and a little bit dazed.

"Don't worry, the next one will be easier," Lucas consoled her as he lent his support with a comforting arm around her shoulders. Miranda had just caught her breath when the band struck up another tune, and she was again whisked into a dance. She found the steps of this dance similar to the first and was soon able to keep herself headed in the right direction. The second dance had barely ended when a man who had been standing on the sidelines stepped in to take Lucas's place. One dance led into another, with yet another eager partner ready to whirl her around the floor. There was no escape, and Miranda began to wonder if the band would ever tire.

Finally the caller sang out the blessed words, "Let's give the ladies a break, gents." Miranda noted as the music ended that every woman in the room began limping toward the punchbowl.

"If we don't get some more women up here, these dances will be the death of me," a plump, middle-aged woman said, panting in Miranda's ear as they left the dance floor. Scanning the room for Lucas, Miranda found him leaning against one wall, holding an inviting cup of punch in his hand. She made her way over to him and took the offered beverage gratefully, downing it in one gulp. It had a mild kick, but she was beyond noticing. Lucas chuckled at her flushed face and went to get her another cup.

"Are American dances always so exhausting?" she asked when she had temporarily quenched her thirst.

"Out here they are, though back East they are a bit more sedate."

"Oh." Miranda took a deep breath. "It really is a lot of fun, though." She looked guiltily at her now-empty cup.

Lucas took the cup from her hands. "I'll be back in a minute."

Miranda was sufficiently rested by the time the band began to play again, singing in slightly off-key voices:

"Hangtown gals are plump and rosy
Hair in ringlets mighty cozy
Painted cheeks and gassy bonnets
Touch them and they'll sting like hornets.
Ha, ha, ha, Hangtown gals . . ."

Lucas led Miranda back on to the dance floor, singing so softly only she could hear the words: "English gals are small and classy, I've got one who's mighty sassy.'' Miranda laughed at his words as they joined in.

After the first dance she did not see Lucas again until the band took another break. Even then, she could only wave from across the room, as her present partner was intent on engaging her in conversation. The evening continued in this manner. The punch was getting stronger as the evening wore on, but Miranda was too tired and thirsty to give it much thought.

It was near midnight when the band finally announced the last waltz. Lucas managed to claim Miranda before anyone else, and she permitted him to guide her exhausted body around the dance floor.

''You're drooping,'' Lucas whispered in her ear. Miranda straightened as she realized her full length was pressed against him. She blushed with embarrassment, but as the waltz played on, she gradually relaxed. A sigh of contentment escaped her lips as the sinewy muscles of his thighs moved rhythmically against hers. Lucas felt lovely, so warm and strong. She nuzzled her head against his chest, taking pleasure in the clean, masculine scent surrounding her. Their bodies moved as one as they glided across the dance floor. She felt tired and light-headed; she could worry about being proper tomorrow, she assured herself.

The dance ended, and the exhausted but happy participants began to wend their way home. Miranda leaned wearily against Lucas, securely cradled in one arm as they walked slowly back to their camp. As they approached, they could hear Miranda's father snoring loudly.

"I hope that isn't a bear," Miranda said with a giggle.

"If it is, he won't give us any trouble tonight." Lucas smiled. "Now be a good girl and give me a goodnight kiss, then it's off to bed with you."

In her slightly intoxicated state the request sounded reasonable enough to Miranda, and standing on tiptoe, she wrapped her arms around Lucas's neck, giving him a long and loving kiss. Lucas moaned softly at this unexpected pleasure, wrapping his arms tightly around Miranda's waist, matching her passion measure for measure. He nibbled tenderly at the trembling lips that parted slightly as they hungrily sought his own, amazed at the flaming response her touch unleased within him. Their tongues met in a slow, sensual dance as their limbs entwined, binding them into one shadow in the moonlight. Miranda's fingers combed through Lucas's burnished mane, sending rivulets of desire rippling down his spine.

The tempting kiss continued, each giving as well as taking delight in their intimacy, until Miranda pulled back, startled by the unfamiliar warmth spreading like fiery fingers through her body. She turned confused eyes up to Lucas's. Seeing the fervid passion there, she turned and retreated to the safety of her lean-to. Miranda had little time to sort out her confused thoughts. Exchanging her gown for a nightdress, she climbed under her covers and fell asleep immediately, the combination of the dancing and punch having taken its toll.

The sun was already high in the eastern sky by the time Miranda poked her tousled head out the end of the lean-to. She closed her eyes tightly against the overbright light, reopening them slowly to allow her eyes time to adjust. Lucas sat near the fire, idly stirring the embers with a stick. "Good morning, sleepy, I trust you had a good night's sleep," he commented, watching her with a lazy grin.

"I'm sorry, I'm afraid the punch last night was stronger than I thought," Miranda apologized, a deep blush spreading up her face. For a fleeting moment she entertained the thought that perhaps Lucas did not remember their parting, but one look at his smug smile shattered that hope. The direction of his thoughts could easily be read on his handsome face.

"Where is my father?" Miranda rubbed her aching head as she looked around for her parent. Perhaps his presence would prevent the conversation from turning in the direction she fervently wished to avoid.

"He said he had some business he needed to take care of in town. Left some time ago." Lucas broke the unwelcome news. "I'll roast you a hunk of bacon if you'd care for some breakfast."

"No, thank you." Miranda paled slightly at the mention of food. "I think I'll just wait for lunch. I'm sure you have things you need to do." The last statement held an almost pleading note.

"No, not really. I had planned to continue our journey today, but neither you nor your father appear up to it. I guess you'll just have to keep me entertained so I don't grow fidgety."

"Lucas . . . I . . . ah . . . what I mean is . . . I . . ." Miranda could not find the needed words.

"If you're trying to explain last night, don't

bother. I enjoyed it, you enjoyed it. Let's just leave it at that.''

''But I didn't mean to—''

''If you try to apologize,'' Lucas interrupted, ''I'll turn you over my knee and give you a sound thrashing. It was a perfectly natural thing, and I hope to enjoy the continued pleasure of your kisses in the future.''

Miranda could not be certain that Lucas was teasing her.

''Now go comb your hair, and we'll take a walk.'' Miranda turned to make a hasty escape, missing the twinkle in her companion's eyes.

Taking her time with her morning toilet, Miranda tried to postpone the walk as long as possible. If she dallied, perhaps her father would return and she could find some excuse to avoid it altogether. Whatever had possessed her to kiss Lucas in such a manner? He clearly intended to pursue the matter further, and she was not sure if she was more frightened of his advances or what her own response to them might be. She had no intention of getting seriously involved with any miner, least of all Lucas. It could only lead to trouble, and she already had enough of that, thank you.

She knew what she wanted out of life: a nice solid British husband, children, perhaps a country home. What she didn't want was to spend her life following some dreamy-eyed man to the four corners of the earth while he chased rainbows. Stability and good manners were what she wanted from a man. The effect of the punch, not Lucas's kiss, had caused her to feel so strangely, she decided. She was in no danger of falling in love with him. Last night meant nothing, and Lucas Adams meant nothing to her, either.

After taking care of her private needs Miranda scrubbed her face and arms vigorously in the cool mountain stream, cupping her hands to drink freely of the water to rinse away the stale, cottony feel in her mouth. Refreshed, she sat brushing her hair, vainly searching for some further reason to delay.

"Put your brush down. I'm tired of waiting," Lucas commanded as he rose from his place by the fire.

"But I haven't put my hair up yet," Miranda protested, knowing Lucas had seen through her ploy.

"I like it better down around your shoulders, anyway." He removed the brush from her fingers, tossing it into the lean-to. "You can put it away later," he told her before the words of protest could leave her lips. Without releasing his grasp on her fingers, Lucas placed her arm on his and led her into the shade of the forest.

Miranda kept a wary eye on Lucas as they strolled along in silence. She wondered why he wanted to take this walk; perhaps he was leading her out here to seduce her. She involuntarily stiffened at the unsettling thought. Lucas merely patted her hand, smiling down at her in a knowing and slightly superior way. They continued until they reached a small clearing carpeted by thin meadow grass and a colorful assortment of spindly wildflowers.

Unable to bear the silence a moment longer, Miranda burst out, "What do you want with me?"

"A kiss will do for the moment."

She turned her face away as her eyes met the inviting glint in the blue eyes, which burned with the intensity of his desire. "I don't want us to form a permanent attachment."

"Neither do I." Lucas pulled her into a strong embrace, touching her lips gently with his as he explored their rose-colored softness. His gentle assault caused her senses to reel. She pushed firmly against his chest, and he released her. Once she was free from the intoxicating contact, her anger gained control.

"I'm sorry to disappoint you, but I have no intention of playing the whore for you. If you expect me to throw my morals to the winds merely for the pleasure of your embrace, you have grossly overrated your seductive powers. My virginity is a gift I guard closely. A gift I will give to only one man, and that man will be my husband." The combination of her unbound hair and flashing eyes made her a most tempting sight.

"Why fight it?" Lucas said reasonably. "Since we are fated to live under each other's noses, it seems foolish not to make this venture pleasurable as well as profitable. You needn't be frightened. I'll be gentle with you."

Miranda slapped his hand away as he brushed his knuckles across her silken cheek.

"Pleasurable for who? Don't pretend you are thinking of anyone but yourself! You're not worth risking my future."

"Suit yourself." Lucas shrugged as if the matter was of little consequence to him. His attitude confused Miranda. She had expected annoyance, even anger, but not total indifference. Somehow that was more devastating than an assault upon her would have been.

She turned to walk back toward camp, feeling empty inside. Yet she knew she could never give herself to a man unless they were bound by the ties of love and marriage. She knew little of physical love, but the act seemed defiling outside the bounds of committed love, and for a woman there was always the possibility of a child. Since there had really been no decision to make, why did she feel so depressed?

The steady crackle of leaves and twigs breaking underfoot let Miranda know that Lucas was close behind as she fought a hopeless battle against the lump in her throat. She was determined not to cry, but the unbidden tears began to roll down her cheeks even as she tried valiantly to muffle her sobs. Lucas's strong arms encircled her from behind, turning her so she could hide her tear-streaked face against the soft flannel of his shirt. She did not resist the gesture and, resting her head against his chest, continued crying softly as Lucas stroked her long, silken hair.

"I'm sorry. I should never have asked," he murmured, shaken by the depth of her emotion. Miranda seemed more like a vulnerable child than a desirable woman as she leaned quietly sobbing against him, and he felt uncomfortably like a villain. Though trail life was hard, she had suffered uncomplainingly, doing more than her share of the work. Never once had she allowed her uncomfortable circumstances to weaken her to the point of tears. On the contrary, she had remained remarkably cheerful. Now, because of his stupidity, she cried as if the miseries of the world were suddenly thrust upon her shoulders. He was a fool to think she might even consider such an alliance. Miranda was a properly bred young Englishwoman. Though she might bend society's rules a bit to allow for her changed circumstances, she was not about to ignore her strict upbringing for the unknown pleasures to be found in the arms of a man.

For the first time Lucas considered Miranda's mother. She must have instilled these values, as her father was sadly lacking when it came to guarding his daughter's virtue.

Lucas continued stroking her hair, trying to give a small measure of comfort. While he could easily understand his physical attraction to Miranda, he was feeling something very different for her now. If he were smart, he thought wryly, he would uproot the emotion before it flowered into anything more than sympathy.

At last her tears ceased, and Miranda began to breathe more evenly.

"Are you all right now?" Lucas questioned with concern. Miranda nodded affirmatively but was reluctant to move out of the comforting shelter of his arms.

"I didn't mean to be such a baby," she apologized, searching her pockets unsuccessfully for a handkerchief. Why did she never remember to tuck one in? Leaning over, she wiped her cheeks with the hem of her skirt, leaving behind a wealth of brown streaks.

"I'm afraid you're not ready for civilization yet." Lucas chuckled at the sight of her mud-streaked face, anxious to lighten the mood. "With your dark hair and those streaks on your face you look like an Indian in warpaint. If you're not careful, you'll scare the townfolk.''

''Do I really look that awful?'' Miranda managed a timid smile as she tried to imagine the picture she must present.

''I'm afraid so,'' Lucas replied, relieved she was regaining her spirits. ''We'll have to stop at the creek and give you a good scrubbing.''

Miranda willingly grasped his hand, glad they were friends again. Lucas continued to tease her about being part Indian, and by the time they reached camp, they were both more comfortable in each other's presence.

Miranda's father did not return until late afternoon. He was unusually quiet, but upon being questioned, he merely stated that he had a bit of a headache. Assuming his discomfort was due to the excess of alcohol he had consumed the night before, Miranda tried to make him as comfortable as possible. However, her attentions only annoyed him, and she soon left him alone.

She and Lucas went about the usual routine of preparing the evening meal and securing the camp against visiting wildlife, much as they would on any other night. Both preferred to put the unsettling events of the last two days behind them.

As they mounted their horses the next day, ready to continue their journey upriver, the sky was an endless sea of blue, broken only by wisps of snow-white clouds.

Miranda took a deep breath of the clean morning air, thoroughly enjoying the warmth of the sun against her skin. It would probably take months to regain the dove-white complexion she had possessed before leaving England. Surrounded by the untamed majesty of snowcapped peaks and endless pines spiraling heavenward, such considerations seemed foolish. *It's strange how I view these mountains more with an eye for their unspoiled beauty than for the dangers that lay hidden within the forests of their slopes*, Miranda thought. She knew the dangers were real. She had seen more bears and wolves since leaving San Francisco than she cared to count, but always they had been at a distance and more fitting in the forest than the endless streams of gold-hungry men. *I'm falling in love with these open spaces*, she admitted to herself. It was a sobering thought.

They began stopping more frequently along the way, to prospect the richness of a likely-looking sandbar or patch of sparkling gravel at the bottom of the creek, hoping to strike pay dirt. The first day's pannings proved a disappointment, but Lucas did not seem overly concerned. They continued making frequent stops for the next two days, never finding enough gold to make staking a claim worthwhile. Miranda's father was becoming increasingly irritable at their lack of luck.

On the fourth day they stopped to exchange news at the camp of some apparently more successful miners. The camp looked fairly permanent, as the men had taken the time to erect sturdy canvas homes.

"Ho, how's your luck?" Lucas called out his greeting as he dismounted. Two miners looked up from the wooden, cradlelike contraption they were working. They abandoned their labors when they spotted Miranda.

"We're doin' pretty good, average at least an ounce a day," one said, offering the sought-after information, as he came forward, drying his hands on his faded trousers. His height barely equaled Miranda's, but he was stoutly built. Gray streaks lightened his brown, blunt-cut hair and beard. "Name's Zachariah Mulgan." The man held out a weathered hand.

"I'm Lucas Adams." Lucas shook the offered hand. "And this is Edward Austen and his daughter, Miranda." The second man's smile broadened at the introduction. He had assumed the younger pair was married. An unmarried lady, and a pretty one at that, would be a welcome addition to their lonely bachelor's camp.

"You're welcome to stay and make camp with us," he offered, looking to Zach for confirmation of his invitation. "There's only six of us, so there's plenty of room along the creek to stake your claim if you'd care to try your luck."

"We'll gladly accept your hospitality for the night," Lucas said, accepting the invitation. "But we'll want to fest the richness of the color before coming to any permanent decisions."

"Good enough. Jess, you help these good people with their gear. I'll let the others know we got company," Zach directed as he headed up the creek.

"I'm Jesse Stollard from Virginia," Jesse volunteered as he helped Miranda from her horse, his pride in his home state evident in the tone of his voice. He was a tall, angular man, and despite the fact that coal-black hair and a beard framed his face with unruly curls, there was an innate neatness about him. Golden lights twinkled in his brown eyes as he continued, "May I say you're the prettiest sight I've seen since leaving my own sweet home." Jesse's smooth southern drawl made his words sound almost musical.

"Thank you for the compliment, Mr. Stollard." Miranda rewarded him with a winsome smile, missing the dark look Lucas threw the eager young man.

"Zach says there be a lady in our camp." A large barrel-chested man came running toward the group, closely followed by a trio of well-seasoned miners. "Name's Stephen Cager. Friends just call me Cager, and I'm hopin' we're goin' to be friends." Cager bowed low over Miranda's hand, ignoring her two companions. Before Miranda could reply, he continued, "The lad's Billy Tucker, this here is Tom Bowman, and the rather scruffy fellow on the end is Jake Dawson."

Miranda's eyes followed his introductions, alighting first on a gangly young man near her own age. He was the only beardless member of the group. Next to him stood Thomas Bowman, his military posture perfectly suited to his stern visage. Lastly, they came to rest on Jake Dawson.

"I wouldn't be sayin' nothin' about bein' scruffy if I were you," Jake, a red-bearded man of enormous proportions, said, returning the good-natured ribbing. "Ain't none of us a fittin' sight for a lady."

"I'm pleased to meet you all." Miranda acknowledged the introductions, somewhat taken back by their enthusiastic welcome. She just couldn't get used to the attention.

"Well, let's stop gawkin' and give these folks a hand," Zach, who appeared to be the unofficial leader of the group, suggested.

Camp was set up in record time. On the trail Miranda habitually slept out in the open between the two men, but since they would be staying among strangers, Lucas again erected a crude lean-to for her.

"I sure hope what you say about these diggings are true," Edward Austen commented as he followed Zach Mulgan to the creek. "I'm getting damn tired of sitting on that horse."

"I imagine you'll do well enough if you don't mind workin' your fingers to the bone," Zach assured him with a pat on the back.

Later that afternoon he and Lucas walked upriver to test the soil. After a few hours of panning they returned, announcing their intention to stay on.

That night they all sat around the camp fire, sharing a communal meal while the men detailed the rules of the camp.

"Zach is the duly elected president of the camp. He presides over any meetings or disputes. If you have a gripe with some other member of the camp, it is settled by a majority vote of the uninvolved parties. All decisions are binding," Thomas Bowman explained. "Each man looks after his own cooking, washing, and so on. New members can join the camp by unanimous consent only. Any thievery or other unlawful activities will be dealt with severely. Any questions?" At the negative nods he went on. "Since

there is a lady in our midst, I move we all agree that
there will be no swearing on Sundays.''

"Here, here." The men readily agreed, eager to
impress Miranda. She thought the rule quite silly but
thanked them all kindly for their concern.

The business complete, Cager produced a mouth
harp, and they passed the remainder of the evening
in song. Miranda learned that Thomas was the only
married member of the group, though Cager had had
an Indian wife up until a year ago. Zach and Jake
were both confirmed bachelors while Jesse and Billy, both still young men, had yet to find themselves
a wife. Lucas told about his home in Oregon, and
Miranda listened intently as he described the life he
and one of his brothers had carved out of the Oregon
wilderness.

It was late when the group finally retired, each
having learned a great deal about their new companions.

The next day Lucas and Edward Austen staked out
their claims, measuring off the allowable footage and
posting the necessary sign. Miranda watched the two
men at work for a while before reluctantly turning
back to camp to do some washing. She waved a
greeting to the other men as she passed, but satisfied
that they were to enjoy her company for some time,
they did not cease their labors.

Toward midafternoon Lucas left his claim, returning to erect two tent houses. Miranda was a bit embarrassed that her father had not offered to help with
this chore but eased her vexed conscience by assisting the best she could.

They selected a small clearing slightly upriver, so

Miranda would have more privacy. The ground was suitably level, and it was conveniently near the water. A small stand of young pines provided a screen between the two camps.

Miranda cut thin strips of rawhide while Lucas felled several small, straight trees and stripped them of their branches. Together they bound the joints of the framing with the leather strips and covered the structures with canvas.

After stringing a line between two sturdy trees downwind from the tents, Lucas secured the horses and mules. Miranda sorted their belongings into piles. She would occupy one tent while Lucas and her father shared the other. Though it lacked the comforts of home, by dusk their little camp had taken on a permanent air.

Chapter 6

The days were becoming increasingly warm, though it had not yet become truly hot; the sky formed a deep blue roof overhead, broken only occasionally by a drift of billowy white clouds.

The men of the camp panned gold six days out of seven, working long, exhausting hours. Each day the miners rose early to take advantage of as many daylight hours as possible. With the exception of Zach and Jesse each man worked alone, washing pan after pan of sand and mud scooped up from the creek's gold-laden bottom, sometimes as many as one hundred a day.

They used heavy iron pans about sixteen inches in diameter with deep, sloping sides. The inside of each pan was japanned with durable black enamel to make the gold more visible. A small portion of sand was scooped up from the sides and bottom of the creek, then the pan was held just below the water's surface and the saucer swirled around and around until the lighter soil and debris washed down the river. The particles of gold would sink to the bottom of the pan along with the heavier stones and pebbles. Once these pebbles were picked out of the pan, all that remained was the gold. Each miner collected his earnings and stored it in a small leather pouch, then he would begin the painstaking process again.

Most of the gold was found in the form of dust, having been gradually eroded over the centuries from veins embedded throughout the mountain rocks. An occasional piece the size of a grain of sand was found, but this was rare.

The other mining device used was a rocker, the cradlelike contraption Miranda had seen when they first entered camp. This consisted of a sloping, oblong box set on rockers similar to a baby's cradle. At the upper end was a box with a perforated sheet of iron, which filtered out large stones. Beneath this stretched a canvas apron. Water washed dirt down this apron to the floor of the rocker across cleats called riffles. These riffles caught the heavier matter including the gold. The process was much more efficient than panning and allowed Zach and Jesse to turn a handsome profit with much less effort.

Miranda spent her days keeping the camp in order, mending shirts, and cooking meals. She continued to practice with the rifle on her own, and her skill had improved to the point where, as often as not, it was she who provided the meat for the evening meal. She was also becoming increasingly skilled at cooking over an open fire and had even managed to make a pie out of some wild berries she had found while on one of her hunting expeditions.

Though the living conditions were rough, she reveled in the freedom life in the wilderness allowed. Here, life was ruled by practicalities and personal preference, not by arbitrary rules set up by society.

She grew used to life in the exclusive company of the
miners and came to regard them as her friends, feeling as comfortable sitting around a camp fire conversing with them as she had been in England in the
parlors of friends enjoying an afternoon tea.

Each man treated her with respect but in his own
special way. They often left a stack of wood or a recently killed partridge as gifts of thanks for a mended
sleeve or a freshly washed shirt. It was a peaceful little community, each member, for the moment, content with the life he was leading.

Sunday was Miranda's favorite day of the week.
It was a day of rest in the camp, and invariably everyone slept late. After a leisurely breakfast they would
all gather together for a prayer and short sermon. The
latter was delivered by Thomas Bowman, his only
claim to the ministry being that he had promised his
wife to attend church every Sunday while he was
away, and this weekly gathering had been the only
way he was able to fulfill his promise. It only took
one Sunday for Miranda to discover that the other
members of the camp attended this meeting more to
humor their friend than out of desire for spiritual
guidance.

Each man, with the exception of Jake Dawson,
who viewed the whole proceedings with less toler-
ance than the others, took turns opening the meeting
with a prayer, thanking the Lord for his goodness and
asking for his guiding hand in the acquisition of a rich
harvest of gold; the most noteworthy feature of these
prayers was that they were short and to the point.
Next Thomas would rise, Bible in hand, to read a
scripture or two and expound on whatever subject his

conscience dictated. Usually he kept his remarks short, but the men had developed a signal of coughing loudly whenever his dissertations began to prove tiresome. Unaware of this, Miranda had been quite confused one Sunday when, after only a few words to introduce his topic, she had innocently coughed, and Thomas had given her a pained look, stopped in midsentence, then started to lead the closing hymn. Later that afternoon Jake had gleefully explained the situation to her, thoroughly delighted that the meeting had been cut short. At future Sunday gatherings Miranda was careful to suppress any urge to cough.

The remainder of Sunday, the men caught up on their washing, wrote letters home, and took a weekly bath. Miranda made it a habit to provide fresh meat and prepared a large midday meal for all to enjoy. The men were most complimentary, making this task more of a joy than a burden. After dinner Cager played his mouth harp, and they would all join in song or perhaps an impromptu jig.

One day, to Miranda's delight, she found a secluded pool a short distance upriver from her father's claim. It was surrounded on three sides by towering granite boulders rising straight up from the water's edge. Over one of these moss- and lichen-covered walls a small waterfall fell in a bubbling mass to the pool below. Access to the watery haven was gained by crossing a narrow point in the creek, then carefully walking down the gradual slope of another granite rock that made up the fourth side. The thick forest provided additional protection from prying eyes.

In a twinkling she retraced her steps; upon reaching camp, she wrapped a clean change of clothing in a towel and, soap in hand, hurried back to the pool. The day was warm, and she intended to take a long and leisurely bath.

Discarding her clothes in a heap, she stood luxuriating in the feel of the warm sun against her bare skin, stretching her arms heavenward as if to embrace it. Placing a toe gingerly into the water, she pulled back from its chilling effect, then, in a burst of bravado, dove into the icy waters, gasping in shock as the cold engulfed her body.

The pool reached just below her shoulders, and she paddled idly about until she became more accustomed to the numbing cold, then returned to the shore to procure her soap. She lathered her skin thoroughly, rubbing the soap over her body until her skin glowed. She soaped her hair, using the gently cascading waterfall to rinse the thick strands, then floated lazily on her back for a while longer, squinting up at the sun as it shone through the canopy of leaves.

At last, thoroughly refreshed, she rose from the water, the perfect vision of an enchanting wood nymph. She squeezed what moisture she could from her hair, then began to dry her skin. As she rubbed the rough towel across the back of her neck, her thoughts were transported to the day she had shared Lucas's horse. Like the towel, his beard had felt rough against her neck, but his lips . . . She brought her fingertips to her own lips. His lips invoked such strange and delightful responses from her body. Her thoughts tickled her flesh to goose bumps.

Still lost in her sensuous daydream, she spread the

towel on the rock and sat cross-legged to brush the tangles from her hair. She did not hear, but rather sensed, a presence come up behind her. Jumping to her feet, she turned to face the intruder, ready for flight.

"My God, Miranda!" Lucas stared in undisguised admiration at her unveiled beauty. Miranda's already rosy skin darkened to a deeper hue as she gazed, mesmerized, into the blue eyes riveted to her, her mantle of dark waist-length hair her only claim to modesty, but those wet strands clung coyly to her, more revealing than concealing. The blood pounded in Miranda's ears as some instinctive part of her recognized the darkening glow in Lucas's eyes.

"You were gone so long, I got worried and came to look for you." Lucas feebly tried to explain his presence, his voice sounding hoarse even to his own ears.

He advanced slowly, one step at a time, until he stood less than an arm's length from Miranda. Reaching out, he grazed the length of one silken arm with his fingertips. She did not recoil but stood gazing into his eyes with an intensity that both questioned and invited. Her small, pink-tipped breasts rose and fell with her rapid breathing. Tentatively he took another step forward.

Miranda stood motionless, feeling strangely disembodied. Some faraway voice urged her to flight, but her limbs stubbornly refused to obey its command. She trembled under Lucas's feather-light touch. She reached up, intending to push him away, but instead her fingers found the buttons of his shirt. Deftly they undid the fastenings until his chest lay bare. The sunlight caught the fiery undertones of the curly mat covering his torso as he let his shirt slip from his muscled shoulders to the ground.

He pulled her to him, his lips hungrily seeking hers. They nibbled at the perimeters before seeking the full draught of her exquisite nectar. Lowering his head, he blazed a trail of kisses from the column of her throat to the peak of one rosy breast. His tongue flicked at a droplet of moisture that had formed there. Miranda moaned softly, closing her eyes as Lucas's searing touch engulfed her in a wave of ardent desire. She held his head to her as he continued his gentle assault on her senses.

He returned his attentions to her lips, leading her to a soft, green spot of earth. A medley of wildflowers perfumed their bed. Drugged by passion, Miranda smiled lazily, running her fingers over the rippling cords of Lucas's back as he plied her with kisses.

She gasped breathlessly as he again turned to her breasts. Pulling gently with his teeth, he urged the nipples into twin, taut buds. The coarse hairs of his beard tickled her soft underbelly.

Again their lips met. Their tongues explored the soft contours of each other's mouths. Lucas nibbled at her bottom lip, then claimed both dewy petals in hungry embrace.

Unable to bear the longing building within her, Miranda's passion blossomed, her entire being welcoming Lucas, as the California poppies unfurl at dawn to welcome the heat of the sun. Without lessening his steady barrage on her senses, Lucas began to ease his trousers from his hips. Miranda continued to knead his muscles as she held him against her.

Abruptly Lucas rolled his weight from her. Miranda cried out softly, bidding him to return to her arms.

"Shh, someone is coming." He pressed his fingers to her lips as he lay tense beside her.

His words had the effect of a bucket of ice water. Her eyes widened with shock. Lying perfectly still, she waited, listening as twigs snapped underfoot mere yards from where they lay. Not until the sound of footsteps receded into the forest did she dare to breathe. Tears of shame filled her eyes to overflowing.

Lucas watched in mute frustration as the passion in Miranda's eyes went cold. It took every ounce of his will not to gather her in his arms and bring what they had started to its natural end.

"Miranda, I'm going to turn my back and allow you to dress yourself." Lucas forced the words out with an effort. "If you do not, that choice will no longer be open to you." He turned, presenting his back as he refastened his belt, and stood, arms folded across his chest, staring blindly into the forest as he willed his breath to a more even pace. He had been a fool to give her a choice. If he pressed the point, he might still be able to rekindle her fire. His aching loins mocked him for his reticence.

He had not intended to seduce her, but living in such proximity was beginning to take a toll on his restraint. The bone-wearying labor of mining in the creek all day had allowed him to push his desires to the back of his mind, but seeing her standing there like some untamed forest creature had brought his hungers painfully to the forefront. He knew he shouldn't have taken advantage of her innocent confusion, but he had been unable to stop himself. At least until now, when his unfulfilled desires tore at his gut. "Damn my moral upbringing," he muttered to himself.

When sufficient time had elapsed for even the most wearisome of women to dress, he turned slowly to face his tormentor. She stood fully clothed, her arms crossed protectively over her chest.

"Come on, I'll walk you back to camp," he ordered more gruffly than he had intended.

Miranda stared at him with wide eyes as she mutely shook her head. A thousand emotions warred within her breast. "I want to be alone . . . please."

Lucas hesitated for a moment.

"Next time tell someone you are going for a bath," he advised before grabbing his shirt and swiftly striding upriver. He felt an urgent need for the creek's icy waters.

Miranda sagged against a tree as she watched Lucas's broad back retreat into the forest. What was the matter with her? Was living so close to nature turning her into a savage? She trembled with the certain knowledge that had fate not intervened, she would have willingly sacrificed her virtue. She had not wanted to deny the primitive urges that had threatened to engulf her, and this knowledge frightened her more than any beast of the forest ever could. Against all she had been brought up to believe and hold as true, against all reason, she had wanted Lucas to take her in his arms and teach her the secrets of love between a man and a woman. She could not understand herself. "It's wrong, it's wrong, it's wrong." She rubbed the back of her hand across her aching brow as her words of protest echoed hollowly in her mind.

During the next few days Miranda avoided Lucas as much as possible, considering the close-knit nature of their community. She busied herself from dawn until dusk in an effort to keep her more disturbing thoughts at bay. At no time did she allow an opportunity for Lucas and herself to be alone.

He was content with the arrangement, having feelings of his own that needed sorting out. He was beginning to develop softer feelings for Miranda, and he knew well the danger in that. Hadn't Mary taught him that lesson well? Dear sweet Mary. Lucas grimaced as he remembered his love of long ago, all goodness and virtue on the outside, with a heart of cold stone beneath the soft, white skin of which she was so proud. He had played the fool well while she led him on a merry chase. Through letters from friends he had learned she had grown fat and spiteful with the years. He pitied the poor man who had married her.

For himself he had found happiness in the wilds of the Oregon Territory, and a serious thought of marriage had not crossed his mind in years. He was contented with the life he had made and wasn't about to let any woman, no matter how desirable, disturb his peace of mind. Dealing with his physical desire for Miranda was easy enough; it was nothing a good tumble wouldn't cure, he reasoned. It was his overwhelming desire to protect her, even from himself, that rankled him. If she would bemoan her state occasionally, it might help, but she faced each new day with such dogged determination, it was impossible

not to yearn to lighten her load when he could. Her
father didn't make matters any better. He had never
seen a more self-centered person in his life. As long
as the man's needs were seen to, he seemed content
to let his daughter fend for herself. Oh, he would occasionally make a show of fatherly devotion, but that
was just what it was, a show. Lucas doubted the man
had the slightest idea what being a father entailed.
Now, if I had a daughter like Miranda . . . Lucas
caught himself in midthought. *Oh, Lord, here I go
again.* He sighed in exasperation.

The tension between Miranda and Lucas was obvious to anyone who cared to look at either of the unhappy pair. They took great pains to avoid contact
with each other; then, when they thought no one was
looking, they sat staring with pensive frowns at the
one who was the cause of so much inner turmoil.
Thomas Bowman, who rather fancied himself the
conscience of the group, was quick to note the strain
and quite accurately deduced that it was caused by
repressed physical desire. The two were obviously
attracted, and feeling it was only a matter of time before they slipped into Satan's power, he determined
that "sins of the flesh" would be the topic of his next
sermon.

That Sunday, after the usual concise prayer,
Thomas launched into his subject with enthusiasm,
little realizing how raw a nerve he rubbed. One look
at Lucas's carefully averted face, and Miranda turned
a fiery red. Had Thomas seen them by the pool? Miranda tried to focus her attention on her hands in her
lap, lacing and unlacing her fingers. Thomas, truly
inspired by his subject, continued blissfully on, to-

tally unaware of the discomfort he was causing. Almost in unison the other more observant members of the party came to the rescue with a loud chorus of coughing. Thomas stopped immediately, a bit hurt that what he had thought to be one of his better sermons had been so poorly received. Miranda was barely able to squeak out the words to "Rock of Ages," and the moment the song ended, she rose to leave, unable to bear the sympathetic, but knowing, glances cast in her direction.

Lucas rose to follow her but was stopped by a firm hand on his arm. "If you're bedding my daughter, you're going to marry her," Edward Austen growled in a sudden show of parental concern, his voice so low only Lucas could hear his words.

Lucas shook off the restraining hand; then, without a backward glance, he retreated down the path Miranda had just taken. It took little time for his longer strides to overtake hers, and hearing him in pursuit, Miranda stopped and waited miserably for him to catch up.

"Lucas, he must have seen us at the pool." Unshed tears of shame glistened in Miranda's eyes.

"I don't think so," Lucas said, trying to reassure her.

"Then how did he know?"

"I imagine it was just a poorly timed sermon, or perhaps he noticed the tension between us and arrived at his own conclusions." Lucas silently cursed the man for his lack of sensitivity. "We've done no more than exchange a few kisses, and that is certainly nothing to be ashamed of."

"But I wanted to do more. You know I wanted to.

I'm no better than the prostitutes I am so quick to condemn." Miranda startled herself by admitting the dreadful truth out loud.

"No, you're different. I would never have stopped if you weren't." His words did little to comfort Miranda, and as he reached to wipe away a stray tear, she skidded out of reach like a frightened rabbit.

"Please . . . don't touch me."

"Okay, little English mouse." Lucas withdrew the offending hand. "You stay here and compose yourself. I guarantee, when you come back, no one will be indiscreet enough to say a word, and if someone is, I promise you I'll flatten him. Now, I'd better go back and explain to your father that you are still the same girl you were when you left England. After the way you took off he is half convinced the deed is already done."

The same girl indeed; the statement was almost laughable, Miranda thought dejectedly. "Lucas," she called as he turned to leave, "thank you."

If there was further speculation as to the extent of the relationship between Miranda and Lucas, it was carried on privately, and life continued normally, each man treating Miranda with the same respect he had shown prior to the unfortunate sermon.

It hadn't rained in weeks, causing the green grasses that carpeted the hills to turn golden under the hot summer sun. Even the nights were becoming unpleasantly warm.

Miranda was surprised that her father had lasted in the gold fields so long. He did not work as steadily as the other men and had yet to make his fortune. In fact, what little gold dust he did find quickly disappeared with each trip to Hangtown to bolster their sagging supplies. Miranda seldom accompanied him on these trips, preferring the quiet peace of their community to the noisy ruckus of the mining town. She felt perfectly safe being left in the care of whoever chose to remain at camp.

Miranda often wondered at her father's tenacity, that characteristic being hitherto so foreign to his personality. She had expected to be on her way back to England by now, or at the very least, back in San Francisco, preparing for such a journey. Whenever she questioned him about when he expected to return home, her father either shrugged noncommittally or brusquely shooed her away. The gold fields were doing little for his disposition.

As time went on Lucas and Miranda slipped back into their former relationship, neither mentioning the incident at the pool again or making any further move to explore the feelings awakened there. Miranda became convinced that Lucas had forgotten the whole thing and even managed to half convince herself that her reaction to him that day had been due to too much sun. In any event, she had no desire to test the soundness of her theory and continued to scrupulously avoid even the most innocent physical contact.

Billy Tucker became sick with bilious fever, a malady common among miners in the back country, and while at first no one was overly worried, his continually weakening state soon gave rise to concern. Billy was the youngest miner in the group, being only nineteen years old, with a round, boyish face that

made him appear even younger than his years. He
had always been rather shy around Miranda and was
acutely embarrassed to have her as his nurse.

One morning Billy awoke with a raging fever. Miranda neglected her other chores to spend the entire
day placing cool rags on his fevered brow and spoon-
ing rice water between his parched lips. He mum-
bled his thanks, then let his head fall back into the
soft lap of his benefactress, slipping into an uncomfortable state of half consciousness. Miranda gently
stroked his tousled hair, murmuring soft words of re-
assurance.

She kept up her vigil through the next two days.
At the end of each day her back ached dreadfully
from sitting in one position for so long, but as her
cradling lap seemed to give so much comfort, she
could not bear to deny it to one who needed solace
so much more than she.

The atmosphere of the camp was tense as real fear
for Billy's continued survival was keenly felt by all.
By the fourth day of his fever, many had begun to
give up hope. Finally, on the fifth day, the fever
broke, and by the sixth, a pale and weakened Billy
was able to sit up for the first time in days. Miranda
continued her tender ministrations, and Billy's
strength returned steadily. After another week of
limited activity he was back at his claim, working as
hard as ever.

During his illness Billy had lost much of his shy-
ness with Miranda. Now he seemed to be present
whenever a fire needed tending or a heavy pot needed
lifting, a fact that annoyed Lucas to no end.

"The next thing we know, that mooncalf will be

moving his tent up here," he complained after witnessing the boy's overlong, undue attentions one day. "He's like a puppy at your heels."

"I know," Miranda agreed. "Sometimes I'm afraid I'm going to trip over him, but I don't know how to send him off without hurting his feelings."

"I'd be glad to do it for you," Lucas offered.

"Don't you dare! He only wants to help, and he isn't hurting a thing."

"I don't agree. Watching him drool over you hurts the pride I have in my own sex, not to mention the fact that his behavior is rather nauseating."

"Why, are you becoming jealous, Mr. Adams?" Miranda taunted, not taking her question the least bit seriously.

"Don't be ridiculous!" Lucas hunched his shoulders and stomped morosely away, incensed with himself for being so transparent. Miranda might be different from most women in that she did not wheedle, cajole, or complain, but she was still a woman, and he didn't want her to start getting any ideas about tying him to her skirts.

Miranda stared at the retreating back. Why was Lucas so angry? Unless . . . She banished the thought. Lucas couldn't possibly be feeling romantic about her.

Miranda decided it was time to find out, once and for all, how long her father intended to stay in the gold fields. She was uncertain of Lucas's intentions and not at all confident in her ability to resist him if he truly set his mind to courting her. Lucas was a man used to getting what he wanted; if he had decided he wanted her, he would pursue her with ruthless determination. If she could not withstand his physical advances, how would she ever manage to ward off an emotional assault?

Her father was working his claim, so it would be a good opportunity to talk to him alone.

"Papa." Miranda waved a greeting, then, smiling her sweetest, she came to sit on a rock near the water's edge. Edward Austen stopped his labor and looked at his daughter.

"What brings you here? Did you come to keep your poor papa company?" His eyes lit up at the prospect of an excuse to cease his labors.

"I need to talk to you."

"Hmm, this sounds serious," her father teased as he stepped out of the water, drying his hands on the upper portion of his trousers.

Miranda came right to the point. "Papa, I need to know how long you plan to stay out here."

Her father scowled. "I'm too busy to be bothered with your foolish questions." Turning his back to his daughter, he picked up his pan and stepped back into the water.

"Papa, I have to know." Miranda refused to be put off again. "I'm not going to leave until you give me an answer."

"You're wasting your time." Edward Austen bent to scoop another pan of dirt from the creek bottom, his face suffused with irritation. Why didn't the girl stop badgering him? He could think of no reason why she should need to know such information.

Miranda's temper had also risen. It was a simple question, and she deserved some kind of answer.

Grabbing the pan from her father's hands, she dumped its contents, then threw the saucer onto the rocks that lined the creek bed. Edward Austen was stunned by his daughter's action. Miranda was becoming rebellious; he vastly preferred her more subservient attitude.

"All right, daughter, I'll tell you when we will leave here." He huffed. "We will leave when I make enough money to pay off our guide and buy passage back to England."

"Papa, surely we have something left!" Miranda was caught completely off-balance. Hadn't she seen the chest full of money her father had kept hidden in his trunk back in San Francisco? It had been enough to keep them for over a year and then some, even with the high cost of living in California.

"It's all gone." Her father confirmed his statement, holding out empty, flattened palms to illustrate how truly destitute they were.

"But how, Papa? There was so much." Miranda was not even sure she wanted to hear the answer, but she asked the question, anyway.

"That night in Hangtown, when you went dancing," he began guiltily, "I ran into a sharper. You remember, I was a bit into my cups. Well, before I could follow you to the dance, he asked me to join him in a friendly little game of cards. Next thing I knew, he had swindled the lot, even let me give him a voucher when he found out I had more back at camp. That's why I went back into town the next day, to pay my debt and try to win a little back, but lady luck had deserted me for sure. I'm sure sorry, Mandy." He looked down at the ground like a small child who had just been caught stealing a cookie, but this was much more serious than a missing treat.

"Have you told Lucas yet?" Miranda questioned wearily.

"Are you mad? Do you want us to be left out here to fend for ourselves, or worse yet, see your papa punished like some sort of criminal? I've been putting Lucas off for weeks, and I finally told him I left all but expense money back in San Francisco and would pay him when we get back. He doesn't strike me as the kind of man who would take kindly to finding out he'd been deceived."

"Papa, you should have told him at the first. You had absolutely no right to retain Mr. Adams under false pretenses!" Miranda couldn't believe she was having this conversation. If her father had gone to Lucas with the truth immediately, she doubted he would have callously deserted them, but now her father's lies guaranteed the worst. "What did you hope to gain by your deceit?" she demanded furiously.

"Time! Time, to find enough of this damn gold to get us out of this mess, that's what. Now let me get back to work, and keep quiet about this." Her father glanced nervously over his shoulder. "I've heard stories. These miners mete out their own brand of justice, and from all accounts, it is swift and stern."

"I will not allow you to take advantage in this way. You created this situation and you should face the consequences."

"But, Mandy, he might get angry." Edward Austen's bottom lip began to quiver.

"After your lies I'm sure he'll be furious." Her

father paled, and Miranda added, ''I'll try to inter-
vene on your behalf, but that is all the help I can offer
you.''

''Just a little more time, Mandy. Please,'' her
father pleaded as she firmly shook her head. ''I'm
sure I'll strike it rich any day now.''

''No.'' Miranda stood her ground.

Edward Austen's lips pursed in an obstinate pout.
Sensing the direction of his thoughts, Miranda
warned, ''If you don't tell him, I will.''

''You're a very brutish daughter, Miranda Austen, to abuse your papa so. I'll tell him.'' Edward
Austen's face continued to show his displeasure.

''When?''

''Within the week,'' he promised. ''I need a little
time to gather my thoughts.''

''Then I'll give you exactly one week.'' Miranda's stern expression gave Edward Austen little hope
that he could extend the deadline.

''It would be better if you told Lucas yourself, but
if you delay, I will not hesitate to do so myself.''
Turning on her heels, Miranda left her father staring
forlornly at her rigid back.

Chapter 7

When Miranda reached camp, she was dismayed to find that Lucas had returned in her absence. She forced the worry lines from her brow as he raised his head to greet her.

"Nice weather we've been having," she commented as she searched her mind for some excuse to quit his presence. She was too agitated to remain in Lucas's company without him noticing her discomfort. She had promised to give her father a week to admit his folly, but she would not lie for him. "I think I'll do a little shooting this afternoon."

"Ah, the great huntress. You put us all to shame with your talent with a gun. I'll fetch it for you." Lucas ducked into the tent he shared with Miranda's father and emerged with the weapon. As he handed it to her their fingers brushed, sparking an immediate physical reaction in her. Their eyes met, and Miranda quickly turned her head. It was too easy to lose her common sense when she gazed into those eyes.

"Well, I'm off." Her voice held an unnaturally gay note as she hurried from the clearing.

She had been gone over an hour and had yet to fire a shot. Her thoughts were too chaotic to allow her to concentrate on the task she had set for herself. Despite every effort on her part to remain unaffected, even a casual touch set her heart pounding and her senses longing for more. She knew Lucas had been avoiding her diligently, but if anything, her attraction had heightened. And now her father had further complicated their relationship. While she frequently acted as a buffer between the two men, she doubted if she could completely shield her father from Lucas's anger. Perhaps he would leave them to their own devices. It would be difficult to find another guide, but it might be for the best. At least with Lucas gone she would be able to think clearly again.

A rustling on the opposite side of a clump of bushes caught Miranda's attention. Raising her rifle, she crept silently around the foliage, coming face-to-face with a man.

The stranger stood a full two heads above Miranda but was almost skeletal in his build. Swarthy skin stretched over flat cheekbones, while the dark shadows surrounding his bloodshot, protruding eyes gave him a decimated look as if he had too often indulged in the vices of mankind.

"You alone?" His eyes raked over her, but he made no move to approach her.

"No." Miranda shifted her weight nervously. "We have a camp not far from here." There was something about the man that made her uneasy. Though he wore some kind of military uniform, his appearance was unkempt, and he carried himself with none of the discipline one would expect of a soldier.

"If you don't mind lowerin' the gun, I'd be much

obliged.'' He bit off a thick wad of tobacco, offering the remainder to Miranda.

"No, thank you,'' she declined with a shake of her head. She lowered the muzzle of the rifle but kept her forefinger poised on the trigger.

"No, I suppose not.'' He shrugged, stuffing his tobacco into his pants pocket. "How many did you say were in your camp?''

"Nine.''

"Claims doin' well?''

"Yes, quite well.''

"You the only woman?'' He spit a stream of yellow juice to the ground.

"Yes.'' Though there was nothing unnatural about his curiosity, his questions made Miranda uncomfortable. She noted that his left leg had begun to twitch. "I really should return to camp. The others will be looking for me.'' Miranda offered the information, hoping it would discourage the man. Her instincts told her he was not a man to be trusted. "If you're camped near here, perhaps we will meet again.'' She forced her voice to sound calm.

"Like as not, ma'am. Like as not.'' The man grinned, revealing a row of uneven, yellow teeth, then, tipping his hat, he ambled off into the forest. He had never even offered his name.

Miranda returned to the camp empty-handed. She had not wanted to linger alone in the forest. However, once she had regained the security of their camp, she pushed her encounter with the stranger to the back of her mind.

The week wore on, each day seeming longer than the last. Miranda chided herself for even considering that her father might come forward a minute before his deadline. He would avoid facing responsibility to the last.

It had been a week to the day, and her father had yet to speak to Lucas. Miranda resigned herself to the unpleasant task of telling him herself that evening after dinner.

She spent the morning hunting and was just returning a shirt she had mended to Cager's tent when she noticed a strange horse tethered to a tree. The men were all working their claims, and since Zach and Jesse had ridden to Hangtown earlier in the week, no one was within sight of the camp. As she came forward to offer the traveler the hospitality of their camp, her eyes scanned the area. There was no one in sight.

Miranda shook her head in confusion as she approached the animal. The poor thing looked half starved. The horse whinnied loudly as she reached up to stroke its nose. Just then a man stuck his head out of the tent Zach and Jesse shared. It was the stranger Miranda had encountered earlier in the week.

The hair on the back of her neck rose as the man approached her. There was something disquieting about the way his eyes darted nervously back and forth as if he were afraid someone were watching him.

"Just keep that pretty little mouth of yours shut," he warned. "I'll just ride out of here, and there won't be no trouble."

Miranda was acutely aware of her vulnerability. She had stupidly left her rifle in her tent. She stood

motionless while he backed slowly to his horse.
Waiting until she judged him to be a safe distance
from her, she dashed up the creek, calling for help.
After her brief, breathless explanation, Jake and
Cager ran for their horses, closely followed by Tom,
Billy, and Lucas. Her father stayed behind in case
the man should return.

The intruder had already put an amazing distance
between himself and their camp. The men rode their
mounts hard, weaving in and out of the trees as they
trailed the rising cloud of dust before them. Gradually they began to close the gap. The man frantically
beat his mount at the sound of thundering hooves
threatening to overtake him. His horse's sides
heaved, and thick foam blew back from its frothing
mouth to splatter his pant legs.

Suddenly a rude hand grasped him roughly around
the collar, causing him to lose his seat on his horse.
He hit the ground with a yelp, barely avoiding the
sharp hooves of his mount as it continued its killer
pace, riderless.

"Up on your feet."

The man gasped hard for his breath as he was
dragged to his feet by a huge, red-bearded man.
Without a word Jake trussed him up like a chicken,
then threw him unceremoniously across the saddle of
the mount Lucas had brought up.

"We ought to hang you just for the way you treat
your horse." Jake eyed the emaciated animal in disgust.

Miranda waited with her father for the prisoner to
be brought back to camp. He landed in the dust with
a thud as he was pulled from his horse.

"You loudmouthed little bitch." He snarled at Miranda from his undignified position.

"Hold your tongue, varmit. You're in enough trouble as it is." Jake gave the man a swift boot in the backside.

"I haven't done a thing," he whined. "I just rode into your camp, and that woman started screamin'."

"Then why were you in such an all-fired hurry to leave?" Jake asked, shoving his hands inside the man's shirtfront and coming up with a small pouch of gold bearing the initials Z.M., and two of Jesse's favorite tobacco pipes. "Don't worry, you'll get a fair trial." He grinned at the now pale and trembling stranger. "But for now you're goin' to be keepin' that big oak tree company."

The prisoner was tied to the tree, all the while staring daggers at Miranda. In his twisted mind she was the cause of his present misery. He silently vowed to get even with the wench.

"It don't seem right to hold a trial without Zach and Jess, seein' how they were the victims of his thievery," Cager stated as the group gathered together to decide what to do next.

"I imagine he'll keep until they get back," Lucas added. "They are expected anytime now. Did the man hurt you, Miranda?" All eyes turned to Miranda.

"No. He just scared me a bit," Miranda reassured the men.

Lucas watched Miranda uncertainly. She appeared unscathed; however, her confrontation with the thief must have shaken her. It would be just like her to conceal her anxiety to prevent the others from worrying about her.

"Well, I, for one, want to get back to work. That no account has already wasted enough of my time. We can draw straws to see who stands guard first, though I doubt he will be goin' anywhere," suggested Jake.

"Don't bother with the straws. I'll volunteer to take first duty," Lucas offered, not wanting to leave Miranda alone. Since no one had any objections, the camp soon emptied.

"Where do you suppose he came from?" Miranda asked as she sat next to Lucas on a log that provided a convenient bench.

"From the ragged uniform I'd guess he is probably a Hound. They're ex-soldiers from the Mexican-American War who virtually ruled San Francisco until the good citizens finally had enough of their ham-fisted ways and threw them out. Many left the area altogether, but a few still roam the back country making trouble. It's best you stay away from him." Miranda had every intention of following that bit of advice.

Late that night Zach and Jesse rode into camp. The prisoner had been quiet the entire day, and no one had troubled with him, except to untie his hands long enough to permit him to eat. Zach and Jesse were clearly disheartened to be greeted by the news of the attempted robbery, not wishing to have the good spirits of their downriver trip spoiled by the necessary proceedings. All agreed the trial could wait until morning, leaving the luckless prisoner to spend an uncomfortable night tied to the tree.

Court convened the next morning around the oak tree. Although the prisoner was released from the tree, his hands and feet remained bound.

"What's your name, man?" Zach directed the question to the prisoner.

"Jeb Lewis." The man glared his hatred at the group sitting around him. He knew that the minute they had caught him, his fate had been sealed.

"Jeb Lewis, this court has been called to decide your guilt or innocence in the matter of thievin' my gold and Jess's pipes. First we'll hear the witnesses against you, then you'll be given a chance to speak for yourself. Miranda, since you're the one who caught the man in the act, why don't you go first."

Miranda stood and gave her account of the previous day's events, explaining how she had stumbled upon Jeb Lewis a week earlier and apologizing profusely for not alerting the other camp members of his presence. Though she kept her eyes carefully averted from Jeb Lewis, she could feel his malevolent eyes burning his hatred into her soul. The sensation was so acute, her flesh prickled and her hands turned clammy. Relieved when her part in the trial was finished, she sat down, unconsciously edging closer to Lucas. Next, each man in turn gave his version of the events, their accounts so similar as to become monotonous. Finally Jeb Lewis was given his chance to defend himself.

"Just get on with it," he muttered, turning his eyes to the ground.

"All present have been heard," Zach continued. "We'll now vote on the guilt or innocence of the prisoner. All those who find Jeb Lewis guilty as charged, raise your right hand.'' Every hand shot up without hesitation with the exception of Miranda's.

"Miranda, you're a member of the camp. You've got a vote too,'' Zach instructed her. Slowly her hand rose to join the others.

"The punishment for thievery is thirty-nine lashes on the bare back.'' Miranda paled at his words. Such a punishment could kill a man. "Those in agreement raise your hand.'' Again the voting was unanimous with the exception of Miranda, though Edward Austen's hand trembled almost imperceptibly as he held it to the square.

"Miranda?'' Zach gently prodded. Staring wide-eyed at the group of men, she shook her head, unable to vote for such a harsh punishment.

"Majority agrees to the punishment. If there's no volunteers, we'll draw straws to see who will administer the lash.'' Though the men had not hesitated in voting for the standard punishment, no one was eager to be the one to carry it out. Straws were drawn, and Miranda watched as relief flooded the face of each man as he pulled a full-length straw. She was grateful no one had even suggested she participate in this phase of the trial.

It was Lucas's turn, and only two straws were left. Miranda held her bottom lip between her teeth as he slowly began to pull a straw. Her heart sank when its end was revealed all too soon.

"The lot falls to me,'' Lucas stated, his voice expressionless.

Jeb Lewis had remained motionless throughout the entire proceedings, but as the men came forward to tie his arms around the tree, he suddenly came to life, struggling with the strength of two men, despite the ropes that bound his hands and feet. It was a hopeless battle, and soon his arms embraced the rough trunk of the oak. Jake parted the back of his shirt with one clean rip, then ducked inside his tent, returning with a large mule whip. Silently he handed the instrument to Lucas.

Miranda sat immobile as Lucas slowly drew back his arm. With a crack the evil lash snaked out, and the bound man screamed as it bit into his back. Lucas continued striking the man, cutting a pattern of long, bloody slashes into his bare skin. As the leather tore at his raw flesh his screams became increasingly agonized, causing Miranda to claw at the rough bark of her seat until her fingertips were raw and bleeding. Jeb Lewis's head fell forward, and still the whip continued to hiss through the air, though the blows had imperceptibly lightened.

Unable to bear the sight any longer, Miranda ran for the protective screen of the woods, her hand pressed tightly over her mouth to hold back the threatening sickness. When she had gone far enough to block out the dreadful scene, she fell to her knees and was violently ill. Her body racked with shudders as she emptied the contents of her stomach. Rising unsteadily, she sought the reviving effects of the stream's cool water. She splashed her face and neck, then, cupping her trembling hands, she slowly sipped the liquid, rinsing the sour taste from her mouth. When she straightened, she could no longer hear the steady crack of the whip.

His punishment complete, Jeb Lewis was untied from the tree. He crumpled to the ground before he felt a pair of strong hands lifting him to the back of his horse. After a firm slap on the rump the horse began walking slowly away from the camp with its hapless burden. The men picked up their shovels and pans and withdrew to their respective claims, subdued but content that justice had been served.

Miranda did not return to the central camp but instead retired to the privacy of her tent. She picked up a petticoat with a small rend that needed mending, but after staring blankly at the well-worn article for some time, she set it aside. How could she ever tell Lucas of her father's deceit? The horrifying vision of her father slumped bruised and bleeding against a tree as a whip shredded the skin of his back to ribbons came unbidden into her already tortured mind. The face of his tormentor was a blur, but as her vivid imagination continued to unfold the scene, the face gradually focused to reveal Lucas, his jaw set in grim determination. She shook her head vigorously to banish the gruesome thoughts. No, she could never risk the possibility of such a fate befalling her father. He was not a hardened miner, and such a punishment would surely mean his death if Lucas ever found out her father had lied to him.

At the first opportunity Edward Austen privately sought out his daughter.

"Mandy, you didn't tell him, did you?" He grasped her hand with trembling fingers. His complexion was alarmingly pale.

"No, Papa." Miranda stroked his face. "With all the excitement I never had the chance."

"Thank God!" Edward Austen sighed with relief. "Did you see what he did to that man? I nearly was ill witnessing such brutality."

"I saw, Papa." Miranda's shoulders sagged in resignation.

"You see, I was right not to tell him."

"No, you were wrong! Your lies got us into this mess." Miranda's harsh words made him wince.

"You aren't still planning to tell him?" he questioned in shocked disbelief.

"No. I'll keep your secret. I can't allow Lucas to hurt you." Miranda's eyes rose to meet her father's. "What we need now is money. Tomorrow I'll start panning myself."

"Good girl, Mandy." Edward Austen gave his daughter a heartfelt hug. "But you better leave finding our fortune to me. Lucas might get suspicious if you took a sudden interest in panning gold."

"I can't stand idly by and do nothing," Miranda protested. Even her father must have realized by now that they were not going to become rich overnight.

"Just keep the man happy, I'll do the rest." Adjusting his hat, Edward Austen returned to his claim, leaving his daughter to stare at his back in vexation.

Miranda avoided Lucas for the rest of the day, afraid he might read the fear in her eyes and discover the terrible secret she and her father shared.

It was a relatively simple task, as he worked hard all day in an effort to block the distasteful task he had just performed from his mind. The punishment had been no more harsh than the man would have received at any other mining camp, but still, it was a hard thing to bring a man to such a state. He had seen the terror in Miranda's eyes as she watched him administer the lash. But he could not have refused to carry out the sentence. It had been a fair trial, and as a member of the camp, he had drawn the responsibility to carry out the will of the majority. Lucas cursed his luck that the lot had fallen to him.

Edward Austen was not unaffected by his firsthand initiation into the workings of frontier law. He threw himself into the business of panning gold with a fervor bordering on obsession. For all his newfound enthusiasm, the work was still backbreaking and the rewards maddeningly sparse. Fear clung to him with the tenacity of a mountain tick, and he could not shake the feeling of impending doom. For the first time in his life Edward Austen truly regretted his gambling nature.

Meanwhile Miranda spent more and more of her day away from the camp. One day she had come upon Jake scratching at a rock with his knife point, and he had explained it was possible to scrape gold from tiny veins embedded in the rocks. Unwilling to leave their fate in her father's hands, she began spending her time among the rock-filled hills, scratching out what gold dust she could. It was tedious work, but she felt every particle of dust, no matter how small, improved their situation.

To avoid arousing suspicion, she always took her father's rifle. If the men noticed that her hunting expeditions were becoming more frequent and less successful, they did not mention the fact. Though her small deception plagued her conscience, she could see no way to avoid it.

As June gave way to July the heat continued to increase. Often the afternoon temperature would reach more than one hundred degrees, so that even the most determined miners had to stop and rest in the shade. The fierce sun reflecting off the sparkling water caused heads to ache and eyes to burn.

On one of Miranda's gold-seeking excursions, she had discovered a natural rock slide less than a quarter of a mile upstream from the claims.

One unbearably hot afternoon, when even the tenacious Cager had chosen the solace of shade over the glitter of gold, everyone agreed that a visit to Miranda's slide was in order. It was no more than a large granite boulder worn smooth over the centuries by the flow of water. The creek narrowed just above the slide, then washed in a wide band down its gradual slope to the pool below. Pines, lining one side of the pool, provided some shade, while lush green ferns and other foliage fed by the abundant water supply added the effect of coolness.

The slide provided a enjoyable pastime. Everyone was in good spirits with lighthearted teasing continuing throughout the afternoon. Miranda found the freedom of joining in the play equally delightful, and she splashed and dunked with as much enthusiasm as the rest. She knew her behavior was not very ladylike, but living in the forest with a bunch of men was no place for a lady in the first place.

She was exhausted by the time the group started back to camp, but she was more relaxed than she had been since the incident with Jeb Lewis. The Lucas Adams she had watched at play seemed worlds away from the grim man who had nearly beaten a fellow human being to death. They had both carefully avoided any physical contact, but the tension between them was less than it had been in weeks.

"I suppose I will have a pile of mending to do if we go there very often," Miranda commented, observing the worn pant seats of the men as they walked along. Eight pair of hands spread protectively to cover their backsides. Miranda laughed out loud as she assured them, at the moment, that their modesty was still preserved.

The long summer day still had plenty of daylight to offer, so most of the men returned to work. Not bothering to change, as her damp clothes helped keep her cool, Miranda decided to pick some berries for dinner. Billy offered to accompany her. She was glad for the company, and the two set off with a basket for a large berry patch Miranda had discovered earlier.

Though he was shy by nature, Billy had nonetheless developed a close friendship with Miranda. However, unbeknownst to her, Billy was also experiencing his first pangs of love and had convinced himself over the weeks that Miranda was the most perfect woman he had ever met. She was small and appeared fragile, arousing his protective instincts, but despite her size, she was strong and never shunned work, though, in many cases, she could easily have gotten one of the men of the camp to perform the heavier duties for her.

They laughed and talked as they picked the berries, more finding their way into their mouths than into the basket.

"Oh, we really are being naughty." Miranda felt a twinge of conscience as she popped another red, ripe berry into her mouth. The sight of her was more than Billy's poor, love-befuddled mind could resist. Gathering her into his arms, he suddenly began kissing her full on the lips. Miranda's immediate response was to use all her strength to pull away, and Billy's arms dropped instantly.

"Forgive me." Abashed, he stepped back, as surprised by his actions as Miranda. He continued to apologize in a muffled voice as he stared at the little puffs of dust the toe of his boot stirred up. He looked so repentant, all thoughts of rebuke deserted Miranda.

"Don't look so embarrassed," Miranda said, comforting him. "I'm not at all offended." Billy lifted his head, his hopeful eyes meeting Miranda's.

"You mean that? I've loved you from the moment I first set eyes on you, but I never dreamed you might come to love me too. Oh, Miranda, could I kiss you again? I can hardly wait to tell the others." His words fell out in an excited jumble.

"Billy, you misunderstand me." Miranda laid a consoling hand on his forearm. "I do love you but not in the way you want," she added firmly, intending to leave no question in Billy's mind as to her feelings.

"I thought it was too good to be true." His shoulders hunched forward. "A woman like you would never be attracted to someone like me. . . . Don't worry, I won't be bothering you anymore." He glowered at her from beneath his lowered brow.

"Billy, you're a wonderful man, and one day some girl will thank her lucky stars she has your love. But I can't pretend the kind of love I don't feel. I know that's not what you want. But, please, don't throw our friendship away. It would be more than I could bear.''

"I'll always be your friend, Miranda." It was Billy's turn to offer comfort. "And, if you ever change your mind about loving me, I'll marry you, anytime, anyplace, unless, of course, I'm already married to that girl you mentioned." The old sparkle was back in Billy's eyes. "Don't worry about me. I'll get over you. I'll just have to start thinking of you as my little sister.''

"Hmm, I do see a family resemblance." Miranda eyed him appraisingly, glad the tense moment had passed. "Come, if we don't get this basket filled, I'll never have time to make a pudding for supper.'' A short time later the two came strolling, arm in arm, into camp, laughing over their private joke.

"You two look mighty friendly," Jesse commented as they passed him.

No one noticed the scowling look Lucas gave the couple, but as he spoke, their attention turned toward him. "May we expect an announcement at any moment?''

"Yes, you may." Miranda ignored his dark look. "Billy has asked me to be his sister, and I have accepted." She gave a low, formal curtsy, before being overcome with a fit of giggles.

"I always thought you two looked like long-lost twins." Jesse came over to slap Billy on the back.

Miranda and Billy were so dissimilar in looks, even Lucas's face broke into a smile. "I'm sure Miranda's father will be surprised to learn he has a son," he commented, placing the knife he had just sharpened back in its sheath.

"Well, I'd better start fixing our dinner, or my father will be more than surprised. He'll be grumpier than a bear." She excused herself. "I'll save a big helping of pudding for you if you would care for some," she said to Billy, who accepted enthusiastically.

Singing to herself, she set about cooking the evening meal. The day had been thoroughly delightful, and, at that moment, Miranda could think of little she would want to change in her life.

Chapter 8

The Fourth of July arrived, and although the Austens' ancestors would have hardly thought the day worthy of celebration, Miranda did not feel the least bit unpatriotic by joining in the fun. A large pot of beans had cooked to tenderness, buried in the embers of last night's fire, and she had managed to keep three pies, baked the day before, safe from the eager men and any night prowlers. With hair slicked and nails clean, all gathered at the center of the camp, each bringing a contribution to the planned feast. For the occasion Miranda had donned her wine-colored gown, and she swirled and curtsied for the appreciative men.

"Your tongue is hangin' out." Jake gave Zach a good-natured nudge in the ribs. "I'd be careful. I don't think our friend Lucas is appreciatin' the show." He nodded his head in Lucas's direction.

Lucas did *not* appreciate the casual way in which Miranda regarded the men. She treated them as though they were childhood playmates, seemingly oblivious of the effect she had on them. He wondered if she could really be so ignorant of the desires she aroused.

She must know the only reason he was avoiding her company was that he found it nearly impossible to keep his hands from her. It was only out of respect for her wishes that he had been able to restrain his desire thus far, and that restraint had cost him untold discomfort. So why did she play the temptress for a group of woman-hungry men if she prized her virtue so highly?

Lucas, though not totally mistaken in his assessment of the situation, was, nevertheless, prejudiced by his own reactions to Miranda. His own need to possess her had grown with each passing day, and if he could have found some way to have her without the threat of marriage breathing down his neck, he would have seduced her long ago. Lucas had no doubt that with one whimper from her, every man in the camp would readily escort him, shotgun in hand, to the altar. Even if he escaped that, his own conscience would not allow him to take unfair advantage of a gentlewoman. He was trapped between his desire for Miranda and his desire for total freedom. Was he going to throw away his convictions on the binding nature of marriage because of his physical desire for a woman, who, more often than not, seemed more like a child than woman?

Though the other men of the camp were not unaffected by Miranda's flirtatious play, none, with the exception of Billy, had ever seriously entertained any romantic designs, and even he was more comfortable regarding her as a sister, despite his claims of love. The men enjoyed Miranda's presence more for the feeling of home she gave the camp. In her they saw the essence of the mothers, sisters, and sweethearts they had left behind in their quest for gold. They were more lonely for the companionship of a proper lady than for a pair of warm arms. A night of love could be easily purchased, whereas gentle conversation was rare indeed.

The festivities began at noon with a twenty-one-gun salute, then Cager rose to read The Declaration of Independence with such fierce pride even Miranda's British heart was stirred. Next Thomas rose to deliver his Independence Day address.

"Fellow friends and countrymen, this is a celebration of that great day in history, when our forefathers risked their homes, their livelihoods, yes, even their very lives, to assure that we, their descendants, could live lives free from the tyrannies of a foreign king. Begging your pardons." Thomas threw an apologetic glance at the two Austens before continuing, "We, the grateful children of those brave men, have the grave responsibility to insure that we never, in the future of our great nation, violate the sacred trust they have given us and allow that hard-won freedom to slip from our grasp. We, in the new state of California, have the added responsibility to see that this new state grows up in the noble heritage of the original thirteen. Many of us plan to return to homes far away, but each of us will leave a legacy here also. Let that be a legacy of truth, justice, and the love of the freedom that has made this country great. Amen."

The speech ended among cheers and hearty pats on the back as each man congratulated Tom on a speech well done.

"If you didn't have a wife back home, you could

stay here and become a senator,'' Lucas complimented the man.

Thomas was pleased with the reception of his
speech, noting with satisfaction that not one cough
had been heard throughout the entire oration.

The end of the speech signaled the beginning of
the feast, and the always-hungry miners headed for
the food. Besides the pies and beans Miranda had
brought, they enjoyed roast rabbit and quail, biscuits, fresh berries, and wild peas. Before long the
whiskey jug was making the circuit, filling one eager
cup after the next. Cager was trying to coax Miranda
into taking a taste when a hand reached across the
makeshift table and removed the cup from her lips.

''That's not a good idea. Miranda can't hold her
liquor,'' Lucas warned, his eyes darkening with remembered delights.

Curious eyes turned her way. She did not appear
to be the sort of woman to indulge; in fact, no one
could ever remember seeing her drink anything remotely resembling alcohol.

''You can all stop staring at me,'' Miranda
scolded. ''I am not a tippler. Mr. Adams''—she
stressed the formal use of his surname—''has undoubtedly confused me with one of his other ac-
quaintances.'' Turning away the offered cup, she
continued without pausing for breath. ''If you
gentlemen are ready, I will serve the pie.'' Plates
were eagerly thrust forward as Miranda dished out
generous portions to everyone except Lucas. When
he brought this lack to her attention, she forced a disconcerted expression on her face as if it had been a
terrible oversight; then, smiling wickedly, she placed

a slice of pie on his plate, which appeared a mere sliver in comparison to the other more generous servings.

"Ah, your generosity overwhelms me, Miss Austen." Lucas returned her smile. "Perhaps you would like me to enlighten our friends on how I came upon my knowledge of your drinking abilities. I'm sure they would find the story most amusing."

"If you so much as open your mouth, I'll . . ." The words spewed forth without thought. Chagrinned, she wished she could learn to keep her mouth shut. Her outburst effectively admitted that what he said was true.

"Yes, what is it you'll do?" Lucas, knowing he held the upper hand, was enjoying himself immensely, feeling a little revenge was in order.

"Oh, I don't know what I'll do! I'll float your socks down the river." Miranda had said the first thing that came to her mind, unaware of how childish she sounded. "I wish you'd all stop staring at me like that. I had a little too much punch at a dance, that's all. How was I to know it was more than fruit juice?" She slammed her hand down on the table.

"Now, Mandy, don't spoil the day with your temper. The man's only teasing you." Edward Austen broke in, trying to appease his daughter. If worse came to worst, he wanted his daughter to be on good terms with Lucas; it was his only hope for leniency.

"Speaking of dancin'," Zach said, seizing the opportunity, "let's clean up these dishes and get down to some serious celebratin'. I, for one, haven't danced with a real woman in longer than I care to admit." His words provided the necessary impetus, and the table was cleared, and pots and dishes cleaned and stored in record time. As Cager blew a tune on his mouth harp Zach grabbed Miranda around the waist, leading her in a wild impromptu dance that wavered between a cotillion and an Indian war dance. Others joined in, and Miranda found herself being whirled from one pair of arms into another until she spun so fast she was totally dazed, only the arms of her frequently changing partners keeping her on her feet.

"Wait a minute," she protested, stopping to gasp for air. "I've been through this before, and I have no intention of discovering just how long it will take you gentlemen to reduce me to an exhausted heap."

"It appears the lady needs a little help, gentlemen. If three of you will tie your kerchiefs around your arms, we'll get on with the dancin'," Cager instructed. Thomas, Billy, and Jake secured red bandanas around their arms but made it clear they were only performing a temporary service.

"Three dances and we change roles," Jake said, stating their position. Miranda was thoroughly confused by the exchange until the three men bent their knees in exaggerated curtsies before the remaining men. Zach called the steps as he joined in the dancing, their number being perfect for the formation of a square.

Miranda had trouble controlling her laughter as she watched Lucas swing the mountainous Jake in his arms. Even Lucas was dwarfed by Jake's size, while the bearded couple was anything but graceful. It was a sight that would have brought a smile to the lips of the sternest of souls. Jesse danced with Billy.

They were no less comical, both being lanky and unable to keep off each other's feet. But it was when she watched Thomas, despite his female role, trying to lead her father in the right direction, that she completely lost control and had to lean against Zach for support. Her father, already uncomfortable with the idea of dancing with a man, had no idea what the calls meant, and Thomas was trying hard to hide his exasperation as he pushed and nudged his bewildered partner in the right direction.

Miranda was laughing so hard she could barely follow Zach's lead.

"I swear, Miranda, you're stepping on my feet as much as Jake does," Lucas complained as he crossed her back over to Zach.

"I'm sorry, but I can't help—" Her answer was cut short by another fit of giggles. As soon as the music ended Miranda dropped down onto a nearby stump, struggling valiantly to regain her self-control. "I really am sorry, all of you. It's just that I've never seen men dancing together before." Another peal of laughter overtook her, leaving the sincerity of her apology in grave doubt.

"I think the woman is having hysterics," Jesse pronounced as he patted her hand. "What she needs is a good dunking in the creek. That should bring her around." He offered his advice with a grin.

"Don't you dare." Miranda pulled in a deep breath, wiping the tears from her eyes. "You have to admit it is a funny sight," she defended herself, taking slow, steady breaths to prevent herself from going off again.

They danced till dusk, when the party split up to

attend to the evening chores. Miranda did a little two-step as she danced down to the creek to wash off the day's grime before retiring. She did not feel the least bit sleepy, and the cool creek water did little to remedy the situation. The morning fire had gone out long ago, but she sat near the small, rocky containment circle, anyway. She bid her father good night as he ducked into his tent, then she leaned back to stare at the star-filled sky.

This was a glorious land, gold or no gold. Clear skies, clean air, everything fresh and new. Life was so straightforward here. A person took what he needed from the land, and the land provided generously. She wondered if it would always be so. As remote as they were, every week, at least one group of miners would stop at the camp to exchange information. The land was vast, but was it vast enough to accommodate the hordes of men who came for no other reasons but to search for gold, leaving the earth scarred in their wake? It was sad to think of such beauty destroyed by man's greed. Perhaps, when the gold ran out, the men would disappear with it, leaving time and the elements to heal the earth. Pock-marked streambeds would again become smooth, and the forest would once more be free from the sounds of man.

"What are you looking so serious about?" Lucas sat down on a stump on the opposite side of the fire circle.

"I was thinking about the land and what we are doing to it," she replied. "It's so beautiful; I hate to think of it being destroyed by man's greed."

" 'And God blessed them, and God said unto

them, Be fruitful, and multiply, and replenish the earth, and subdue it: and have dominion over the fish of the sea, and over the fowl of the air, and over every living thing that moveth upon the earth.' It's man's destiny to rule the earth. We couldn't stop it if we wanted to,'' Lucas said in reply.

"I suppose you're right. I just hope we can subdue the earth without destroying all that is truly of value.'' Miranda tried to explain her feelings even as she wondered at Lucas quoting the Bible with such accuracy.

"I think we will, but there will be plenty of mistakes along the way. Man doesn't mean to destroy the land; it's just that most times he acts before he thinks. The land was put here for our use, and for the most part, I think you will find we use it wisely. I would never have come out to Oregon if I hadn't believed this was so. It would be a mortal sin to desecrate a gift as wondrous as this Western territory. It will be up to those of us who see more than potential wealth to guide the less discerning.''

"Is Oregon like California?'' Miranda asked, curious about Lucas's home.

"In some ways, but Oregon is much greener, and it was settled more slowly than California. Trappers have been in the area for years, but it was only during the last decade that families came out to make their homes. It's a more settled life than here, probably because we have more women.''

Miranda smiled at his last statement. "Well, I hope you are right about the future of this country.'' Miranda returned to her musings, turning her gaze back to the star-filled sky.

"It's late, and we both should be getting to bed," Lucas gently chided her. "Besides, you'll get wrinkles trying to divine the world's future."

As Miranda rose to go to her tent she suddenly missed the nights she had slept under the stars with Lucas by her side.

All claims were beginning to pan out, and there was much talk in the camp of moving on in hopes of finding more profitable diggings. Miranda's father rarely worked the creek now, preferring to go crevicing among the rocks with Miranda. While he found the work wearying, it was not nearly as backbreaking as panning the sand of the creek bottom. It was even less profitable than his claim on the creek, but Miranda refrained from questioning the wisdom of his decision. She feared the hard physical labor was taking a toll on his health.

The first shadows of dusk were beginning to fall several weeks later, and Edward Austen had still not returned from his day in the hills. Miranda stood cutting large chunks of potatoes and dropping them into a steaming pot of rabbit stew. She had returned to the camp earlier in the afternoon, leaving her father in the hills to work during the remaining daylight hours.

At the sound of crackling underbrush, she looked up from her work, turning in the direction of the sound. Her father took two staggering steps toward her, then fell to the ground, his face ashen. The knife and still-uncut potato slipped from her paralyzed fingers.

"Papa!" She ran to her father's side, cradling his head in her lap.

"Go get Lucas," he commanded, his voice barely audible. Miranda gently laid his head upon the ground and ran in the direction she had last seen Lucas, calling desperately. He was not far.

"Lucas, it's Papa. Something has happened to him," she said, urging him back to the camp. Lucas needed no prodding. The stricken look in her eyes was enough to let him know that something was seriously wrong.

"Edward, tell me what happened." Lucas spoke the words with deliberate slowness into the man's ear. He was not even sure he was still conscious.

"Rattler, left leg." Though they were not spoken above a whisper, the words rang like a death knell in Miranda's ears. Lucas wasted no time, but from experience he knew it was already too late. He slit Edward Austen's pant leg, cutting a cross into the discolored, swollen flesh surrounding the twin puncture marks in his leg. Sucking at the site, he tried to draw the poison out, but too much time had already elapsed, and the poison had spread its life-choking fingers throughout Austen's body. After binding the wound with his handkerchief Lucas raised sympathetic eyes to Miranda.

"I'm sorry. There is nothing I can do."

"Can't you ride for a doctor?" Miranda did not want to accept the finality of his statement.

"Even if I could find one, there is nothing he could do. The poison has spread. There is no way to get it out."

Miranda turned her entire attention to her father, blocking out all but his presence. Dry-eyed, she stroked his brow, crooning a childhood lullaby as she cradled his upper body in her arms, rocking him with motherly care. The scene tore at Lucas's heart, forcing him to turn away.

"Mandy . . . sorry to leave . . . you . . . mess." Her father struggled to get the words out.

"I'll be fine, Papa. You know I can take care of myself, and we have friends here to help me. You just rest," Miranda said, trying to comfort her father. At the moment she could not spare a thought for her own future.

"Lucas . . . strong man . . . stay with him. Make a good . . . husband . . . not like . . . me." The words cost dearly, and he slipped into unconsciousness.

Miranda's complexion was as pale as her father's as she continued to rock him. He did not speak again, except to call out his wife's name as he drew his last breath. Even after his spirit had departed his body, Miranda did not relinquish her hold but continued to rock to and fro, mouthing the words of the lullaby. The loneliness she felt devastated her. She was not ready to give up her father, not like this, not in some wild country. Lucas, respecting her need, forced himself to leave her. He willed his leaden feet to carry him away from the sorrowful scene to inform the others of the death.

When Lucas returned an hour later, Miranda had not moved from the spot. She had had enough time to say good-bye, and Lucas lifted her from the ground as Zach and Jake took the body from her care and wrapped it in a blanket. Miranda did not resist. She stood, leaning against Lucas, her arms wrapped tightly around his waist as if she were afraid she would be left alone in the world if she loosened her hold. Her strange silence worried Lucas more than hysterical sobbing would have. He held her close, stroking her hair as he willed her to release her grief and allow him to share his strength with her.

"We can bury him in the morning," Zach stated quietly when he and Jake returned from laying the body in the tent.

Miranda suddenly came to life. "The wolves! You won't let the wolves have him?" She faced the men, her eyes wide with panic as the image of the tattered corpse they had seen along the river flashed in her mind.

"Of course not," Lucas said, trying to soothe her. "We'll bury him deep so nothing will disturb his rest." Miranda closed her eyes again, clinging to Lucas's stabilizing presence, willing to give the responsibility of preparing the body for burial over to the men.

"If you need any help with the little miss, just give a holler." Jake patted Miranda's shoulder before he followed the others out of the clearing.

Lucas sat Miranda down on a log near the fire and removed the pot of stew from the flames. Dishing her a small portion, he came to sit beside her. "I want you to eat this," he commanded, handing her the cup and spoon. She obediently took the food but made no attempt to raise the spoon to her mouth.

"Miranda, you have to eat whether you want to or not. Making yourself sick will not bring your father back." Taking the spoon, he brought a small sip of the broth to her unresponsive lips. "Miranda, listen to me." He tried to penetrate the protective fog she had surrounded herself with. "Your father is dead. You have to accept that."

"But I don't want him to be dead." Her lips began to quiver. "I'm afraid to be alone. I need to have someone to care for." Miranda fell into his arms, sobbing out her misery at being abandoned by her only parent.

"It's okay, angel. I'll always take care of you." Lucas made the promise unthinkingly, relieved that she was finally allowing her tears to wash away some of the pain. He held her, whispering soft words of comfort until the sobs subsided. When she looked at him again, her eyes were clear, and he knew she had started to accept the reality of the situation.

"Don't leave me tonight, Lucas." It was the plea of a frightened child. "Sleep with me under the stars again."

Lucas nodded his agreement, then went to gather their bedding. When he returned, she spread it out on the ground while he scraped the plates of stew back into the pot, clearing the area of any food that might attract predators.

They retired immediately, though neither felt like sleeping, and lay side by side, staring at the star-studded sky. A falling star brought fresh tears to Miranda's eyes, but after a moment she was able to blink them back. The surrounding beauty gave her peace as she tried to concentrate on the sounds and smells of the forest: the clean scent of pine, the chirp of a cricket, the sighing of the wind through the leaves, all helping her accept the fragile nature of the gift of life. As she drifted off to sleep she dreamed of a chorus of angels welcoming her father into their midst.

When Lucas awoke with the first rays of dawn, he found Miranda curled snugly against his side, one leg draped casually over his thigh. He wondered if she had awakened during the night and sought out the comfort of his presence, or if she had moved to him in sleep with an unconscious need to touch another living being. Her head lay in gentle repose on his shoulder while her silken hair spread out like a fan blanketing them both. Lucas cursed himself as he felt a familiar quickening in his loins. Only an inhuman monster would take advantage of her in her present condition.

He tried to concentrate on other things, but the soft feminine scent of her skin continued to invade his senses, bringing his attention back to the woman in his arms. He was unable to resist placing a feather-light kiss on her upturned lips. Immediately he regretted giving in to the urge. Stretching like a contented house cat, she rolled over, lying full length on top of him; then, with a sigh she fell back into a deep sleep. He muffled a tortured groan as he felt her soft breasts pressing through the fabric of his shirt. Miranda needed to sleep, and he was loath to wake her, but he did not know how long he could endure this intimate position. He chided himself for not making sure their bedrolls were placed at a more respectable distance before retiring.

He ached with his need to caress Miranda's satin skin. He hoped when she awoke that she would not feel his urgent need. The hardness of his desire was all too evident to him. He would have to depend on her innocence to protect her from the knowledge, or she might never seek further comfort in his arms. He was unwilling to deny her any comfort he could give.

The sun was considerably higher in the morning sky when, at last, to Lucas's profound relief, Miranda began to stir. He quickly rolled to his side, slipping her onto the ground beside him. He gritted his teeth as she yawned, stretching against him, before finally blinking her eyes open. Her eyes focused on the handsome face so close to hers, then, with a contented smile, her heavy lids dropped back over her eyes. Moments later she was wide awake as her compromising position penetrated her sleep-fogged brain. Tensing against the strong arms that held her, she searched Lucas's face. Finding only sympathetic concern, she again relaxed.

"I'll make us some coffee." Lucas disengaged himself, grateful to be released from the torture chamber his bed had become. Noticing how her eyes misted with tears when she glanced in the direction of the tent where the still form of her father lay, he helped her to her feet, to distract her. She quickly turned and began rolling up their bedding.

They were sipping the last of their coffee when the other men began to wander respectfully into the clearing. Miranda was grateful for the bitterness of the brew; the slightly acrid taste helped her steel her nerves for what was to come. Each man offered his condolences, relieved to see that the faraway look had cleared from her eyes.

Zach cleared his throat before he spoke. "We chose a spot a bit back from the creek. The soil isn't so sandy there."

"Thank you." Miranda was aware of the comfort his words were meant to give.

"If you're ready now, miss, we'll get on with it," he continued.

"I'm ready." She nodded her permission, following closely behind as Jake and Cager carried the body to its prepared resting place. The grave was deep, as promised. Miranda felt Lucas's comforting arm slip around her shoulders as they lowered the body into the ground.

All knelt around the grave as Thomas offered up a prayer. "Lord, we gather here to lay to rest the body of our friend, Edward Austen, who yesterday was struck down . . ."

Miranda stared down into the gaping hole that would serve as her father's final resting place. He would never achieve his dream of endless wealth. How sad his hopes should end this way. She would miss the way his eyes danced with enthusiasm each time a new scheme caught his fancy. Poor quixotic Papa.

Lucas watched Miranda from under carefully veiled eyes. He was worried how her father's death would affect her. Theirs was a strange relationship, and though he felt Miranda would probably be better off without the responsibility of caring for a self-centered father, he could take no comfort in the thought. Though he had little affection for the man, he knew Miranda had loved her father despite his many shortcomings.

The service ended with the recitation of the Twenty-third Psalm, then Billy and Jesse picked up their shovels and began to fill the grave. It was not until the first shovelful of dirt splattered the blanket that served as her father's shroud that her tears began to fall, washing away the sharper edge of her pain. Miranda had no doubt that her father now resided with the angels and was far happier than he could ever have been on earth. His troubles and cares had been lifted from his shoulders. As Miranda thought of the loving welcome he would receive from her long-departed mother, she smiled.

Chapter 9

The next few weeks were a healing time. Miranda threw herself into the life of the camp with new vigor; mending, washing, and lending a hand wherever she could, in an effort to keep her mind off the future. By living life day to day, she was able to put her loss behind her and regain some of her cheerful spirit.

Every man in the camp was especially mindful of her needs during her first and most difficult week without her father, but it was Lucas she invariably turned to when the sadness threatened to overcome her. It became a common sight to see him holding her gently in his arms, coaxing a smile back onto her face. He alone had the power to give her the sense of security she so badly needed. As she worked out her grief, Miranda did not stop to ponder why this was so.

She had always had someone who needed her. Her lost feeling had as much to do with a vague feeling of uselessness as it did with finding herself truly alone in the world. Unconsciously she began to direct her nurturing instincts toward Lucas, rubbing his shoulders at the end of a long day, making sure he always had a fresh shirt to wear or simply listening attentively when he had something to say. Though Lucas recognized her actions for what they were, and her tender care was not unwelcome, it gave an uncomfortably domestic air to their relationship.

Lucas was glad she was handling her father's death so well. Her mature acceptance of what she could not change heightened his respect for her. Here was a woman who was not only pleasant to look at but intelligent, uncomplaining, and adaptable as well. He was glad he could comfort her and sure that they were both too level-headed to read more into it than that.

The day Miranda planted wildflowers on her father's grave, she turned her back on the past and focused her full attention on the future. She cultivated the young plants with the tenderest of care to insure that they would survive to produce seeds for the next season. It gave her great comfort to know that even in this isolated place, her father's grave would have fresh flowers in the coming years. What she herself could not provide, nature would provide for her.

It was time to start making decisions. Her efforts among the rocks netted her little, and each day she remained with Lucas, her debt to him increased. She needed to return to San Francisco, and she needed to find a job. The problem with this decision was that there were two unpleasant results: she would have to leave the relative security of the mining camp and all of her friends and she would be forced to inform Lucas that he would not be paid for his services.

Her course was set, but Miranda could not quite bring herself to implement her plan. Once they returned to San Francisco she would have to learn to face life alone. She knew she was not a burden to the other members of the camp; she always did her share of the work and, in addition, performed many little domestic chores that gave the men some small taste of home. It was only where Lucas was concerned that she felt guilty. His solicitous care of her served to make her feel more in his debt with each passing day. Left on her own, she was not even sure she could support herself, let alone save enough money to repay her father's debt.

Though she knew Lucas would be in the gold fields regardless of her presence, her conscience was not eased. She had no excuse to delay telling Lucas the truth, except that she had come to rely on his strength. She couldn't imagine what he would do when she finally confessed, and the anxiety she felt was frightening.

Meanwhile, she kept the camp spotless, and she approached the task of preparing their daily meals with new enthusiasm. Allowing her imagination to run free, she created many new and delicious meals out of their supplies and the wild plants and animals available in the forest. She became so zealous in her attempts to keep Lucas's clothes in good order, he teased her that she was going to wear them out with so much washing.

Lucas, though he would be loath to admit it, had grown too comfortable with Miranda's daily presence, and he was in no hurry to part company. He had decided to insist she keep the money her father owed him, reasoning she would have far more need of it than he. He wondered if she planned to return to England immediately or if she would stay awhile in San Francisco. She was better educated than most.

Perhaps he could persuade her to return to Oregon with him and become a schoolteacher. He smiled at the idea of Miranda in a schoolroom with a dozen eager children pulling at her skirt. He told himself that his only motivation for this idea was his desire to see to her welfare now that she was alone in the world. Or maybe it would be better if they went their separate ways. Things could become complicated if they got too close.

The day Jake announced it was time for him to move on brought the beginning of change in Miranda's life. He left within two days to try his luck on the Yuba River, sent on his way amid good wishes and a tearful hug from Miranda.

"You take care of yourself." Jake crushed her to his massive chest. "You're a rare one, Miranda Austen."

"I'll miss you, Jake, Godspeed." Miranda waved a last farewell as they watched Jake ride out of sight, trailing his mule behind him. She knew she would never see him again.

Within the week Cager decided it was time he, too, moved on to greener pastures, though he preferred to try his luck south on the Mokelumne River. Billy decided to join him, further reducing their numbers. When Thomas began talking more and more frequently of giving up the gold fields altogether and going back home to his wife, Miranda knew it was time to talk to Lucas.

One morning, after she had scoured the breakfast dishes with handfuls of sand from the edge of the creek, she followed him up to his claim. Sitting on a rock, she hugged her knees to her chest, watching him work as she tried to find the right words to begin. Finally, realizing that no matter what words she chose he was going to be upset, she forced herself to speak.

"Lucas, I need to talk to you about returning to San Francisco."

"I was wondering when you would decide it was time to go back. The diggings here are becoming so sparse, there is really no point in staying. We can leave whenever you're ready." Lucas stepped out of the creek, laying his pan aside.

"I really don't mind staying if you want to."

"No, it's time I get you back to civilization. We can leave on Wednesday." Lucas's cooperative attitude was making this even harder for Miranda. She wished she had told him the truth immediately after her father's death.

"There is something else . . . I can't . . . I mean, there isn't . . . There isn't any money in San Francisco to pay you."

Lucas stared at her in silence for what seemed an eternity; then, meeting her eyes and holding them with the intensity of his own, he quietly asked, "You knew?"

Miranda could only nod her head in answer.

Her face blurred, and in its place Lucas saw the mocking image of Mary Blake. Miranda was no different. She had helped her father trick him, knowing full well the man had no intention of paying him. They were no more than a couple of swindlers, charlatans from across the sea, and he, fool that he was, had let a pretty face and an innocent smile take him in. He should have known that no respectable Englishman would take his daughter into the gold fields. His self-disgust knew no bounds.

Suddenly the incidents that had caused him to respect Miranda so deeply took on new light. It was all an act to keep him trusting; her character of the long-suffering English gentlewoman was all part of the game. No wonder she had been so distraught by their encounter by the pool. If they had played the scene to its conclusion, he would have discovered she was a fraud. She was no more innocent than one of the girls of Madame Countess. His hands tensed into tight fists.

His rage at being so easily duped, when he, of all people, should have been wary of such professed innocence, made him want to punish the girl who sat, head bowed, before him.

"You've seen what the punishment for petty thievery is." His voice was deceptively calm, though he could barely contain his rage. "Have you stopped to consider what it might be for a coldly calculated swindle?" He smiled derisively as the color drained from her face. "I imagine thirty-nine lashes, at least, and perhaps the loss of one of your pretty little ears as a warning to your future victims. I'm sure the others would be most interested to learn we have a thief living among us." His eyes flashed with his desire for revenge, and he traced his thumb around the contours of her left ear. She shivered uncontrollably, silently pleading for understanding. Lucas was deadly serious. She doubted that the sting of the lash could possibly hurt more than the look of disgust in his eyes. "Lucas, please. It's not what you think . . . . ."

"No, I am thinking more clearly than I have in

quite some time, though I can understand how that fact might cause you some distress. But don't worry.'' His smile sent chills down Miranda's back. ''Your secret is safe with me. I have my own special plans for you. We will not be returning to San Francisco. I think I'll try my luck on the American River. There is still plenty of good weather left. What? No objections? I thought not.''

Miranda sat trembling, making no further effort to explain. It was hopeless. How could she defend herself against his charges when she had known for so long that there was no money? While she would hardly term herself a calculating swindler, she was guilty, by her silence, of deceit, even if at first it had been out of a desire to protect her father. Lucas was intent on believing the worst, and nothing she could say now would sway his opinion of her. He was not interested in her excuses; he was interested in his money.

She could not guess what Lucas had planned for her, but the lash meant almost certain death, and her strong instinct for survival would not permit her to consider admitting her folly to the remaining members of the camp. If Lucas, who understood her so well, believed her a criminal, surely they would also.

Lucas depended on Miranda's fear to keep her silent. If she went to the other members of the camp, he knew she would not be punished. The contract had been between her father and himself and generally unenforceable under the present state of California law. Further, the dire shortage of women made it almost impossible to convict a woman of a crime, no matter how heinous. That Miranda was unaware of these facts was obvious. He would make sure she continued in ignorance until he was satisfied she had paid sufficiently for her part in the deception. It would give him added pleasure to tell her of her mistake once he was through with her. For now it gave him a necessary hold on her.

Miranda avoided Lucas the rest of the day, hoping once he was over his initial anger, she would be able to reason with him. She now knew she would have to find some way to pay Lucas the money owed him, but after so many months, the sum seemed enormous and the task nearly impossible. Wondering if she could convince him she would pay the debt off a little at a time, as she was able, she remembered the forbidding expression on his face and had little confidence he would agree to such a plan. It was frightening how quickly her circumstances had changed.

The thought of slipping away while no one was looking did not even occur to Miranda. She had never been the type of person to run away from her problems. To stay and face what she must was the only course she considered. Given time, Lucas was bound to become more reasonable. She would just have to be patient.

Lucas continued to work his claim until the heat of the afternoon sun became unbearable, then, gathering up his tools, he returned to camp. He had been content to leave Miranda to her own devices, though it was his faith in his ability as a tracker, rather than a belief that she would not choose to run, that prompted his confidence. If she did choose to leave, he could easily find her. She would have gained nothing and lost much.

He noted with neither surprise nor satisfaction that Miranda was still at the camp, going about her afternoon chores as if nothing had happened. Making no attempt to speak to her, he set about the task of packing for their journey. The sooner they left the others, the less chance there was that Miranda would discover how slender his hold over her really was.

Miranda stared forlornly at Lucas's back as he bent to his task. He did not look one bit more friendly than when she had left him at the creek. He was already making ready to break camp, which meant he wanted to waste no time implementing the plans he had made. She wondered what he would tell the others.

That night, as they joined the men, which was their usual habit after the evening meal, Lucas placed his arm firmly around Miranda's shoulders. The gesture had once given her comfort, but now it only made her feel trapped. She steeled herself for what was to come.

"Evening Zach, Jess, Tom. We've come to say our good-byes." Lucas guided her until they stood before the others. "Miranda and I have decided it's time we move on."

Zach eyed the couple curiously. Though he knew they were mutually attracted, he had rarely seen them display any public affection. Now they stood before them, Lucas's arm draped casually across Miranda's shoulders as he absently touched her ear. She did not make the slightest protest, though she seemed stiff and uncomfortable with his attentions.

"I imagine you're headed down to San Francisco," he commented as he tried to understand this strange new familiarity.

"No, we're heading north to try our luck while the weather holds. After that, I don't know."

The implication was clear to Miranda. Lucas would keep her with him as long as it suited his purpose; then, without warning, she would be left on her own. She watched the look of disapproval pass over Thomas's face. He understood she had little choice but to travel with Lucas back to San Francisco; that she would choose to accompany him without a chaperon was clearly shocking to the man.

"If you need an escort back to the city, I'll be glad to take you," Thomas invited. "It wouldn't be any trouble. I've been thinking of returning home for some time now."

Miranda raised questioning eyes to Lucas. His expression remained immobile. She swallowed the hard lump in her throat. "Thank you, but I think I'll stay in the gold fields."

Thomas shook his head. There must be more to the couple's relationship than they had been led to believe. It saddened him to think that even properly bred ladies were inevitably weakened by the immoral climate of this rough land.

Miranda held her tongue despite her desire to scream out her denial of the conclusion she knew Thomas had reached. How could she tell him Lucas was forcing her to accompany him without betraying herself? Lucas was purposely leading her friends to believe they were carrying on some kind of tawdry affair, knowing she was powerless to deny it. Her lips whitened with anger.

"If it's money you need, I'd be honored to help you out. I know your father didn't do as well as he'd hoped," Jesse offered. He had the distinct impression that the last thing in the world Miranda wanted to do was stay in the gold fields with Lucas Adams.

"I've plenty of money for my needs," Miranda lied. If Jesse had any idea how much money she needed or why, she doubted he would be so generous. She wished they would all stop offering their kindness. If they didn't leave soon, her conscience would force her to confess.

Though they stayed only a few minutes, it seemed hours to Miranda. She bid each man a sincere, if somewhat stiff, farewell, then forced herself to leave their presence at a sedate pace. She refused to look at Lucas as they walked along in silence. She would not give him the satisfaction of knowing how much his brutish behavior had hurt her.

When they reached their clearing, Miranda escaped to the privacy of her tent, wishing her troubled thoughts were left behind as easily as the man who caused them. Lucas had given her no clue as to how he planned to punish her, but she was becoming increasingly alarmed at the prospect of finding out. His behavior toward her seemed out of proportion to the gravity of her crime. She could only pray that a good night's sleep would make him more rational.

They left at dawn, traveling due north toward the south fork of the American River. Neither spoke unless it was absolutely necessary. Miranda was exhausted, having slept little during the night, and she had trouble keeping her attention on the trail. After her horse had wandered in the wrong direction for the third time, Lucas took the reins from her with an ex- asperated sigh and began leading her mount. If her eyes had not been so obviously swollen from lack of sleep, he would have sworn she was purposely trying to slow their progress.

Her eyelids continued to droop throughout the morning, and she fought a constant battle to stay alert enough and keep from slipping from her saddle. She was greatly relieved when they stopped for their midday meal.

They washed down day-old biscuits with a gen- erous amount of water, then, leaning comfortably against the base of an oak, Lucas decided it was time to inform Miranda of her fate.

"I think it's time we discuss the terms of the re- payment of your debt," he began, giving Miranda cause for hope. She reached into her pocket and handed him the small pouch of gold she had hidden there. It was all she had in the world, but she readily parted with it. She leaned forward eagerly, hoping he was willing to listen to her now.

"I'll write my father's solicitors as soon as we reach San Francisco, and I'm sure I can find some sort of employment. I'll pay you every penny just as quickly as I can."

He weighed the pouch in his hand before tossing it back. Did she really think she could repay him with gold? It was too late for that. It had been pure torture living with her under his nose yet denying himself the pleasure of her embrace.

"The sum you owe is enormous. Do you think I would have taken on a man like your father unless the fee had been irresistible?" he continued, barely acknowledging her gold or her offer. "There is only one profession in which you could possibly make that kind of money, and for the moment, I prefer to sample your charms myself. You are welcome to turn—or is it return?—to that profession when I am through with you."

Miranda's hand flashed up and made contact with the bearded cheek; the sound reverberated in her ears as she stared in horror at her reddened palm. He was only taunting her. She trembled at the thought of what this burst of temper might bring her.

"I believe I warned you against doing that." His deadly tone brought her eyes up to meet his.

"I'm sorry."

"I'm sure you are, but you understand that I cannot let such insolence go unpunished. Do you have any suggestions, or do you prefer to leave the matter to me?"

His words hit a raw nerve. How dare he insult her, then suggest she was the one who had committed some grave offense? He deserved to be slapped for what he had said. Her only regret was that in her fear she had apologized. She might owe him money, but that was all.

"I apologized, which is more than you deserve. Our meal is long finished. I suggest we remount and continue on our way." Miranda was quite pleased with the haughty tone she managed despite the trembling of her knees as she rose. The vulnerability of her position was not lost to her, but at the moment, her indignation overrode her common sense.

Lucas had to admire her spunk, but he could not allow it to sway his purpose. He was committed to

teaching her a lesson, and teach her a lesson he
would. "Ah, I see you choose to bow to my superior
wisdom in the matter." He followed her to his feet,
reaching out to capture the soft flesh of her upper
arm. He had denied himself too long and was intent
on rectifying his mistake. "I think a sampling of your
charms might be in order."

Miranda stared at him as if he had gone mad. "I
am not your whore, no matter what you choose to
think . . . . Lucas, your hand is hurting me." Unwanted tears sprang to her eyes.

"Excellent. The tears add a nice effect. And just
to show you I appreciate a good performance, I will
settle for a kiss. Though I warn you, next time I will
not be so lenient."

Miranda knew she had lost. Rising on tiptoe, she
placed a kiss hardly worthy of a not too dearly loved
maiden aunt on his cheek. She realized that if she
provoked him further, he might be unwilling to settle
for a mere kiss. She was wise enough to realize he
could overpower her, if he so desired.

"Not good enough." Lucas made no effort to
loosen his grip.

Miranda sighed and tried again but with little noticeable improvement.

"I'm losing my patience, Miranda," he said
slowly, with just the right hint of a threat.

Miranda closed her eyes. Her teeth tugged at her
bottom lip, then, after taking three slow, deliberate
breaths, she opened her eyes and kissed Lucas full
on the lips. The contact was electrifying, and she
drew back as if she had been burned. She should hate
him for what he was doing to her, but she had re-

sponded to his touch. Running for her horse, she almost fell in her haste to mount. Lucas was playing a dangerous game with her, and she had no idea what the rules were, only that his purpose was to make her feel cheap and vulgar. At the moment she almost wished she had chosen the lash.

It was dusk when they stopped to make camp. Miranda made a stew of dried beef and potatoes, which Lucas ate with relish, but the entire meal could have been straw, and it was unlikely she would have noticed. After cleaning up the remains of the meal she unrolled her bedding, placing it as far away from Lucas as she dared without arousing his wrath. As an afterthought, she placed her father's rifle beside her before climbing beneath the covers.

Lucas laughed at her efforts to protect herself. "You may be a lying little witch, but I'd wager you're no murderess. If you'll rest any easier, you have my word I won't touch you tonight. I don't want you falling off your horse tomorrow from lack of sleep."

The only acknowledgment Miranda gave his words was to pull the covers up higher under her chin. The day had taken its toll, and moments later she fell asleep, serenaded by the now-familiar sound of howling wolves.

Lucas watched the gentle rise and fall of her breasts. In sleep she looked so much like a child, he had to remind himself that, in fact, she was no more than a calculating woman blessed with an innocent face to aid her in her schemes. What a fool he had been! But if he had been injudicious, so had the Austens. They could have attached themselves to any group of miners and found their way to the gold fields without him. He wondered if Miranda realized how dearly she would pay for so little.

He planned to try his luck for four weeks, no more, then head back to San Francisco to take a ship home before the winter storms began. His year was up, and though he had not found gold mining unprofitable, the rewards were far from what rumor had promised. Making a fortune required a lot of luck and even more hard work. He did not regret the time he had spent here, but he was ready to go home.

His thoughts turned back to Miranda. He intended to keep her for his personal pleasure while he remained in the gold fields. After that he would return her to San Francisco and release her from her debt. It amused him that she still kept up the act of the untouched virgin; he could not fathom what she hoped to gain by it. He had no intention of abusing her, just gaining a little compensation for his trouble. Well, she could play her games. Now that he viewed her realistically, he had no doubt he would emerge the victor.

Miranda awoke refreshed, noting with satisfaction that Lucas had kept his word. Perhaps he was just trying to frighten her and really had no intention of forcing her into a compromising relationship. Yesterday he had still been angry and perhaps not thinking clearly. She would have to be careful not to rekindle his anger.

After washing the last remnants of sleep from her eyes, she set about the task of preparing breakfast in a somewhat cheerful manner. Her sudden change in attitude surprised Lucas, but not one to question his good fortune, he simply smiled in anticipation of the pleasures the night would bring. He would have to be especially careful to humor her throughout the day.

As the day wore on, Miranda began to relax. Lucas was again acting like his old self, asking after her comfort and behaving in a most gentlemanly fashion. She, in turn, was especially mindful of his every need, afraid that with the slightest provocation he might turn on her again. By the end of the day she had ceased to feel wary and even managed to engage in a bit of lighthearted banter.

The sky was filled with twinkling stars when Miranda stopped trying to stifle her yawns and excused herself to retire. While she still placed her bedroll a more-than-respectable distance from Lucas's, she omitted the addition of the rifle, confident it was only the beasts of the forest she need fear.

She had barely settled in under her blanket when Lucas came over to stand beside her. Raising herself up on both elbows, she strained to hear what he had to say. He bent down to gather her in his arms as he slid down beside her.

Before the first word of protest had left her lips, he claimed them with a hard, passionate kiss that gave evidence to the urgency of his need. The warm glow in the pit of her stomach fanned into a consuming fire as he continued to explore the softness of her lips with slow deliberation. Of their own accord her lips made a timid response, then, as Lucas's intent began to sink in, her mind rebelled: he had lulled her into a false security just so he could catch her off-guard. She pushed against his chest with a sudden burst of strength, rolling out of his reach before coming to her feet, her eyes flashing indignation.

"What the . . ." Lucas stared up at her flushed face.

"How dare you!" Miranda stomped her foot in frustration, unable to get the names she longed to call him past her lips.

"What do you mean, how dare I? I told you what I expected from you. Did you think I was joking? I expect you to pay your debt in full, and I'm offering you a way to pay it that can be pleasant for us both." He smiled confidently. "Don't deny that you want me. I didn't imagine your response. Now come back to bed, and I'll try to forgive your outburst." Lucas patted the place beside him, lifting the blanket invitingly. "Your little virginal act is getting rather boring."

"You must be out of your mind." Miranda finally found her voice. "I'd sooner rot in hell than give you what you ask. Do you think I'm some mindless ninny you can order into your bed? I assure you, I am not."

"You *are* tiresome. Didn't your father teach you when it is time to give up the game?" Lucas rose to his feet. "Now get over here before I lose my patience and drag you back."

Miranda did not need further encouragement. She turned on her heels and ran into the forest, as if her life depended on escaping the handsome man who taunted her. She gave no thought to the beasts that might find a lone human easy prey.

Cursing her, Lucas picked up his rifle, then slowly followed her into the darkness, wondering why he bothered.

Chapter 10

An hour later Lucas found Miranda sitting high atop the branch of an ancient oak, her legs dangling in the moonlight. Beneath the tree the tracks of a large bear encircled the trunk, though by the scarcity of prints, it was apparent the animal had only a passing interest in such a scrawny morsel.

"If you are quite through playing the idiot, I think it is safe to come down." He looked up at her frightened face.

Miranda cautiously scanned the trees for any sign of the shaggy beast that had precipitated her hurried ascent, then, satisfied the animal was gone, she peered down at Lucas, unsure of whether he was rescuing her or still pursuing her. "Do you promise not to hurt me?"

"I should just leave you here." Lucas turned as if to go. Miranda bit her lip to prevent herself from begging him to stop. She was desperate to know his intentions and terrified to be left alone in the dark. He took a full dozen steps before turning back to face the tree. "Come on. I'll help you down."

"You promise?"

"Yes, dammit, I promise. Now get out of that tree

before I come to my senses.'' Lucas clenched his teeth in frustration. He could hardly leave her defenseless in the forest. She hadn't even had enough sense to grab her rifle before she made her hasty retreat.

Miranda sighed in relief and scurried down the tree before he could change his mind. Grabbing her around the waist, Lucas lowered her to solid ground again, taking in her bedraggled appearance with a groan. Shallow scrapes covered the palms of her hands and the tip of her nose. As she limped gingerly beside him he surmised that her knees probably shared the same fate.

''I fell,'' Miranda said, answering his unspoken question.

''I'm sure I will live to regret rescuing you, but for now let's get you back to camp, so I can tend to your cuts. I can decide in the morning whether or not I want to give you back to the bear.'' Lucas's comment drew a reluctant smile from Miranda. He shook his head at his own foolish desire to cheer her.

By the light of the fire Lucas determined that Miranda's wounds were only superficial. After cleaning away the dirt and rubbing ointment into the abrasions, he tucked her back into her bedroll. Turning to his own lonely pallet, he wondered if this constant lack of relief for his desire could cause him permanent injury.

The stars were still bright in the night sky when Lucas was awakened by the sound of a series of long, piercing screams. Instinctively grabbing his rifle, he raced to Miranda's side. He was relieved to discover that she was frightened by nothing more than a bad dream. Folding her protectively in his arms, he rocked her gently to and fro until her lids became heavy and she was again breathing evenly. As he lowered her to the blankets he lay down with her. Her eyes immediately flew open in alarm.

"Shh . . . I'm not going to hurt you." He smoothed her hair back from her face. "Just go to sleep. I'll stay to chase the bad dreams away." Miranda was afraid to trust him, but she needed his presence and could not find the will to argue. In no time they were both asleep, wrapped securely in each other's arms.

The bright morning sun disturbed the sleeping couple. Unwilling to give up the comfort of Lucas's arms, Miranda feigned sleep long after she became fully awake. Lucas's presence filled her senses: the rhythmic rise and fall of his chest; the scratchy tickle of his beard against the tip of her nose; and, most of all, the strong masculine scent that was his alone. She wondered if each person possessed his own unique scent. She had certainly never noticed such a thing back in London. But then, she had never been so close to any other man. She blushed at the thought, betraying her wakeful state.

"Good morning." Lucas smiled lazily as he looked into her eyes, sensing she, too, was enjoying their shared closeness. His ardor had risen, but he forced himself to bide his time, so as not to frighten her again.

Miranda stiffened slightly, once more on her guard before shyly replying, "Good morning," as she tried to suppress a yawn.

"You see, sleeping in my arms is not so unpleasant after all." His voice was softly seductive.

"It's not sleep I'm afraid of. If all you wanted was to sleep with me, I would gladly lie in your arms night after night," she replied, surprising Lucas with her admission.

"And are you sure the other would be so bad?" Lucas asked, wondering if some clumsy man had once hurt her in some way. If so, it would explain why she denied him even while her own response invited him.

"Without love, without commitment, yes, I think it would be bad. How can you ask me to do a thing that goes so much against my beliefs?"

It frustrated Lucas to no end that she insisted on keeping up this charade even after she admitted she found his touch pleasurable. "Then what about the others? Why wasn't it wrong with them? Because you had something more than a few moments of pleasure to gain? Surely you don't expect me to believe you are a virgin. Women in the business of taking other people's money rarely retain that virtue for long. Sex is too valuable a tool to be ignored."

"There have been no others, you thickheaded oaf," Miranda ground out from between clenched teeth as she tried in vain to push Lucas away. "And if you think I'm willing to prove the fact to you, you are sadly mistaken. You offer me nothing but a few weeks of dubious pleasure, then abandonment. When I give myself, it will be with the covenant of marriage."

So that was her game. If marriage was her goal, it was imperative she convince him of her inexperience. At last Lucas had a clue to her motivation, but if she sought to trap him, she had grossly overestimated her charms. He should have realized that without her father she would need a protector. In her present circumstances he was her only available prospect. While he was sure she would have preferred a more pliable sort, she was obviously willing to make due with what she had.

Satisfied he had unraveled the mystery of what seemed to be her totally irrational behavior, he was free to make his plans. He would continue his slow, seductive assault on Miranda's senses until she came to him willingly. The challenge might prove interesting. Though his body craved relief, he was not a man given to rape, no matter what the circumstances. When he won the game, and he had no doubt he would, it would be a pity to let her loose on society, where she would have no trouble finding a husband, but he could not be expected to be his brother's keeper. And so the challenge began, and if Miranda could have guessed what Lucas was planning, she would have run from him and never looked back.

Even in the mountains the weather was still warm, though the umbrella of trees provided some relief from the fierce afternoon sun. They traveled up the American River, passing a string of small camps, usually numbering no more than ten men. As was the custom, they stopped to exchange news and occasionally share a meal, but Lucas refrained from making camp with any of the other miners. He wanted Miranda to himself, and the wistful sighs of many a man as he introduced Miranda irritated him beyond reason.

Miranda was not oblivious to the longing and sometimes openly hungry looks of the men they met on the trail. She would have been tempted to try to find her own way back to San Francisco, but she feared these other men more than Lucas. At least she knew he kept his word.

Since the night of her flight into the woods, Lucas had not again suggested she become his mistress. Miranda wondered if her words had finally penetrated his thick skull. He did not refrain from touching her; however, after a few initial complaints, she soon grew accustomed to idle fingers combing through her hair or a casual pat on the fanny when she was bent to some task. She knew it was not proper to allow such liberties, but they seemed to pacify him, and she was afraid if she pressed the issue, he might again demand more. She found that as long as she could anticipate these light caresses, she could control her reaction to them. It was only when she was caught off-guard that her body behaved with a will of its own.

Against her will, Miranda found herself drawn more and more to Lucas's touch. By the time they had spent several days stopping to test the color of various locations along the river, she came to sit near him without hesitation, as eager for his light caresses as he was for more intimate contact.

After five days of travel Lucas found a sandbar that met with his satisfaction. He paced off his claim and posted a sign of ownership while Miranda began setting up camp in a more permanent fashion. She was

glad they were finally stopping. Though she loved
the rugged terrain they traveled through, she was
tired of spending so much of her day on horseback.
She laughed out loud at the thought of striding into
Mrs. Penchamp's parlor dressed in her now-faded
blue prairie dress and her father's wide-brimmed hat.
She had started wearing his hat after his death. It provided not only protection from the sun but also a
comforting link with the past.

"What's so funny?" Lucas asked as he came to
help her with the heavier packs.

"Just look at me." She set down the roll of bedding she had just unloaded from her horse and spread
her arms so he could view her fully. "You can't
imagine what would happen if I walked into a proper
English parlor looking like this. Why, the whole
room would probably faint dead away."

"Hm, you look fine to me, all soft and warm with
the sun on your skin. You look healthy and alive,
though I must admit the hat is not quite the thing. It
hides too much of your face." Lucas reached out to
cup her chin in his hand. She did not scold him when
he brushed his lips lightly across hers.

She could not understand why he had become so
complimentary of late. Like any woman, she enjoyed being told she was pretty, but Lucas did not
seem the type given to casual compliments. Don't
borrow trouble, she warned herself.

"As long as it doesn't rain, I'm not going to bother
with tents," Lucas informed her. "I prefer sleeping
under the stars."

Miranda nodded. She was a bit uncomfortable
with their sleeping arrangements, but so far, no harm

had come of it. Since her nightmare, Lucas had insisted on placing his bedroll directly next to hers. Though he never made any conscious move to touch her, often in the morning she would find they had rolled together in sleep and awakened wrapped in each other's arms. It was such a pleasant sensation, Miranda found it hard to protest with any amount of conviction. Besides, Lucas constantly reminded her that she herself had said she would gladly *sleep* in his arms, and as it was impossible to argue with the truth, she had relented on this issue also.

What Miranda didn't realize was that she was falling into Lucas's plans for her perfectly. Though their continual close contact was a strain on him, it was also weakening her defenses as she gradually came to accept more and more physical contact. Often he would awaken to find her studying him, her desire plain, but she never did more than stroke him with her eyes. His stubborn refusal to believe that she was inexperienced prevented him from understanding her reluctance to give into the consuming pleasures to be found in his arms.

The next day Lucas began working his claim in earnest and was more than pleased with the results. Though he found the challenge Miranda presented infinitely more enjoyable than standing knee-deep in a mountain stream bent over a pan of sand, his ostensible purpose was to find gold. The rivers were at their lowest this time of year, making it the most profitable season for working the diggings.

Miranda's mind was not idle while she cleared the remains of the breakfast. She needed to find a way to pay Lucas the money she owed him, as much to

soothe her own conscience as to have him regain his
good opinion of her. Though he had as many faults
as the next man, she had a higher opinion of him than
any other member of his sex. Even the fact that he
had come to the gold fields no longer weighed so
heavily against him, as his reasons for coming were
well thought out, and he was not risking his entire
future on the outcome of the venture. He worked hard
and he kept his word. Despite his poor opinion of her
morals, he had not pressed his advantage when he
could easily have taken her by force. He was a stubborn man but a good one.

As she packed away the tin plates her eyes wandered over her father's tools. The solution to her
problem was obvious. She could not believe she had
overlooked it for so long. She would stake a claim
and pan enough gold to pay Lucas back; maybe she
could even save a little for her future. If her father
could pan gold, then she could do it too. Without a
second thought she snatched up the pan and shovel
and started for the river.

Lucas looked up as he heard her approach, raising
a doubtful eyebrow as he took in the pan and shovel.
Miranda set the tools down at the edge of Lucas's
claim. She paced off a forty-foot square, then
scratched her name and the date into the trunk of a
tree standing near one corner of her claim. That task
complete, she picked up her pan and waded out into
the lazy current. She had watched others enough that
she knew how to begin, and soon she bent studiously
over the remains of her first pannings, picking out
minute particles of gold.

It was an exhilarating experience to have some

control over her own future. Even if the claim was a poor one, if she worked hard, she would at least be able to reduce her debt. She glanced briefly at the man to whom she owed so much. Lucas was watching her with such a condescending smile that she turned her attention to her task with new vigor, determined to prove to him that she was up to the challenge.

By noon she began to have serious doubts about her plan. Every muscle in her body ached. Her feet were numb from the cold water, and when she looked up from its glistening surface, bright spots danced before her eyes. To make matters worse, her labors had not even produced a bulge in the little leather pouch she had tied to her waist. Dragging herself from the river, she momentarily leaned against the trunk of a tree, then slid down its length, unwilling to expend the energy it took to stand. She glanced up as Lucas approached.

"If you want some lunch, I'll get it in a moment," she offered with all the enthusiasm of a condemned man.

"You look a bit tired." Lucas laughed at the bedraggled heap at his feet, earning himself a murderous glare. "Perhaps I should do the honors today."

"No, that's my responsibility." Miranda jumped to her feet. It was important that she continue to keep up her other duties in the camp, or she would build on her debt, something she could not afford to do. "I'll have something ready in a few minutes." She stumbled off in the direction of their supplies. Lucas watched her go, shaking his head at her stubborn determination. He could not even try to guess what she was up to this time.

Lunch turned out to be a plate of leftover biscuits and a pot of reheated coffee. Though not very appealing, the meal was adequate, and after a brief rest, Lucas rose to return to the river, a reluctant Miranda trailing behind.

The afternoon was even worse than the morning. Miranda spent more time leaning over her pan, her eyes glazed with exhaustion, than she did actually panning gold. By late afternoon she had had enough. Though Lucas continued to work, she excused herself by saying she needed to prepare dinner and quit the river.

She had no idea what she prepared, accomplishing the meal through habit alone. After serving Lucas she took her own plate on her lap, using a tree to support her back, and began to eat. Only a few bites reached her lips before the spoon lay still in her limp hand as she drifted off into a sound sleep, at last released from the ache of her labors.

Setting his plate aside, Lucas prepared her bed, then carried her to the more comfortable resting place. The hem of her dress was still damp. With great care, so as not to disturb her, he eased the garment over her head. Through her thin cotton chemise he could clearly see the outline of the body he had once gazed upon in its unveiled glory. His physical reaction to the sight was immediate. He toyed with the idea of finding release for his needs here and now, knowing she could put up little fight if she woke up at all. The last thought was not very flattering to his manly prowess and served to cool his ardor to a more

manageable level. With the help of the cold river he
could bide his time a bit longer. The night was warm,
but he covered Miranda with a blanket, more to protect himself from temptation than to give her warmth.
He then returned to his cold dinner.

Miranda stretched with the first rays of dawn, immediately regretting the action. She had thought a
restful night would ease the ache of her muscles.
How was she ever going to force herself back into
the river today? she wondered dismally. Turning
carefully onto her side, she studied Lucas's peacefully sleeping form as he lay beside her. She had new
respect for the man now that she knew firsthand what
truly hard work panning gold was. That he, or anyone, could go back to the river day after day, week
after week, was amazing. Without thinking she
reached out to stroke his tan cheek and the coarse
brown-red beard covering the lower half of his face.
Lucas's arms reached out to encircle her, bringing
her to rest full-length on his chest, their legs inter-
twined. His hands captured her head, guiding her lips
down to meet his own. The kiss was studied, seductive, not betraying the urgent need of the man beneath her.

Caught off-guard, Miranda did not fight but returned the kiss in full measure, pressing her body
against Lucas in an effort to imprint every inch of him
onto her skin. She did not want to think about what
she was doing; she only wanted to be in his arms.
Lucas opened his eyes to gaze into the intense gray
ones above him as his hand stroked lazily down Miranda's back. He gradually inched her to her side,
allowing him access to her soft breasts, lightly

brushing their first swellings with his fingertips. The contact caused rivers of delight to flow through her veins. She could not have stopped him if she had wanted to.

Rolling her to her back, Lucas again claimed her lips while his hand pursued a more direct assault on the pink-tipped mounds. Miranda did not resist, giving herself fully to the warming sensation his lips and hands caused. Not until his hands grew bold, reaching down to caress the soft flesh of her buttocks, did her reason return. With an indignant shriek she disengaged herself from the compromising situation and jumped to her feet.

"I thought we settled all this." She stood above the reclining form, arms crossed before her, her eyes blazing. She couldn't seem to catch her breath.

"Sorry, my mind must have still been befuddled with sleep." Lucas grinned up at her, enjoying the display her thinly clad form provided.

"Sleep, my eye! You were perfectly aware of what you were doing."

"And what was I doing?"

Miranda had an uncontrollable urge to feel her fist make contact with that maddeningly nonchalant smile. "You were trying to seduce me. Stop trying to play the innocent. You're a sneaky man, Lucas Adams, and you know it." She stomped her foot at him in frustration, refusing to acknowledge that she might be partially responsible.

"Believe what you will." He shrugged his shoulders with feigned indifference. "I think I'll try to get another hour's sleep." With that he turned on his side and pulled his blanket up over his shoulder, mentally congratulating himself for his near victory.

Miranda suddenly became aware of her state of undress. Quickly her eyes darted around until they lighted on her dress hanging neatly over a branch. She had the dress smoothed protectively in place with amazing speed.

As she surveyed Lucas resting comfortably under his cover, a devilish twinkle began to glow in her eyes. If he thought to dismiss the issue so easily, he thought wrong. Humming a merry little melody, she grabbed the coffeepot and headed for the river. Upon returning, she ceased her tune, creeping silently until she stood over Lucas's bed.

"Lucas," she called softly. When he turned his face upward to see what she wanted, he was greeted by a potful of icy water. With an oath he shot to his feet, but anticipating the move, Miranda had already removed herself to a safe distance. As he took a menacing step forward she placed herself behind the protection of a large fir tree.

"Now, Lucas, I only thought you needed a little cooling off." She tried to look contrite, but a smile of triumph kept fighting its way to her lips as she watched the water drip from Lucas's hair and beard onto his flannels.

"You, little girl, are in big trouble." Lucas lunged around the tree, but Miranda managed to scamper to the other side before he could catch her.

"You only got what you deserved, and I'm not the least bit sorry I did it." She really was quite pleased with herself.

Suddenly Lucas roared like some injured forest

creature. The sound startled her, putting her momentarily off-guard. It was all the advantage he needed. With one fluid motion his arm shot out to capture hers, then he threw her over his shoulder like a sack of flour.

"Lucas, I was only teasing you." Miranda beat against his back as she tried to twist out of his grasp.

"But you find such delight in the water. I thought you might enjoy a little yourself." They were at the river's edge, and his intent was clear.

"Lucas, that's not fair. You're bigger than I am. Besides, I only got you a little bit wet."

"I'm afraid you should have thought of that before you started this little game. I always play to win. If the deck is stacked in my favor, so much the better." Bracing his feet on two stable rocks, Lucas straddled the water, shifting her from his back to the cradle of his arms. He held her over the water. "And now, madame, I believe it's time for your morning bath."

"Oh, Lucas don't . . . I'll bake a pie for you if you'll let me go," she pleaded.

"Hmm . . . a pie." Lucas paused to consider the offer. "If you sweeten the deal with a kiss, I'll accept."

"The pie is enough."

Lucas abruptly dropped her several inches nearer to water's surface. Miranda's arms tightened around his neck.

"Okay, one kiss but nothing more," Miranda warily agreed. She could not understand this constant desire he had for her kisses. When he made no effort to release her from her precarious position, she added, "Well, put me down."

"The kiss first."

"Oh, all right." Miranda reached around his neck as he drew her against his chest. She applied her lips lightly to his, not protesting when he increased the pressure. Her eyes closed as she savored the fiery heat his kisses invariably invoked. Reluctantly he released her lips, peeling her arms from around his neck. Again he held her out over the water.

"Lucas, you promised!" Miranda gasped in dismay.

"I believe the deal was a kiss and a pie if I let you go. Well, I'm letting you go." With that he withdrew the support of his arms, and with a splash Miranda hit the water's chilling surface. Though the water was not deep, she was soaked from head to toe.

Rising dripping from the river, she muttered a string of unladylike oaths beneath her breath as she stomped toward the camp. Why did the man always have to remind her how much power he had over her? It was obvious she was at his mercy out here in the middle of nowhere. Did he have to keep rubbing her nose in the fact? He had tricked her with her own words, knowing very well what she had meant. If he thought she was going to make him a pie, he was deluding himself. Rummaging through her pack, she pulled out a fresh dress and dry underclothes, then started for the cover of a nearby bush.

"Wait. I'd like to come watch." Lucas grinned at her.

"And I'd like to put your eyes out, but it appears we will both have to forego our fondest dreams this morning.'' With that, she turned on her heels and left him standing in the middle of camp, his laughter ringing through the forest.

When Miranda returned, a pot of coffee and the never-varying pan of mush were already on the fire. It was lucky Lucas had decided to start their morning meal, as she was in no mood to serve him in any way whatsoever. By the time the coffee had boiled, Miranda's temper had cooled.

''Truce?'' Lucas handed her a steaming cup. She nodded as she took it, unable to suppress a snicker as she remembered his expression when he had risen dripping from the bed.

''You really looked quite funny, you know,'' she explained.

''No more so than you. Why, if I hadn't known better, I would have mistaken you for a water rat. Though I must admit, I've never heard a rat utter such language.''

They cleaned the remains of the meal together companionably. It was with some reluctance that Miranda picked up her pan and shovel and followed Lucas back to the river. She did not want to get the skirt of her only dry dress wet, so after a quick review of her alternatives, she hiked up the hem and tied the skirt so that it fell just above her knees. While Lucas appreciated the display he found it a bit distracting; however, Miranda was working too intently to notice his frequent leers.

Biding his time was proving more difficult than Lucas had originally thought. He found himself sniffing after Miranda like she was a mare in heat and he a full-blooded stallion. It was disconcerting that he desired this one woman so intensely. Never in his life had he been willing to invest so much time and energy in procuring his pleasure. It wasn't as if he desired a long-term relationship. All he wanted was the comfort of a pair of warm arms until he returned to San Francisco. If he didn't bring Miranda around to his way of thinking soon, the opportunity would be lost altogether.

Miranda managed to survive her second day of mining better than the first. While her muscles were not nearly as sore, by the end of the day she was again thoroughly exhausted. She did not have the energy to grace their evening meal with conversation, witty or otherwise. Even when Lucas teased her about the noticeable lack of a pie on the menu, the retort she managed was hardly worthy of the effort it took to utter it. Sighing, Lucas helped her with the dinner dishes. Her chores completed, Miranda climbed into bed, not even bothering with her usual evening toilet.

By the fifth day Lucas could stand no more of her foolishness. At the end of each day she practically had to crawl to her bed, and her hands were becoming red and chapped from constant exposure to water. It was not only his concern for Miranda's health that prompted Lucas's decision to put a stop to her attempts at mining, though, in truth, that was his major concern. The weather was becoming increasingly cool, and his time was running out. If he ever hoped to have Miranda, he would have to do it soon. He found it impossible to chip away at her defenses when she was so tired, she was barely cognizant of his existence. The glimpses of her fiery nature made him long to discover what flames a night of passion in his arms might spark.

The next morning when Miranda went to gather her tools, they were not where she had left them. She searched the camp in frustration before turning to Lucas.

"Have you seen my pan and shovel? I distinctly remember setting them over by the base of that tree yesterday, and now I can't find them anywhere."

"They're gone," he stated without explanation.

"What do you mean, they're gone? They couldn't have just up and walked away." Her brows drew together in vexation.

"I threw them away. I'm tired of watching you kill yourself off day after day in that damn river," Lucas calmly explained. "If you need money that badly, I'll give you some."

"Well, you can just go get them. I need those tools. How do you ever expect me to pay you back if I don't work?" Hands on hips, she squared for battle. Didn't he realize the purpose behind her labors?

"You know how I want you to repay me. I'm not interested in the money anymore," Lucas said patiently, as if he were explaining matters to a not overly bright child.

"Lucas Adams, your arrogance is only exceeded by your stupidity if you think I'll ever agree to that. I honor my debts, and I intend to pay you every penny owed you, but if you think I am going to fall into your bed, you're sun-crazed. Now give me back my things."

"No."

"Lucas, you're being unreasonable." Lucas's

expression remained cool. It annoyed her that he was able to carry on a heated argument without the least sign of agitation.

"No, I'm being sensible. I have no intention of being saddled with a sick woman. If you go on as you have been, before long I will have to spend my days playing nursemaid. Many men can't stand up to the rigors of a miner's life, and look at yourself." He paused, running a finger lightly down the bridge of her nose. "You're no bigger than a child. I can't stand back and let you abuse yourself, all for the sake of a few dollars."

Miranda brushed away his hand, wrinkling her nose to banish the sensation.

"But it is important that I pay you back."

"Not to me it isn't."

She shook her head in disbelief.

"Then what am I doing here? If you have so little concern for the money, why didn't you just leave me back at the mining camp when you moved on?" Lucas's reasoning was totally irrational as far as Miranda was concerned. He'd been so angry when she had first told him about the money that she had been terrified, and now he was telling her he didn't care one whit about it.

"Maybe I just like your company," he commented dryly.

"Don't be ridiculous. Nobody would drag a woman through the forest, against her will, just for the company. You're not making the least bit of sense."

"I didn't say I brought you only for company. I expected other things as well, but I must admit you have been rather slow to deliver.'' Lucas's eyes twinkled in expectation.

''Is that all you ever think about? I pity the poor woman who marries you. She'll probably never leave her bed again.'' Miranda could not believe they were on that subject again. The man was unbelievably dense.

''An interesting idea, but I've told you I have no intention of marrying, ever. So rest assured, I will not be condemning one of your fair sex to such a fate.'' Lucas hoped his statement would crush the idea of marriage once and for all. If she knew there was no hope, they could get down to the business of enjoying each other.

''Well, what a relief. I was afraid I would have to spend the rest of my life following you around, warning poor innocents of your unnatural nature. Now, it's getting late, and I need to get to work, so hand over the tools.''

''You seem to be having a little problem understanding me.'' Lucas groaned at her in exasperation. ''I told you, I will not allow you to continue panning gold. Now, you are well aware that I have the power to enforce my will in the matter, so I suggest we end this foolish conversation. As you said, it is getting late.'' With that, Lucas rose, jammed his hat on his head, and, tools of the trade in hand, he headed for the river.

Despite the fact that she had lost, Miranda had found the confrontation oddly exhilarating. Matching wits with Lucas was always a challenge, and though she hadn't won the battle, she had every intention of winning the war. She might not be able to continue panning, a fact she greeted with a mixture of regret and relief, but she would still find a way to repay Lucas without submitting to his compromising suggestion.

Retrieving her knife, she started for a likely-looking jumble of boulders. Crevassing might be a slow method of mining gold, but it was preferable to doing nothing. She would prove to Lucas Adams that she was not so easily thwarted.

That night she made sure their beds were placed at a discreet distance. Things had already progressed much farther than they should have. She hated to admit she was going to miss Lucas's touch, but if she intended to keep her virtue intact, she could not let things continue as they were, or one morning she would wake up and find the deed done despite her good intentions. She had no expertise in dealing with such a persistent man. As far as she could determine, everything she did seemed to arouse him. Though she couldn't stop living, she could curtail any physical contact between them. Though she knew she could never bring herself to use it against Lucas, she placed her father's rifle as a barrier between the two bedrolls. It added a nice touch and made her intentions perfectly clear.

Lucas realized he had lost ground as he watched Miranda prepare for bed, but he was not daunted. Perhaps he was going about this all wrong and should try a more direct approach. It was becoming clear that as long as he allowed it, she would continue to play the reluctant virgin, though he was certain she no longer possessed that virtue. He was tired of being patient. If she would not come to him, he would go to her. He knew enough about the art of lovemaking to be confident that she could not resist him for long.

He was just settling into his own bed, having determined that a midnight approach would be best while her mind was still befuddled with sleep, when Miranda shot straight up in bed.

"The horses!" Her voice was incredulous. "Why didn't I think of the horses?"

"What are you talking about?" Lucas asked in genuine confusion. "The animals are fine."

"Lucas, if I sold the horses and the mule, how much could I get for them?" she asked, amazed that she had again overlooked the obvious.

"I don't know. They're in fairly good shape, maybe sixty-five dollars apiece for the horses and forty for the mule," Lucas said, giving her his best guess.

"How much would I still owe you after that?" She was not quite sure of the exact terms of the contract her father had made with him.

"I told you to forget the money. You'll need what you get from the sale of the animals to live on once you get back to San Francisco." She was the most stubborn woman Lucas had ever come across. For a swindler's daughter she certainly seemed overly concerned about setting things right between them. It didn't make sense, but then, little of what she did made sense to him.

"Lucas, the only way I can ever convince you that you are wrong about my character is to pay you the money my father owed you. It will release me from my obligation to you, so I can be free again. I'll find some way to get by, and I will do it without your charity. We have gone over and over this matter. Nothing you say will ever convince me to stop trying to pay you your due.''

"You are either the best little actress I have ever met, or you are truly sorry for your part in this scheme. I wish I knew which one it was, Miranda. I really wish I knew.'' Lucas turned his back to her, grumbling to himself about how complicated his life had become of late.

Chapter 11

Once Lucas decided on the direct approach to solving the problem of Miranda's continued resistance, he set about planning his strategy with the zeal of an army commander. After pondering the midnight approach, he discarded it as having too many potential obstacles. Though he doubted Miranda would use the gun against him, he deemed it wisest to avoid the confrontation altogether. In addition, she was in a defensive mood tonight and might not prove as tractible as he would like. He was planning a seduction, not a rape, and if too many complications arose, he would lose the game.

It was Miranda's habit to bathe in a tree-shrouded pool slightly downstream from their claims. He would wait until she was thoroughly engrossed in her bath then come to join her. His plan set, Lucas waited for his opportunity. Whenever a twinge of guilt threatened to overturn his plans, he deftly squelched it, confident she wanted him as much as he wanted her. It was only her foolish failure to abandon this marriage scheme that kept them apart. Actually he would be doing them both a favor by ending the charade. All day he kept careful note of Miranda's movements while he pretended to concentrate on the business of panning gold. At last he saw her head downstream, a bar of soap and towel in her hand. When he was sure she was out of sight, he threw down his pan, then, gathering up the buffalo robe that served as his bed, he quietly followed her.

He concealed himself in the brush while she discarded her clothing, sucking in his breath as she removed first her dress, then her chemise. Her body was even more beautiful than he remembered, and he knew he would have to keep a tight rein on himself or he would move too quickly, losing all that he hoped to gain. Once Miranda was busily splashing in the water, he carefully spread out the robe in a shady knoll near the water's edge, testing the bed for comfort. He didn't want pine needles or rocks distracting her. Satisfied that all was ready, he discarded his own clothing in a pile and waited impatiently for the right moment to make his move.

The wait was maddening. Unaware that she was being observed, and having nothing pressing to accomplish, Miranda used her bath as much as a pleasant pastime as a way to get clean. She floated and submerged with languid movements, enjoying the feel of the water as it flowed across her bare skin. From his hiding place Lucas caught frequent glimpses of a rosy breast or a long length of leg as she floated lazily upon the glistening water. He was hard-pressed to bide his time as he continued to view this tantalizing display. When he thought he could stand the exquisite torture no more, she finally began to lather her hair. His sigh of relief was audible. As soon as she submerged to rinse the bubbly soap from her hair, he wasted no time. Slipping into the water, he swam with ease toward his resplendent goal.

Miranda had just finished washing the last of the soap from her hair when she heard a small splash at the water's edge. Giving her face an additional rinsing to be sure no soap remained to sting her eyes, she turned toward the sound, hoping it was nothing more than a falling pine cone. She gasped in surprise to see Lucas gliding purposefully toward her.

"I thought I'd join you in your bath today," he informed her, as if it were an everyday occurrence.

Miranda knew a moment's indecision. Should she stay in the water and remain at least partially concealed, or run for her clothing, heedless of what she might reveal in her flight? As Lucas advanced upon her with determined strokes her decision was made. Frantically she swam for the shore, panting in apprehension as she felt Lucas's hands close around one slim ankle. As he pulled her toward him her eyes widened with shock when she felt his manhood brush against her leg.

"Let me love you, little one." Though his arms locked her against his chest, his request was gentle.

"I can't." Miranda's eyes pleaded for understanding. She felt strangely dizzy and clung unconsciously to him. Pulling her tighter against him, Lucas claimed her lips, nibbling at their softness until they parted, inviting a more thorough exploration. He did not hesitate to accept the invitation, running his hands down her back as he eagerly consumed the sweetness of her lips. Miranda shivered, but whether it was because of the hands that kneaded her spine or from the coolness of the water, she did not know. Her reason told her to fight, but she could not seem to will her rebellious body into action.

Scooping her up in his arms, Lucas carried her from the river, continuing to tease her lips with his. Once she was out of the water, reason returned. She struggled against the iron arms that held her, but that served only to excite Lucas further. His eyes darkened with passion.

"Lucas, no, you mustn't." Her protest fell on deaf ears. Rage mixed with fear, and fear mixed with desire; she was overwhelmed by the emotions that warred within her as Lucas laid her down on the forest bed, using the weight of his body to hold her there.

"Be still. I won't hurt you," he soothed, smoothing the damp strands of hair from her face.

"Lucas, I beg you—" He silenced her words with another kiss, exploring the moist contours of her mouth with his tongue, bringing her further into his power. She pushed in vain against his lightly furred chest, trying to escape the responses of her own body as much as the man who caused them.

"Miranda, I have waited too long. I need you too much," Lucas said, denying her plea. Pulling one hand to his lips, he kissed each work-roughened fingertip, then applied his mouth to the sensitive palm, pausing to nip lightly around its perimeters before continuing down her arm. The pressure of his firmly muscled body so intimately molded to hers, skin burning against skin, banished her reason. Though she fought valiantly to retain the only defense she had against Lucas's bittersweet assault, her own need for release from the constant tensions of their daily contact was as great as his.

She closed her eyes, trying to focus her attention away from the sensual onslaught, but the trail of warm, moist kisses Lucas forged left her trembling with desire. Her awareness of the delightful warmth of his kisses intensified. When he settled his attentions on her small white breasts, all reason deserted her, and she gave herself up to the luxurious sensations that enveloped her.

As if instantly cognizant of her surrender, Lucas released his hold on her arms, freeing them to encircle his neck, though his attentions never wavered from the taut pink button he teased with gentle nibbles. Instinctively Miranda arched against him, moaning softly with pleasure. She was swept away on a tide of passions too long denied, aware only of her desire for the man lying above her and the strong scent of pine that perfumed the air. It was a scene as old as time itself. Man drawn to woman in an inexplicable desire to be one.

Lucas continued his studied seduction, steeling himself to be patient. His beard tickled the delicate satin skin of her belly as he rained kisses upon its softness. Firmly he stroked the inside of her thighs until she cried out softly in her need for him to release her from the pleasurable prison of passion where he had led her with such expertise. His lips again claimed hers. They tasted the salty sweetness of each other's skin, and she pressed herself against him with a need to fill the vague feeling of emptiness she did not understand.

Still drinking in the nectar of Miranda's lips, Lucas reached down and gently parted her thighs. Raising himself above her, he guided his manhood into the moist softness of her. He groaned at what he discovered there but did not withdraw. She stiffened in shock at the brief moment of pain, and then she was overcome with a wonderful feeling of fullness, of being so much a part of the man in her arms that they were no longer two beings but one gloriously complete entity.

As her hips pressed expectantly against his, Lucas began to move within her, slowly at first, until she matched his rhythm with more intensity. They strained against each other, oblivious to all else but the increasing passion building within them. Driven near wild with desire, Lucas plunged into Miranda, reveling in the feel of her moist, satiny flesh warmly caressing his every stroke. His eyes clouded as he lost himself in the scintillating sensations of their coupling.

She clung to him, her legs encircling his as she locked him against her. Her mouth sought out his, and their lips united in hungry embrace, their tongues echoing the movement of their hips. She felt as if the pressure building within her would tear her asunder, yet she welcomed the feeling. Her soul was no longer her own as Lucas's bold strokes spiraled her senses to dizzying heights. Her skin began to tingle, then, as she received one final thrust of Lucas's hard maleness, the fire within her exploded in a shower of white-hot sparks. Undulating waves of delight engulfed them both, rolling them over and over like a piece of driftwood caught in a cascading current, their release heightened by the months of restraint.

Their passion spent, Lucas rolled them to their side, brushing a strand of damp hair from Miranda's eyes. She kept her eyes closed, savoring the sensation of his nearness, but as the beating of her heart slowed, her sanity returned. The enormity of what had just occurred hit her with such force, it knocked the breath from her. With a strangled cry she jumped to her feet, tears swimming in her eyes as she stared at Lucas with a mixture of horror and accusation. Her now-clear mind took in the conveniently supplied bed, and she knew that what had occurred between them had been no accident.

"How could you?" The words were barely above a whisper but so thick with emotion, they cut the air with their intensity.

"Miranda." Lucas rose and reached out a hand to comfort her. She drew away as if it were a snake. "We shared something beautiful—"

"Beautiful!" She did not wait for him to finish. "You call rape beautiful? How could you destroy the only thing of value I had left in the world."

"Rape? It was not rape, and you know it," Lucas stormed back, angered that she would describe the precious thing they had shared with such a vulgar term. Never had he felt such emotions in the arms of a woman. How could she say the act of sharing their mutual desire had been no more than the physical abuse of some sex-maddened animal? He could not have imagined her surrender, nor her response.

Miranda turned her back to him, her very soul racked with silent sobs. She was unable to deny the truth of his words, but she needed her anger as a shield against her own emotions.

Instantly sorry he had spoken so roughly, Lucas came up behind her, placing his hands on her trembling shoulders. She jumped as if burned, her eyes blazing, the need to vent her anger at him great.

"Don't you ever touch me again you . . . you . . ." She could not find a word she deemed foul enough to describe his despicable behavior. "I hope you found destroying my virtue as pleasurable as you anticipated. Is revenge as sweet as they say?" Her smile was so forced, it distorted her features into a grotesque mask.

"If I had known you were a virgin, I would never have pursued you so relentlessly." Lucas tried to justify his actions as much to himself as to her.

"If you'd known I was a virgin? How can you plead ignorance? I've lost count of how many times I informed you of that fact. No, you were bent on this course from the moment I told you my father had no money. Well, the price of my virginity is high. I doubt if you will ever have so expensive a tumble again." Miranda searched in vain for her clothes. "Where did you put my clothes, or do you plan to abandon me naked in the woods now that you have had your fun?"

"Miranda, stop being ridiculous." Lucas retrieved her bundle of clothing from under a bush, tossing it to her. He tried to reason with her as she hurriedly donned the garments.

"I'll admit I was a cad to take advantage of you, but I had reason to believe you were playing me false. You'll have to admit I had cause to doubt your honesty. I'm sorry for what's been done, but I couldn't undo it even if I wanted to, and in all honesty, I can't even say I would want to. I'm a normal, healthy male. You could not expect us to live together month after month without it coming to this."

"I expected you to be a gentleman, but it appears I grossly misjudged your character. Had I even suspected what a truly loathsome man you are, I would have gladly thrown myself on the mercy of the court, regardless of the outcome. Surely they would have been more merciful than you. Was it my fault my father was fool enough to lose all our money? No. But you took ample pleasure in extracting your pound of flesh, didn't you? As far as I am concerned, you can stay in these hills and rot." Miranda started to stomp away, but an unyielding hand reached out to stop her.

"What do you mean, your father lost his money?" Lucas spoke the words slowly, willing her to give him answer.

"He lost the money in Hangtown, the night of the dance," Miranda explained through trembling lips. Suddenly she felt too miserable to fight him. She wanted nothing more than to be alone so she could sort out her thoughts.

"Why didn't you tell me he lost the money, you little ninny? I would have understood." Lucas tightened his grip unmercifully as the truth of the situation began to sink in.

"I was afraid." Miranda fought back the tears of pain that threatened to spill. Then, finding that her only source of strength was her anger, she straightened her back and added icily, "And, if you will recall, when I did try to tell you, you weren't interested in explanations."

"Oh, that I had turned and run the first moment I laid eyes on you!" Lucas groaned in frustration, realizing the enormity of his mistake. He released her, bringing his hand up to rub the back of his head. Miranda wasted no time in making her escape, leaving Lucas standing naked and alone by the rumpled bedding.

As soon as she had put a safe distance between herself and the man she had suddenly come to loathe, the last shreds of her composure shattered, and she crumpled to the ground, beating her fists against the dry earth as she sobbed out her misery. She cried out her anger at fate for allowing her life to come to such a sorry state. Why had she allowed her father to bring her here, to force her to accept the companionship of this man? Why had she allowed Lucas to take her off alone into the forest, knowing he was determined to hurt her? And worse, why had she responded to Lucas's touch the way she did? Surely no proper woman would have responded in such a manner. Was there no area of her life where she could exercise control?

Her tears spent, she still was unable to find the answers to her questions. Raising herself from the dust, she straightened her skirt. The only thing Miranda was sure of was that it was time she took control of her own fate. With her jaw set in determination she walked into camp.

Lucas stood watching Miranda's retreat into the forest, feeling more of a fool than he ever had in his life. She had every right to feel as she did toward him. She truly was the innocent she had claimed. That he had deliberately deceived her, so he could bring her to this end, rode hard on his conscience. Reaching down, he absently began to dress. When had he thrown reason to the wind and begun to play the fool? Was it anger or lust that had blinded him to the truth?

Probably a healthy dose of both, he surmised. The problem now was, what was he going to do about his mistake? Though he was not the least bit eager to enter that state, marriage seemed the only gentlemanly solution. As he remembered Miranda warm within his arms he smiled. Perhaps it would not be so bad a solution after all.

When he returned to camp, Miranda was nowhere to be seen, but reasoning that she needed time to be alone, Lucas was not concerned. He neatly packed his robe away, certain that any reminder of their afternoon together would only add injury to insult. At length Miranda returned. It was obvious she had been crying for quite some time. Lucas turned his attention back to the stew he was preparing. It would be best to determine her mood before he presented his proposal.

She walked directly to her packs and began arranging the contents therein, content to let Lucas prepare the evening meal. She had spent enough time and energy seeing to his needs. When she had the pack arranged to her liking, she rose to her feet and approached him.

"Lucas, I am going back to San Fráncisco. I'd like to trade my father's mule for enough food to get me there."

"There is no need. We can start back in the morning," Lucas assured her.

"I can manage on my own," Miranda stated with false confidence. "I think we should part company immediately."

"I can't let you go off into the woods alone. You'd be in trouble before you got a mile out of camp. I do feel some responsibility toward you,'' Lucas said patiently.

''Be that as it may, I do not desire your help.'' Miranda had no intentions of altering her plans. It was imperative that she remove herself from Lucas's influence.

''If you're afraid I'll take advantage of you again, you have my word I'll not touch you; besides, I think you may forgive me when you hear what I have to say,'' Lucas went on confidently, sure she would be grateful for his proposal. ''I have decided to marry you.''

''You what?'' Miranda shrieked at him. Her outrage knew no bounds. Where did he get the nerve to make such a ludicrous proposal?

''I've decided to do the honorable thing and marry you,'' Lucas explained, a bit irritated by her outburst. ''It's the least I can do.''

''You must be demented. Whatever made you think I would consider marriage to you? After what you have done I'd sooner fry in hell.''

''Suit yourself. I'm not terribly eager to be tied down to some ill-tempered chit. I made the offer because I am a gentleman, not because I desire you as a wife.'' Lucas was more than a trifle taken back by her blunt refusal. He had been willing to sacrifice his precious freedom for her, something he had sworn never to do, and she was acting as if his offer insulted her. Though he told himself he should be glad he had escaped so easily, he only managed to half convince himself that escape was what he truly desired.

''You call yourself a gentleman? Where was that gentleman this afternoon?'' Miranda stared directly

at him with cool gray eyes. ''If you were a gentleman, we would not be having this conversation.''

''A reasonable point.'' Lucas had again regained
control of his temper. ''But, regardless, I will escort
you back to San Francisco. After that I will relieve
you of my company.''

''I can't prevent you from following me.'' Miranda shrugged her shoulders. ''If you choose to return
to San Francisco, it is none of my business.'' Turning her back on him, she began sorting through their
supply of food, placing what she deemed necessary
in a small pile to one side.

They consumed their evening meal in strained silence, Miranda pointedly ignoring Lucas's very existence. Lucas could not help smiling at her childish
antics. Her nose in the air, she sat regally on the end
of an upturned log as if it were a throne and she a
queen. He was hard-pressed not to reach out and caress the stiff back she presented to him. He idly wondered how long she could keep up her act of
indifference.

That night Miranda placed her bedding on the opposite side of the camp from Lucas. After smoothing
the covers in place she made an elaborate show of
checking her rifle to be sure the gun was loaded,
sighting several small targets before she climbed into
bed. She tucked the gun close to her side. Lucas,
watching this display, wondered if she was angry
enough to use the gun against him, then quickly decided he was in no mood to find out. With a casual
wave of his hand he called, ''Sweet dreams.'' His
only reply was the chirping of the crickets.

Chapter 12

Having slept little during the night, Miranda awoke bleary-eyed. Lucas was already up, busy loading the packs on their animals. She could smell the aroma of coffee boiling on the fire and did not have to look to know the second pot contained a thick, nourishing porridge. Though not the least bit eager to face the day or the porridge, she forced herself to rise.

"Good morning," Lucas called over his shoulder as she began to roll her bedding. "Breakfast is ready if you're hungry." He had decided to ignore her peevish mood, feeling that in a day or two her temper would cool.

Pointedly ignoring his greeting, Miranda served herself a generous bowl of the cereal. Though she did not feel hungry, she knew she would need to keep up her strength for the days ahead. It would be necessary to be constantly on guard to defend herself against Lucas or, if he changed his mind and left her on her own, to protect herself from the dangers of the forest. Miranda was not confident she could do either. Though her skill with a rifle was impressive, it had never been tested in a crisis situation. And where Lucas was concerned, she felt even more vulnerable. Not only had she failed to ward off his advances, but her own body had turned traitor. She blushed with mortification as she recalled the way she had responded to his lovemaking. What she needed was a healthy dose of civilization. Living so close to nature was definitely weakening her moral fiber.

She downed the bowl of lumpy gruel in silence, foregoing the coffee, then set about the task of making sure all was ready for her journey. Lucas, with his usual efficiency, had left nothing undone. As she checked the bindings on her pack she knew she would find them all securely tied. Instead of feeling grateful, she was angry. In her mind she had cast Lucas in the role of a villain, and she did not want to concede that he might have some points to recommend him. Still silent, she pulled her oversize hat into place and mounted her horse.

A sharp tug accompanied by a whistle started the animals into motion. Anticipating a hasty departure, Lucas had already dumped the coffee, scraped the remains of the porridge, and tucked the cooking vessels unwashed into a pack. There was nothing to delay him. Mounting his horse, he followed the little train winding its way down the bank of the American River, led by a forbidding, but nonetheless feminine, guide.

The sun rose warm in the sky, but the oppressive heat of August had abated. Birds called their protest overhead as the humans disturbed the quiet of the forest with their passage, but Miranda was too immersed in her own thoughts to take note of their scolding cries. She knew if she kept to the river, she would not become lost and would eventually arrive in Sacramento City, though she had no idea how long the journey would take. She was determined to remain independent of Lucas. She stayed as close to the banks of the river as possible, straying only when the terrain demanded, then quickly returning to within sight of the river. If she got lost, she would again be at Lucas's mercy, and that was something she was determined she would avoid at all costs.

She stopped only once during the day and then only to give her animals a much-needed rest. She busied herself picking clusters of wild, blue-black grapes from vines entwined around the trunk of a dead oak. The fruit sufficed as her lunch. Its juicy sweetness provided a welcome relief from a diet overladen with starch. Though Miranda's figure did not show its effects, she was thoroughly tired of the never-ending procession of beans, biscuits, and porridge.

By dusk the relentless pace she had set was beginning to tell on her. After selecting a suitable place to make camp she slid from her horse onto less than steady legs.

Lucas watched her with amusement. She had turned her head away from him whenever he came into view and had not spoken one word to him the entire day. He wondered how much longer she would be able to keep up her vow of silence.

Once he was sure she would not try to travel further, he unloaded his animals, relieving the beasts of their burdens. He then began gathering dry tinder to start a fire, keeping an eye on Miranda as she struggled to remove her own packs. She managed the first one with little difficulty, but as the second slid off the back of the mule, both pack and woman landed with a thud in the dust. The sight was more than Lucas could bear, and he burst out laughing, coming forward to give her assistance. Miranda gave him a withering glare before rising to her feet to brush the dust from her skirt.

"I said, I don't need your help." She slapped away his hand as he reached for the pack.

"You have got to be the most stubborn woman I have ever run across." He ignored the indignant fire in her eyes as he easily carried the pack to the base of a nearby tree to join the others. "You make these mules seem to be the most obliging creatures." Miranda was not the least bit flattered by the comparison.

She was not about to let his remark go unchallenged. "Well, I'd rather be kin to an ass than some hoary beast that roams the forest abusing innocents. I don't know why I didn't notice it before, but you bear a striking resemblance to a grizzly."

"I see you have finally found your voice, though I fear I should mourn the fact." Lucas's smile was maddeningly pleasant, as if they were discussing the price of tea in China, not exchanging insults.

"*Mr. Adams.*" Miranda stressed the name. "You may mourn all you like, but I will say and do whatever I please. You have had your payment, and I am through being under your thumb." Miranda presented her back.

"If we are going to deal as equals, I suggest you start preparing our dinner. If you recall, I did the honors last night." Lucas wisely resisted the temptation to give her buttocks a playful swat.

"I have no intention of serving you in any way. I will prepare my own meal. Whether you eat or not is your concern," Miranda said, stating her position, her head held high.

"That arrangement is fine with me, but I think you will find it less than satisfactory. You see, I have the only matches, and unless you are willing to share your cooking skills with me, I am not willing to share my fire with you." Though he did not mind cooking his own meals, Lucas had grown too comfortable with their former domesticity to give it up without a show of resistance.

Tears of frustration welled in Miranda's eyes. Why did he always have to have the upper hand? It just didn't seem fair. But then, she was fast coming to the realization the world was not a particularly fair place. There was nothing fair about the way she was uprooted from her native country against her will, nor was fairness a consideration when she was forced to pay for her father's foolish nature. There was simply no way she could get by without a fire, but she would not let him know how much his small victory was costing her. Blinking back her tears, she schooled her features into an expressionless mask before setting about the task before her. With a satisfied smile Lucas turned his attention to the fire and began piling branches into the small circle he had cleared.

A generous handful of jerked meat flavored the broth of the thick dumpling stew Miranda prepared. She dished out a generous portion for herself, as she was quite famished. She was about to call Lucas when she was blessed with a deliciously spiteful idea. Making sure Lucas's back was still turned, she tossed

a healthy portion of pepper into the pot still simmering on the fire, stirring the black flakes into the contents so they were not readily visible. The lateness of
the hour and the color of the broth aided her efforts.
She smiled her first sincere smile of the day, then,
with an effort, suppressed her good humor. She took
her plate and sat cross-legged on the ground before
she called Lucas. "Your dinner is ready." She was
careful to keep her voice neutral.

Lucas immediately approached the pot, leaning
over to ladle out a healthy portion for himself. Miranda watched him out of the corner of her eye as she
nibbled on one of the fat dumplings. As she again appeared in a less than talkative mood, Lucas applied
himself to the meal without saying anything.

He spooned a dumpling into his mouth with a generous coating of broth. Instantly his mouth was on fire,
and his eyes watered. Looking up at Miranda, ready
to berate her for wasting a perfectly good pot of food
as soon as he could get the peppery mass down his
throat, he was surprised to see her placing a dumpling
in her own mouth, chewing it as if there were not a
thing wrong with the dish. Since he had served his own
portion, he did not think hers could be so different from
his. Determined not to be bested, he bit back the words
of reproach he was about to utter and stared down at
his plate with grim determination.

He forced a second bite down, almost choking in
the process, but when he looked up, Miranda only
gave him a small smile of concern before popping
another bite into her mouth without the least sign of
discomfort. He frowned at her in consternation as she
took yet another bite, to all appearances enjoying the

meal immensely. Could she possibly be unaware of the overseasoned state of the food? It seemed unlikely unless her throat were made of iron, but even if it were, it would not do to insult her cooking. Still, unable to keep silent he ventured, ''These dumplings have an interesting quality.''

''Yes, I hope you like them. Our meals have become so monotonous, I thought I'd try something new. We had a Spanish cook once, and this is just the way she made them.'' Her expression was so innocent, Lucas believed the lie.

Her temper seemed much improved, and unwilling to spoil her docile mood, he replied, ''Yes, they're quite tasty.'' Then forcing a smile, he ate another spoonful.

Miranda continued to consume the meal, keeping her eyes cast down to her plate but snatching frequent covert glimpses of Lucas. It was all she could do to keep a smile from her lips as she watched him force down the peppery mess. This was better than she had planned. She had only sought to make the food inedible, but Lucas believed she truly found nothing wrong with the meal and was eating it all. His pride was causing him even more discomfort than she had intended. She had a momentary twinge of conscience but efficiently squelched it. He deserved every bit of revenge she could mete out and more, for what he had done to her.

When he finally managed to consume the contents of his plate, Miranda looked up at him and smiled innocently. ''There is plenty more in the pot if you're hungry,'' she offered with all the mercy of an assassin.

''Thank you, but I'm quite satisfied,'' Lucas said,

managing to force the words out of his tortured mouth. Miranda had not bothered to make coffee, so he had even been deprived of the benefit of liquid to wash the peppery provender down.

"I'll wash up," he offered, rising to his feet before Miranda could reply. He was eager to get to the river where he could drink his fill in private. Besides, he wanted to be sure what remained in the pot was discarded. Another meal like that one and he would have holes burned through his stomach. Already he was beginning to feel the first sharp pains of the heartburn he felt sure would attack throughout the night.

As soon as Lucas was out of earshot Miranda gave in to the fit of giggles that had threatened to overcome her during the entire meal, pressing her hand across her mouth to prevent the sound from carrying to the river's edge. At last she had bested that arrogant man, and the surge of power she felt made her almost giddy. She was not doomed to be putty in his hands but could fight back and win, albeit in small ways, but she had won nonetheless. Buoyed by the success of her ploy, her mind began to search for new areas to assert her independence.

It was obvious the pepper could not be used again without arousing suspicion, so it would be necessary to find some way to get the matches. It would be Lucas's turn to cook tomorrow, giving her almost two full days to procure them. She had seen Lucas slip the small tin box containing their supply in his pockets, but perhaps there were more in the packs. A quiet search after Lucas had fallen asleep was in order.

Lucas returned from the river with the clean utensils, having quenched the fire in his mouth, if not in his belly. He watched Miranda for any signs of discomfort as he laid out his bedding, but she went about her nightly routine almost gaily, not showing the least sign of pain. "The woman must have the stomach of an ox," he grumbled as he tried to make himself comfortable on his earthen bed. In the back of his mind he had the niggling feeling he had somehow been the brunt of a joke, but he could not quite put his finger on how it had been accomplished. Clutching his midsection, he rolled to his side, wondering if it would not have been a good idea to eat separate meals after all.

Miranda awoke early the next morning. Finding Lucas still sleeping soundly, she determined that now was as good as time as any to check the packs. She made a thorough search of every pack but was disappointed in her effort. It was apparent Lucas was the sole possessor of their supply of matches. It made things more difficult, but Miranda was far from defeated. It was his habit to sleep in his long johns, and she was not above going through his pockets while he slept. After all, desperate times called for desperate measures. Lucas was just beginning to stir as she finished replacing the contents of the last pack she had searched, making it necessary to postpone further action until a later time.

Lucas did not even suggest she prepare the morning meal, fearing what she might create in her new experimental mood. This morning nothing sounded more appealing to him than a nice, dull bowl of porridge.

It did not take long before they were again on the trail. Though they passed several camps, they did not stop to converse with the miners. Miranda wanted to

get back to San Francisco as quickly as possible.
Once there, Lucas would have no excuse to continue
their acquaintance. The sooner they parted company, the better for her peace of mind.

The day passed much as the last. Though Miranda
was far from friendly, she was a little more civil than
the day before. Discovering that Lucas was not invin-
cible softened her feelings toward him more than a little.

It seemed to Miranda that the sun would never
touch the mountaintops, signaling the end of the
day's ride. She was anxious for nightfall, so she
would have another opportunity to try for the
matches. Camp was set, but it seemed forever before
they said their good nights. Miranda lay gazing into
the starry sky as she waited to hear the sounds of Lucas's breathing slow to deep, even breaths. She had
to strain her ears to catch the sound over the chorus
of night noises. Frogs croaked happily in the moonlight, accompanied by a choir of clicking crickets.
Overhead an owl screeched in the trees. From a distance wolves howled their mournful melody.

Creeping silently from her bed, Miranda cautiously peered at Lucas to be sure he was truly asleep.
He was. With care for the carpet of twigs that
crunched underfoot, she crept toward her goal, a pair
of worn trousers silhouetted in the moonlight against
the tree where they hung to air out. She was just
reaching into the first pocket when a large twig
snapped underfoot.

"Hold!" Lucas's roaring command was accompanied by the sound of a rifle hammer being cocked.

Miranda instantly spun around, looking as guilty

as a cat caught at an empty bird cage with a feather in its mouth.

"Are you trying to get yourself killed?" Lucas slowly released the hammer and laid the gun aside. His scowl was ominous.

"Of course not," Miranda replied, annoyed by his menacing tone.

"Then what are you doing going through a man's pockets in the middle of the night?" Lucas was not the least bit amused by his discovery. Just when he had convinced himself Miranda really was the innocent she claimed, he had to catch her rummaging through his pockets like a common thief. It seemed unlikely he would ever discover just what her true character was.

"I was looking for the matches," Miranda shot back in defiance, surmising that bravado might be the best way to handle the situation.

Lucas stared at her incredulously for half a moment, then burst out laughing.

"It's not funny." Miranda stomped her foot. "I need those matches."

"I thought we decided to share the cooking chores," Lucas replied calmly, relieved that he did not again have to revise his opinion of Miranda.

"No, you decided to share the cooking. I was merely forced into it for one night. Now give me my half of the matches . . . unless, that is"—she smiled at him slyly—"you'd like another pot of peppered dumplings, though it does seem a pity to waste good food for the sake of your ego."

"So it *was* a trick, you little witch." Lucas started to rise, a vengeful gleam in his eye.

"You're a bully, and you only got what you deserved." Miranda took a cautious step backward then, snatching the pants off the tree, she beat a hasty retreat across the camp, at the same time dexterously continuing her search of his pockets. Triumphantly her hand seized the small metal box she sought, and without a second thought she discarded the trousers in a heap on the ground.

Lucas was only a few steps behind, stalking her with slow, deliberate steps. He bent to retrieve his trousers, casually tossing them across his shoulder. When he reached Miranda, he held out his hand. "Hand over the matches, Miranda."

She was not about to give in. She had backed down too many times, and she was painfully aware of what timidity had gained her.

"No." She faced her opponent with blazing eyes, clutching her treasure all the more tightly in her hand.

"Now, Miranda, don't be foolish," Lucas cajoled. "You're a bright girl. You know I'll get the matches back in the end." His calm voice did not reflect the rapid pounding of his pulse in his ears. He was suddenly overcome with a burning lust for the woman who faced him with such fierce defiance. He had thought that once he'd had her, his ardor would cool, but the hardness straining against the cloth of his long johns laid false his assumption. He was uncomfortably aware of how revealing his present state of undress was.

As if aware of his thoughts, Miranda's eyes strayed downward. With a strangled cry she threw the matches at him, snatching up the rifle that had become her nightly bedmate. She waved it threateningly at the man before her.

Lucas realized his mistake, but for the life of him he couldn't fathom how he could have controlled his physical reaction to her.

"Get away from me," Miranda directed as she pointed out the direction of retreat with the muzzle of her rifle.

"I really had no intention of—" Lucas cut off his explanation as she centered the bore of the gun on his chest. She was too agitated to be trusted. A loaded gun pointed at one's heart was no laughing matter. Cautiously Lucas backed toward his bed, slipping under the covers without taking his eyes off the gun.

When she was sure Lucas had no intention of rising again, Miranda breathed a sigh of relief. She knew full well she could never bring herself to shoot him no matter how much he might deserve it, but it was to her advantage that he believe otherwise.

Having succeeded in protecting herself from his advances, she had given up the matches in the heat of the moment, and she was thoroughly disgusted with herself for her rash gesture. If she had kept her head, she could have retained both the matches and her self-respect.

She wondered how long she could survive on uncooked food. Jerky and even oats could be eaten without cooking if necessary, but the thought was not very appealing. Perhaps if he saw she was not going to relent, Lucas would give in and share the matches with her. It was a slim hope. Presently she drifted off to sleep, her hand resting on the butt of the rifle.

Chapter 13

Lucas wisely did not suggest that Miranda prepare their meal the next morning. Her tight expression was fair warning that she was in no mood to discuss the issue in a sensible manner. While she could see no reason to refuse to eat the food Lucas prepared, her acceptance of the meal was anything but gracious. Neither had any desire to dally, and in no time they were settled into their saddles, winding their way down the river's edge. Miranda continued to lead the way, carefully nurturing her air of independence.

Lucas smiled as he watched the gentle rocking of Miranda's hips as she guided them along the river. He had to admire her determination. This was the third day they had spent on the trail, and she had not relaxed their pace one whit. Not once had she sought his assistance or shown any sign that she could not have managed perfectly well without him. He tipped his hat in silent respect. He had rarely seen a more capable woman.

In the early afternoon Miranda's horse stumbled while climbing a steep grade. Though not seriously hurt, her mount favored the injured leg, and after continuing a short distance, Miranda deemed it wise to make camp for the day. No matter how anxious she was to come to the journey's end, she could not continue at the risk of permanent damage to her animal. Lucas concurred with her decision, grateful he had not had to suggest they stop. In her present mood she was likely to go against anything he suggested just to avoid agreeing with him.

After tethering the animals and relieving them of their burdens, Lucas rubbed a soothing salve into the tender fetlock of her mount. Miranda knew nothing about caring for an injured horse, and she was not foolish enough to allow her stubbornness to stand in the way of the horse's well-being. After carefully examining the injury Lucas assured her that there should be no problem in continuing their journey on the morrow, a fact that relieved her considerably. After last night's display she felt as if she were sitting on a powder keg. She could not make the mistake of trusting Lucas. The knowledge of her own wanton surrender was still fresh in her mind. It was not a part of her nature she wanted to examine too closely.

She had many emotions that needed thinking through, but at the moment she did not feel up to exploring any of them. She had always blocked out unwanted thoughts with activity, but unfortunately, at the moment there was nothing pressing she had to do. Unwilling to sit and muse, she decided to oil the butt of her rifle. It would keep her occupied; also, knowing Lucas respected the potential power of the weapon in her hand gave her a sense of security.

Lucas leaned against a tree, relaxing as she went about her task. He was pleased she took enough pride in the weapon to keep it in good condition. So many women did not think past the most obvious maintenance of a gun. Before long his eyelids began to droop in the warm afternoon sun. Not even the sight of Miranda bent intently to her task was enough to keep him awake. Last night had afforded him little sleep. Having spent most of the night wrestling with his unflagging desire, he was badly in need of a nap. Soon he was sleeping soundly. Glancing in his direction, Miranda smiled upon seeing him look almost angelic. In repose he in no way resembled a heartless cad. Scolding herself for her gentle thought, she returned her attention to the gun.

Suddenly there was a loud crashing in the underbrush; then she heard a rifle shot, followed by a terrible bellow of pain. Leaping to her feet, she watched with horror as a huge shaggy bear stood on its hind legs, towering over Lucas as he jammed another bullet into place. Before he could fire a second shot the beast struck him with one monstrous paw, raking its claws across his chest. The force of the blow threw him several yards from where he stood. With a triumphant roar the bear approached Lucas's motionless figure, intent on finishing what he had begun.

A high-pitched scream diverted his attention to Miranda. She could see the blood lust in the animal's eyes as he charged her. Raising the rifle with trembling arms, she sighted the beast's massive head, knowing that a direct hit was her only chance. The sound of the shot reverberated in her ears as she stood, momentarily transfixed, watching the gigantic bruin pitch forward. She stepped back, reloading the rifle. The mountain of brown, yellow-tipped fur did not move. She could see its lifeblood surging out of the gaping hole in its skull.

Convinced it could cause no further harm, she forced her leaden feet toward Lucas's still form. She was sure he was dead but was terrified of being confronted with the reality of his lifeless body. Kneeling beside him, she gently rolled him to his back. A large lump on his forehead oozed blood, and his chest was a bloody mass of shredded skin and cloth. His flesh was still warm. Blinding tears flowed freely down her cheeks as she stared sightless at the carnage the bear had wrought with a single blow.

"I'm sorry for the way I've treated you, Lucas. I know it was my fault too. . . . Please forgive me. Please forgive me." She knew her words were too late. She had treated Lucas with such contempt, and now he was dead. He would never know her anger was directed at herself as much as at him. He had been her strength when her father had died, and she had never thanked him properly. Her tears mixed freely with Lucas's blood as she bowed her head over his still form.

"Don't bury me yet, woman." Lucas tried to raise his head, but as the world began to spin, he immediately gave up that idea. He forced a crooked smile.

Miranda stared at him as if he were a ghost. Then, regaining her grasp on the situation, she began a closer survey of the extent of his injuries. "Lucas, I'm so glad you're not dead." She smiled through her tears and offered a silent prayer of gratitude.

"I think I hit a rock when I fell," Lucas said, explaining his stunned state as he slowly raised a hand to examine the swelling above one eye. His chest ached abominably, and he felt as weak as a kitten.

"Oh, do be still." Her worry made her tone sharper than she had intended. Then, continuing on a softer note, she confessed, "Lucas, I don't know what to do."

Lucas reached for her hand to give it a reassuring squeeze. It was as cold as ice. "You'll have to clean away this bloody mess to see how bad the damage is. The bear may have broken a few ribs, and I'll probably have need of your sewing skills." His steady, reassuring voice gave Miranda the confidence she needed to take command of the situation. In truth, Lucas was far less certain of his survival than he sounded, but it would not do to frighten Miranda any more than she already was. If he were to recover, he would need her to be calm and levelheaded.

"I'll be back in a minute," Miranda assured him as she went to quickly gather the items she would need to attend to his injuries. She returned momentarily with a bucket of water, cloths, her sewing kit, and a flask of whiskey.

"I want to get you off the dirt and onto this blanket," she explained to Lucas as she spread the blanket beside him. "If I help, can you roll onto your side for a minute?"

Lucas nodded, and a few moments later he was again on his back, lying on the blanket. Miranda stripped away the remains of his shirt and underwear, baring his chest before she began sponging away the gore with a damp cloth, pressing against the wounds to stem the flow of blood.

"You have me just where you want me," Lucas

forced himself to joke. Miranda was as pale as a ghost. He had to keep her calm. She spared him an exasperated glance, then fought hard to swallow her rising gorge as her ministrations revealed several long, loose flaps of skin.

"Lucas, will you be able to hold still while I stitch you?" she asked, wondering how she would be able to do the necessary sewing. A rend in a garment was one thing, but mending a man was something entirely different.

"I'll manage." Lucas steeled himself for the procedure. "But first let me have a taste of that whiskey."

Miranda obediently lifted the flask to his lips, letting him take a healthy draught before lowering his head to the ground. His wounds continued to seep blood, but she had managed to staunch the flow enough to see what must be done.

Taking the flask of whiskey in her hand, she held it over the wounds until Lucas nodded his consent. A scream of agony tore from his throat as he bucked in an effort to escape the fiery liquid. Miranda bit her lip so hard she could taste her own blood. She was grateful when Lucas was finally unconscious and oblivious to his pain.

She threaded her needle, tying a strong knot in one end. If she could complete her task before Lucas awoke, it would make things easier for them both. Gritting her teeth, she made the first stitch. Though his bruised flesh did not resist the prick of the needle, the feel of her thread drawing through human skin was almost more than she could bear. She struggled to gain control of her trembling hands. Unless she got a grip on herself, the task would prove impossible.

"Think of a quilt," she told herself. "I am merely stitching together the pieces of a quilt." The illusion helped, and she was able to continue. For over an hour she worked in grim silence, making small, neat stitches as she pulled the edges of his skin together. When the last knot was tied securely in place, she again bathed the wounds in whiskey to ward off infection.

After retrieving a clean petticoat from her pack she tore the garment into strips and tightly bandaged Lucas's chest. It was no mean feat working the bandages under the back of an unconscious man, but she had no choice but to manage. Reaching for her scissors, she cut away the remains of Lucas's undergarments at the waist, then covered him with a blanket and began to clean up.

Her dress was stained with blood. After a quick glance over her shoulder to be sure Lucas was still unconscious, she hastened to replace it with another, pausing long enough to wash the blood from her arms. She swiftly returned to his side to await his awakening. It was not long before he started moving restlessly.

Miranda greeted him with a smile.

Lucas blinked his eyes. He lay silent staring up at the sky, until a thought suddenly entered his mind. "What happened to the bear?"

"I shot him."

"Thank you." Lucas relaxed, smiling up at her with pride. She had kept her head and probably saved both of their lives. A wounded bear was a very real threat. Lucas was grateful he had taken the time to teach her how to use the rifle.

"Lucas, how do you feel?" Miranda was satisfied she had done all she could, but he had lost a lot of blood. If there were internal injuries, or infection set in, all her work would be for naught.

"Sore, but I think I'll mend." The effort it took to speak was draining, and Lucas was already starting to drift back to sleep. Miranda tucked the cover up around his neck, then sat down beside him, to keep a careful watch over her patient.

As she at last began to relax, all the horror of the afternoon flooded over her. She began to shake uncontrollably, fighting back hysteria. Even though the late-afternoon sun was still radiating its warmth, she felt chilled to the bone. Hugging her arms around her, she tried to hold in what little warmth there was. She had the dreadful feeling she was going to pass out.

"You're supposed to faint during a crisis, not after," she gently chided herself. It was ridiculous to suddenly become vaporish after she had managed so well up to this point. Taking a firm grasp on her nerves, she turned her attention back to Lucas.

He was resting easy, but it was frightening to see such a vital man lying pale and as still as death. She reached out to brush a stray lock of hair from his brow. He looked so vulnerable, not at all like the villain she had painted him. Watching the rise and fall of his chest, she realized he was neither devil nor angel but a man with strengths and weaknesses like any other man. It was foolish to think of him otherwise. Though she could not quite bring herself to forgive him for what he had done, she could understand that living together in such proximity might put a strain on him, bringing out his less gentlemanly feelings. It still did not excuse what he had done. She felt he could have controlled himself if he had desired to do so, but she could grant that he might have been motivated by something more than a cruel desire for revenge. With one exception he had always been fair with her, and it was uncharitable not to admit it was so. She was abruptly aware of how empty her life was going to be when they parted company.

"Oh, Lucas, how can I hate you and love you at the same time?" Without realizing it she spoke the plaintive question out loud. *No, I can't love him. There is no way we could build a life together. Lucas does not want a wife, and I . . . I don't know what I want anymore.* She sighed at the impossibility of her situation. *Whether I want him or not makes no difference. I cannot have him on my terms with love and commitment.* Without that life would be meaningless. She was suddenly struck with a melancholy thought. Lucas could very well die here in the wilderness. She pushed away the possibility. "Not if I can help it he won't." She again spoke out loud but, this time, daring fate to deny her will.

Seized with a burst of energy, she jumped to her feet. There were plenty of preparations that needed to be completed before nightfall. Her sitting and staring at Lucas was not going to make him heal any faster. Making a mental list of what she needed to accomplish, she started working with renewed determination. She was in charge now. It was up to her to insure their survival.

Both mules and Miranda's father's horse had broken loose during the bear's attack. She could not leave Lucas to search for them now. Luckily they had not run off with any of their provisions.

She would need a pot of broth for Lucas when he awoke. Though she would have preferred a fresh fowl to flavor the stock, she settled for jerky. When she had laid the fire and fetched the water, she crept silently back to Lucas. The matches were still in his pocket. Folding back the edge of the blanket, she gingerly slipped her hand into his pocket. His thigh felt warm and hard to the touch, causing her to blush at her own boldness. He sighed in his sleep. Clutching her prize, she immediately withdrew her hand.

When Lucas awoke, Miranda had a fire crackling a few feet from him. He could see she had dragged their packs nearby. Her bedding was spread next to his, and her rifle was propped against a pack within arm's reach. She leaned over a pot, stirring what he assumed would be dinner.

When she heard him stir, Miranda came to place her hand on Lucas's brow. It felt warm but not alarmingly so. Though his face was colorless, his eyes were clear and alert. "Are you feeling any better? I've made some broth if you're hungry."

"I could use a cup of soup." Lucas ignored her question, for, in truth, he felt as if he had been run over by a hay wagon. It hurt to move; it hurt to talk; it hurt to breathe.

"Do you think you can sit up? I can drag a pack over to give your back support."

"If you help me, I can manage," Lucas assured her, though the thought of any kind of movement filled him with dread. He knew he needed to eat to keep up his strength, and the thought of being spoon-fed while he laid flat on his back was intolerable.

Miranda moved the pack into position, then, lifting him from behind, she shoved the pack under his shoulders with her legs. Lucas gritted his teeth against the pain and went a shade paler, but in a few moments he was recovered enough to accept the broth. He only managed half a cup before exhaustion overtook him.

"I'm afraid I'm not very good company." He tried to make light of his weak condition.

"Would you like to lie back down?" Miranda was on her feet, ready to help ease him down.

"No. It's best I sleep sitting up." Lucas forced himself to think clearly. "We're too close to the bear carcass, and I'm afraid we might have visitors to-night. Load my rifle and bring it here."

"But, Lucas, you'll hurt yourself if you try to fire your gun," Miranda protested, once again filled with fear. She had forgotten that the scent of blood might attract predators to the bear's carcass and their camp. There was simply no way she could move the remains of the huge beast, and Lucas was in no condition to be moved to another site. She searched her mind for a solution to the dilemma but found none.

Lucas tried to reassure her. "Don't worry. I hope I won't need to use the gun. We'll keep the fire high, and with a little bit of luck, the wolves won't bother us."

Miranda was not convinced it was all going to go so smoothly, but she did not intend to waste what little strength Lucas had arguing with him. Remembering she had never retrieved his gun from where it landed when the bear struck him, she searched the brush for the rifle. It was not far from where he had fallen. The light of the fire made it fairly easy to locate.

Rummaging through a pack, Miranda found their supply of ammunition and filled both pockets of her dress with bullets. By the time she returned her attention to Lucas, he was again sleeping soundly. With a tired sigh she reloaded his rifle and laid it beside hers. Before settling in for the night, she built up the fire, then moved the horses nearer the flames, double-checking her knots after tying them to a tree; they could not afford to lose any more of their animals. Sitting cross-legged on her bed, her rifle lying across her knees, she waited for what the night would bring.

Every small sound caused her to start. She was acutely aware of how vulnerable and alone she would have been if Lucas had allowed her to have her way and she had set out for San Francisco alone. Not only would she have been at the mercy of the beasts of the forest, but she would have been easy prey for men too long in the gold fields. She shuddered to think what her fate might have been. Grudgingly she acknowledged that she had been relieved when he had insisted on accompanying her. She was so exhausted, she felt as if her eyes would drop at any moment, but tonight, for both their sakes, she must avoid sleep at all cost. Failure to do so could cost their lives.

The horses whinnied nervously, straining at their bonds as the expected feral beasts began to edge to-

ward the camp, their low, throaty growls announcing their arrival. Across the fire Miranda counted first
one, then two, then five sets of gleaming yellow
eyes. The animals paid little attention to the two humans on the other side of the fire. Their goal was
more immediate. With savage jaws the wolves began to tear at the thick hide of the grizzly, laying bare
tough, blood-rich muscles. They gorged themselves, snapping viciously if a comrade ventured too
near a choice piece of meat. Blood dyed the thick
gray fur of their faces and chests a muddy red.

Miranda sat propped on her heels, her rifle leveled
in the direction of the shadowy hulks. She could not
see the beasts clearly, but the savage sounds of their
feasting was enough to make her blood run cold. She
was afraid to move lest the wolves turn their attention to her. It was unlikely she could kill them all before they attacked. She could almost imagine the feel
of the wolves' sharp fangs tearing at her flesh and had
to force back an hysterical scream. She risked a quick
glance at Lucas. He was still sleeping soundly, but
it was an unnatural sleep. His brow was beaded with
droplets of perspiration. It worried her that the snarls
of the wolves, which sounded deafening to her terrified ears, did not wake him. He needed cool com-
presses to break his fever, but she could not risk
relaxing her vigilant guardianship to tend to him.

She leaned forward, tossing more brush into the
fire. The rising flames momentarily caught the attention of the wolves, but after pausing to sniff the
air, they returned their attention to their meal.

Fighting sleep was no longer a problem. Miranda

stared wide-eyed into the darkness, praying the beasts would leave. The night wore on endlessly.

At last the wolves were satiated. They began to drift back into the forest; however, one unfortunate wandered too close for Miranda's comfort. Squeezing the trigger, she shot at the bold one. Lucas stirred restlessly but did not awaken. Without hesitation she grabbed the second rifle and took aim, but the wolf had eaten his fill, and the sound of the shot sent him slinking off with his companions. Miranda did not lower the rifle but sat poised for his return. Dawn was fully upon them before she deemed it safe to lower the gun. Her arms ached from the weight of the weapon. As she tried to rub some feeling back into her numb limbs, Lucas began to stir.

When he opened his eyes a few minutes later, he was startled by the sight that greeted him. Miranda looked worse than he felt. Her face was pale and drawn with large blue-black circles under her eyes lending the only color to her face. Thick strands of hair had escaped her usually neat bun, but she seemed oblivious to her disheveled state.

"Didn't you sleep well?" He reached out a hand to her. Miranda looked at him incredulously for a moment, then burst into a fit of half sobs, half laughter, which quickly dissolved into quiet weeping. Lucas winced as he forced himself to sit upright.

"Miranda, what's wrong?" Before he even finished the question, his eyes fell on the tattered remains of the bear, and he knew the reason for her distraught state. Large tufts of blood-soaked fur lay scattered around the partially exposed skeleton of the grizzly. How had he possibly slept through such carnage? He ached to take Miranda in his arms and chase away the visions of the night that haunted her, but in his present state, such comfort was beyond his ability to give. He was forced to content himself with stroking her back until the weeping ceased and her chest began to rise and fall in exhausted slumber.

He tucked his blanket over her shoulders, then reached for the rifle that lay beside her. The exertion was telling on him. He paused to rest a few minutes before checking the loading mechanism. All was in readiness. He settled back against the support of the pack. Though he did not expect further trouble, it was always best to be prepared for the worst. Miranda had valiantly defended him twice within the last twenty-four hours. It was time he took over and gave her a much-needed rest.

Miranda continued to sleep until well after noon. Though Lucas dozed off and on throughout the morning, he remained alert for trouble. But nothing further happened.

When Miranda awoke, Lucas was sitting up watching her sleep with a strange expression on his face. She immediately sat up, rubbing the sleep from her eyes.

"I'm sorry, Lucas. I must have dozed off. I'll get you some breakfast." She looked up into the afternoon sky, shaking her head in confusion.

"It's the middle of the afternoon. You've been sleeping for hours," Lucas explained. "After last night you needed the rest."

"I'll boil some rice in yesterday's broth," she offered, unwilling to recall last night's events. "I don't think you should have anything too heavy just yet."

"I'm willing to eat anything you prepare. I'm as hungry as a bear." Lucas immediately regretted his poor choice of words. He watched a brief expression of fear dart across Miranda's face before she leveled him with a rebuking glare.

"I'll gather some brush." She rose, smoothing the wrinkles from her skirt. "You just rest."

"Whatever you say. For the moment, at least, you're the boss." Lucas smiled at her beguilingly, causing her heart to beat more rapidly. She could see the respect in his eyes.

"You look like you're feeling better," she commented as she rebuilt the fire. "When do you think we can be moving on?" It was not her haste to return to San Francisco that prompted the question but her desire to leave this particular camp.

"I'm sorry, but it will be a few days at least." She had defended him so bravely, he had thought her feelings toward him had softened, but apparently he had misjudged. She was just as eager as ever to rid herself of his company. It was probably only her sense of decency that prevented her from abandoning him to his fate. He would be sorry when the day to part company arrived. Miranda was a remarkable woman.

Lucas ate heartily, feeling a little of his strength return with the nourishment. Miranda only sipped spoonfuls of the concoction. Throughout the meal her eyes kept drifting to the carcass of the bear. If Lucas could not move, she would have to remove what was left of the bear. However much she dreaded touching the remains of the animal, she doubted her sanity could survive another night like last night. The mere thought of the upcoming task effectively squelched her appetite.

As soon as she finished toying with her food Miranda set another pot of water on the fire to boil, tossing in a generous handful of jerky. She was sorry she couldn't offer Lucas anything better than another pot of boiled dumplings, but without fresh meat, it was hard to vary their menus. And she could not yet leave him alone to go hunting.

Finally, determined to complete the dismemberment of the bear as soon as possible, she approached the carcass, butcher knife in hand.

She shuddered as she leaned over the remains of the bear, to cut away the first large portion. A wave of nausea passed over her as the stench of blood and saliva rose with the swarm of flies. She swatted at the annoying insects as they buzzed around her head. For the most part the wolves had done her work for her, but there was still a large pile of heavy bones to be hauled away.

From his bed Lucas watched her, sympathizing with her plight. She had not been raised to deal with this, and he could see how difficult it was for her. Of late her education of life in the wilderness had taken a rather overwhelming turn. Still, she always managed to face what must be done. His thoughts began to drift, and he closed his eyes. The sun felt warm against his skin.

When Miranda looked up from the bear's carcass, she found that Lucas had fallen asleep again. She turned her full attention back to her chore, confident for the present that he would have no need of her.

After the bones were all moved a safe distance

from camp, Miranda took a shovel and turned the earth where the bear had lain, trying to mask any remaining scent of blood that might attract the wolves. Satisfied she had done all that was possible, she went to the river's edge and vigorously scrubbed away the stains of the bear.

When she returned, Lucas was awake. He smiled at her thoughtfully. "You handle yourself well. I think you'd make a good pioneer."

"I don't think so," she replied, a bit disconcerted by the warm way he looked up at her. "I'm afraid all this is a bit out of my realm."

"But you managed, anyway, didn't you? How many women do you know who can claim they shot and killed a grizzly bear?"

"Not a one," Miranda replied with a grin. It pleased her that Lucas was so proud of her, and she felt a fresh surge of confidence. She *had* managed despite her fears. Maybe she wasn't doomed to be at the mercy of other people all her life. Surely once she was back in San Francisco, circumstance could not offer her anything nearly so challenging.

"Just think of the stories you'll be able to tell your grandchildren," Lucas continued though his eyes had fallen shut again.

The laughter left Miranda's eyes. How could he tease her about grandchildren when he had effectively ruined her chances of marriage?

"I doubt I will be having any grandchildren," she stated blankly.

Lucas's eyes abruptly blinked open; he was taken aback by her sudden change in mood. He had extended her a compliment, and she suddenly turned cold.

"Why not?" There was a sharp note to the question. He was too tired and sore to try to discern her quicksilver moods no matter how grateful he was that she had saved his life. He was trying to be nice, not start an argument. It was taking every ounce of his strength just to stay alert.

"Because . . ." Miranda could not believe he was making her explain the obvious. "To have grandchildren you must have children, and to have children it is preferable to be married, and you, sir, have closed that avenue to me."

"That's ridiculous. You can still marry just about anyone you want. No one out here would be concerned with one little indiscretion." Lucas massaged his aching brow. "In case you haven't noticed, the state is hardly overflowing with available women. Besides, you're a remarkable woman. A hundred virgins couldn't hold a candle to you. Any man who can't see that doesn't deserve to have you. Why, I bet that Hiram fellow back in San Francisco would snap you up in a minute if you but said the word."

"Did it ever occur to you that I might want to return to England? I can assure you that the lack of my virginity would very much concern a future husband there. Do you think I could deceive a man about such a thing?" Despite her words Miranda was not nearly as angry as she sounded. Her new understanding of Lucas did not allow her heart to condemn him with any amount of conviction. They had shared too much.

She was suddenly depressed by the fact that they were arguing again. It seemed that was all they did anymore. The emotional strain of the last two days had left her little energy for a battle of tongues. With an almost pleading note she asked, "Please, Lucas, can we just not talk about it?"

"Okay, the subject of grandchildren is off limits. Maybe we can talk about dinner. I'm still starving, though I don't know why. I haven't done a thing all day." Though it irritated him that she would not look at her situation logically, Lucas forced himself to smile brightly as he gingerly offered his hand in friendship. He had offered marriage. What more could he do to make amends?

Miranda accepted his hand, banishing her melancholy thoughts.

"What are we having?" He was as eager to change the subject as she.

"Dumplings."

A pained expression passed across Lucas's face, and Miranda could not help but laugh.

"Don't worry. I couldn't be so cruel to an invalid. If you want, you can watch me put in the seasonings, so you'll know I haven't tried to poison you."

"As you say, I am a poor invalid. I'll have to trust to your better nature not to put me in more pain than I'm already in." Lucas gazed up at her with pathetically sad eyes.

"Save your energy for getting well. You're overacting. If I want to see a play, I'll go to the theater." Miranda rumpled his hair before adding, "If you take too long to mend, I might leave you out here to fend for yourself."

"The woman has a heart of stone." Lucas started to raise his arms in supplication to the trees, then quickly thought better of it. "She would abandon a man half dead to his fate. It would have been better if she had let the bear have me." It was a performance designed to wring tears from the driest of eyes.

"Your injuries have affected your mind." With a stiff back Miranda turned her attention to preparing their dinner, but she could not suppress a giggle.

As soon as the meal was consumed and the camp secured for the night, they both retired. Despite spending the majority of the day sleeping, both badly needed the rest. Miranda made sure both rifles were loaded and ready, then snuggled down into her bed. She had left it next to Lucas's. In his present condition she feared no advances from that quarter. Their defense would be easier if they were together, and if Lucas again became feverish, she wanted to be near at hand.

Though Miranda tried to stay awake in the event that the wolves returned, it proved impossible, and she was soon sound asleep. Lucas smiled at her figure in repose, resisting an urge to run his hand down the soft hip that lay within his reach. Nothing but trouble would come of it if she awoke. He would respect her wish not to be touched.

A short while later he, too, was asleep, contentedly dreaming of a small, soft woman nestled warmly in his arms.

Chapter 14

The next day Lucas was noticeably stronger. His gashes were healing well thanks to Miranda's skill with the needle, though he would always have scars to remind him of his encounter with the grizzly. He could now assume with a reasonable amount of surety that he had suffered no broken ribs. He was sorer than the devil and still weak from the loss of blood, but in all, he was lucky to have escaped as lightly as he had.

Miranda took care of him with the devotion of a mother hen. She shouldered the entire responsibility of the camp, insisting he spend all of his time in bed. Lucas tolerated this confinement for two days but, after that, insisted on walking a little every day and helping with a few of the lighter chores. He knew prolonged inactivity would weaken him as much as the loss of blood. Despite his rapid recovery, he did not feel up to facing a day on horseback, and as Miranda made no further mention of her desire to be on her way, he did not broach the subject. Though he did not understand her change in attitude, if she was content to stay with him, he was more than happy to have a few additional days to recover.

Three days after the bear attack Miranda's mule wandered back into camp. She had made several attempts to find the animals but with no luck. Apparently the mule had tired of foraging and returned of its own accord. Miranda was greatly relieved, not only because they needed the mule to carry their packs, but also because she would need the money from its sale in the future.

Lucas weathered his convalescence with tolerable good humor, snapping only occasionally at Miranda when she became too helpful. It rankled him that Miranda was forced to carry so much responsibility. He was a man. He should be caring for her.

Their relationship had regained some of its former friendliness. Miranda was confident that Lucas's injuries would prevent him from taking advantage of her, so she relaxed her guard. She continued to sleep near Lucas, ostensibly as a defense against further intruders from the forest, but she was honest enough with herself to admit that she enjoyed their shared closeness.

Once they reached San Francisco, they would go their separate ways. It was unlikely they would ever meet again. In the short time left to her she wanted to store up memories to last a lifetime. If Lucas offered marriage again, she was tempted to accept. She doubted she could ever find a better man. The problem was she wanted him to want to marry her out of love, not out of a sense of guilt or duty. Such an offer would never come, so she contented herself with making what time she had left with him as pleasant as possible.

A week after the frightful incident Miranda could

find no further excuse for delay. Lucas was strong enough to travel and managed to get around quite well on his own. It was impossible not to mention the possibility of continuing their travels without Lucas becoming suspicious that she did not want to leave him at all. After breakfast the next morning she brought up the subject.

"Lucas, when do you think you will feel up to traveling again?"

"We can leave today," Lucas replied. He was just as reluctant as Miranda to start the journey that would put an end to their relationship, but he did not feel he had the right to delay their departure for his own selfish reasons.

"If you're sure, I'll start breaking camp." Miranda greeted the news with less enthusiasm than he had expected.

Miranda insisted that Lucas rest while she loaded the animals. With the loss of her father's horse and Lucas's mule, it was necessary to rearrange their packs to distribute the weight of their belongings equitably among the three remaining animals. It was fortunate their supplies were running low or they would have been forced to leave some of their provisions behind. Miranda purposefully asked Lucas to lead the way so she would be able to watch him for signs of fatigue. The jarring motion of the horse was bound to cause him some pain.

They had only traveled a few hours before Miranda insisted on stopping for the day. Though she gave the excuse of wanting time to hunt for fresh meat, Lucas knew it was her concern for his health that had prompted her insistence.

After setting up their camp in the new location Miranda filled one pocket with a handful of bullets and set out to validate her excuse. Lucas offered to accompany her, but she was adamant in her refusal. He smiled at her determination to see that he rested. Settling under the shade of a pine, he relaxed against the trunk, grateful for a chance to rest. He was perturbed that riding even that short distance had fatigued him, and that he was still a burden to Miranda. His self-respect demanded he do something to lighten her load.

Seized with an idea, he left his resting place and skillfully fashioned himself a fishing pole from a long stick, some string, and a piece of wire. If Miranda's hunt was successful, they would have a feast. If not, they would both welcome the trout. Threading a worm onto his makeshift hook, he settled down at a likely-looking place by the river for an afternoon of fishing.

As he lazily watched his line drift in the current, his eyes fell upon a wild rosebush across the river. It immediately reminded him of Miranda. Unlike the stately, cultivated roses, its blossoms were not perfectly symmetrical or showy but possessed a simple beauty, no less breathtaking for its subtlety. Miranda was like those yellow roses, bringing sunshine and beauty into his life with elegant understatement. He had learned a lot about the priggish English girl he had met in San Francisco. Most startling was the fact that she was not at all what he had originally assumed but a woman worthy of respect and admiration with an underlying wildness that was in vivid contrast to her gentle manners.

A tug on his line brought Lucas's attention back to the river. With little effort he had a trout in hand. He strung the fish on a stick, then rebaited his hook, frowning as he thought of the time in the near future when he would have to say good-bye to Miranda. He had mistreated her from the beginning. If he had acted the gentleman, he might have had a chance to win her affection, but now it was too late. He could hardly expect her to be eager to spend her life with a man who had abused her at every turn. Was it any wonder she viewed his marriage proposal with such revulsion?

By the time Miranda returned with two plump quail, Lucas had managed to land four large trout. He set his pole aside, carrying his catch back to camp when he saw her approach.

"It looks like we'll eat like kings tonight." Miranda eyed the trout appreciatively. She would have preferred Lucas to have spent the afternoon napping but reasoned that a quiet afternoon of fishing had probably done him no harm. He looked rested.

"After I clean these fish I'll pluck the birds," Lucas stated.

"No, I can do it." Miranda leaned her rifle against the trunk of a tree.

"Then I'll gather wood for a fire."

"Just sit still and relax. You've had a hard day."

"And I suppose you've done nothing all day." He looked down at Miranda in exasperation. "Miranda, I want to help you."

"Help me by taking care of yourself," she chided.

"I am not some sickly child who requires my every

need to be seen to. The chest is a little sore, but I'm perfectly capable of pulling my own weight.''

Miranda shook her head at his determination. She searched her mind for an appropriate task. ''If it will make you happy, you can sit by the fire and turn the birds while they roast.''

''Hmph!'' Lucas scowled as Miranda gently pushed him to a sitting position. ''You're getting too bossy.'' Despite his protests, he did as he was told.

The evening passed pleasantly. The next morning they rose early to continue their journey. Again Miranda insisted they travel slowly, stopping frequently for long rests. The bruise on Lucas's head had faded to a greenish yellow, and his coloring had returned to normal, but Miranda was taking no chances with his health. Though he took great pains to hide it from her, she knew his chest still caused him discomfort.

It took them four days to reach the settlement of Coloma. They stopped to make camp slightly downriver near Sutter's Mill, the sight of the first gold discovery.

Walking along the trace of the abandoned sawmill, Lucas related the story of how James Marshall had been building the sawmill for John Sutter when he discovered the small granule of gold that set off dreams of endless wealth and the mad rush to the land of El Dorado. It was incredible that the chance discovery of such a small bit of metal could affect so many lives throughout the world. Men had left businesses, wives, families, all for the chance of filling their pockets with the precious yellow metal. Even she, living thousands of miles away, had had her entire life disrupted by this one small event.

It took three days to reach Sacramento City after leaving Sutter's Mill. Even in the few months they had been gone, the city had grown noticeably. More permanent buildings had been added to the cityscape, but saloons and gaming hells still dominated the scene. As they passed one such establishment, a combination hotel-saloon, Miranda eyed the rooms longingly. She would almost be willing to sell her soul for a real bed and a hot bath. It had been so long since she had had either, she could barely remember what they felt like.

Lucas, not blind to the look of longing in her eyes, brought the horses to a halt but hesitated to suggest that they rent rooms. The establishment was not the type a lady should patronize, yet there was such yearning in Miranda's eyes, he decided to risk offending her.

"Would you like to take rooms here?"

Miranda's eyes instantly lit up, then, remembering her lack of money, she slowly shook her head. Even after she sold her animals she would not be able to afford to indulge in such a luxury.

Sensing the direction of her thoughts, Lucas offered, "My treat. A sort of thank-you for nursing me back to health." His smile was beguiling.

Miranda knew she should not accept, but for the life of her she couldn't bring herself to turn him down. "Thank you, Lucas. I'd love to sleep in a real bed." She smiled in gratitude.

The matter was settled. They hitched their animals to the post in front of the hotel and stepped inside to inquire about lodgings.

The lower floor of the building was occupied by a bar and gaming tables. A small dining area was set to one side. Three roulette wheels were spinning for patrons willing to risk their gold on a game of chance. In addition, various card games were in progress at the tables set around the room, while scantily clad women hovered about the players in hopes of distracting them from the game. The room was lavishly decorated, and a huge gilded mirror hung behind the bar, reflecting the activity of the room. Cut-glass bowls filled with cigars, lemons, and peppermints were placed at even intervals down the length of the bar. To the right a staircase spiraled its way to the second floor. Although the room's decor was rather overstated for Miranda's taste, the place was definitely the most richly appointed she had seen in California. She cringed inwardly at the thought of what a night's lodgings in this hotel would cost.

She stood near the door while Lucas approached the man behind the bar. He returned a few moments later, two keys dangling from his hand. Lifting the two small bundles containing their personal articles, he offered Miranda his arm.

"Miss Austen, our rooms await."

"Lucas, are you sure you want to do this?" Miranda questioned. "This place looks terribly expensive."

"Everything in California is terribly expensive," he countered, his eyes twinkling. "But for tonight we will ignore the fact and think of nothing but our own pleasure. After that we can become sensible again.''

"Then lead on.'' Miranda placed her hand on his arm, deciding to take his advice and forget about the more practical side of life for the night.

"I have taken the liberty of ordering a bath to be brought up to your room,'' Lucas informed her. "I hope you don't take offense at the gesture.''

"Offense? I could almost kiss you!'' The words burst forth before she had time to consider them.

"Almost, huh?'' Lucas eyed her with a half smile. "I wonder what I have to do to win the prize?''

"Behave yourself, Mr. Adams. Your chest is healing nicely. I would hate to have to cause it further injury.'' Miranda smiled as she made the threat. The thought of a long, hot bath put her in such good humor that even Lucas's teasing could not irritate her. Having proven to herself and him that she was a capable woman with a will of her own, she no longer felt so threatened by his slightly suggestive humor.

"If good behavior will win me a kiss from your fair lips, I must be doubly sure to mind my Ps and Qs.'' They had reached the door of her room, and handing Miranda her bundle, Lucas turned to his room directly across the hall.

"You know that's not what I meant.'' Miranda spoke the words to his back, slightly piqued by the way he had purposely misread the meaning of her words.

Lucas entered his room. He turned his head toward her, letting out an exaggerated sigh of longing, then quickly closed the door before she had a chance to remark on his gesture.

Smiling, Miranda entered her own room. She was delighted to find a generously proportioned, raised bed covered with a thick quilt. The room was also furnished with a dressing table and a small washstand with a brightly painted porcelain bowl and pitcher, but it was the bed that held Miranda's interest. She sat on the edge, testing its softness and sighing with pleasure as she ran her fingers over the feather tick.

A knock at the door interrupted her reverie. She reluctantly rose to answer. In walked two rather burly men carrying a bathtub, followed by a third with two large buckets of steaming water. Their irritation at being asked to carry the heavy tub up the stairs immediately dissipated upon seeing Miranda's smile of pleasure. They set their burden in the middle of the room, then excused themselves, the third man promising to return with more water.

When the additional water had been provided, along with a rough towel and a large bar of soap, Miranda closed the door against further intrusion, then poured the steaming water into the tub, adding just enough cold to make it bearable. She planned to soak a long, long time and didn't want the water to cool too quickly. Satisfied with the temperature, she laid out fresh undergarments along with her wine-colored gown. Discarding her soiled clothes in a heap on the floor, she eased into the inviting water, reveling in the sensation of the warmth enveloping her skin.

The ends of her long, dark hair spread out like a

fan on the water's surface as she rested her head against the rim of the tub, relaxing and finding a simple joy in the water's silky smoothness.

When she could no longer ignore the fact that the water had become tepid, she opened her eyes and reached for the soap. She scrubbed off the layers of dust until her skin blushed with a healthy glow. Turning her attention to her hair, she lathered it with the same enthusiasm, using the water she had reserved in one of the buckets for the final rinse.

She had spent a good hour in the tub, but still she left it with reluctance to dry herself and put on clean clothes. She applied the towel vigorously to her hair, not wanting to stay in her room long hours while she waited for it to dry, and she tied it at the nape of her neck with a ribbon. She had just begun to pick up her soiled clothing when she heard a knock at the door. Assuming it was the proprietor coming to retrieve the tub, she called out, bidding him enter. Turning, she saw Lucas enter her room, looking as fresh and clean as herself.

"I was beginning to think you might have drowned," he teased her, glancing at his pocket-watch. "It's lucky this hotel has more than one tub, or the rest of the guests would have been left to sit in their own dust."

"It's been months since I had a proper bath," Miranda said, defending herself, then adding with a mischievous grin, "It took awhile to scrub off all that dirt."

"The effect was well worth the wait." Lucas smiled his approval. To his mind Miranda would look ravishing in a flour sack; when dressed fashionably, she was truly dazzling. "If you're ready to join me for dinner, I'll tell you what I've been up to while you had your soak in the tub."

His words made Miranda realize she had grown quite famished. After a final glance in the mirror to be sure her hair was presentable, she allowed Lucas to escort her down the stairs to the hotel dining area. It was set to one side of the saloon. The small round tables were covered with white linen and set with sturdy white china.

They ordered a steak dinner, Lucas topping off the meal with a generous slice of apple pie. Miranda, much too full to even think of dessert, sipped blissfully at a long-denied cup of tea. During the meal Lucas informed her he had found a buyer for her horse and mule if she were still interested in selling them. In addition, he had arranged passage back to San Francisco by steamer, explaining it would take less time to make the trip by boat.

Miranda readily agreed to both plans, though with San Francisco within reach, she was suddenly filled with a fear of the future. For the first time in her life she would be truly on her own, without family, without friends. Even after her father's death she had not felt so alone. She had had Lucas, no matter how stormy their relationship, and the friendship of the other miners. She wondered how long Lucas would be staying in San Francisco before he returned to his home in Oregon. Regardless, she knew she would not seek him out once they had parted company. In a day or two they would say good-bye and never see each other again.

A shadow passed over her eyes as she realized how

much she was going to miss Lucas's daily presence. With new insight she realized it had not been her father she had turned to for guidance and protection in the gold fields but Lucas. Even in his anger he had not left her or submitted her to the rough brand of justice in this land, which he might very well have done. Even then he had protected her. In her heart she knew that the supposedly forced seduction was partly her fault. She had allowed him too many liberties. Lucas was obviously the sort of man who could not stand too much temptation. The lion's share of the blame still fell on his shoulders. But she had unwittingly tempted him beyond control, so she still must accept some of the blame. That she had responded to his advances still disturbed her. She could not understand why she had not fought him to the bitter end. In her mind it made her less of a lady than she would have liked to believe herself. While one might excuse Lucas's behavior as the natural lust of a man, women of breeding were not supposed to be affected by such things. No matter how he made her feel, she should have resisted him.

"You're very thoughtful tonight," Lucas said, interrupting her musings.

"I'm sorry. I didn't mean to be rude." Miranda looked up at him. "I was just thinking about the last few months in the gold fields. It really is finally over, isn't it? I'm glad, but I just don't know if I can fit back into normal society. I've changed so much."

"Are you sorry you came out here?" Lucas questioned gently.

"In many ways, yes, but still, I'm glad I came. I've seen so many wonderful things I would never have seen if I hadn't . . . and maybe, I'm just a bit wiser than when I started out. I suppose one should never wish away her life experiences. They all seem to have some value." Miranda took a sip of her now-cold tea.

"I believe you've turned philosopher," Lucas commented with a grin, then continued more seriously. "But you're right. It's the opportunities I let slip by more than the mistakes I made that I regret the most. At least I can learn something from my mistakes, whereas the other availed me nothing."

"So you're not sorry you agreed to guide my father and I?"

"What?" Lucas's blue eyes gave her a thorough perusal. "And miss watching a proper little English maid turn into a seasoned mountain woman? Before we started out, I would never have believed it. You still look as though a feather could blow you away. But underneath that prim and proper exterior lurks all kind of surprises." Though Lucas had not intended his statement as anything but a compliment, the remark hit too close to the truth Miranda was not quite willing to accept.

"If I am no longer proper, it is because you made me so," she returned rather acidly.

"You're the touchiest female I ever met." Lucas was quickly becoming exasperated with her habit of misinterpreting his words and taking offense. He could hardly speak anymore without fear of insulting her in some way. He had neither the inclination nor the energy to plan everything he said.

Rising from his seat, he suggested, "Since we're both finished, let's get out of here. If you like, we can go for a walk; otherwise, I'll take you back to your room.''

Miranda looked up at Lucas in indecision. They had so little time left together, and she wanted their relationship to end on a friendly note. Still, letting her feelings toward him soften had already caused her irreparable damage. ''I think I'll go back to my room.'' She spoke the words with regret, which he did not notice.

He was not pleased with her choice. ''Then I'll take you up.''

''I can find my own way, if there is something else you'd like to do.'' He looked so grim, Miranda wished she had decided on the walk.

''Then I'll leave you here.'' Lucas's tone was even, but she knew she had irritated him. He was absently rubbing the back of his neck as if it pained him.

''Good night,'' Miranda said as she started up the stairs. When she was halfway up, she turned back, seeing Lucas head for the bar, she reconsidered and continued her ascent.

Once inside her room she changed into her night shift, but not even the anticipation of the invitingly soft bed could lift her spirits. Despite what she had said earlier, she wished she and Lucas could have met in a different place, under different circumstances. He could have courted her gently and perhaps . . . No, it never would have happened. Lucas did not want marriage. Though he had proposed it once, he had never mentioned the subject again. At the time he had made his offer out of guilt and remorse, not out of any desire to have her as his wife. She could never accept marriage to him on those terms.

"And me, what do I feel?" She spoke out loud to her reflection in the mirror. "At least Lucas knows what he wants. I can't even decide whether I love him or hate him. It seems I have cause for both." It was true. He was hardworking, sober, and, above all, responsible. But the one major flaw in his character could not be easily overlooked. He was not a gentleman. He had taken advantage of a situation no gentleman would have allowed in the first place.

Oh, what did it matter? Once she reached San Francisco she would never see him again. That thought was so depressing, Miranda threw herself across the bed with a sob and cried herself to sleep, unmindful of the downy softness of her resting place.

Lucas slid onto the seat before the bar and ordered a whiskey. He was not a man given to hard liquor, but at the moment a drink seemed in order. His eyes involuntarily drifted up the stairs.

A voice to his left caught his attention. "Woman trouble, huh? She sure is a pretty one."

"What?" Lucas turned his head toward the voice. It belonged to a thin, sinewy man with a grizzled beard. "Yes, she is very pretty." Lucas's hand continued to massage the back of his neck.

"Well, that whiskey should help dull the pain, though I can't say as I can feel too sympathetic. Most men 'round here, includin' myself, would give plenty just for a woman to have trouble with. Name's John Smith, originally from Arkansas." The man offered his hand to Lucas.

Grasping the knobby member in a firm shake, Lucas chuckled. "Are you advising me to count my blessings?"

"You might say that." John Smith grinned, exposing uneven, yellow teeth as he returned Lucas's grip with strength surprising for a man his size. "I don't mean to be nosy, but where'd she come from? She don't look like none of the gals from these parts."

"She's from England. She came here with her father, but he died in the gold fields. I've sort of been taking care of her since then." Lucas could not fathom why he was telling a stranger all this, but he felt he could use a friendly ear, and this John fellow seemed more than willing to listen.

"And she wants you to marry her to make the relationship respectable? 'less you've got a wife waitin' back home, if you don't mind me sayin' so, you could do a whole lot worse . . . . Of course, I don't know the woman. Perhaps she's a nag. There ain't no greater hell on this earth than to be married to a whinin' woman." John, looking a bit shamefaced, pulled a handkerchief from his pocket and wiped it across his brow.

"Do you speak from experience?" Lucas asked, intrigued that the little man spoke on the subject with such conviction.

"Had a wife once in Arkansas. Pretty as a picture but with a tongue that would make the devil himself cringe. Take my advice, son. If the woman's a whiner, hightail it out of here and don't never look back." It was advice given from the heart.

"Where is your wife now?"

"Don't rightly know," John admitted. "Left her

years ago . . . . I suppose she's still naggin' away somewhere. By now she's probably given me up for dead and married some other poor fool. Me, I'm just sort of a free spirit. Had me a few good women since. Best was an Indian from the Shoshone tribe. Liked her so well I married her, but she died a few years ago of the fever. But here I'm ramblin' on 'bout myself, and you're the one with a problem,'' John apologized.

"You can rest easy. Miranda is not a whiner. Most uncomplaining woman I ever met. But she's temperamental. She'll turn on me, and half the time I don't even know why . . . . And you're wrong about her wanting marriage. I offered once, and she turned me down flat. Not that I really wanted to marry her. I was just trying to do the decent thing.'' Lucas took advantage of the opportunity to unload his troubles.

"Then I don't see what your problem is. Enjoy her while you can, then walk away when she gets to be more bother than she's worth,'' John counseled, as if it were the most obvious thing in the world.

"I can't do that. I feel so damn responsible for her. The woman saved my life. How am I supposed to just walk away and never look back?'' Lucas questioned, exasperated by the man's inability to grasp the complexity of his problem. He suddenly wished John would leave him alone.

"Well, if you're in love with her, there ain't nothing I can tell you.'' John rose from his chair, sensing that his presence was no longer wanted. "There's no helpin' a man in your condition.'' He patted Lucas on the back sympathetically before walking across the room to pull up a chair and join in a game of monte.

Lucas stared into his half-empty glass for a few moments, then downed the remainder of its contents in a single gulp, ignoring the fiery sensation of the liquid as it burned down his throat. What John Smith had said was ridiculous. His problem was not that he was in love with Miranda, it was that he needed a woman. For a long time she had been the only one available. Naturally his attention had focused on her. What he needed could be easily bought, then he would be free of this obsession that had ruled his life of late. Turning his back to the bar, he surveyed the room until his eyes came to rest on a voluptuous blond leaning provocatively over a table as she served the men their drinks. When she straightened, he caught her eye, motioning her to approach him.

"What can I do for you, lovey?" Her eyes perused him invitingly. "Are you a bit lonely tonight?"

Lucas took in the view of her amply displayed bosom as she pressed toward him but felt no quickening in his loins. All he could think about was the look of hurt and disapproval Miranda would give him if she could see him now. With a muffled groan he raised his eyes to the woman's face.

"I'm sorry I bothered you." He rose from his seat, eager to quit the place. "I just remembered I was supposed to meet somebody, and I'm already late."

"Maybe some other time." The woman waved him on his way, a bit disappointed. The man had recently taken a bath, something not many of her patrons could boast.

Lucas took the stairs two at a time, eager for the solitude of his room. As he reached the door the sound of muffled weeping caught his attention. He crossed the hall, hesitating before Miranda's door, then, deciding against entering, retraced his steps and entered his own room. He felt grumpy and out of sorts. John Smith's words continued to haunt him as he undressed for bed. What he felt for Miranda was respect and a goodly amount of desire. He enjoyed her company, and that was all. He draped his shirt and trousers over the back of a chair before sitting on the edge of the bed to remove his boots. Realizing how thickheaded he was being, he threw himself across the bed, wincing as he made contact with the mattress.

Of course, you love her, you idiot. What was love but friendship and respect? His burning desire for Miranda was a natural result of his desire to be a part of her life in every way. It was pointless to deny he loved her, just as it was pointless to think anything would ever come of it. He had made too many mistakes.

Miranda awoke the next morning to the sound of loud knocking on her door. "Just a minute." She quickly rose and dressed before answering the door.

"I hate to disturb you, but we've quite a lot to do before we catch the steamer," Lucas greeted her, thinking how beautiful she looked with her hair framing her face in wild disarray. God, he was going to miss her!

"I'll be ready in a minute." Miranda yawned as she pushed a strand of hair from her eyes. She poured some water from the pitcher into the bowl on the washstand and splashed the cold liquid over her face and neck. She hoped her eyes did not betray last nights tears. Taking up her brush, she smoothed the tangles from her hair before plaiting it and securing it into a neat bun at the nape of her neck.

After a quick check in the mirror she announced, "I'm ready."

"Then we're off." Lucas guided her out of the room with a firm hand placed on the small of her back.

They ate a light breakfast, then went to meet the man who had agreed to buy Miranda's horse and mule. He was also persuaded that used equipment was just as good as new, and considerably cheaper. When the transaction was complete, Miranda had enough money to see her through for a month, maybe two, if she were exceptionally frugal, which would give her the time she would need to find employment. It helped bolster her spirits a little.

Lucas had also found a buyer for his horse. After completing their business with him they were left with little more than their personal belongings, though both were considerably heavier in the pocket.

At noon they gathered the few belongings they had left at the hotel, then walked to the docks to board the steamer. The ship was not crowded on the down-river trip. Miranda stood by the railing, watching with mixed feelings as a chapter of her life drifted out of sight with the fading view of Sacramento City.

Chapter 15

The trip downriver, though uneventful, was strained. Miranda's emotions seemed to churn with the water, and as each rotation of the paddlewheel brought them closer to San Francisco, her newfound confidence began to dissolve. Lucas was unusually withdrawn. For once his ready wit had deserted him. Was he relieved that he would soon be rid of her? Try as she might, she could not divine his thoughts. Though she tried to present a cheerful countenance, more often than not, her conversations with Lucas were short, to the point of being curt.

That night she sat on the berth in her cabin watching the undulating shadows cast on the floor by the swinging lantern overhead. In the morning they would arrive in San Francisco. The past two days had been horrible. Her nerves were on edge. She wanted their remaining time together to be pleasant, but instead she had been all but openly rude to Lucas. It shouldn't end like this.

What she needed to do was to go to Lucas and tell him she had forgiven him. He had given her so much during the past months. She needed to tell him how grateful she was for the time they had had together. Jumping from her bed, she ran out of her cabin.

She hesitated at the door of the adjoining cabin, then, before she lost her nerve she knocked firmly on the door. A moment later it swung open, but as she gazed up into Lucas's blue eyes, words deserted her. He was clearly surprised to see her.

"Did you need something?" Lucas questioned.

Miranda nervously shifted her weight from foot to foot. It wouldn't do to stand in the doorway staring at him. She searched for an excuse to explain her presence.

"I've come to check your stitches." She stepped into the cabin. "I might not have another chance before we disembark."

"The wounds are almost healed, but you're welcome to see for yourself if it will make you feel better."

"Yes, I really would feel better. If you'll remove your shirt and lie on the bunk, this will just take a minute." Miranda couldn't believe what a mess she was making of what she had intended to be a simple apology. Why wouldn't her tongue cooperate? A simple "thank you for all you've done" and she could be on her way.

Lucas laid his shirt across the back of a chair, then stretched out on the bed. Miranda was acting oddly tonight. It seemed strange that she just didn't wait until morning to check his chest. There would be plenty of time before they reached San Francisco.

She sat on the edge of the bunk and began a careful inspection of Lucas's wounds. She moved her fore-

finger cautiously over each seam, testing to be sure
the skin was knitting together properly. She watched
Lucas's expression as she pressed on the wounds.
His face registered little pain. His chest was so beautiful. She ran her fingers lightly through the soft hairs
covering his powerful muscles. Even the scars did
not diminish his manly appeal. She needed him so
much, wanted him so much.

Rising from the bed, she reached up and doused
the lantern. Her clothing slipped from her shoulders
to the floor. She joined Lucas on the bunk, snuggling
against his side as she lay her head on his shoulder.

"Miranda?"

She silenced his lips with her fingertips.

Lucas could not see her expression in the darkness. When he made no move, Miranda's lips sought
his, gently at first, but her kisses quickly increased
in intensity. Rising on her knees, her hands slid to
his waist, and she removed his trousers, returning to
lay full-length against him, flesh caressing flesh.
Slowly his arms encircled her, holding her to him in
silent embrace. He no longer cared why she had
come to him. She was here, next to his heart, where
she belonged.

They lay quietly, stroking each other, tasting each
other's flesh. Theirs was a slow loving, a studied
loving. They left no inch of each other unexplored.

He massaged the soft cheeks of her buttocks,
molding her more intimately to him. Warm lips caressed her toes, her breasts, the hollow at the base of
her neck. His tongue teased hers as their lips embraced.

She, in turn, kissed his eyes, his lips. She nibbled

the lobe of one ear. His beard tickled her nose as she burrowed her face to his neck. Her hands kneaded the hard muscles of his upper arms and stroked the sensitive flesh of his inner thighs.

When Lucas entered her, there was none of the impassioned frenzy of their earlier joining. Instead their hips swayed to the rhythm of a slow, sensual dance. Neither desired to rush to passion's peak, preferring to stoke their mutual fire leisurely, drawing pleasure from each moment they remained locked in intimate embrace.

When, at length, they could delay the consuming flames no longer, they found release together, their passion burning to a bed of smoldering embers. Still joined, they drifted off to sleep.

It was still dark when Miranda awoke. She slipped quietly from the bed and donned her clothes. She had forgiven Lucas the only way she knew how. By openly giving herself to him, she had erased all blame. Taking care not to wake him, she placed a parting kiss on his cheek before returning to her own cabin.

A short time later Miranda stood by the ship's railing, watching the tree-lined shore drift by. The sun had risen above the treetops, lighting the September sky. She looked up as she heard footsteps approaching, then averted her eyes as Lucas came to join her.

"I missed you when I awoke this morning," he said, greeting her with a contented grin. "Have you had breakfast yet?"

"Yes." Miranda did not turn to face him as she spoke.

"Want to eat again?" Lucas invited, his eyes

twinkling merrily. When she did not respond, his mood sobered. He studied her in silence for several minutes. Miranda was clearly unhappy.

"I think we should talk."

"We've nothing to say." Miranda wished he would just let things be. She had no intention of discussing the previous night. In the light of day she doubted that her actions could bear close scrutiny.

"But, Miranda, if you're unhappy . . ."

"Lucas, I am not unhappy. Go have your breakfast." She turned to face him. Her eyes were dark and unreadable. "I really should go organize my belongings. I want to be ready to leave the ship when we dock. I'm starting a new life as an independent woman today." She forced herself to sound eager about meeting the challenges awaiting her. Before Lucas could respond, she left him standing alone at the railing.

Lucas shook his head in confusion as he watched her retreat. Why was she acting so cool this morning? After last night he had thought . . . What *had* he thought? He had not understood her last night any more than he did now. One simply could not apply the rules of logic when trying to discern what motivated the woman. The only thing he could assume with reasonable certainty was that Miranda did not desire his company this morning. He forced himself to respect her wishes.

Miranda remained in her cabin until she heard the steamer grind to a halt. It had taken less than five minutes to gather her belongings. The remainder of the morning she had spent thinking, a pastime she found highly disturbing. It had been a mistake to go to Lucas's cabin last night. What if he guessed the truth? She could not bear to have her feelings ridiculed, or worse yet, have Lucas stay with her out of a sense of obligation. The man valued his freedom above all else, but she knew he credited her with saving his life. If he discovered she had fallen in love with him, it was very possible he would feel dutybound to burden himself with her care. She must never let him know how strong her attachment to him was.

Her belongings in hand, Miranda walked out on deck. Lucas came to join her, relieving her of her small bundle. Together they stood waiting for the gangway to be secured in place.

San Francisco had grown while they were away, but it still possessed the character of an unruly teenager, having grown up too quickly and without discipline. Schooling her expression to one of cheerful anticipation, Miranda willed her knees to cease their trembling and followed Lucas off the ship.

They walked in silence to Mr. Clark's store. A new brightly painted shingle hung over the doorway.

"Well, this is where we say good-bye." Miranda took her bundle of belongings from Lucas's arms. She swallowed the hard lump in her throat.

"I'll see you get settled," Lucas offered, opening the door for her.

"No, I can manage." If he stayed a moment longer, she might lose her composure and beg him to stay with her. In all her life she had never wanted anything so badly. "You had better see to your own lodgings . . . . Godspeed, Lucas." Before Lucas could reply, Miranda entered the store, closing the door firmly behind her. She paused, taking a firm grip on her emotions.

Mr. Clark was not in the front of the store. After waiting a few minutes for him to appear she stepped into the doorway of the back room.

"Mr. Clark, are you here?" she called to the figure on a ladder at the back of the storageroom.

"Be right with you," he replied from his perch.

Miranda stepped back into the front of the store. The shelves were well stocked with a wide variety of items. It appeared Mr. Clark was doing well for himself.

"Now, may I help you?" Mr. Clark entered the room, dusting his hands on his pant legs. He stared at Miranda for a moment, then burst into a smile. "Miss Austen, is that you?"

"Yes, Mr. Clark, it's me. I've finally come back from the gold fields." Miranda returned his smile with an effort. She hoped he wasn't in the mood for a long chat, as she knew she would not be able to maintain her cheerful mask for long.

"I suppose you'll be wanting your trunks. If you'll tell me where you're staying, I'll have some lads bring them around. How did you father do? I don't see him with you." He raised a knowing eyebrow. "I suppose he couldn't wait to spend some of his newfound wealth on a little entertainment."

"My father died in the gold fields, Mr. Clark. I'm afraid he never struck it rich."

"I'm sorry, miss," Mr. Clark said, offering his condolences.

"I was hoping I could have our old room back. I will be staying in San Francisco for a while." Miranda did not want to dwell on the fact that her father was no longer with her.

Mr. Clark hesitated.

"If you're worried about the rent, I have enough to pay you. I'm not asking for charity," Miranda quickly explained.

"It's not that," Mr. Clark began, looking uncomfortable. "The room is already rented out. As far as I know, the fellow is comfortable with the place and plans to stay on indefinitely."

"I see." Miranda tried to hide her disappointment. "Could you suggest some other suitable place I might find lodgings?"

"There is always the hotels, but they are a bit steep."

Miranda shook her head to this suggestion.

"The only other place I can think of is a boardinghouse for single women. It's near the docks, but I'm afraid it's no place for a respectable lady. Most of the boarders are . . . members of a . . . a profession that is ..."

"I understand, Mr. Clark." Miranda came to his rescue. "Is the rent reasonable?"

"As low as you'll find in this city, but I think you should consider a hotel. The neighborhood is a bit rough."

"I'm afraid my funds don't allow me to be too choosy. If you will give me directions, I'll be on my way. I can send around for my things when I get settled."

Mr. Clark gave her the necessary directions, and after a polite farewell, she set off to find the boardinghouse. It was easily located. As Miranda eyed it

in indecision she thought that Mr. Clark had painted
a rather rosy picture of the place. It stood crowded
between two other unpainted, clapboard structures,
showing ample evidence that it was built near the
weathering sea. Though everything in San Francisco
was new, one would guess it to be at least a hundred
years old, judging by its appearance. The two-story
building had a slight tilt, though Miranda could not
determine if it was the ground or the building itself
that sat at an angle. Squaring her shoulders, she
stepped up to the door and knocked.

After she waited an appropriate amount of time she
knocked again. A few moments later the door was
answered by an unkempt woman in her mid-forties.
The bright red of her lip paint clashed with the purple
of her dress, cut to reveal more than was wise for a
woman with a fading figure. Her graying hair strag-
gled about her face.

"What do you want?" she asked in irritation.

"I came to see about a room," Miranda informed
her, forcing herself not to draw back as she was engulfed in the cloud of perfume that surrounded the
woman.

With a snort the landlady motioned her inside an
untidy parlor. "Rent is eighteen dollars a week. You
can use the kitchen, but you got to clean up your
mess. I don't put my nose in your business; I expect
you to do likewise. Payment is due in advance." She
held out a plump hand.

Telling herself she was in no position to be particular, Miranda paid the woman, then followed her up
the stairs.

"This is it." The woman threw open one of the

doors lining the hall. Without further comment she ambled back down the stairs.

Miranda shuddered as she entered the room. It reeked of stale urine. Striding across the room, she threw back the shutters of the paneless window, sucking in deep breaths of fresh air. With grim determination she searched out the source of the offensive odor, a badly stained chamberpot. Picking up the malodorous article with her thumb and forefinger, she glanced out the window to be sure the alley was free of foot traffic, then tossed it out. That accomplished, she turned her attention back to the room.

It was furnished with nothing but a washstand and cot-styled bed, both covered with a thick layer of dust. The bed had a feather mattress but no linen.

Miranda sat on the edge of the bed staring forlornly around the room. This was not exactly what she had planned. She had counted on the room at Mr. Clark's. Lucas was gone; she was reduced to living in a sty, and she had no source of income. It was too much. Burying her face in her hands, she gave up her last threads of composure. It was a long time before she roused herself enough to prepare for bed.

After leaving Miranda Lucas had found comfortable lodgings in a modest hotel. Remembering their last night together, he had decided he was not going to give Miranda up without one last effort. He would be leaving for Oregon on the first ship out, and he wanted her with him. They belonged together. It was with this goal in mind that he determined to visit her and again ask her to become his wife. After quickly downing a hearty breakfast the next morning he set out for Clark's store.

"Morning, Mr. Clark. Is Miranda up and about yet?" he said, greeting the proprietor. Having decided on a course of action, Lucas was eager to implement his plan.

"Oh, aren't you that friend of hers? I'm afraid she's not staying here, but I'll give you directions to where she said she was going." Mr. Clark was relieved someone was looking after Miranda. It helped ease his conscience.

Lucas was surprised by this news. "Tell me where she's staying."

Mr. Clark gave him directions to the boarding-house, then added as a second thought, "If you're going directly there, maybe you could take her trunk. She will probably be needing some of her things."

Lucas followed Mr. Clark into the storeroom to retrieve the trunk, then set off down the street. The area where he eventually found himself was not one he thought of as suitable. Stopping before Miranda's new home, he shook his head in disgust. Inquiring at the door, he made his way up to her room.

"Coming," Miranda said in answer to the knock at her door. She was dresssed and about to leave to buy a generous supply of cleaning items to make her room habitable. Opening the door, she was startled to see Lucas standing on the threshold with her trunk.

"May I come in?" he asked, his face clearly showing his opinion of her new lodgings.

"Yes, please do. You can put the trunk over by the bed." Miranda opened the door wide so he could enter. What was he doing here? She couldn't face another farewell scene.

When he had set the trunk on the floor, Lucas turned to her. "What are you doing in a place like this? I thought you had better sense."

"The rent is low."

"It should be." Lucas wrinkled his nose. Despite her sleeping with the window open, the room still smelled. "I wouldn't let a dog sleep in a place like this. Do you know this is a boardinghouse for prostitutes?"

"I know it needs a thorough cleaning and the neighborhood isn't the best, but it's affordable. Once I find some sort of employment, I will look for a better situation." Miranda tried to reassure herself as well as Lucas.

"Do you expect me to let you stay in this hellhole?" Lucas questioned in exasperation. It would be like leaving a lamb in a den of wolves. Miranda was too trusting. It would be a simple matter for her more worldly neighbors to take advantage of her naïveté. Look how easily he had been able to deceive her and use her for his own selfish purposes.

"The decision is not yours to make." She knew how bad her circumstances were. What right did he have to make her feel any worse than she already did? She didn't want his pity. She refused to be a burden to him anymore.

"Miranda, stay with me." Lucas took a step forward and reached out for her. "Let me take care of you. You deserve better than this."

Miranda blinked back tears of pain as she shook her head. More than anything in the world she wanted to accept Lucas's offer, but her pride wouldn't let her. "I don't want your help."

"I'm offering marriage, not some sordid arrangement," Lucas explained, thinking she might have misunderstood his offer.

"I know," Miranda returned in a cool, even tone. "I thought I had made it quite plain. I have no desire to become your wife." It took more effort than Lucas could ever know for her to retain her composure. He was offering her exactly what she wanted, but in a way she could not accept. His words made it clear he felt obligated to see her to her welfare. Lucas might be willing to spend the rest of his life paying for his mistakes, but she would prefer a life of loneliness to the role of jailer. He would come to hate her. A marriage could not be built on such a sorry emotion as pity.

"Then I will take my leave," Lucas responded to her statement with a coolness that matched her own. "Good-bye, Miranda, I hope you get what you want out of life." He turned on his heels and walked out of her life, closing the door firmly behind him.

"I want you to love me." She spoke the words to the closed portal. "I want you to love me." Refusing to give in to another fit of tears, she forced herself to sort through the contents of her trunk. She hung her dresses on a row of nails provided on one wall but left the other items folded neatly in the chest.

Though she knew she should set out immediately in search of employment, she hadn't the heart for it. Instead she let the condition of her room serve as an excuse to put it off.

After a brief trip to purchase the necessary cleaning materials and enough groceries to see her through a day or two, she attacked the filth of her room with a vengeance. Nothing was left untouched. By the end of the day the room, though far from homey, had given up the lingering odors of its former occupant and was probably cleaner than it had ever been. Miranda surveyed the room, satisfied with the change she had wrought. She went downstairs to fix herself a light supper; then, having nothing better to do, she retired.

She awoke the next morning to a dreary, gray drizzle that was a perfect reflection of her mood. She knew Lucas would not return. Again she excused herself from looking for work, reasoning after trudging through the rain and mud that she couldn't possibly present a very promising picture to her prospective employers.

She wandered around the boardinghouse part of the day. While most of her fellow boarders were friendly enough, it seemed everyone had a place they needed to be in a hurry. No one had time to spare in small talk with the new boarder. Consequently she spent the majority of her day alone in her room, brooding. She tried not to attribute her dejected state to the absence of the rough, bearded man who had been such an intimate part of her life but rather to her distressful circumstances. Until recently she had never dreamed she would be forced to seek employment, and she had not the slightest idea how to go about it.

She had the education to be a governess, but if there was one thing in shorter supply than women in California, it was children. Besides, without references she couldn't imagine anyone trusting her with the education of their children.

She had yet to see a woman working in one of the supply stores, but maybe that was by choice and not because they were not welcome.

Sewing was another possibility; however, she would have to find some shop willing to hire her, as she had no capital to open her own. Even renting ground to set up a tent in the business district was well beyond her means.

There were only two areas of employment that held any great promise: the gaming hells and brothels. She could not imagine ever becoming so desperate that she would accept work in either quarter.

The rain continued, and it was almost a week before Miranda was able to rouse herself enough to begin her search for employment. She soon discovered that while the proprieters of the many stores she applied to were sympathetic, they either did not need help or they required the services of an able-bodied man who could lift the heavy crates of merchandise. Even Mr. Clark had nothing to offer.

Though her skill as a cook was questionable, she made inquiries at some of the smaller cafés. Only one was interested in hiring her, though not for her services as a waitress or cook. Miranda let the proprieter know in no uncertain terms what she thought of his proposal, then treated him to a decidely uncomplimentary appraisal of his character.

Next she returned to the shop where Lucas had had her dresses made. The woman could not offer her work but gave her a lead to two other places where she might inquire. At the end of a week she was no closer to finding work than before, and her spirits sunk to new depths.

In desperation she returned to Mr. Clark and persuaded him to allow her to put up a sign in his shop advertising her willingness to mend clothes for anyone needing such a service. His approval was only secured on the condition that he be given a percentage of her profits. Mr. Clark was a businessman first and never allowed sentiment to interfere with making a profit.

Each day Miranda would check at the store to see if there was any work for her. At first only a few items trickled in, but eventually, through word of mouth, she soon had enough sewing to keep a roof over her head and food on the table. It was not what she had hoped for, but until she could come up with a better plan, it had to do.

Besides producing a barely adequate income, sewing for a living had another bothersome drawback. Miranda spent hours alone in her room with no other companion but her thoughts. And those thoughts were forever straying in an undesirable direction. She kept recalling little details about Lucas. The way he rubbed his neck when he was perplexed, the patient way he had taught her to fire the rifle, even the comforting sound of his rhythmic breathing as he slept. She supposed he was gone from San Francisco by now. It frustrated her that she could not seem to banish him from her mind. Peevishly she hoped he felt as lonely as she did.

One day blended indistinguishably into the next. Miranda began to admit to herself that her melancholy had as much to do with Lucas's absence as it did with being trapped in this unsatisfactory way of life. Though she knew he must have left San Francisco long ago, she still caught herself scanning the streets for his familiar face.

One rainy afternoon, as she was hurrying to Mr. Clark's store with her latest bundle of repaired items, she spied a familiar face. The person to whom it belonged was standing on the opposite side of the street under an overhang as if she were waiting for someone.

"Lizzy! Is that really you?" Miranda ran across the street, totally oblivious to the mud.

"Miranda Austen, I thought we'd never meet again." Lizzy threw open her generously fleshed arms to embrace her. "How are you?"

"I'm fine." Miranda glossed over her question. "But look at you." She took in Lizzy's new periwinkle-blue silk dress. The gown boasted yards of expensive French lace and a ponderous bustle. A large, wide-brimmed hat provided the crowning touch. "You're dressed as fine as a queen. Don't tell me you struck it rich?"

"We sure did. And the first week out too. We're so rich, I hardly know what to do with all this money." She grinned wickedly. "But I'll think of somethin'. Can't have ol' Ed squanderin' it on foolishness."

"I'm so happy for you." For the first time in weeks Miranda's smile was genuine.

"What about you? How did your pa do?" The instant she asked the question, Lizzy knew something was wrong. Miranda looked as if the weight of the world had fallen on her shoulders. "What's the matter, Miranda? Didn't things work out for you and your father?''

"My father was killed," Miranda stated. "By a rattlesnake.''

"Poor dear, and now you're on your own. When did it happen?'' Lizzy put a comforting arm around her.

"In July.''

"You've been back in San Francisco all this time, and I never knew. Well, there's no help for that. We'll just have to make up for lost time. Why don't we get out of this weather? We can have a cup of tea at my place. It isn't far from here,'' Lizzy offered. Miranda had lost her sparkle. Lizzy was worried that her friend was having such a hard time accepting her father's death.

"That sounds wonderful, but I have to drop these off at Clark's store first. Why don't you wait here where it's dry. It won't take me more than five minutes,'' Miranda explained, hoping Lizzy was not in a hurry.

"Be glad to wait. Ed should be along any minute, and I need to let him know I decided to go back to the hotel.'' Lizzy had a way of making a person feel she was never inconvenienced but rather that Miranda's happening by fit in perfectly with her plans for the day.

"Then I'll be back in a minute.'' Miranda waved as she hurried down the street. Though in fact the sky had darkened, the day suddenly seemed brighter.

True to her word, Miranda was back in no time, in her arms a fresh stack of well-worn clothes needing the attention of a needle and thread. The rain was beginning to fall in earnest, and the two women wasted little time making their way to their destination.

Lizzy and Ed had taken a suite in one of the better hotels in San Francisco. Lizzy stopped at the desk long enough to order a pot of tea brought up, then the two women made their way up the stairs to her apartment. Once inside, Miranda set down her burden and removed her wrap.

"Oh, Lizzy, this is wonderful." Miranda surveyed the richly decorated room. "I'm glad things turned out so well for you."

Lizzy laughed as she removed her hat. "You know, it was almost too easy. We'd barely staked out our claim when Ed came a runnin' with a hunk of gold in his hand that fairly made my eyes pop out of my head. Ed and I worked like mules for a month. By then we were so rich, I couldn't see the sense in gettin' any richer. We sold our claim and headed back to San Francisco. For the first time in our lives we can enjoy the finer things."

"If anyone deserves this success, you do," Miranda told her generously.

"And why is that?" Lizzy quizzed her.

"Oh, just because you're you, I suppose. Don't complicate things by asking sensible questions." Miranda giggled, sinking into a soft, overstuffed chair in the sitting room.

"Speakin' of sensible questions, would you mind tellin' me why you're carryin' around a pile of old clothes?"

A knock at the door momentarily interrupted their

conversation. Lizzy answered it, returning with a tray bearing a pot of tea, cups, and a plate of sweets.

"Sugar and cream?" she asked as she poured the steaming brew into the delicate china cups.

"Both please." Miranda took the cup. After taking a cautious sip she set it aside to allow it to cool a minute or two.

"Now, you were about to tell me about the clothes," Lizzy prompted.

"They're my job," Miranda explained. "I have a sign in Mr. Clark's store. Men bring in their clothes for me to mend."

"What happened to all your father's money? I thought you two were well set." Lizzy had a hard time believing that Miranda's fortune could have changed so drastically in such a short time.

"Some of it went for supplies and such. The rest he lost gambling before he died. I'm afraid I'm rather strapped as they say."

"Oh, dear." Lizzy knew too well how foolish men could be. If it wasn't for the tight rein she kept on their purse strings, Ed might have easily squandered their fortune. "Don't you have any relations back in England who could send you enough money to get home?"

"I have an aunt, but she could never afford to send such a large sum. Besides, it would take well over a year for funds to be forwarded. I have written my father's solicitors, but I am not optimistic," Miranda confessed. "But don't worry, I get along just fine with the money from my mending." She did not add that she had little hope of ever being able to save enough to afford decent lodgings, let alone buy passage home.

"And you have been takin' in mending since July?" Lizzy could not imagine how Miranda could make enough to survive with the high cost of living.

"No. I've only been back a few weeks." Miranda did not elaborate.

"Now, I know it's none of my business," Lizzy could not keep from asking, "but if you weren't here, where were you?"

"I stayed in the gold fields," Miranda stated simply, wishing Lizzy would drop the subject, but knowing she wouldn't until all the facts were out.

"Not by yourself?" Lizzy looked at her incredulously. "Not even I would have the nerve to do that, and I imagine I'm a bit more experienced with rough livin' than you."

"No," Miranda reluctantly admitted. "My father hired a guide before we left. I stayed with him."

Lizzy eyed her friend curiously. She was certainly not naive, but she found it hard to believe that Miranda would involve herself in such a relationship. It was totally out of character.

"And where is this man now?" Lizzy had to ask. If the man had gotten Miranda into trouble, she would have to persuade Ed to find him and make him aware of his obligations.

"I don't know. I suppose he's back in Oregon by now." Miranda shrugged her shoulders, trying to look as if his whereabouts didn't concern her. The gesture was futile. Lizzy was too keen not to notice the mist in her eyes.

"Miranda, did he get you in trouble?" Lizzy asked with characteristic bluntness.

"More than you know," Miranda answered, then, realized her friend wanted to know if he had gotten her with child, she quickly amended her answer. It must somehow show, she thought forlornly. How could she ever hope to find respectable employment if people could tell just by looking at her. "How did you know we did that, Lizzy?"

"You told me," Lizzy protested.

"I only said we were together. I didn't say we did anything improper. Can everyone tell just by looking at me?" Miranda questioned, thoroughly humiliated by Lizzy's discovery.

"Of course not." Lizzy patted her hand. "I just assumed since you were in his care, you two became intimate. Unless there is something wrong with the man, it was bound to happen. But, what I don't understand is why you stayed with him in the first place. Are you in love with him?"

"No." The reply sounded too sharp even to Miranda's ears. She picked up her tea and concentrated on the contents of the cup. "I had no choice."

"I realize I'm being rude pryin' like this, but, Miranda, that doesn't make sense. Why on earth would you have to stay with him?" Lizzy liked to have her facts well ordered. At the moment she wasn't even sure what the facts were. Miranda obviously cared for the man, though she was trying hard not to show it. She guessed that her friend's present lassitude might have more to do with the absence of this man than with her father's death. It seemed while fortune had smiled on Ed and her, fate had done nothing but turn her friend's life topsy-turvy.

Miranda sighed, then began to explain. "I told you my father lost all our money. Well, he had been lying to Lucas, telling him he left his money back in San Francisco for safekeeping and would pay him when we came back. You see, Papa hoped he'd strike it rich, and no one would be the wiser, but things didn't work out. Then a man came to camp and stole a few things from two of the other miners. Lizzy, Lucas almost beat the man to death. By then my father had told me about the money, but I was afraid to tell Lucas for fear that same would befall my father. Then Papa died and I felt so alone. Lucas was so kind to me, I kept putting off telling him. When I finally did, he said I had to stay with him or he'd tell the other miners, and I'd be whipped and have my ear cut off. I didn't have the nerve to face that, so I agreed to stay with him." Miranda paused. It all sounded so sordid, as if she sold herself to avoid justice. "Oh, I'm explaining it all wrong. I really didn't know Lucas planned to seduce me, at least not at first, and for the most part he really is a good man."

"I hate to disillusion you, but that good man is a liar." Lizzy snorted in disgust. "If he had told the other men, nothin' would have happened to you. His agreement was with your father. Besides, women are scarce around here. There is not much we can't get away with. I'd wager he knew all along and was just usin' the whole thing as an excuse to bend you to his will." Lizzy was incensed that the man had taken advantage of Miranda's naïveté, then, after Miranda had developed an attachment to him, he had left her.

Miranda sat quietly digesting this new information. "Do you mean he tricked me? Why, that . . . that . . ."

"I can think of a few words to help you out, but they wouldn't be very ladylike," Lizzy said in consolation. "I think you are lucky to be rid of him."

"Lucky?" Miranda stared up at her. "I must be the unluckiest person on earth." She burst into tears, all hope of ever seeing Lucas again destroyed. In the back of her mind she had cherished the thought that he might discover he truly cared for her and return. It would have been hard, but they might have worked out a future together. But it was all a dream. Lucas was a scoundrel of the worst ilk, a liar, a seducer, and heaven knew what else. For all she knew, he had never set foot in Oregon.

The thought gave her a moment's pause. If that were true, perhaps he was still in San Francisco. If she ever saw him again, she planned to let him know just what she thought of his little game. How could she ever have made excuses for him? He was a thoroughly detestable man.

Drying her eyes, she looked up at Lizzy. "I hope you're right about women being above the law here, because if I ever set eyes on Lucas Adams again, I'll kill him." Her words seethed with indignation. His concern for her welfare had been a ruse. He was probably still gloating over his victory. How he must have laughed at her gullibility! She was so intent on imagining Lucas's execution, at first, she missed the startled look on Lizzy's face.

"Don't worry, Lizzy. I'm sure he is long gone." Miranda misinterpreted the reason for Lizzy's dis-

tress. "Besides I doubt if I could really bring myself
to kill him no matter how much he might deserve it."

"No, I'm sure you couldn't." Lizzy looked
around the room, a bit distracted, then, regaining her
composure, she rose from her chair. "I really do hate
to run you off, Miranda, but Ed and I are supposed
to meet someone for dinner. I'm afraid it's business
or I'd invite you to join us."

Miranda was more than a little hurt by her friend's
sudden desire to be rid of her. She immediately rose
to fetch her wrap.

Realizing that her actions were being misunderstood, Lizzy added, "Leave me your address so I can
find you. I'm free most of tomorrow. If you like, we
can spend the day together."

"That would be lovely." Miranda sighed in relief. She had not offended Lizzy after all. Having so
few friends, she was loath to lose her valued friendship.

"I'll be around about ten then." Lizzy glanced at
the slip of paper Miranda handed her as she bustled
her out the door.

Lizzy sagged against the door as soon as it was
closed. She and Ed were meeting a Lucas Adams that
very night to discuss investing in his sawmill. Until
Miranda had inadvertently mentioned his name, Lizzy had not dreamed that Miranda could have been
talking about the same Lucas Lizzy had gotten to
know over the last few weeks. The man she knew
was from Oregon, too, but he was a businessman.
Lizzy prided herself on being a good judge of character. She would swear that the Lucas Adams she
knew was a good decent man. Perhaps there were

two Lucas Adamses. Adams was a common enough
surname, though for them both to be from Oregon
seemed a bit of a coincidence. She had a strong suspicion Miranda cared deeply for her Lucas Adams,
despite her denials. She would soon get to the bottom
of this mess. If they were the same man, a little well-
intentioned meddling might straighten things out.

Lucas sat at a table slowly sipping a bourbon.
Though he had twice had the opportunity, he still had
not left for home. He used the excuse of business to
stay in the city, though he had taken care of all es-
sential matters the first week back. Now he was just
filling his time with inconsequentials to justify his
reluctance to leave. But the *Arabelle* was in port and
would be sailing within the week. Though he hated
to admit it, the real reason he had stayed so long was
Miranda Austen.

It put him out of humor to realize she held so much
power over him. Though he had first offered marriage out of remorse for his actions, he knew he now
wanted her for his wife, because without her daily
presence, his life seemed flat. She was a remarkable
woman, worthy of any man's love, but she had already turned him down twice. In face of that rejec-
tion he was not willing to bare his feelings to her and
subject them to possible ridicule. But he would have
to come to some decision soon. He was already long
overdue at home. Though he had sent letters, with
the unreliability of the mail service, he could not be
sure they had reached their destination. He would
either have to forget Miranda or convince her to become his wife. Since the former was proving impos-

sible, he was bound to pursue the latter. He had never before courted a reluctant woman, and he was not sure how he should approach the matter.

Whatever he decided to do, it could wait until tomorrow, for tonight his business was of true importance. Since returning to San Francisco he had become friends with Edward and Elizabeth Decker, two of the newly rich of California. The couple had wisely decided to invest their newfound wealth, though he imagined the decision was more at the wife's insistence than the result of the financial finesse of the husband. He liked both Ed and Elizabeth, but Elizabeth, or Lizzy, as she liked to be called, was definitely the more canny of the two. At times her manner of dealing with her husband seemed a bit heavy-handed, but it was obvious she cared for him in her own way. Since her husband rarely complained about her treatment, he assumed he was content to let her rule the roost. In any case, it was none of his business.

What was his business was the fact that the Deckers had expressed an interest in one of his sawmill operations. With the rapidly expanding market for lumber in California, expansion was logical, but that would require capital. Though he was reasonably certain he and his brothers could come up with the necessary funds, outside investments would help lighten their private financial burden, freeing their capital for other ventures. The sawmill was a relatively safe investment, and he felt no qualms in encouraging the couple to part with some of their gold. He knew the mill was well managed. Though all investments held an element of risk, he was reasonably certain this one could do nothing but increase the couple's wealth.

Glancing up, he saw the objects of his thoughts enter the room, Lizzy in the lead, as usual. Rising he waited until she was seated before resuming his seat. They exchanged pleasantries, then ordered their meal.

Lizzy bode her time, waiting until everyone was engrossed in the dinner. "I ran into an old friend of mine today."

Lucas looked up, feigning interest.

"Poor little thing, she's really down on her luck. She's all alone in the world and barely scratchin' out a living mending clothes for a bunch of dirty old miners. Such a sad fate for a lady." Though appearing to make casual conversation, Lizzy covertly watched Lucas for his reaction to her words. She could see he was still more interested in his food than her conversation.

"The worst of it is, some man held her a virtual prisoner out in the hills. It's unspeakable what some men will do to a defenseless woman. Don't you agree, Mr. Adams?" Lizzy smiled at him expectantly.

Lucas shifted in his seat. He had the feeling Lizzy was setting him up for something. He found it somewhat amusing to watch her maneuver Ed. It was not so amusing when she tried it with him.

"Now, Lizzy, I doubt Mr. Adams is interested in your friend's problems. We're here to discuss a sawmill, not some girl." Ed broke into the conversation.

"Oh, but I believe he *is* interested," Lizzy continued, undaunted by her husband's censure. "Can you believe the man actually threatened to have her ear cut off if she didn't submit to him?'' Lizzy could not suppress a satisfied grin as Lucas choked on a piece of meat.

Ed stared at his wife as if she had gone mad.

''She told you that, did she?'' Lucas lay down his fork, giving Lizzy his full attention. He had forgotten that Miranda had once mentioned having a friend named Lizzy Decker.

''Yes.'' Lizzy looked at Lucas expectantly.

''Would someone mind tellin' me what is going on?'' Ed asked in a plaintive voice. He was the first to admit that his wife had the better head for business, so he was usually content to hold his tongue, but this didn't sound like business to him.

''Would you like to explain to Ed?'' Lizzy was thoroughly enjoying the way Lucas squirmed uncomfortably in his seat.

''No, I wouldn't. It's not any of his business or yours, either, for that matter.'' Lucas was in no mood to discuss his personal affairs. Memories of Miranda constantly came unbidden into his consciousness, and of late, his dreams of her were so realistic, it was bittersweet torture to lay his head upon his pillow. He had not left San Francisco because he could not bear to break his last tie with her. At least while he was still in the city he could check on her well-being through Mr. Clark.

''It's my business because I care about my friends,'' Lizzy stated bluntly. ''Did you ever stop to think that she might get with child? Those sort of things do happen, you know.''

''Oh, God.'' Lucas shook his head in consternation. He hadn't thought she might get caught so easily. "I guess she'll have to marry me now. I'll go talk to her in the morning."

Lizzy couldn't have been more pleased with his reaction and concluded that her original assessment of Lucas's character had been correct. Convinced he could be counted on to do what was best for Miranda, she relented a little. "No, she's not pregnant, but I can tell you she's miserable. Why did you take advantage of her like that and then leave her? She's not the sort of woman you can toy with—"

"Now, Lizzy," Ed interrupted. "Even if the girl is your friend, you can't go tellin' the man how to run his life. We're suppose to be talkin' about a sawmill, remember."

Lucas was grateful that at least Ed was on his side, but he couldn't resist setting Lizzy straight. Miranda had obviously told her of their relationship in a light that had painted him without conscience. "Perhaps Miranda neglected to tell you I offered to marry her. Twice. She's the one who wanted to part company." He leaned back to watch Lizzy's reaction.

"I see." Lizzy digested this new bit of information. This situation was more complicated than she thought, but now that she was convinced Lucas was not some kind of ogre, she was determined to find some way to get the couple together. Lizzy liked marriage. It only seemed fitting that these two should end up at the altar.

"I wonder why she did that?" Lizzy mused out loud.

"You'd have to ask Miranda, though I believe it has something to do with loathing me." Lucas was amused by the play of emotions that crossed Lizzy's face. He had a good idea she was planning some sort of matchmaking scheme. He had seen that gleam before and had skillfully avoided many a marriage trap; however, this time he was not so sure he wanted to. Perhaps Lizzy was the answer to his problem. He seemed bound to Miranda as much as if he were her husband. It would be much easier to keep an eye on her if she were close at hand. Besides, there were some aspects of marriage in which he was eager to indulge. In more ways than one Miranda was a woman worth holding on to.

"I don't think Miranda really hates you, even if she's told you so. You forget, she's from another country, and who knows how they do things over there? I believe what we're dealin' with is nothin' more than a slight misunderstanding." Lizzy emphasized the word *slight*. "If you're still willin' to marry her—and I think you are—I might be persuaded to help you convince her." Lizzy looked directly into Lucas's cool, blue eyes, her own sparkling with delight as several possible plans began to form in the back of her mind.

"Lizzy." Lucas began to chuckle as he realized he was actually going to accept her help. For a confirmed bachelor he was certainly making an abrupt turnabout. Not only was he willing to get married, but he was willing to enlist the aid of an determined matchmaker to arrange it. "I know I will live to regret this, but I'm willing to go along with whatever you plan. Though Miranda and I are quite capable of making each other miserable when we're together, we're even worse off apart. My ship, the *Arabelle*, is in port and sails within the week. If you can arrange things by then, I would be grateful."

"If you two are goin' to spend all evenin' planning how to shackle this man to some girl I barely remember, I'm movin' to another table." Ed started to rise.

"Oh, all right Ed, we'll change the subject. Until I work out the details of my plan I prefer to keep it to myself, anyway." Lizzy relinquished the hold she had on the conversation. "Why don't you two discuss the sawmill? Though if Mr. Adams runs it as poorly as he does his personal life, I fear it may not be a wise investment."

"I assure you, madam, except where Miranda Austen is concerned, I have always managed to keep a logical head. It is a good investment with the new market for lumber in California. I don't see how you could help but make money." Lucas was again the businessman, and for the moment, all thoughts of Miranda were pushed to the back of his mind.

They continued to discuss business for the remainder of the evening, and Miranda was not mentioned again until they were about to part company.

"Lucas." Lizzy caught his arm as he turned to leave. "Don't go see Miranda just yet. When I talked to her this afternoon, she swore to shoot you on sight."

Lucas raised his eyebrows heavenward, but he assured Lizzy he would follow her advice.

Chapter 16

Jeb Lewis had been back in San Francisco since August. While the wounds on his back had healed, the memory of the pain he had suffered scarred his mind more than the stripe had his back. He prayed daily for a chance for revenge. He was living in a dingy shanty near the waterfront, making a living as a thimblerigger. With sleight of hand he had bilked many an unsuspecting miner out of his hard-earned gold.

He could not believe his good fortune when, one autumn day, he spotted the dark-eyed oval face that was etched forever in his memory. He stopped to take a second look. It was the same woman all right. She was dressed in finer clothes, but it was definitely her.

Being careful to stay out of sight, he followed her. She went into a general store, then came out a few moments later with a small bundle in her arms. Jeb was careful to turn his back to her as she passed. He did not want her to recognize him just yet. He continued to follow her until she entered a rather sleazy boardinghouse. After waiting a good half hour, he concluded she would not be coming out again and went on his way.

It seemed strange that Miranda Austen would be staying in such a place. He had gathered that the Englishman was her father, but this house was for single women. Her dress did not indicate she was down on her luck but rather that her circumstances had improved. Perhaps, after making his fortune, her father had died. Many a tenderfoot had succumbed to the fever. Whatever her situation, he would have to move slowly. Avenging himself against a lone woman was one thing. If she had a protector lurking in the background, it would be an entirely different matter.

The next few days Jeb Lewis kept a careful watch on his quarry. Her comings and goings were incredibly dull. Other than frequent visits to the general store, where he had first spotted her, she went nowhere and saw no one. If she was attached to some man, he was unavailable at the moment.

The fifth day of his surveillance was the first time Jeb saw Miranda talk to a soul. She had met another woman on the streets. Observing their greeting from a discreet distance, he concluded they had not seen each other for some time. It could only hinder his plans if they renewed their friendship. The time to strike was now. Jeb grinned as he thought of how he would make Miranda Austen pay for what she had done to him.

Miranda dashed up the stairs, her hair wrapped in a towel. All the boarders shared a single tub set in a small closet just off the kitchen. She had discovered that if she wanted to take a leisurely bath, mornings were the best time, because most of the other women slept late.

Lizzy was expected at ten, and Miranda wanted to be ready when she arrived. Despite her room's improved state, it was still not a fit place to entertain company.

Stepping across the threshold of her room, she kicked the door closed with her foot. She froze as she felt the blade of a knife pressing against her ribs, her nostrils wrinkling as they were assailed by the odor of whiskey mingled with unwashed body.

"Move over to the bed," a gruff, but somehow familiar voice ordered.

Too frightened to do otherwise, Miranda did as she was told, though it was an effort to force her quaking limbs to obey.

"Now put yer hands behind ya."

Again Miranda obeyed. She was painfully aware of the knife point in her side. A small cry escaped her lips as a rough rope bit into the tender flesh of her wrists.

When her hands were securely bound, her assailant shoved a filthy rag into her mouth, causing her to gag. He removed the knife from her ribs, yanking the towel from her head as he spun her around. Miranda blanched as she came face-to-face with Jeb Lewis, his vile eyes gleaming with evil anticipation.

"It's time to pay up fer the pain ya caused me, ya little bitch. I told ya to keep yer mouth shut, and by the time I'm through fixin' ya, yer sure gonna wish ya did." Jeb threw his head back and laughed out loud.

Miranda took a step backward, but the backs of

her legs came up against the edge of the bed. Her eyes widened with terror.

"I couldn't believe my luck, findin' ya all alone in the world." He grinned, savoring the fear he saw in her eyes. "And yer landlady was so helpful. Told her I was yer brother just back from the diggin's, and I wanted to surprise ya. . . . Are ya surprised?" His smile lacked all trace of human warmth.

Miranda tried desperately to spit the foul rag from her mouth. She could barely breathe. Her panicked mind raced in circles. She had to call for help. If she did not escape, she doubted she would live to see another day. She could read her death in his eyes.

Noticing her futile attempts to dislodge the gag, Jeb frowned at her with false sympathy. "I really wish I could remove the gag, but someone might intrude on our privacy. It's a pity I'll be havin' to miss the pleasure of yer screams fer mercy, but it can't be helped." Without warning Jeb gave her a vicious backhanded slap across the face, causing her to stumble against the wall.

Blinking the tears of pain from her eyes, Miranda righted herself. Her eyes fell on the rifle standing in the corner. It was not loaded, and with her hands tied, it would be impossible to use it as a club. She desperately searched the rest of the room for anything that could be used as a weapon.

Watching the expressions of hope, then despair, play across her face, Jeb smiled in triumph. He reached out to stroke the already discoloring skin on her cheek. "A pity to ruin such beauty," he mused out loud. "Maybe I should enjoy it first." Reaching out, he yanked Miranda to his chest. She shuddered as he pressed his rough, wet lips against the base of her throat.

The kiss was enough to break her bonds of fear. She would prefer death to submitting to this man. If he did succeed in abusing her body, she intended to be past all feeling. With that purpose in mind she brought her knee up hard between his legs. Though her aim was less than accurate, the action secured her release. Jeb lunged forward, his knife eager to taste blood, but she managed to sidestep his thrust, and he fell to the floor with a growl. Miranda was at the door, fumbling with the latch, before he could rise. She stared in numb fascination as the knife whistled through the air toward her breast. Suddenly the stubborn latch released and the door swung open, sending her sprawling to the floor. The knife sailed past her ear and lodged in the door.

Standing in the doorway, like an avenging angel, was Lizzy, a small pearl-handled Derringer pointed at Jeb Lewis's head.

"Don't think I don't know how to use this," she warned as Jeb took a step toward her.

Miranda scrambled to her feet and came to stand beside Lizzy.

"Now get your filthy carcass out of here," Lizzy ordered, moving to clear a path to the door. She kept the gun trained on Jeb's chest as he edged slowly to the door. Once he had exited, she stepped into the hall to watch his rapid descent down the stairs.

"Waterfront scum." Lizzy wiped her hands as she stepped back into the room. Prying the knife from the door, she cut the ropes that bound Miranda's hands, then pulled the gag from her mouth, throwing the offensive cloth on the floor.

"Lizzy, how can I ever thank you?" Miranda threw her arms around her friend. She could not stop trembling.

"I'm sure glad I decided to come a little early." Lizzy patted her back. "Who was that slime, and how'd he get into your room?"

"His name is Jeb Lewis." Miranda paused to try to spit the foul taste from her mouth. "And my landlady let him in. He told her he was my brother."

"Brother, my foot." Lizzy snorted in disgust. "The woman must be blind. The only thing that man might be brother to is an alley rat. . . . Well, it's obvious you can't stay here anymore." Lizzy made no attempt to hide her disapproval of her surroundings. "Pack a few things. I'll send Ed around for the rest later."

"Thank you, Lizzy." Miranda gratefully accepted her offer of sanctuary. "You're just the friend I need right now." She sniffed back a tear.

"Don't go gettin' teary on me," Lizzy chided, always being one to be embarrassed by a compliment. "Now get your things. After a nice hot bath and a cup of tea you'll feel like a new woman."

Miranda quickly complied, anxious to leave the scene of her narrow escape. When she was ready, Lizzy tucked her arm under hers, then led her down the stairs, careful to keep the Derringer ready in her hand in case Miranda's attacker was still lurking about. The two women cautiously made their way through the streets until they reached Lizzy's hotel, then, upon entering, went directly upstairs. Even so,

Miranda's rather battered appearance caused an eyebrow or two to rise.

Once Miranda was safely settled into their suite, Lizzy arranged for a bath and tea to be sent up. She had planned to treat Miranda to lunch at one of San Francisco's more elegant establishments, but considering the events of the morning, she deemed it wise to postpone her plans. Miranda was too shaken to enjoy such a meal, and until the bruise on her cheek faded, Lizzy doubted if she would want to be seen in public. As an afterthought, she left word at the desk for Ed to spend the day out. He would only get in the way, and she wanted to give Miranda time to recover before she was forced to face anyone.

Within a half hour of arriving at the hotel, Miranda was soaking in a hot tub. Despite the fact that she had bathed only a few hours earlier, she scrubbed viciously at her skin to remove any reminder of Jeb Lewis. While any trace of his foul scent remained she felt defiled. Fresh from her bath and wrapped in a dressing gown, Miranda entered the sitting room to find Lizzy busily working on a sampler.

"Feel better?" Lizzy asked, looking up from the piece.

"Much."

"I've ordered tea." Lizzy indicated the tray on the table, then surveyed Miranda with a critical eye. Except for the bruise, she appeared unharmed. "I've got some salve for that bruise." Lizzy rose to fetch the ointment.

"Lizzy, you're like a mother hen." Miranda felt comforted by her friend's solicitous care.

Lizzy returned from the bedroom, handing her the

cream and a small hand mirror. Miranda groaned as she studied her reflection.

"It'll fade," Lizzy assured her, settling back in her chair. "Do you want to talk about it? It might help."

"Not now." Miranda looked to Lizzy for understanding. "Maybe in a day or two, when it isn't so fresh."

Lizzy respected Miranda's need for time and steered their conversation to lighter topics. They spent the day recounting their various adventures since arriving in California. Though Lizzy did most of the talking, she was able to coax enough information out of Miranda to piece together a fairly accurate picture of her experiences. The conspicuous absence of any mention of Lucas Adams only confirmed Lizzy's suspicions that Miranda cared deeply for the man.

Miranda retired early, having been exhausted by the events of the day. Lizzy had arranged for her to stay in the room adjoining hers. Though Miranda knew she should protest the cost, she was too frightened of being alone to mention the subject. Someday she would find a way to repay Lizzy for her generosity.

In light of the attack on Miranda, Lizzy was forced to rethink her plans. She had been appalled by the conditions under which Miranda had been living and decided it was unsafe to leave her to her own devices. Even though she had managed to frighten off that Jeb Lewis character, there was always a chance he might return. Unfortunately Lizzy knew that once Miranda had controlled her initial fear, she would no longer accept her charity. The best plan seemed to be to get her out of the city as soon as possible.

The first thing Lizzy determined to do was to convince Miranda she should return to England. She did not think it would be very difficult, considering the present state of the girl's life. Miranda had mentioned she had an aunt in England. She would use that information to her advantage.

Throughout the next few days Lizzy skillfully interjected remarks about the comforts of living near one's family, emphasizing how older relatives could often give wise counsel to their less experienced, younger relations. When she was satisfied Miranda was properly primed, Lizzy presented her idea.

"Miranda, I've been thinkin' you should go back to England. There is no future for you here, and perhaps your aunt could help arrange somethin' for you."

"I have been thinking a lot about going home. I don't seem to be managing very well on my own." Miranda was honest enough with herself to admit that since returning to San Francisco, she had just been going through the motions of living, finding joy in nothing. It was an effort just to drag herself from bed to face another day. Even Lizzy's companionship helped only a little.

"I hate to agree with you, but I do." Lizzy patted her hand. "Why, that place you were stayin' in was hardly fit for a girl like you. I imagine your aunt would have a thing or two to say about the companions you've been keepin' too."

"Aunt Elenore is quite strict. She would not approve at all," Miranda admitted, remembering her aunt's stern visage. "I suppose if I ever manage to save enough money, I will go back. Perhaps I could live with my aunt's family while I look for a position. She could probably help me obtain references, so I could secure a place as a governess or perhaps a companion."

Lizzy hid her distaste of the idea of Miranda locked in some stately mansion, looking after someone else's spoiled children. She could not imagine a more dismal future for her friend, but she kept silent on the matter. "I think you're makin' a wise choice; however, it could be years before you manage to save enough to buy passage to England. That is why I'm goin' to insist you accept a ticket home as a gift from Ed and me."

"Lizzy, you're the best friend a person could have, but I could never accept such a generous gift," Miranda protested.

"You can, and you will," Lizzy insisted. "There's a ship in port at this very moment that will do nicely."

"But, Lizzy . . ."

"Not another word," Lizzy admonished as she swept out the door. "Unless, of course, you'd like to say thank you." Without giving Miranda a chance to say more she hurried down the hall.

Miranda suddenly realized what Ed must feel like much of the time. Somehow she was about to sail for England, and she wasn't even sure that was what she wanted to do. Lizzy's advice was reasonable, but still, she felt as if the decision had been taken out of her hands. Oh, well. She sighed. *At least I'll know how to deal with life in England.* It was not until she was preparing for bed that she wondered how Lizzy knew a ship bound for England was in port.

Lizzy practically skipped down the street as she headed toward Lucas's hotel. Miranda had fallen in with her plans with amazing ease. All she needed to do was convince Lucas that her idea would work and she could add another triumph to her list of successful matches.

"Good mornin'' Lucas," Lizzy said in greeting as he opened the door to his room. "You'll be glad to know everything's arranged."

"You mean, Miranda agreed to marry me?" he asked, surprised Lizzy had managed it all so easily. Apparently she understood Miranda much better than he did.

"Well, not exactly," Lizzy admitted, then went on to explain her plan.

Two days later Miranda was standing on the deck of the clipper ship *Arabelle*, watching San Francisco drift out of sight. She had not had to do anything to arrange the trip except be ready with her trunk on the appointed morning. Lizzy had insisted on arranging everything, tactlessly pointing to the fading bruise on Miranda's cheek when she threatened to protest the high-handed manner in which Lizzy had taken over her life. Their farewell had been tearful, each knowing this would be their final parting.

"Good-bye, Lizzy. Thank you for everything." Miranda threw her arms around her friend's ample figure. "As soon as my father's estate is settled, I'll repay you for all you have done."

"This voyage is a gift." Lizzy smiled through

misty eyes. "The happiness it'll bring you will more than repay me. The captain's here. Take care, and remember me with a charitable heart."

"How could I do otherwise?" Miranda smiled through her tears.

Lizzy released her to the care of the captain, who escorted his fair passenger onto his ship. After indicating the door to her cabin he guided her to the railing, then excused himself to attend to his duties. Miranda leaned against the railing. Her life had been filled with nothing but good-byes since coming to this country. She had lost her father, she had lost Lucas, and now she was losing Lizzy. It was unrealistic to hope they would ever meet again.

San Francisco had become an indistinct blur by the time the brisk sea breeze urged Miranda below to her cabin. She sat in her quarters on the edge of the soft bunk attached to the wall. Lizzy had certainly spared no expense. The cabin, though small, was richly decorated with a table, washstand, and wardrobe, all fashioned from oak and polished to a warm sheen. The only pieces of furniture not bolted to the floor were the two chairs set near the table. At least she would pass the months on board in comfort. In a way she was glad she would have time to prepare herself for her return to her homeland. Try as she might, she couldn't muster the least bit of enthusiasm for the future she had planned for herself.

The sound of a knock at the door broke into her thoughts, and she rose to answer it. Before she reached the door, it swung open. She stepped back, staring in openmouthed disbelief. There stood Lucas Adams, looking just as she remembered him, except all that remained of his beard was a neatly trimmed mustache. Without his beard he was devastatingly handsome. His jaw was firm and square, and his chin had just the hint of a cleft. He grinned, revealing a row of straight, white teeth.

"What are you doing here?" Miranda asked when she had regained her wits enough to speak.

"Why, this is my cabin," he stated as he entered, closing the door firmly behind him. Miranda's heart began to race. His mere presence kindled her desire. She fought to suppress this dangerous attraction she felt toward him.

"It can't be." Miranda stared at him in confusion. "Why are you going to England? You're supposed to be in Oregon."

"I'm afraid you're a bit confused. The *Arabelle* is bound for Oregon," Lucas replied, straight-faced.

"No, Lizzy would never make such a mistake. She arranged . . ." Miranda's voice drifted off as a terrible suspicion began to surface. Lucas's presence was no mistake. His face had not registered the slightest surprise when he saw her standing in the cabin. He knew she would be there. She was again the victim of some kind of deception.

"I'm afraid Lizzy did. We became acquainted through some business dealings. The Deckers were considering investing in one of my sawmills. When she met you and saw how unhappy you were, she suggested it was my duty to make amends."

"She wouldn't have done that to me. You're just trying to trick me." Miranda refused to believe that Lizzy would betray her. "Please get out of my way. I am going to see the captain and have you removed from my cabin, by force if necessary.''

Lucas continued to block the doorway. ''I'm afraid he won't help you. You see, my brothers and I own the *Arabelle*; the ship is named after our mother. I doubt the captain would risk losing his ship for you.''

Listening to this high-handedness Miranda's temper reached the boiling point. ''How dare the two of you presume you have the right to run my life,'' she shouted. ''What a bunch of arrogant fools you Americans are. There is only one flaw in your little plan. I have no intention of cooperating. I'll throw myself overboard before I agree to become your mistress.''

''I'm not asking you to be my mistress. I'm telling you, you are going to become my wife.'' Lucas's tone left no room for argument. ''Whenever you're ready, the captain will marry us.''

''I will not be bullied into marrying you.'' At what price had Lucas been willing to sell his freedom? He must have been desperate for Lizzy's money. Miranda squared her shoulders. ''As soon as we reach port we will part company. I have no intention of sacrificing my life to satisfy whatever whim prompted this insane idea of yours.''

''How?'' Lucas questioned. ''You have no money, and I assure you, I am quite capable of keeping you with me by force if necessary. I can't make you to marry me, but I assumed you wanted respectability. If you prefer the other, it is fine with me, though the respectable women of Oregon City are likely to snub you.''

''How can you expect me to marry a man I can't trust? You lied to me!'' Miranda's bottom lip protruded slightly as she looked up at her captor. ''It was despicable the way you used me. You've had all the fun you are going to at my expense.''

''It's true, I lied to you. I needed some way to keep you with me so I could punish you. I was furious. I thought *you* had used me. How was I to know you were just a frightened little girl? Believe me when I say my desire for revenge had little to do with you. . . . Sometimes a man acts like a fool.'' Lucas shrugged his shoulders.

''Why should I believe anything you say? You explain nothing except that you are a fool, and that I have already concluded for myself,'' Miranda flung at him.

''Someday I'll explain but not today. Let's just say you took the blame for something that happened to me a long time ago. Now be sensible. I am really the best option left to you.'' Lucas successfully concealed any trepidation he was feeling. Lizzy had warned him that Miranda would probably fight the idea of marriage, but she assured him her arguments were only a screen to hide her true feelings. As much as he wanted Miranda, he would never have considered this course of action if he had not believed she also wanted him.

''Lucas, why are you doing this to me? Why can't you just leave me alone?'' Miranda pleaded.

''I want you,'' Lucas replied. ''You are a warm, exciting woman, and I want you to share my bed. There are worse things than being married to me.''

''Name one.'' Miranda instinctively put more distance between them. So it was lust that motivated him, lust and greed. Again she wondered how much

Lizzy had agreed to invest in order to persuade him to make their relationship legal. Undoubtedly the price of his freedom had been high.

"How about living in some dingy dockside boardinghouse, rubbing elbows with a bunch of prostitutes, or perhaps you enjoy being surprised by knife-wielding scum in your very room?"

Miranda's hand instinctively rose to cover her cheek.

"I was told you didn't care for that sort of life. Of course, Lizzy could have been lying, but judging by your pallor and your scraggly condition, I'd say she was telling the truth. You look awful." Lucas was blunt in his assessment of her appearance. His eyes momentarily darkened in anger. Jeb Lewis had left the city without a trace. It rankled that he could not make the man pay for his assault on Miranda. He would have seen that Jeb Lewis never had another opportunity to inflict his foul presence on the human race.

Miranda brushed a stray wisp of hair back in place. It was true she had taken little notice of her appearance of late, and she hadn't been eating well. Regardless of her appearance, Miranda did not think Lucas had the right to criticize it. "If you don't like the way I look, I suggest you leave my cabin."

"And where do you suggest I go? I told you, this is my cabin." Despite the fact that they were arguing, Lucas found Miranda's presence exhilarating, and he smiled broadly.

"I suggest, sir, you go to hell." Miranda turned her back to him as he burst into laughter. She might not have survived brilliantly on her own, but she was not about to turn over control of her life to Lucas. Despite the fact that she had once wanted the very marriage he now insisted upon, she would not be foolish enough to trust him again. After all, she had ample reason to distrust anything he said.

"Tsk, tsk, Miranda, such language. The good citizens of Oregon will think I found you in a gutter. Didn't your mother ever teach you that proper ladies don't use such expressions?" Lucas could not contain his good spirits despite Miranda's forbidding appearance. He felt more alive than he had in weeks. Besides, he was depending on her damnable pride to bring about the end he desired. No matter how much Miranda might protest the marriage, he knew she was too proud to be presented as his mistress.

"As you well know, I am no longer a proper young lady, so I will use any sort of language I please. If my words offend you, you have my permission to leave." Miranda turned to face him again. "And quit smiling like that!" She stomped her foot. "You've lost, Lucas. Admit it."

"I'll admit you are reacting just the way I thought you would when Lizzy told me of this plan. I was for the direct approach, but Lizzy was convinced you wouldn't listen to reason. Since Lizzy is a woman, and your friend, I bowed to her superior knowledge of these things. Considering how beautiful you look when you're angry, I think she did have the better idea." Lucas appeared invigorated by their heated exchange.

Miranda could barely contain her frustration. "I'm trapped in a cabin with a madman! First you tell me I look awful, then you say I'm beautiful. And as for Lizzy being my friend . . . no friend would ever put me in such a compromising position. I'd say Lizzy is more your friend than mine, though I can't help but wonder what sort of lies you told her to win her to your side.''

"Don't judge Lizzy too harshly," Lucas advised. "She only did what she thought would make you happy. Who knows, someday you may thank her for her meddling.''

Miranda doubted that very much, though in all honesty she had to admit that some small part of her was enjoying the challenge of this confrontation, but she would have to keep her wits about her if she was going to extract herself from this mess. A change in tactics seemed in order.

"Suppose I did decide to marry you." Miranda's smile was suddenly too sweet, and Lucas braced himself to do battle. "What kind of life are you offering me? Is Oregon a wilderness, or does it offer a wealth of cultural pursuits to which I am accustomed? I assure you I have no intention of becoming the wife of some backwoodsman.''

The barb struck home, and Lucas was momentarily taken aback. He had not considered that Miranda might object to living in the relatively primitive conditions that still existed in Oregon. She had found such joy in nature, he had assumed she would fit into such a life with ease.

"Oregon is still relatively wild," he admitted. "But someday I'm sure it will offer all the refinements one could desire. Perhaps you could help speed the development of such things, if that is where your interests lie.''

"Perhaps." Miranda toyed with a strand of hair. "But right now I would like to be alone so I can think. If you don't mind?" Miranda gazed up into his eyes, as if seeking his permission.

"Of course. I'll be on deck if you should need me." It was Lucas's first taste of being subjected to Miranda's womanly wiles, and he was devastated. At that moment he would have denied her nothing.

Miranda waited until she could no longer hear his footsteps in the corridor before she turned the key in the lock.

"Now what am I going to do?" she asked herself. How could Lizzy have believed she would be willing to marry Lucas on any terms? She didn't want a loveless marriage. Besides, the man was a proven scoundrel. Lizzy should have had more sense. Miranda stared in frustration at the cabin door. It only served as a temporary barrier. She couldn't stay locked in the cabin the entire voyage. Without food and water she couldn't reasonably expect to survive. Apparently Lucas had planned well. There was no way she could escape him while they were on the ship. She did not believe that Lucas's promise to hold her prisoner was an idle threat. She still intended to go to the captain, but if Lucas's family really did own this ship, it would be too much to hope that her honor would carry more weight than his authority.

No matter how she viewed the problem, she always arrived at the same two options. She could agree to marry Lucas or live with him without the bonds of matrimony, and that was no choice at all.

She stayed in her cabin the remainder of the day, trying to discover some solution she had overlooked, but to no avail. She was still deep in thought when a knock at the door startled her. When she did not answer, the knocking came again, this time a bit more insistent. A few moments later she could hear the rattle of the door handle, then the sound of retreating footsteps. She sighed in relief. She had expected Lucas to cause an embarrassing scene when he discovered she had locked him out. Perhaps he was already having second thoughts.

A few minutes later she was surprised to again hear the door being tried, but this time it swung open, and Lucas stepped in, dangling a key from his hand. "I've come to escort you to dinner," he stated, ignoring the fact that she had locked him out. "The captain has invited us to join him at his table."

"And, of course, you accepted the invitation." Miranda was piqued that Lucas had gotten around her ploy so easily.

"Of course. It is an honor to be asked to dine with the captain. Dress in something pretty." Lucas stepped over to her trunk and pulled out a dark blue velvet gown with a high neckline trimmed in white lace. "This should be suitable for the occassion."

"How do you expect me to face the man? I can imagine what he thinks of me, considering that he thinks we are sharing the same cabin."

"He will think you are my reluctant bride. He has already been apprised of your situation and is quite anxious to perform our wedding ceremony. Although he may not approve of our present arrangement, he will not interfere."

"If you will leave, I'll dress for dinner," Miranda

instructed, still determined to try to convince the captain to help her.

"Oh, no. I'm not giving you the chance to lock me out again. I'll just wait here." Lucas leaned nonchalantly against the door.

"I'm not going to change in front of you."

"You may as well get used to it. Wives often dress in front of their husbands. Besides, I've already seen you in the altogether. I assure you I won't be shocked by the sight of your petticoats."

"Lucas, you are the most exasperating man I have ever met. Stay if you must, but have the decency to turn your back. And I warn you, if you so much as twitch your eyebrow, I'll scream the timbers of this ship down around your ears."

Lucas bowed gallantly before turning his back toward her.

Miranda changed her gown with a haste unbefitting a lady's toilet. Unwilling to appear compliant, she exchanged her gray silk for the blue velvet. In truth, she would have preferred the blue gown, but she was not about to let Lucas tell her what to wear. When she was dressed, she turned her attention to her hair. If she had her way, Lucas would be left staring at the door for a very long time.

Lucas waited patiently long past what he considered ample time for even the most meticulous of women to dress. He did not want to turn too soon. Checking his pocket watch for the tenth time in the last hour, he decided enough was enough, and he would risk offering his assistance if that was what was necessary to speed her along. The sight that greeted him sorely tested his self-control. Miranda sat daintily on the edge of a chair, unconcernedly reading a book. She raised her eyes from the page, smiling innocently up at him.

"Why, you witch! I can see I'm being much too understanding. I warn you, if your little game has made us late, there will be the devil to pay. I'll not have you insulting the captain." Lucas forced just the right amount of menace in his voice to expedite a speedy departure.

Captain Jameson greeted her respectfully and assisted her to her chair. They were barely seated before the first course of their meal arrived. As soon as the steward had left she decided to get right to the point.

"Captain Jameson, there is a slight problem regarding my quarters," she stated, staring defiantly into Lucas's amused face.

"I am sorry, Miss Austen. If it is within my power, I will have it corrected at once." The captain's cooperative attitude gave Miranda new hope.

"I knew you were a gentleman. I'm sure it was just an oversight, but this man insists he was assigned to my cabin."

Captain Jameson blushed under her penetrating stare. He was most uncomfortable with the situation between his only two passengers but did not feel it would be wise to interfere. Lucas Adams's intentions were honorable, so it was not as if he were a party to destroying this young woman's virtue.

Seeking to avoid a confrontation, he sidestepped the issue. "I'm afraid there is only one cabin available on this ship. The *Arabelle* is a cargo ship and wasn't designed to carry passengers."

Miranda cursed herself for not paying more attention to the ship when she was boarded. The fact that it was a cargo ship should have warned her that something was amiss, but then, she never suspected Lizzy of any underhandedness.

"Surely you could find him some place. Perhaps with your men. I'm sure Mr. Adams wouldn't mind the inconvenience."

"I'm sorry, Miss Austen. I know you've been under a great strain lately. After dinner I'll be glad to marry you and Mr. Adams. I hate to leave you in this compromising situation a minute longer than necessary."

"No!" Miranda had to force herself to remain seated at the table. "I'll manage. I need more time." It was a lame excuse, but it was all she could think of to offer at the moment.

The arrival of the second course interrupted their discussion, and she lapsed into silence, content to let the conversation drift in another direction.

The dinner was delicious, and having missed lunch, Miranda ate with unladylike appetite. If the captain had been wavering in his support of Lucas's cause, witnessing the enthusiasm with which she consumed the meal convinced him Lucas was right in insisting the girl marry him. Captain Jameson personally preferred a rather plump figure on a woman. To his mind Miranda's naturally slight figure appeared emaciated. Yes, considering how young and alone she was, it was a good thing a man like Lucas was taking her under his wing. He knew all of the Adams brothers to be hardworking, honest men. A woman could do worse than marry into that family.

Some time later Captain Jameson rose from the table. "I'm sorry to have to break up this little party. If you'll excuse me?"

"Thank you, Captain, it was a lovely dinner." Miranda extended her hand. The captain had looked so uncomfortable throughout the evening, she couldn't bring herself to be rude to the man.

"Excellent meal, John. We'll be seeing you in the morning." Lucas guided Miranda out of the cabin. When they reached the deck, she paused to gaze at the beauty of the night sky. Noting her interest, Lucas led her over to the railing of the ship where they stood in silent companionship.

After a time he spoke. "Beautiful, isn't it?"

"Yes," she replied softly, continuing to gaze up at the light-filled sky. "I could stand here forever."

"Is it the stars you find so intriguing or the fact that you wish to avoid returning to our cabin that makes the night so appealing?" Lucas leaned his arm casually against hers.

Miranda glared at him in irritation. He had broken the mood. She had made an innocent remark, and he had turned it into a challenge. Turning on her heels, she stomped into their cabin. She knew Lucas would follow, and she immediately regretted her hasty retreat. The single bed seemed to overpower the room, mocking her for her stupidity. She backed away from it. Blushing, she turned to face Lucas.

"You don't intend to . . . I mean, we're not married and . . . you don't intend to force yourself upon me, do you?"

Lucas chuckled at her distress. "That all depends.

If you'll agree to marry me on the morrow, I'll behave in the most gentlemanly fashion. If not . . .''

"I am not going to marry you, tomorrow or ever,"
she stated emphatically.

"In that case . . ." Lucas pulled her against his
chest, teasing her lips with his as he ran his fingers
down her spine.

Caught by the delicious shivers running through
her, Miranda did not resist his caress. It was enough
to convince Lucas that somewhere, buried beneath
her pride, she desired him as much as he desired her.

"No, Lucas, please." She strained against the restraint of his arms. He was robbing her of her will.

"Then promise to marry me."

"No."

Miranda found her lips again captured by his. Try
as she might, she could not keep from responding to
the insistent pressure. If she did not stop him now,
she would be lost. While she despised the thought of
a loveless marriage, her becoming his mistress was
unthinkable. And it was down to a choice of one or
the other.

"I promise."

"Tomorrow?"

"Yes, tomorrow." Tears of frustration welled in
her eyes.

Abruptly Lucas released her, drawing in a ragged
breath as he pushed her toward the bed. Gathering an
armful of blankets from the bottom of the wardrobe,
he made a pallet upon the floor, turning his back to
Miranda as much to protect himself as to give her
privacy.

Miranda quickly changed into her nightclothes and

slipped in under the covers of the bunk. She lay staring at the ceiling for a long time.

"This marriage is a mistake, Lucas. We may both regret it for the rest of our lives," Miranda said softly as she listened to Lucas shift restlessly on the floor.

"Perhaps not," he replied, wrapping his covers more tightly about him in an effort to keep out the chill seeping through the timbers of the floor. At length, the sound of his even breathing filled the room.

Chapter 17

The next morning Miranda awoke with a feeling of hollow dread in the pit of her stomach. Why, against all reason, had she agreed to bind her future to a man who had tricked and used her at every opportunity? What insanity made her melt under his hands when she knew his tender caresses were just a means of bending her to his will? She had fallen in love with him once. What if it should happen again? It would be too dangerous to resurrect the feelings she struggled to keep buried. She could not allow him to know how vulnerable her feelings for him made her. It would just give him another weapon to use against her. Miranda rubbed her aching brow with her fingertips. How long would it be before he tired of her? Lucas had repeatedly told her how much he valued his freedom. It would seem that much more dear once he was saddled with a wife he did not love. If she had any sense at all, she would refuse to go through with this mockery of a marriage.

''Good morning,'' Lucas said, greeting her, when he heard her stirring. He was already up and dressed in a dark, handsomely tailored suit.

Miranda had never seen him dressed so elegantly,

and she was momentarily taken aback. Gone were the last vestiges of the rugged frontiersman, and in his place stood a man so polished, he would fit in at any formal gathering with ease. She had to admit Lucas was strikingly handsome. It would be so easy to forget the past and pretend he really did love her.

"I'll see about getting you some breakfast, then I'm afraid I must leave you. I have a few things I need to arrange."

Miranda acknowledged his comments with a nod and watched as he exited the cabin, his steps evidencing his good humor. As soon as the door closed she jumped out of bed, determined to be dressed before he returned. As she opened her trunk it struck her that whatever she chose to wear might very well be her wedding gown. She paused to contemplate her choice more thoroughly.

Before she could make her decision, there was a knock at the door. Miffed at her own indecision, she yanked on her dressing gown just as the door opened. What did it matter what she wore? she chided herself. It was not as if this was a proper marriage. The thought came to her that the marriage might not be legal at all. She had heard that sea captains could perform marriages, but she was not sure under what circumstances such a ceremony was allowed. Struck by a possible solution to her problem, she raised her eyes to meet Lucas's as he carried a tray of tea, biscuits, and oat porridge to the table.

"Lucas, I want a church wedding," she stated firmly. Without breaking her word she hoped to be able to buy the time she would need to convince Lucas to abandon this foolishness.

"I am hardly able to provide you that here in the middle of the ocean, though I assure you I have no objections to being married in a church. I'm afraid you'll have to settle for the good captain and a couple of seamen for witnesses." Lucas turned to leave, confident the request was just a ploy to postpone the wedding in hopes she might escape it altogether. If Lizzy was wrong and Miranda's reluctance to marry him had to do with a genuine lack of affection and not her indomitable pride, his forcing her would be a mistake. But he doubted Miranda could be forced to wed a man she truly abhorred. Lizzy had been un-wavering in her certainty of Miranda's love for him, patiently explaining that a woman like Miranda would never have allowed any intimacies between them if she had not loved him.

"We could wait until we reach Oregon to be mar-ried," Miranda offered hopefully.

"I don't want to wait."

"But, Lucas, I'm not sure this is legal. This could be another trick of yours."

"I assure you it is quite legal. Besides, if I wanted to take advantage of you, I could have done so last night, and you will remember, I was the perfect gentleman despite the hardness of the floor." Lucas rubbed the small of his back.

"But last night I would have fought you. When I am your wife, it will be my duty to . . . submit to you." Miranda blushed as she mentioned the most intimate duty of a wife, and gazed at the floor.

"I was rather hoping you would view it as a pleas-ure and not as a duty," Lucas commented dryly. "But if it will make you feel more secure, we can have a second ceremony in a church. It will give me a good excuse to throw a party to show off my new wife. I'm sure Emily would love that.'' Lucas smiled, remembering his sister-in-law's love of parties.

''Who is Emily?'' Miranda had not heard Lucas mention the name before, and she was immediately suspicious.

''My brother's wife. She's been after me to marry for years. You have no idea of the ribbing I am going to take when I come back married after all these years of swearing I'd never tie the knot.'' Somehow the prospect didn't bother Lucas in the least.

''You could always avoid her teasing if you would be sensible and give up this idea of our marriage.''

''But then I'd have to give you up. No, we will be married today as planned. Now, if you'll excuse me.'' Lucas bowed himself out of the room, cutting off any further argument.

Miranda stared at the tray before her, taking a nibble of one biscuit. Two biscuits and a cup of tea were all she could manage to swallow. Not allowing herself to ponder the choice of gowns any longer, Miranda selected a light blue silk with long, fitted sleeves and a high neckline. A short, attached capelet softened the lines of the shoulders, and the whole was trimmed with yards of milk-colored lace. A down bustle and the addition of several petticoats gave the skirt a fashionable fullness. If she could not be an eager bride, she would at least be a beautiful one.

She pulled the top of her hair back from her face and fashioned it into a snug knot at the nape of her neck, then twisted the hair left loose at the sides of her face into several thick ringlets. Surveying herself as best she could in her small hand mirror, she could not help but be pleased with her appearance. She hoped Lucas would find her appealing. Catching herself, she gave herself a mental scolding for such a traitorous thought. The only chance she had of surviving this marriage unscathed was to keep herself distant. Wanting Lucas to find her beautiful would certainly not achieve that end. She momentarily considered changing her hair and gown to achieve a more remote appearance, but her vanity would not allow it. *I'm dressing to please myself,* she reasoned in an effort to justify her decision.

There was nothing left to do but wait for Lucas to return. In an effort to distract herself, she picked up the book of poetry she had been reading the day before. Though she was too agitated to comprehend a word she read, she appeared to be calmly engrossed in her reading when Lucas came for her.

He offered his arm, taking note of what a beautiful bride she made. Miranda blushed under his roaming eye. She intended to plead one last time for her freedom, but seeing the determined set of his angular jaw, she knew her words would fall on deaf ears. Placing an icy hand on his arm, she allowed herself to be led from the room.

"You'll never know what a happy man you have made me," Captain Jameson said when he greeted her at the door of his cabin. He was genuinely relieved that his conscience would again give him peace.

Miranda followed him into the room, looking

every bit the reluctant bride that she was. Tight-lipped, she nodded briefly to the two seamen who stood waiting to witness their vows. Lucas did not deem it wise to delay the ceremony. Miranda looked as if she would bolt at any moment.

"I think we should get started, Captain."

"Of course," the captain agreed, glancing nervously in Miranda's direction.

The ceremony began. Lucas repeated his vows in a clear, unwavering voice. For a man giving up his beloved freedom, he seemed unnaturally calm. Miranda did not make her own vows with such confidence but in a voice so meek, the captain, though standing within arm's reach of the pair, had to strain to catch her words. The ceremony was brief, and before Miranda had time to comprehend the enormity of her surrender, she was being asked to sign the necessary papers. She did as she was instructed, surrounding herself with a numbing fog, so she could present a calm, if not joyous, countenance to those present.

Too soon Miranda found herself being escorted back to their quarters. The cabin seemed to have become repressively small in their absence. She felt like a mouse cornered by a cat, waiting helplessly to be tortured before she was finally consumed. Now that they were married, it was her duty to submit herself to Lucas. She was terrified of the emotions his touch evoked. When she turned to face him, the apprehension in her eyes made it clear she thought he intended to consummate their marriage immediately. She sighed with relief when he said, "I've ordered a private luncheon to be brought to our cabin." He loosened and discarded his cravat. "I'm afraid a ship isn't a very private place to start a marriage, but we'll have to make do."

As if on cue, there was a knock on the door. Lucas relieved the crewman of his tray and once again closed the door against intrusions. He set plates of poached fish, bread, and cheese on the table, along with two glasses and a bottle of wine, and held out a chair for Miranda.

"Are you going to remain silent all day? I assure you it is not something I require of my wife. If I ever find your conversation trying, I will inform you," he teased as he seated himself on the opposite chair.

"I don't know what to say," Miranda replied frankly, keeping her gaze lowered to the plate before her.

"Then I will have to keep up both ends of the conversation." Lucas grinned mischievously, then asked, "How do you like your fish?"

Before Miranda could reply, he answered himself in a high-pitched mimicry of a feminine voice, "Oh, it's quite lovely."

His voice again assumed its natural pitch. "And does married life agree with you?"

"My, yes, at first I was a bit reluctant, but now I see I was quite right to agree. My husband is such a gentleman, and helpful too. Why, if I don't feel like talking, he will do it for me."

Though Miranda struggled to maintain a stern face, she could not help but laugh at his antics. "I hope, sir, my voice is less grating than your imitation. Otherwise I will have to give up talking altogether." She began to relax.

"I assure you, your voice is most melodical, and I much prefer it to my own imitation." Lucas smiled beguilingly, causing her heart to melt just a little. "Now eat your food. You've grown too thin in my absence. I consider it my personal duty to see you put a little more flesh on your bones. Not too much, mind you. I still want to be able to put my arms around you."

"And if I do grow too fat for your liking?"

"Then I will have to starve you back to a more suitable figure. But you are far from that sorry fate, so eat. If you like, when we're finished, we can walk around on deck for a while."

The offer instantly gave Miranda more appetite. Apparently she was to be allowed at least a few hours to get used to the idea of being married.

Storm clouds had been gathering all day; the canvas sails flapped noisily in the wind. As they stood together Lucas explained the names of the sails and a little of the workings of the ship. He carefully avoided any personal conversation, considering it best to keep their topics light. Miranda was as nervous as a virgin bride, and though he would rather be doing something other than talking of ships, he wisely chose to postpone his pleasure.

Presently a light rain began to fall. Though it was a minor storm, it was enough to drive the couple indoors. Before Miranda's apprehensions could get the better of her, Lucas produced a deck of cards.

"Would you like me to teach you a game? Traveling this time of year, we may have to spend a lot of time in here."

"Do you expect the weather to be rough?" Miranda asked as she sat down at the table.

"Not dangerously so, but we get a lot more rain up north. I think I'll teach you monte. It's very popular in the gaming hells because the rules are simple."

It was an enjoyable afternoon, and for a brief while Miranda was able to view Lucas as an entertaining companion and put the circumstances of their marriage out of her mind.

They again joined the captain at his table to share another delicious evening meal. Though Miranda was unusually talkative in hopes of extending the after-dinner conversation as long as possible, the meal inevitably ended. Duty called the captain, and once again she found herself being escorted back to the cabin. Once inside, she kept her eyes carefully averted to the floor.

Lucas cleared his throat to gain her attention. "I'm going up on deck for a few minutes, so you may have some privacy to prepare yourself for bed."

Miranda did not miss the double meaning behind his words. Her reluctance was obvious. He was going to allow her time to prepare herself mentally as well as physically.

"Thank you." She could not keep her lips from trembling as she tried to smile at him. Lucas abruptly turned on his heels and was out the door.

Miranda stared at her trembling hands in disgust. This was no time to turn coward, she scolded herself. Lucas was being more considerate of her feelings than she had thought he would be. It would not do to anger him and have him lose patience with her.

"It is not as if I am a virgin," she told herself aloud; still, it was precisely because she did know what to expect that she was so frightened. It was too easy to lose control when Lucas touched her.

Selecting her least worn nightgown, Miranda changed, neatly packing her clothing in the wardrobe. The nightgown was hardly appropriate for her wedding night, but she was too proud to come to her husband in patches. She had no money to replenish her wardrobe since returning to San Francisco. As she continued her evening toilet she catechized herself on the duties of a wife, mentally rehearsing every scripture and word of advice she had heard on the subject in an effort to convince herself that it was not only her duty but her moral obligation to submit her body to Lucas's without a fight. To deny him would make further mockery of the vows they had spoken.

Her toilet complete, she approached the bed with grim determination. She had almost won her internal battle when a light knock at the door, followed by Lucas's entry, caused her to lose all courage and back instinctively from the bed.

Lucas groaned inwardly. He had a small sense of the war raging within her; nevertheless, he had hoped she would be more reconciled.

"Climb into bed, Miranda," he directed. "I'll turn down the light before I undress." Without pausing to see if she would obey, Lucas turned down the oil lamp until it gave a faint glow. Miranda stood riveted to the spot, watching with growing fear as he removed each item of clothing and laid it across the back of one chair. He came to stand before her, his manly outline silhouetted in the dim light.

Without a word he lifted her up in his arms and laid her upon the bed. Slipping in beside her, he pulled the quilts up to his waist to conceal his nakedness. "You needn't be so frightened. It is a natural thing between a man and a woman."

Miranda lay perfectly, afraid to trust her voice to speak. She knew she was handling this badly but was powerless to change her reaction. How could she explain that she was frightened of the pleasure he would give her? She could not risk surrendering her heart. She had to resist him.

Though Lucas was grateful she had not chosen to fight him, this quaking mouse in his bed was hardly what he had dreamed of. She looked at him with such fear in her eyes, he felt like a villain for even desiring that they consummate their marriage. The sleeping gown she had chosen wasn't helping matters, either. It made her look too childish, adding to his discomfort. No matter, he had no intention of waiting for his wife to admit her feelings for him. Considering Miranda's stubborn nature, it could be a long and frustrating drought. It would be better to settle the matter here and now. Casting aside all doubt, Lucas turned his full attention to the pleasure of making Miranda truly his wife.

Though he patiently plied her with tender kisses, he could feel the wall she had built between them. She accommodated him in every way but did not respond to his caresses. At last, unable to hold himself back any longer, Lucas released his seed. This had been no more than the physical joining of two bodies, totally devoid of the almost spiritual union that had made their previous coupling so satisfying. Rolling to his back, he lay staring at the ceiling, wondering if, indeed, he had made a mistake by forcing the marriage.

Miranda lay beside him, equally miserable. She had carefully steeled herself against all outward show of response, fearful of the delightful sensations poised to overcome her with tingling waves of pleasure. She could not allow herself to become involved with Lucas again. It would destroy her when they parted company. Marriage or no marriage, she felt that their parting was inevitable. Their marriage cup was an empty vessel. It was only a matter of time before Lucas tired of playing the devoted husband.

Despite the fact that she had been victorious in controlling her body, Miranda felt strangely tense when Lucas rolled from her. It was if she had betrayed not only him but herself as well. She could tell by the set of his jaw that Lucas was displeased, but she could find no words to explain to him that if she gave herself fully to him, she would be destroyed. Lucas might be able to view their relationship as a game, but she could not remain so detached. When he had left her in San Francisco, the emptiness of her life had been almost unbearable. She could not let herself become so vulnerable again. In time the two discontented lovers fell asleep, finding a peace in each other's arms they could not achieve in a wakeful state.

When Lucas awoke the next morning, he found a delightful creature cradled against his chest, her leg draped intimately between his thighs. That he was married to the woman in his arms only increased his pleasure in her. Unable to resist, he placed an inviting kiss on the delicate, pink lips that lay slightly parted in sleep. To his surprise Miranda's arms came up around his neck, and she returned the kiss with a passion that surpassed his own. After last night he had not thought to assert his husbandly rights so soon again, but Lucas was not a man to question his good fortune. This was a different Miranda from the one who had shared his bed last night.

Responding eagerly to her invitation, Lucas claimed her lips with more force, then began a languid trail of kisses from the base of her throat to the bud of one small, cream-colored breast. Miranda sighed and arched against him, shifting so that her soft nest lay directly above his manhood and her breasts pressed into the fine fur of his chest. Lucas stretched, reveling in the sensation of the pressure of her silken flesh against his skin. He lay content as Miranda boldly explored his flesh, her fingertips relearning the textures of his skin as she left no part of him untouched. She paused to trace the scars that striped his chest, then, smiling momentarily, relaxed against him. Her hips began to move instinctively against his, as if searching for his presence within her. Sensing that she was ready for more intimate contact, with a skillful hand Lucas guided his throbbing member to its home.

Miranda purred with satisfaction, unwilling to awaken and give up the titillating sensations of her dream. She was lying atop Lucas, and in her dream she was able to respond to his intimate ministrations without fear. She felt wonderfully warm and safe enveloped in his strong arms and was loath to give up comfort for the confused state of reality. Lucas's kisses became more insistent, and she felt her own desire building within her. At last the aching need in her grew too strong to bear, and she boldly sought out the hard member that could release her from this prison of delights. As she felt the object of her search enter its sheath her eyes flew open, and she realized that this was no dream at all; she was brazenly pursuing the pleasures of Lucas's flesh. The revelation hit her with such force, she started, inadvertently breaking their intimate joining. Lucas moaned softly and attempted to guide himself back home, but instead of assisting him as before, Miranda avoided him. With a growl he rolled her to his side. This was no time to be playing games.

"Woman, you would try the patience of a saint. Explain yourself!" Lucas narrowed his eyes in irritation.

Miranda tried to put more distance between them, but his arms held her firmly in place. She was so confused and mortified, she didn't know how to answer him.

"If you have nothing to say, I suggest we continue what we were doing." He tried to pull Miranda back on top of him, but shaking her head, she pulled back.

"Damn! What are you trying to accomplish? Last night you could have been dead for all the response you gave, then, this morning, I suddenly find myself in bed with a seductress who brings me to the heights of desire, then cruelly casts me aside. I warn you, I will tolerate no such games. I expect you to be a warm and loving wife. You possess a passionate nature. Don't you know you hurt yourself as much as me by this foolishness?''

His tirade angered Miranda. Forcing herself to appear calm, she coolly responded, ''If you will remember, I didn't want to become your wife.''

''So to punish me you will force me to lie in a bed of thorns. Well, remember, we share the same bed. Take care that in your desire to spite me you do not hurt yourself even more.''

Wondering if it was possible to feel more miserable than she did at this moment, Miranda turned her back to Lucas, pulling the covers up over her head. Unbidden tears began to fall, and though she tried to be silent, her attempts to gulp back her sobs only resulted in a strangled cry.

Sorely tested by his sudden change in fortune, Lucas was in no mood to be sympathetic to a woman's tears, especially when she had brought her misery upon herself. Rising from the bed, none too kindly he instructed, ''I'm going to get something to eat. Don't come out of this cabin unless you can manage a face befitting a joyous new bride.''

Lucas dressed and departed, leaving Miranda alone with her tears.

Chapter 18

Unwilling to face the curious stares of the captain or crew, Miranda did not venture out of the cabin all day. Though she had tried her best, she had not been able to wash the last traces of red from her eyes, and not wishing to risk provoking Lucas further, she chose to remain closeted in their room.

She was convinced she should never have agreed to this marriage no matter what threat Lucas had used. After only one day there was ample proof of that fact.

Although Miranda was too upset to care about breakfast, by the time her lunch was past due, a gnawing hunger added to her misery. Lucas did not return, and she saw this as evidence of what her future would be: days, weeks, maybe even years alone while Lucas pursued his own pleasures. She would never be free to find a loving relationship for herself. Their marriage vows eliminated that possibility for her, though she had little hope that Lucas would feel so restrained.

Perhaps he already had a favorite mistress waiting for him at home. Miranda clenched her fists as a wave of possessiveness washed over her. Why should she sit passively back and tolerate his infidelities? He was the one who insisted on this marriage. She would demand that he honor his vows.

Another wave of despair washed over Miranda. No one could demand love and respect. It had to be given freely.

When Lucas returned at the dinner hour, he found Miranda sitting in a chair, wearing her light blue day dress, and looking pale and drawn. She had left her hair loose, and the curls softly framed her face, making her appear even more ethereal. He felt a momentary twinge of guilt for leaving her alone all day, but she needed to be taught a lesson. The sooner she accepted the reality of their marriage and made a real effort toward making it a healthy one, the better it would be for them both.

He had spent the day going over some old ship logs, finding everything in order, as he knew he would. Captain Jameson was an excellent captain and a honest man. There was really no need to check the records, but it had kept him occupied for the day and helped him concentrate on something besides his stubborn wife.

"Would you like to dine with the captain, or do you prefer to have a private supper?" Lucas questioned, giving no explanation for his long absence.

"Would it be all right if we ate alone tonight?" Miranda asked. She had a terrible headache, but whether it was from her worries or from the fact that she hadn't eaten all day, she could not say.

"Of course. I'll go arrange it with the steward." Lucas left, and Miranda wondered how long he would be gone this time. But he was back in but a few minutes.

"You look tired." Lucas sat on the edge of the bed, leaning casually against the wall. He resisted the urge to take her in his arms.

"I am, a little," Miranda admitted, not explaining that her fatigue was caused by worrying about her future with him. If only he loved her, she could give herself to him fully and allow her love for him to blossom into full flower. During her long hours alone with her thoughts she had reluctantly admitted to herself that she still loved Lucas despite all he had done. She had probably never stopped loving him. It was a frightening discovery. If Lucas loved her, things could be different, but in all his proposals he had spoken of obligation, of desire, even of Lizzy's money, but never of love.

"What did you do with yourself all day?" Lucas questioned, hiding his interest by casually studying his fingernails.

"Nothing, really," Miranda replied, then added, "I did read for a while." She did not want Lucas to think she had spent the entire day languishing over him. To her chagrin her stomach began to make low, rumbling noises. She tried to ignore it, but the gurglings were all too audible.

"Didn't you eat much lunch?" Lucas eyed her suspiciously. Miranda had a penchant for starving herself of late.

"No, I guess not." Miranda deliberately avoided the truth.

"What did you eat?" Lucas was not ready to drop

the subject. If Miranda didn't start taking better care of herself, she was going to become ill.

"Nothing."

"And breakfast?"

Miranda shook her head slowly in reply.

"Miranda, why on earth didn't you eat? I can't watch you all day to be sure you take proper care of yourself." Lucas sighed wearily.

"But you're the one who told me not to leave the cabin," Miranda protested. "I was only doing what you said. If anyone would have offered me food, I would have eaten."

"What am I going to do with you?" Lucas shook his head at her as if he were dealing with an obstinate child. "I didn't mean you couldn't come out at all. I just don't want the whole ship speculating about our relationship. When a woman emerges from her first night in her bridal chamber with swollen eyes, it is bound to cause talk. I am not the sort of man who likes to have his personal affairs made public."

"And what about you?" Miranda countered. Don't you think anyone wondered why you neglected me all day? I think you defeated your purpose by your own actions."

"I had some books to go over," Lucas explained. "No one would think it odd that I have to spend some time attending to business."

It irritated Miranda that he always had to have the last word.

A knock announced the arrival of dinner, and Lucas rose to open the door. The thin little steward scurried in, setting the table and laying out an assortment of delectable-smelling dishes. As soon as

he left Miranda seated herself at the table, too eager
to wait politely for Lucas to perform the amenity. She
was too intent on filling her plate to notice his gentle
smile as he joined her.

They ate with enthusiasm, speaking only occasionally. If Miranda had not been so hungry, she
would have been embarrassed by the amount of food
she consumed. Lucas, too, enjoyed the meal though
not with equal gusto, but not wanting to curb Miranda's appetite, he made no comment.

At last satiated, Miranda surveyed the empty platters and bowls a bit guiltily. Meeting Lucas's gaze,
she found him smiling at her, his eyes twinkling.

"Shall I order more?"

"No, thank you." Miranda felt her cheeks grow
warm. Then, as an uncomfortable thought occurred
to her, she added, "Unless you didn't get enough."

"I'm quite satisfied," Lucas assured her, removing the napkin from his lap and placing it beside his
plate.

Miranda tried in vain to stifle a yawn. Now that
her stomach was full, she wanted nothing more than
to curl up in a ball and go to sleep.

"As soon as the steward returns for the dishes you
can go to bed," Lucas suggested.

She greeted his offer with mixed feelings, not sure
if he was offering her sleep or letting her know his
intentions for the evening. She had little say in the
matter, anyway, and in truth she felt so sleepy, she
would welcome a soft bed under any circumstances.

The steward returned and left again. Miranda
wasted little time preparing herself for bed. When
Lucas made no move to join her, she sighed in relief,

then, curling on her side, turned her back to the room. It was no more than a minute before the sound of her slow, steady breathing filled the cabin.

Lucas leaned back in his chair as he watched the gentle rise and fall of the quilt. Tonight he would let her rest.

He reminded himself that he had known it would take time for Miranda to forgive the way he had maneuvered her into this situation. It was her stubbornness that caused her so much misery, and he was determined to make her admit she loved him. This morning, though a thoroughly frustrating experience, had proven one thing: When her guard was down, she gave herself freely. Lucas understood Miranda well enough to be certain that if she had no feelings for him, such abandon would never have been possible. It would be a challenge to scale the wall she had erected around herself.

He tried to fill his evening by reading a book, but his eyes frequently strayed to his sleeping wife. Soon he, too, began to yawn, and after taking time to douse the light, he removed his clothing and slid in beside Miranda. She turned in sleep, snuggling close to the warmth of his body. The impulse to wake her was great, but tonight she seemed so fragile, his desire to protect her was even greater than his own needs. Cradling her head on one arm, he toyed with a lock of her hair, enjoying its silky softness until he, too, fell asleep.

Miranda awoke the next morning feeling wonderfully refreshed, and since Lucas was still asleep, she felt safe in openly enjoying the closeness of her husband. There was no denying that he was a beautifully made man, and her eyes lovingly roamed the length of him. She almost wished she could accept their marriage on his terms and enjoy what happiness she could while he offered it. But the price for that would be high, and she did not know if she was willing to pay it.

Pushing these more serious thoughts from her mind, she concentrated on the more pleasant subject of Lucas's lips. They were straight and firm with just the right hint of color for a man's complexion. She remembered their feel against her own and was surprised at her own physical reaction to mere thoughts. I really must be a shameless woman to feel such things just by thinking about a kiss, she mused, but for the first time she wondered if she was mistaken in her assessment of the physical side of love.

"Good morning, sweet. Do you approve of what you see?"

Lucas's words startled her, and she blushed, averting her eyes from his naked form.

"I don't mind." He gave her bottom a playful pat. "I enjoy looking at you. It seems only fair that you should be allowed the same privilege. Only, at the moment, you have me at a disadvantage. If you would remove your nightgown, I would be much obliged."

Obediently Miranda did as she was told but defeated his purpose by pulling the covers up high under her chin.

"Hmm." Lucas eyed the blanket speculatively before yanking it off the bed altogether. "Now that's better." He leaned on one elbow as his eyes boldly raked over his unclad wife. "Have I told you this morning how beautiful you are?" He stroked the length of her belly, sending delightful shivers dancing over her already heightened nerves.

Miranda smiled shyly up at her husband, searching his eyes for just a trace of the love she so desperately wanted him to feel for her. She could easily read desire there, but if it were mingled with love, she could not tell.

Lucas slowly lowered his lips to hers, feasting on their sweetness. With an effort of will Miranda forced her fears from her mind. She was tired of thinking. She would lose herself in the consuming sensations of their lovemaking. It was foolish, she knew, but for now she would pretend that the vows spoken between them had been vows spoken in love. Wrapping her arms around Lucas's neck, she gave herself up to the world of sensation.

Lucas grinned as he stood on the deck, taking in the crisp sea air. This morning Miranda had responded to him as he had long dreamed she would, and he was feeling very pleased with the world. Now she was truly his wife, and he discovered he did not find the married state burdensome at all. On the contrary, the addition of a wife seemed to round out his life. Though Miranda had been strangely quiet after their lovemaking, he knew she had felt the specialness of their union. It was more than a physical joining; it was an integral mingling of bodies and souls. Their lovemaking had left him drained and, at the same time, rejuvenated. He had never experienced such emotions with any other woman.

The remainder of the voyage passed, the wind in the sails blowing them steadily toward Lucas's home. More often than not they had dinner with the captain. Miranda enjoyed listening to the stories the two men told of their adventures. The captain was a longtime acquaintance of the Adams family, and through their conversations she learned a great deal about her husband. Lucas was the fourth born in a family of five sons. She already knew his brother, Matthew, lived in Oregon, but was surprised to learn that the other three brothers made their homes on the East Coast. It seemed strange for a family to be separated by an entire continent. Despite the distance, the brothers kept in touch and were joint partners in a variety of business ventures, each an expert in a different field. Lucas's specialty was in the lumber industry. Miranda was always particularly attentive when the conversation turned to Lucas's family. She wanted to learn as much as she could about the man she had wed.

Their days were spent watching the scenery when they were close enough to land or enjoying a game of cards if the weather forced them indoors. Lucas taught Miranda a variety of games, and she was delighted to find she invariably won.

But in bed she felt she never had the upper hand. She seesawed between keeping herself aloof from Lucas's lovemaking and giving herself with wild abandon in an effort to block out the fears that haunted her continually. Lucas was confused by this state of affairs, but he did not press her for an explanation of her strange behavior.

After two weeks the *Arabelle* reached the mouth of the Columbia River. It was raining, and a strong wind caused the sails to flap, straining under the wind's pressure. The crew dropped anchor and tightly trimmed her sails to await better weather. Lucas explained that this would be the most treacherous part of their journey. Many a ship had foundered helplessly on the ever-shifting sandbars.

The *Arabelle* rode at anchor for five days before the captain considered it safe to enter the river. They traveled through a narrow channel to the north, and though progress was steady and uneventful, it was painfully slow; it was necessary to continually sound the channel to avoid running aground. To Miranda the most notable feature of their location was the almost deafening roar as the waters of the Columbia poured into the Pacific Ocean. She was astounded by the immensity of the river.

The crew breathed a sigh of relief as they finally glided through the channel into calm waters. The roaring sound gradually faded into the background, making conversation once again possible, and Miranda's attention turned to the tree-lined shore. The trees were huge, some measuring as much as forty feet in circumference and towering to heights exceeding three hundred feet. A profusion of plant life formed a thick mat of intermingling shades of green, reminding Miranda a little of the lush Panamanian jungle.

Lucas stood beside her, his arm draped around her shoulders. As they traveled upriver he pointed out Fort Astoria to the south, briefly explaining its history. Miranda strained to get a better look at the rustic log structure, wondering if her new home would look like this. She could feel Lucas's excitement at being home again. It was obvious from the pride in his voice as he pointed out various items of interest that he felt a deep bond with the land.

At length, the rain changed from a light mist to a true downpour, and they were forced to take shelter in their cabin.

"Lucas, how long will it be until we reach your home?" Miranda asked as he helped her out of her sodden wrap.

"If all goes well, we should pass Portland sometime tomorrow morning. From there we'll turn south and travel the Willamette to Oregon City. *Our* land is located south of the city," Lucas explained as he, too, removed his coat, spreading it out to dry.

"Is it a large city?"

"It is the largest city in these parts and the capital of the territory, though other cities are growing fast. New towns seem to spring up along the river every day. It didn't offer opera when I left, but we do have a school, a library, and our own newspaper." Lucas suddenly felt uncomfortable about bringing Miranda to such an undeveloped area. In face of what she must have been accustomed to in London, Oregon must seem primitive indeed. "The area will grow," he assured her, trying unsuccessfully to mask his uneasiness.

"Oh, I was just curious." Miranda was touched that he would care what she thought of his home. She gave his hand a reassuring squeeze.

The next morning they passed Fort Vancouver and Portland as Lucas had predicted. At Portland they left the Columbia, turning south into the mouth of the Willamette River. A short time later the *Arabelle*'s hull was scraping against the dock at Oregon City.

Miranda stood at the railing, surveying the city
while they waited for the gangplank to be lowered.
The town was situated on the banks of the Willamette River just below a waterfall. It was a neat little
town with buildings of whitewashed clapboard lining its streets. While most of the homes were modest, it boasted several stately houses. Of all the towns
they had passed since entering the Columbia, Oregon City appeared the most progressive.

''We can go ashore now.'' Lucas directed her attention to the gangway. ''I'll rent a wagon, then return for our trunks.''

Miranda followed Lucas off the ship. Their first stop
was a livery stable where Lucas rented a horse and wagon. He introduced them both to the owner, a new-
comer during Lucas's absence. Next they stopped at
Abernathy's store to pick up supplies to stock the
shelves of their home. Lucas and Mr. Abernathy
greeted each other, warmly exchanging news, and the
storekeeper was most enthusiastic in welcoming the
new bride to Oregon. After paying for their purchases
they quickly returned to the wagon. The overcast sky
was darkening, and Lucas was hoping to reach home
before they were caught in the storm.

They made a brief stop at the docks to pick up their
belongings, then drove toward the edge of town. The
road they followed veered from the river, becoming
little more than a track crossing the meadow. After
an hour perched on the hard seat of the poorly sprung
wagon, Miranda was sure that every joint in her body
had dislocated.

''How long before we reach your home?'' Miranda questioned, holding tightly to her seat as they hit yet another rut.

"Another hour," Lucas apologized. "We should have spent the night in town. In my eagerness to arrive home I've neglected to think of your comfort. We can stop and rest if you like." He slowed the wagon.

"I don't think we had better." Miranda glanced nervously at the sky. "Besides, I'm eager to get settled myself. It's been a long time since I have been a place I could call home."

"All right, but if you get too tired, let me know and I'll stop."

They passed widely spaced farms set along the track, and Lucas gave her a brief history of the families who owned each parcel. He was becoming increasingly nervous. Why had he never noticed the roughness of the road or how long it took to travel to town? And what would she think of the home she was so eager to see? He had never gotten around to building the stately, two-story house he had planned. He was comfortable enough where he was, and there were always other seemingly more important things to attend to. A wife had never been in his plans, so he hadn't given a thought to anything but his own comfort.

He cursed himself for not having planned better. They could have stayed in Oregon City while he sent word to Matthew to air out the house and make it more welcoming. When all was ready, Matt could have picked them up in a well-sprung buggy instead of this poor excuse for a wagon. Well, it was too late now. He would have to live with the consequences of his poor planning.

Chapter 19

Lucas pulled the wagon to a halt before the one-story, log house that up until now he had been content to call home. With Miranda sitting quietly beside him, dressed in her well-tailored traveling dress, it looked shabbier than he remembered, almost forlorn, with its shutters barred tight. He made a mental note to have her look over the plans he had drawn for the new house and make any changes she wanted. They could begin building in the spring.

"Well, aren't we going in?" Miranda interrupted his thoughts as he sat staring in dismay. "I'm anxious to see my new home." When he made no move to assist her, Miranda climbed down from the wagon seat without his help.

"I think we should stay at my brother's home until I get the place aired out," Lucas suggested as he joined her on the ground. "The house has been closed for over a year."

"Unless we can walk there, I'd rather stay here. I'm afraid I couldn't bear another bone-rattling moment on that wagon. Besides, I want to see the house," Miranda insisted. Though the cabin was not what she had dreamed her first home would be, in its own way it was a charming dwelling, blending into the backdrop of pines with a comfort no stately mansion could ever achieve. It was revealing that Lucas would chose such a home, and she was anxious to see what new insights into his character the furnishings within would disclose.

Unlatching the door, Lucas left her standing in darkness while he opened the shutters. The windows were all in need of a thorough washing, but they let in enough light to illuminate the interior. Miranda found herself in a large room that served as a combination kitchen, dining room, and parlor. At one end of the room stood a large open fireplace. Removing the dust covers from the bulky shapes arranged before it, Miranda discovered a settee and chair upholstered in matching gold brocade and a large, rather rustic rocking chair with a solid brown cushion tied to the seat. At the other end of the room stood a trestle-style table with two benches of equal length flanking either side. Beyond them sat a cast-iron cook stove. The rest of the far wall was taken up by a built-in cabinet. Miranda guessed it contained cooking utensils, dishes, and various other articles necessary for the running of a household. However, the item that caught and held her attention was a small upright piano standing against the back wall.

"That," Lucas informed her as he saw her eyes light up, "is a wedding gift to you from my mother."

Miranda turned to him in confusion.

"All my brothers married, and it was a sore point with my mother that I had not yet followed them to the altar. In her will she left me her piano, directing that I was to place it in my home and upon my marriage present it to my wife. It was her way of continuing to remind me she was displeased with my unattached state. I think she hoped the piano would haunt me into finding a bride," he explained with a grin. "And now it's yours."

Miranda could not help laughing at Lucas's mother's attempt to prod him into marriage even from the grave. She must have been a fascinating woman. Miranda was saddened that she would never get a chance to meet the woman who had raised Lucas. She tried to imagine her husband as a small boy, but the image eluded her.

Crossing the room, she ran her fingers over the dusty keys. Though the piano was slightly out of tune, she delighted in its tinkling sound. It had been ages since she had sat down to a piano, and she couldn't resist the urge to play a simple little melody. When she finished, Lucas applauded loudly. She acknowledged his praise with a regal curtsy.

"I see you have hidden talents. My mother would be pleased to know her gift was so well given. Why don't you look over the rest of the house while I bring in our trunks. It's starting to rain." He nodded toward the open doorway.

Not needing further invitation, Miranda opened the door nearest the piano and found herself in a large bedroom. Dominating the room was a huge four-poster bed. After crossing the room Miranda opened the shutters and was surprised by the richness of the furnishings. A large armoire stood against one wall and to the side of it sat a mirrored dresser of equally immense proportions. Miranda felt comfortable with the masculine atmosphere of the room but wondered how Lucas had managed to bring such furnishings with him. He had told her he had first come to Oregon by the overland route. It did not seem possible that he could have brought such pieces over the mountains. She would have to remember to ask him.

Leaving the bedroom, she tried the only other door leading out of the main room. This one led to a pantry lined with shelves. Returning to the front of the house, she closed the door behind Lucas as he entered with the last of their things.

"I want to ride over and let my brother know I've returned. Would you be frightened if I left you for a bit? There really is no reason for us both to get soaked."

"Should I be frightened?" Miranda questioned, wondering if she had overlooked some hostile element in her new surroundings.

"No," Lucas replied frankly. "But, if you get uneasy, you have your rifle. Just fire a shot in the air and I'll ride back immediately. I'll only be at the next farm."

"You go ahead. It will give me a chance to get settled." Miranda gave her home another quick survey, determining that the first order of business would be a thorough cleaning.

"I'll lay a fire and bring in some extra wood before I go," Lucas said as he stepped out the door.

With the fire crackling merrily and Lucas out of the way, Miranda set about the task of tidying her new home with enthusiasm. She had been too idle on the ship and was glad to have something to occupy her body as well as her mind. Locating a broom in the pantry, she rummaged through her trunk until she found one of the faded but sturdy dresses that had served her so well in the mining camps. In no time she had the little house sparkling.

Lucas had left their trunks by the front door. She had to empty them of their contents so she would be able to drag them into a corner of the bedroom. She smiled as she placed the last of her undergarments in a drawer next to his, feeling strangely content in her new domestic role.

The sound of the front door opening announced Lucas's return. Though disappointed she had not had time to change before he returned, she stepped out of the bedroom, eager to greet him. She stopped in mid-stride, mortified by her appearance. Standing next to Lucas was a man of equal height. His coloring was a shade lighter and, from the twinkle in his eyes as he grinned down at her, she knew instantly he was Lucas's brother.

"My wife, Miranda. Miranda, this is Matthew Adams, my brother." Lucas did not seem the least bit disturbed by her shabby appearance; if anything, he was amused.

"It's a pleasure to meet you, ma'am," Matthew said, greeting her warmly.

Miranda self-consciously wiped her hands on her skirt before extending her hand. "The pleasure is mine, though I must apologize for my appearance." She threw an accusing glance at Lucas. The least he could have done was warn her that he intended to bring his brother back with him.

"I'm innocent," Lucas protested with a helpless shrug. "Matt's curiosity got the better of him, and he insisted on coming to meet you."

"I shouldn't have intruded on you unannounced," Matt apologized, looking only slightly repentent. "But after all these years of trying to get Lucas to settle down, I just had to see the girl who could convince him to marry her. You must be a remarkable woman."

"I'm afraid Lucas has given you the wrong impression, Mr. Adams." Miranda smiled sweetly at Lucas before turning back to Matt. "You see, I was the one reluctant to marry. It was only after Lucas threatened me with dishonor that I agreed at all."

For the first time since she had known him, Lucas looked truly embarrassed, but before his brother could question him on the matter, he deftly changed the subject. "The house looks lovely, Miranda. You've done wonders, though you should have waited for some help."

"Thank you." Miranda was genuinely pleased with his praise. Their eyes met for a brief moment, then Miranda turned to Matt. "I'm forgetting my manners. Mr. Adams, would you care for a cup of tea?"

"No, thank you, I really can't stay. Please call me Matt. After all, I'm your brother now. My wife, Emily, bids me to invite you to join us tomorrow for dinner. I'm afraid her curiosity is aroused. I almost couldn't persuade her that it might be a bit overwhelming if we arrived with the whole brood at your doorstep when you've only just arrived." Matt beamed proudly as he mentioned his family.

"How many children do you have?" Miranda took an instant liking to her brother-in-law. He was ready to welcome her with open arms, and she liked his friendly, easygoing manner.

"Let's see." Matt held up one hand and began to count off his fingers. "I believe there's five now. Though I'd have to line them up to be sure."

"I don't think I'd be able to recognize Emily unless her belly was round with child," Lucas added with a wink.

"Well, I'd better be getting home and let you two get settled. You will come to dinner, won't you?"

"We'd love to." Miranda accepted the invitation after receiving a nod of approval from Lucas.

"Let's get the wagon unloaded." Matt tipped his hat and started for the door. "I'll be interested in hearing more about your courtship tomorrow."

As soon as the men stepped outside Miranda put away her broom and rags, then stepped into the bedroom to tidy herself the best she could. She made a face at the bedraggled reflection in the mirror. What she really needed was a bath.

With that goal in mind she retrieved the bucket and started for the well. On her second trip Lucas stopped her and insisted on filling the large kettle hanging over the fire. While the water heated he pulled out a small brass tub from its storage place in the pantry and set it before the fire.

"I can't take a bath in here," Miranda protested, noting the lack of privacy with dismay.

"Why not? It's the warmest spot in the house," Lucas called from the pantry where he was busy loading the shelves with the provisions he had procured from his brother's storehouse. Matt had had a good year, and there was plenty for all.

"I had thought to take my bath in private," Miranda told him bluntly.

"How much more privacy do you need? Our nearest neighbors are a mile away." Lucas purposely ignored her true meaning, seeing no merit in denying himself the pleasure of watching her bathe.

"Then I presume you intend to sit in the pantry so I may have some privacy?"

"I intend to thoroughly enjoy the sight of you bathing, so don't plead modesty to me. I have seen all there is to see of you. I intend to exploit my rights as a husband to the fullest." Walking over to the fireplace, Lucas tested the water. Finding it sufficiently hot, he poured it into the tub along with enough cold water to bring the water to a comfortable temperature.

Knowing it was pointless to argue, Miranda turned her back, quickly disrobing and sinking into the relative safety of the water. Glancing around her in frustration, she noticed that in her haste she had forgotten to fetch the soap. With great reluctance she brought the oversight to Lucas's attention.

"If you like, I can scrub your back," he offered hopefully as he approached the tub, making no effort to disguise his growing ardor at the sight of her unclad body glistening in the firelight. It was all he could do not to pluck her from the water and carry her to his bed.

"I can manage. Don't you need to go chop more wood or something?"

"What kind of wife would banish her husband out into the rain?" Lucas feigned incredulity.

"A reluctant one," Miranda returned, causing

Lucas to lose a bit of the pleasure in the game at her reminder.

In more private circumstances Miranda would have lingered in her bath. Once again fully clothed, she felt less vulnerable. While Lucas took his turn in the tub, she busied herself surveying the now well-stocked larder and selecting the items necessary for the preparation of their dinner.

For the remainder of the evening Miranda plied Lucas with questions about her new home and his brother's family until Lucas, chuckling at her inquisitive nature, protested the lateness of the hour and suggested they retire.

The bed was wide, and much to Lucas's annoyance, Miranda hugged the edge on her side, leaving a distinctly unpleasant distance between them. Lucas wondered if the chasm in their marriage bed was Miranda's way of telling him she found the new life he offered insulting. She had been friendly enough this evening, but her quicksilver moods kept him off-balance. Shrugging his shoulders, he turned his back to her, and presently the room was filled with the sound of his deep, rhythmic breathing.

Sleep did not come as easily for Miranda. She was filled with a mixture of excitement and dread. Despite its rustic appearance, she loved Lucas's home on sight, feeling a sense of belonging she had never experienced before. The house, like the man, was an odd mixture of the crude and the elegant. Despite her previous experiences, she began to play with the idea of trying to win Lucas's love. Though he had hurt her badly by his deceptions, the more she learned about him, the less she was able to convince herself that his actions were prompted by cruelty or a selfish nature. She was torn between her desire to protect herself from further hurt and a desire to risk all in order to win her husband's love. Sleep enveloped her before she could decide which course of action she should pursue.

Miranda dressed with special care in the blue velvet dress that was Lucas's favorite. She wanted to make a good impression at her first formal meeting with his family, though she doubted if all the primping in the world could erase Matt's first vision of her as she stood faded and filthy from an afternoon spent on her knees scrubbing.

Lucas, dressed in a casually elegant suit of wool, surprised her by handing her up into a smart, black buggy instead of the expected poorly sprung wagon.

"I am forever trying to decide if I married a rustic or a gentleman," she commented as he assisted her to her seat.

"Perhaps I'm both," he suggested. "A person is seldom one thing or another, but rather a mixture. That's what makes life interesting." His words gave Miranda cause for thought.

It did not take long to reach the home of Matthew and Emily Adams. Unlike the log home she shared with Lucas, their house was a white, two-story clapboard structure that stood elegantly on the crest of a low rising hill. It had French windows set at even intervals across all sides, and at each end rose tall brick chimneys. A long porch graced the front of the house. As Lucas pulled the buggy to a halt the door opened, and out streamed four small children followed by a petite woman with a baby in her arms and Matthew Adams.

Before Miranda could alight from the buggy, a little girl, whom she guessed could be no more than five, climbed up on her lap. Smiling up at her with enormous blue eyes, the child stated firmly, "You're my new auntie."

"Yes, I am." Miranda returned her smile. "And may I ask who I have the pleasure of meeting?"

"I'm Mindy. Do you think I'm as pretty as my mama? Papa says so," she inquired, then waited expectantly for her answer.

"Now, Mindy, let your aunt get down and don't bother her with silly questions," her mother instructed. "I'm sorry, but as you can see, Mindy is a very forward child."

"She's perfectly lovely." Miranda handed Mindy down into Lucas's waiting arms. Mindy threw her arms around his neck, planting a wet, childish kiss on his cheek before letting him lower her to the ground.

When Miranda's feet were firmly on the ground, Lucas began the introductions. "May I present Matt's family: Emily, my sister-in-law; James; Joseph; and John." He named the boys in descending order of age. "You've already met Mindy and Matt, and I'm afraid I don't know the baby's name."

"Jesse," Emily supplied.

They all exchanged greetings before entering the house. Emily ushered them into a cozy parlor, admonishing the children to mind their manners before seating herself on the settee next to Miranda.

"I'm so glad you could come," she said sincerely as she absently arranged the material on her skirt. She was dressed quite fashionably in a pale blue silk that complimented her blond hair and fair complexion. Though she had given birth to five children, she had kept her figure. Miranda noted that Mindy was a miniature version of her mother.

"Thank you for inviting us. It will be nice having your family as neighbors," Miranda returned politely.

"Forget all this formal pish-posh and let's get down to some real conversation. Now, tell me how you two met." Matt broke into their conversation, startling Miranda with his bluntness.

"Ah, now I see the real reason for this invitation," Lucas teased. "It's not that you want our company; you want to get the jump on the local gossips."

"Now, of course we want your company," Emily protested, then she added with a gleam in her eye, "But as your family, I feel we do have a right to all the particulars first."

"Well, you might as well begin your interrogation." Lucas came to stand behind Miranda. "But remember, if you get too personal, we can always go elsewhere for our dinner." His statement was spoken in half jest, half warning.

The next hour was spent recounting their acquaintance as they answered various questions. Miranda was grateful that Lucas's account made their previous relationship appear much more innocent than it truly was. The only uncomfortable moment came when Miranda was asked to explain her rather blunt statement of the day before, but again Lucas came to her rescue, explaining that she had wanted to wait for a church wedding. He had persuaded her to be married by Captain Jameson to avoid any spec-

ulation about the fact she was traveling with him
without a chaperon.

It was not until Lucas recounted the tale of the
grizzly attack that the older boys took more than a
passing interest in their new aunt. She answered their
questions the best she could, trying not to spoil the tale
by letting it show that she found the experience far from
the exciting adventure they seemed to think it was.

At length, a middle-aged woman announced dinner, and the group moved into the dining room, filling the vacant chairs with amazing speed. Then Mrs.
McNay, their cook, housekeeper, and nanny, served
platters heaped with roast venison, potatoes, peas,
and fresh-baked bread. There was wine for the adults
and milk for the children. When everything was on
the table, she took little Jesse from his mother's arms
and left the room.

Eating with four small children was a new experience for Miranda, and she watched with interest the
various ways the youngest found to get his food from
his plate to his mouth. Though the children were polite, they had not yet developed the coordination strict
table manners required. Their parents seemed to be
content to let their children learn by example rather
than criticism, and dinner passed pleasantly.

The meal concluded with a delicious apple cob-
bler that Mindy proudly announced she had helped
her mother bake. Emily and Mindy basked in compliments until Miranda thought the little girl would
burst with pride. Immediately after dinner Emily excused herself to nurse Jesse and help Mrs. McNay
tuck the children in bed. The young Adamses followed their mother reluctantly up the stairs, but only

after being reassured by Miranda and Lucas that they could come visiting anytime.

The adults returned to the parlor, and Emily soon joined them. Lucas and Matt began to discuss business, and Miranda and Emily became engrossed in topics of more concern to women. It was near midnight before anyone noticed the lateness of the hour. Though Matt suggested they spend the night, they declined the invitation. At their reluctance to stay Matt and Emily exchanged knowing winks, then fetched their guests' wraps and saw them to the door.

"Well?" Lucas asked as they started toward home. "What do you think of my family?"

"They're all very nice," Miranda responded enthusiastically. "Do you think they liked me?"

Lucas's laughter rang through the still night air. "What a goose! Of course, they liked you. You even managed to impress the boys."

Content with his answer, Miranda snuggled against him for added warmth, letting her eyes droop as they rumbled home.

During the next few weeks life settled into a routine. Lucas was busy working at the sawmill while Miranda occupied herself with household chores and frequent visits with Emily. The two were becoming close friends. Miranda learned much about housewivery from Emily, who loved her role of wife and mother. She made no pretense of the fact that she was still very much in love with her husband. Miranda envied them.

While her parents' marriage had been a love match, it had not possessed the underlying friendship and common purpose of Matt and Emily's relationship. Her father had seen her mother more as a pretty jewel to be admired by his friends than as a partner in life, and she was content with this role. When the strength of their marriage had been tested by her mother's poor health, both had felt more comfortable living apart. Miranda could not imagine Emily and Matt ever drifting apart, no matter what the trial. She wished she could say the same about Lucas and herself.

Emily was aware that all was not right between Miranda and Lucas, but as Miranda seemed reluctant to discuss the situation, she did not pry. Whenever either of the couple discussed the past, they left much unsaid, arousing her curiosity no small amount. There was something sad in the way they looked at each other. It was a look of longing, as if they each had something important to say but were afraid to speak. She hoped they would be able to work out their problems before long, as it saddened her to see their unhappiness.

Personal concerns were soon pushed aside as the Christmas season drew near. Miranda did not mind the long hours Lucas spent at his sawmill as much, because she needed the time to sew the shirts she was making as her gift to him. She had accompanied Lucas to town one day, and after handing her a hefty pouch of gold, he sent her on her way. She spent the day buying Christmas gifts and was thoroughly pleased with her frivolous selections for the children, remembering how, as a child, she had truly loved the gifts with no other purpose but to give pleasure.

Lucas had not disapproved of her purchases as she

feared he might. In fact, he took such great interest in a set of toy soldiers she had chosen for James, she teased him about taking her back to town so she could buy a second set for him.

Miranda filled the house with the sounds and smells of Christmas. She baked cookies for their neighbors, and in the evenings, as they relaxed after dinner, she played Christmas carols and hymns on the piano. It was a time to set worries aside and enjoy the spirit of life.

She had ceased to resist Lucas's lovemaking, and had found that her appetites matched his own. While locked in an intimate embrace, she could forget that their marriage was built on a foundation of sand. Though they rarely argued now, it gave her little peace. Her fear of abandonment still gnawed at her. She ignored her fears, hiding behind a mask of contentment.

Christmas Day dawned bright and cold. Miranda lingered under the warmth of her covers longer than usual. She could hear Lucas building up the fire in the next room. She snuggled deeper into her quilts, knowing that if she waited long enough, the fire's toasty warmth would permeate the snugly built house.

"Merry Christmas," Lucas greeted as he entered the bedroom. "Do you plan to stay in bed all day?"

"No. Just until you've got the house warmed up," she admitted. "Are you terribly hungry?"

"I suppose I can wait for my breakfast today. Mind, I won't always be so tolerant of an indolent wife." He reached out to tousle her hair. "Of course, I won't give you your presents until you get up." Striding out the door, he closed it behind him, effectively cutting off the warmth that was beginning to fill the room.

With a laugh at the effectiveness of his ploy Miranda pulled on her dressing gown and slippers to follow him.

Lucas had strewn the house with mistletoe, making it impossible to stand anywhere in their home without being under one of the inviting boughs, so Christmas morning began with a series of kisses as Miranda made her way toward the fire.

"May I have my present now?" Miranda questioned as she curled up on the settee. Lucas was in an unusually playful mood, and she intended to enjoy this day to the fullest. Rummaging through the packages under the tree, he lifted a huge wrapped package onto her lap, then settled into the rocker to watch her reaction.

She wasted little time with the ribbons, folding back the tissue to reveal a thick, shaggy fur of silver-brown. Pulling it from the paper, she spread the fur.

At her continued silence Lucas explained, "It's the skin of a grizzly. I thought it would make a nice rug. Since I couldn't save the pelt of the bear you killed, I bought this one. It is sort of a badge of courage among the trappers to keep the skin of the first grizzly they kill."

As Lucas explained the purpose behind his unusual gift, Miranda filled with pride at the thought he had put into selecting it. The rug was her medal of bravery, a symbol of the confidence Lucas felt in her abilities.

"Thank you, Lucas." Miranda threw her arms around his neck. "It's a lovely gift. Will you help me spread it on the floor?"

Lucas was relieved she had accepted his gift in the spirit it was intended. After purchasing the rug he had had second thoughts about its appropriateness. He knew killing the bear had been a frightening experience for Miranda and feared the skin might rekindle old fears instead of symbolizing the pride he felt in his wife.

"Now, I suppose you are expecting your gift. I know that's the real reason you dragged me out of bed." Miranda retrieved her package from beneath the tree, holding it behind her back just out of reach. She deftly avoided Lucas's eager grasp for several minutes before relenting and placing the package in his hands.

Tearing the paper with a single rend, he beamed at the stack of neatly stitched shirts, appreciative of the fact each one represented hours of painstaking work, each stitch straight and evenly placed.

Lucas gave Miranda a wordless hug before exchanging the shirt he was wearing for one of his new ones. "Fits perfectly," he pronounced, running his hands across the fabric. "I'll be the best-dressed man in the territory. And now for your final gift." He reached into his pocket and withdrew a slim wooden box, placing it in her hands. Within the box, on a bed of black velvet, lay a necklace of perfectly matched pearls and a set of matching earrings.

"They're lovely, Lucas," Miranda whispered in awe.

"Not as lovely as you." He came to sit beside her. "They were my mother's."

"But are you sure you want to give them to me?" Miranda protested. They were the loveliest set of pearls she had ever seen.

"And who else would I give them to?"

It was a dangerous question to answer, so as not to spoil the mood of the day, Miranda answered him with a kiss. Someday Lucas might regret his generosity, but it would be foolish to bring up the possibility when they were getting along so well.

"Thank you. I'll wear them to Christmas dinner." Miranda looked up from the pearls and smiled.

"I was hoping you would."

After attending Christmas services at a church in Oregon City, they followed Matt and Emily home in the buggy. The families exchanged gifts and consumed enormous amounts of wild turkey, potatoes, peas, squash pies, and a variety of other sweet and savory dishes skillfully prepared by Emily and Mrs. McNay. The house was in a state of happy confusion, but despite the noise, Miranda found she thoroughly enjoyed being a member of a large family. They stayed until well after dusk, then the tired but happy twosome said their farewells.

"I sometimes wonder how Matt stands all the noise," Lucas commented as he drove toward home.

"I rather liked it," Miranda returned, remembering the silent Christmases of her childhood. "Somehow children make the holidays seem more festive."

"You're probably right, but nonetheless, I'm glad our Christmas will end on a quieter note. I don't envy them the task of getting that brood to settle down enough to go to sleep tonight."

Chapter 20

The holiday season passed and with it the spirit that had kept Miranda's more troubled thoughts at bay. The routine was not unpleasant; neither was it wholly satisfying. She was happy in her new home and found the neighbors she had met pleasant and friendly. Whenever she desired, she could visit Emily or take the buggy into town. Lucas made sure she was always well supplied with money, and she quickly discovered that he could afford luxuries like white flour and coffee, something most of their neighbors' tables could not boast except on special occasions. She had everything she wanted except the one thing Lucas would not give her—his love. She knew he desired her physically and was grateful for the domestic services she performed, but not once had he spoken words of love.

Yet she had more than many women. Perhaps the kind of marriage she yearned for existed only in fairy tales. But every time she saw Matt's eyes light up when they touched his wife, she knew that was not true.

Meanwhile Lucas's frustration grew. Though Miranda was no longer openly antagonistic, she still held a part of herself back. She had adapted to her new life with remarkable ease, never complaining, but he knew she was not happy. Often he would come home to find her playing a melancholy tune on the piano, though when he questioned her, she always insisted she was quite content. It was maddening not knowing what he was up against. More and more he began to feel that forcing her to marry him had been very unwise. He had been an arrogant fool to believe she was merely too stubborn to admit her love. How could she admit what she did not feel?

For over a month Miranda had suspected that something was changing within her body. She felt tired, clumsy, and a slightly nauseous feeling haunted her every step. She couldn't accomplish the most simple task without some mishap. She burned biscuits, spilled water, overseasoned the meat. At night she was too tired and listless to respond to Lucas's lovemaking. When she missed her second monthly flow, her suspicions were confirmed, filling her with fear.

She had no doubt she was with child, and if that were true, how long would it be before she was forced to take to her bed? As an impressionable young woman she had watched her mother slowly fade and die as the result of a pregnancy. To her the news was catastrophic. Staring at her figure in the mirror, she could see startling similarities to her mother's. She could not picture Lucas in the role of nursemaid. If she were unable to meet his physical needs, how soon would he begin to look elsewhere for his creature comforts? Considering his appetites, she could not imagine it would be long. As she dragged through her daily tasks every remark Lucas had ever made about children and noise and freedom played on her mind until by the time her husband returned home, she was near despair. All it took was one remark about her tired appearance to send her to their room in a flood of tears. Lucas followed her but later emerged from the room, none the wiser for all his concerned questions.

He tolerated her behavior for over two weeks, but when he came home unexpectantly one afternoon and found her stretched across the bed sobbing her heart out, his patience came to an end.

"Miranda, you have to tell me what is making you so unhappy," he demanded.

The sound of his voice startled her. Sitting up, she wiped the tears from her eyes. "I'm just being silly. Really, I'm fine."

"Woman, I have had enough of your evasive answers. I have never had any skill in mind reading, and I am through listening to lame excuses. If you don't tell me what is wrong with you, I'll beat it out of you." Lucas was in no mood to be put off again.

With a look of pathetic resignation Miranda whispered, "I'm with child," then buried her face in her hands.

She did not see the look of wonder and pleasure that momentarily passed over Lucas's face before it was replaced by a hard mask. It was true. She only tolerated their relationship out of necessity, else why the bitter tears when she learned she was carrying his child? Recalling the almost childlike delight with which Emily greeted such news despite the fact that

René Garrod

she had already given birth many times, Lucas knew
he had lost. Whereas Emily viewed each child as a
special gift from her husband, Miranda was so re-
pulsed by the prospect, she could not contain her
grief. He had seen her delight too often in his brother's children to believe she did not like children in
general. It was the thought of carrying *his* child that
caused her so much unhappiness.

"I'm sorry, Miranda." He spoke the words with
true regret before walking out the door.

Miranda sat silently waiting before the fire until it
became apparent Lucas would not be returning for
dinner. She picked at her own meal, then curled before the fire with a sampler, though she had little enthusiasm for stitching it. When the clock upon the
mantel struck midnight, she could no longer ignore
her fears. Lucas had simply decided not to come
home. He rarely spent the night in town, and always
before, he had let her know in advance if he would
not be returning. But before, he had not been faced
with a pregnant wife. She fought to stay awake, but
soon she was dozing before the fire.

Morning arrived and still there was no sign of Lucas. Miranda forced herself to eat for the child's sake,
trying to keep busy with various household tasks.
While they occupied her hands they left her mind free
to worry.

After the second night had passed without a word,
Miranda began to pack her things. Lucas had made
his position clear by his long absence. She would go
into town and find him. Once he learned she did not
intend to be a burden, he could return to his home.

He had always been generous with her, so she doubted she would have trouble persuading him to give her enough money to pay for passage to some other part of the world and keep her until she could find work. Beyond that initial assistance, she would ask for nothing. Her bags in hand, she stood imprinting every corner of their small cabin in her mind, reliving in memory the good times as well as the bad.

Lucas sat on the edge of the bed in the hotel room he had slept in the last two nights, rubbing the back of his head. He had to face the fact that their marriage had been a mistake, but he could not quite bring himself to face the final parting. He would always love Miranda, but he would not force her to live with him any longer. It hurt almost more than he could bear, to think of his life without her. At least he would have their child. Miranda would not want to be encumbered with a reminder of their unhappy relationship. He would set her free after the baby was born, seeing that she would never want for the physical comforts of life. Steeling his emotions for the scene to come, Lucas picked up his hat and started for home.

Opening the door to the cabin, Lucas stepped inside. His face was covered with a stubble of a beard, and his eyes were surrounded by dark circles. He registered no emotion as he took in Miranda standing in the middle of the room, baggage in hand.

"There's no need to leave immediately." He spoke the words with deliberate calm.

Miranda felt her knees go weak beneath her. He had not even made a pretense of wanting her to stay.

"I want to leave now," she stated numbly. How could she stay, knowing he had already cast her aside? Her decision to leave immediately might not be practical, but it was the only way she could hope to save her sanity.

"Please, stay until the baby is born. Then you will be free to go." It frightened Lucas to think of Miranda leaving so soon. He had assumed she would want to be among her friends during her confinement.

"I can't." Why was he doing this to her? Couldn't he see that every moment she was with him, knowing she could never have him, was tearing her apart?

"I'm going to take you to Matt and Emily's. I want you to stay there a few days and think about this. Then, if you still want to go, I'll help you in any way I can." Lucas took the bags from her hands, setting them outside the door while he went to hitch up the horse.

Miranda did not move from the spot where he had left her until he returned to guide her to the buggy. They traveled in silence across the field, stopping before the porch of Matt's home.

"Miranda needs to stay with you a few days," he informed Emily as he handed down his wife and her baggage. Without further explanation he resumed his seat on the buggy and, with a flick of the reins, drove off.

"I'll show you to the guest room." Emily picked up one of the bags and led the way into the house. The ill-kept appearance and strain of the couple did not portend a casual overnight visit.

Miranda followed her sister-in-law up the stairs with her second bag, trying with all her might not to burst into tears. Hadn't she learned during the past two days that tears could not erase her pain? Once they had entered the guest room, Emily firmly closed the door and turned to Miranda.

"Now, tell me why you are here."

"Lucas doesn't want me anymore." Miranda tried to say the words calmly. "He only married me out of a sense of obligation, and now I have become too heavy a burden."

"What kind of foolish mess have you two managed to get yourselves into?" Emily asked with a sigh. It was obvious to anyone that Lucas was in love with his new bride. How had Miranda ever come to believe such rubbish?

"Our marriage was a mistake," Miranda said with a defeated shrug of her thin shoulders. "And now I'm with child. What if I should die? Who will take care of my baby?"

"I don't know what you are talking about. If you're pregnant, you and Lucas should be home celebrating, and what's this nonsense about dying? Are you ill?"

"No, I'm fine," Miranda assured her. "But for how long? I remember my mother. She was confined to her bed for months, and then she lost her baby. He only lived a few hours, and she died giving birth to him."

"It's true many women die in childbirth, but that doesn't mean you're going to be one of them. Look at me. I've given birth five times, and I'm as healthy as a horse. There wouldn't be many babies born if every woman who got with child died in the process. You're young and strong. There's no reason to believe you won't have a large family."

Miranda could not find a flaw in Emily's argument.

"You might feel a bit queasy and tired at first, but if you take care of yourself, that passes in a month or two," Emily went on to explain, feeling quite knowledgeable when it came to the subject of childbearing.

"You're probably right," Miranda conceded. "But that doesn't change the fact Lucas doesn't want us." Miranda tried to swallow the hard lump that had formed in her throat.

"I'm sorry, but I just can't believe that. Lucas loves you, and he loves children," Emily protested, shaking her head.

Miranda did not have the heart to tell her friend that Lucas found children noisy and burdensome. The knowledge would only hurt her and cause tension between Lucas and his family. Instead she asked, "Emily, can I be alone for a little while? I know you want to help, but what I really need is time to myself, so I can make some plans for the future."

"I understand." Emily gave her hand a pat before she turned to leave.

Emily wasted little time finding Matt, for the moment the needs of her children taking second place. Mrs. McNay was capable of seeing to them while she concentrated on the more immediate problem. She located Matt in the barn, inspecting the hoof of one of their horses, and came right to the point.

"Matt, you've got to go have a talk with that

brother of yours.'' The tone of her voice immediately caught his full attention.

''What's wrong.''

''He's given Miranda the impression he doesn't want her. She's upstairs now.'' Emily gave him a brief summary of the situation.

''Don't you think we should let them work out their own problems?'' Matt asked. It wasn't like Emily to meddle in other people's affairs.

''Normally I'd agree with you, but Miranda doesn't seem to know he loves her, and from the looks of him when he brought her over, I'd say his view of their relationship is equally morose.''

The expression of concern on Emily's face convinced him. ''All right, I'll ride over there, but remember, it's their problem, and we can't work it out for them no matter how much we might want to.'' Matt set his tools aside and saddled his horse.

''I know.'' Emily planted a kiss on her husband's lips. ''And thank you.''

Lucas was chopping at a piece of firewood with a vengeance when Matt rode up to the cabin. ''Ho, brother, you don't have to kill it before you burn it,'' he called as he dismounted and approached the chopping block.

''Morning, Matt.'' Lucas set the ax aside, then wiped the sweat from his brow. ''I didn't realize I was being so brutal.''

''I could hear that piece of wood screaming from my place. Thought I better come over and see what the trouble was.'' Matt gave his brother a quick appraisal, deciding that Emily's assessment of the situation was quite accurate.

"Miranda wants to leave me." Lucas did not mince words. "But I'm sure you already know that."

"Actually that's not the version I heard. Miranda told Emily you don't want her anymore."

"That's a lie! I want her more now than I ever did. But if that's the story she wants to tell, I guess she has the right." Lucas's shoulders hunched forward.

At his words Matt burst out laughing.

Lucas glared at him. "I'm glad you find the fact that my wife is leaving me so funny. You'll forgive me if I don't join in your amusement. In fact, if you don't mind, I'd just as soon you leave."

"I'm sorry Lucas, but I was just wondering how you two ever managed to get married in the first place, because neither of you has the slightest idea what the other feels. I've got your wife over at my house producing more water than an Oregon rainstorm, and I find you trying to murder a log. Don't you two ever talk, or do you two find some sort of perverse pleasure in making each other miserable?"

"You don't understand, Matt. I forced Miranda to marry me. I thought I knew what I was doing, but obviously I misjudged her feelings. I had hoped things would work out, but when I saw how upset the prospect of having my baby made her, I knew it was pointless to keep hoping. Face it, Matt. I gambled and lost. But at least I'll have the child to remember her by."

"Listen, big brother, my standing here talking to you isn't solving a thing. Saddle up your horse and come talk to Miranda. Tell her how you feel. I can't see that you have a thing to lose."

"Does Miranda want me to come?" Lucas questioned, a glimmer of hope in his voice.

"No, Emily sent me," Matt answered honestly. "And if I come back without you, she'll probably come over here with a rope and drag you back herself. She's fond of Miranda, and she's not willing to sit idly by and do nothing."

"All right, I'll come." Lucas started for the bars. "It was wrong of me to bring your family into this."

A light rap at the door roused Miranda from her misery enough to sit up and wipe her tearstained eyes. "You're needed downstairs," Emily informed her, ignoring her disheveled appearance.

"Emily, I'd really rather not—" Miranda's words were cut off rather sharply.

"I said you were needed. If you're going to stay in this house, you can't expect to lie around in your room all day." Emily allowed herself a secret smile as she marched out of the room briskly.

Miranda, confused by Emily's brusque manner, tucked a few stray curls into place before reluctantly following her. When she reached the bottom of the stairs, she realized she had been duped.

"Hello, Lucas." She kept her eyes averted from his.

"I want you two to take a long walk." Emily pushed the couple out the door. "And don't come back until you've talked this thing out." She watched them walk silently toward the trees, then called as an afterthought, "You might start by telling each other 'I love you.' "

"She's well meaning," Lucas said, apologizing for his sister-in-law.

"I do love you." Miranda's words were barely audible.

"What?" Lucas stared at her in confusion.

"It was nothing important." She closed her eyes as she shook her head.

When they were out of sight of the house, they stopped walking, and Lucas turned Miranda to face him so he could look directly into her eyes. "If I ask you a question, will you answer it honestly?"

Miranda mutely nodded.

"Why do you want to leave me?" He waited in silence for the answer, searching her eyes for the truth.

"Because you don't want me," Miranda whispered, lowering her eyes from his to stare blindly at the ground.

"How can you think such a thing?" Lucas cupped her chin in one hand, forcing her liquid eyes to meet him.

"You don't love me, and when I told you I carried your child, you said you were sorry and left me." Her voice trembled, and she paused to regain control. "I know you married me out of pity, and I promise the baby and I won't be a burden to you. If you'll just help me until I can find some sort of work, I'll give you your freedom."

"Matt was right. We don't talk enough, at least not about the important things. If I did marry you out of pity, it was pity for myself. I was miserable after we parted company in San Francisco. You let me know in no uncertain terms that you didn't want me for a husband, so I kept my distance. Then Lizzy came up with her harebrained scheme, and I suppose I agreed because I felt it was the only chance I had. I hoped, given time, you might come to love me as much as I loved you.''

''You married me because you loved me?'' Miranda stared at him in disbelief. ''Then why didn't you ever tell me?'' The old fire began to flicker in her eyes.

''I thought I had by the way I held you in my arms at night or strutted proudly down the street with you on my arm. Was it so important to hear the words?'' Lucas cringed as she stomped her foot at him.

''Was it so important? I would have given my life a hundred times over just to hear you say those words once. How could you let me go all these months, wondering how long it would be before you tired of me? Lucas Adams, I ought to . . .''

''Kiss me?'' Lucas offered helpfully, taking her in his arms and sampling the sweetness of her lips. In a rush of joy he cradled her head between his hands, raining a shower of kisses on her upturned face before his lips returned to hers. They locked in a languid embrace, melting into each other's arms; touching, tasting, savoring each other with unrestrained rapture.

Miranda pulled away to catch her breath. ''Oh, Lucas, I love you too. I would never have married you if I hadn't. My idea of an ideal husband was hardly some bearded miner from the wilds, you know.'' She grinned up at him mischievously.

''If you love me, why did the thought of having my baby make you so upset?'' Lucas was again serious.

''Because I was frightened,'' Miranda admitted. ''Frightened of becoming too much of a burden. When my mother conceived, she was bedridden for months. I was afraid if I got sick and couldn't take care of your needs, you wouldn't want me anymore.''

"Have you been ill?" Lucas questioned, panic in his voice. Had he been so preoccupied with his own feelings that he hadn't noticed?

"I'm really quite fine. It was just some silly notion I had. Emily assured me that if I take care of myself, I'll be as healthy as she. . . . But do you really want this baby?''

"Only if it's a girl and just like her mother; otherwise"—he paused as if pondering the problem—"we'll send it over to Matt and Emily's. They have so many, they shouldn't notice one more.''

"But I want a boy. Just as handsome as his father, only not quite so stubborn.''

They stood hand in hand, unraveling the web of misconceptions they had unwittingly woven, speaking the words of love both had held back for too long. The sun was low in the sky when they reluctantly started back to the house.

"You know, you never have had that church wedding you wanted,'' Lucas commented as he guided her toward the house.

"I just have.'' Miranda smiled up at her husband, her eyes a window into a heart brimming with love. "Can't you see the church spires?'' She turned back, motioning toward the treetops. "Didn't we just speak our vows of love? No bride ever had a more splendid wedding in a more beautiful church.''